When Dreams Break

When Dreams Break

Book 3 of The Ripple Affair Series

Erin Cruey

To God, who gives hope when we feel hopeless.

To Tina, a.k.a. Girly, my second mom and fellow knitting buddy who makes the best chocolate chip cookies around, and Tara, my third mom and the best crockpot chicken chef – thank you both for your unending love and support. I love you both very much!

A Cast of Main Characters

From the Kingdom of Audlin...

Maria Engel, the Queen Mother:
Supportive of her son, the king, Maria sets out to aid him in his rise to the throne. Distrustful of Malina's growing influence, she advises Edward in hopes of helping him have a secure reign.

Edward Engel, the King:
Rebuilding his reputation after a scandalous affair, Edward begins a new chapter in his life as king of Audlin. Eager to continue the legacy of his late father, Edward seeks to establish a reign of justness and fairness, though how much he can accomplish depends on his wife.

Malina Engel, the Queen:
Far from being like her domestic predecessor, Malina enters the role of queen with an eye for power and domination. Seeking the approval of the nobility, Malina works hard to win favors so she can supplant her husband and take the throne.

Marcus Peterson, the Bowman:
The youngest member of the royal guard, Marcus is the friend and confidante of King Edward. Loyal and brave, he devotes his life to keeping the king and his heir safe.

Samuel Rikert, the Sage:
One of the older members of the royal guard, Samuel is a wise and seasoned veteran known for his efficiency in battle. Originally sent away after warning Edward to not enter Verloris, Samuel may find his wisdom needed once again.

From the Kingdom of Edeland...

Susanna van Echt, the Mother:
The queen of Edeland, Susanna is determined to marry off her eldest daughter, Antoinette, to Prince Arnold of Liegen after an embarrassing failed marriage attempt in Audlin. Determined to let no one alter her plans, Susanna is not opposed to going to extreme lengths to make sure her daughter is married off.

Antoinette van Echt, the Bride:
Once engaged to King Edward, Antoinette finds herself being forced into a marriage with a man she barely tolerates. Unwilling to marry Prince Arnold, she turns to her childhood friend, Emmerich, who offers to elope with her in hopes of escape.

Bernette van Echt, the Support:
The younger sister of Antoinette, Bernie works diligently to keep the elopement secret from both family and friends. Loyal and protective of her sister, she has no problems using words and actions to keep Antoinette happy.

From the Kingdom of Hugellia...

Aldaric van Ketten, the Father:
The father of Emmerich and husband to Anna, Aldaric is an ambassador from Hugellia with much experience working in Edeland. Knowing of the planned elopement between his only child and Princess Antoinette, Aldaric is concerned with the dangers the marriage could bring should Queen Susanna ever find out.

Emmerich van Ketten, the Groom:
Engaged to the woman he has loved since childhood, Emmerich is willing to forsake all warning and reason to save Antoinette from a marriage to Prince Arnold.

From the Kingdom of Liegen...

Arnold von Liegen, the Fiancé:
The youngest prince from the country of Liegen, Arnold is engaged to Princess Antoinette as part of an arrangement with her parents. Charming, clever, and cruel, Arnold cares for nothing but himself.

From the Kingdom of Verloris...

Vacius, the Assassin:
A member of the Velori and a lover to Queen Malina, Vacius is starting to grow tired of waiting for Edward's demise on the throne.

Malum, the Leader:
The mysterious head of the Velori, Malum is clever, calculating, and cold. A man of many secrets, he oversees his plans with perfect precision, waiting for opportunities to present itself to further his plans.

From the Lands of the Recu...

Bohden, the Chief:
The young and mysterious chieftain of the Recu, Bohden is an ally of Aldaric. Gifted with prophecy, his words are often sought after, though sometimes his message may be anything but uplifting.

Chapter Index

When Dreams Break

"In love, there is hope."

The story continues...

Chapter 1: The Man Who Waited

For ten years he waited.

Waited for her to notice him so she could see how much he cared. Waited for her to touch him so they could be closer instead of further away. Waited for her to look at him with the eyes of a lover instead of the eyes of a friend.

For ten years he waited for the woman he loved. And now, after frustration and heartache and thinking the world would look with favor on everyone but himself, she arrived. Emmerich van Ketten's wait was over, and for the first time in his eighteen years of existence, he could say he was happy.

It was morning, just after dawn, when he awoke in the parlor he met her in the night before. The fire had long gone out in the hearth and the air was starting to get cool, but his body felt nothing but warmth as Antoinette snuggled close against him, her cheek nestled in the crook of his neck and her arms wrapped around his chest. He had kept her close throughout the night, wrapped in blankets so she wouldn't get cold, and he held her as she slowly fell asleep. He soon followed, dozing off as his head rested atop hers, and as he slept, his mind was filled with dreams of the future. Their wedding day, as simple as it would be. Their wedding night, where two would become one. A home. Children. A life full of warmth and happiness that made him forget all the hurt and rejection of the past.

For the first time he was thankful, and the future never looked so bright.

Antoinette stirred, experiencing her own dreams as she slept, making Emmerich pull her close and kiss her forehead. He didn't want to wake her. She never was much of a morning person, as was he, but if palace tradition was anything like it used to be when he visited Edeland, a maid or two would be checking the princess' room to wake her for breakfast. With Antoinette absent, the palace would be astir, but with both princesses absent, the palace would be in an uproar. Antoinette's sister, Bernie, slept lopsided in a chair near them and gently snored, but doubtless she would be wakened once the maids came in to find the sisters.

Emmerich couldn't afford to be discovered - at least not yet. Not until after the elopement.

He gently shook Antoinette and she moaned in disapproval. "I'm sorry, darling," he said quietly as he stroked her cheek. "I need you to wake up."

Antoinette's eyes slowly opened and it took her a moment to focus on what was going on. She blinked before offering Emmerich a smile and looking at him. "Good morning," she said.

He smiled back as he watched her expression, his heart giving a flutter as she met his gaze. "Good morning," he answered back. "I'm sorry to wake you, but if tradition is still the same, there should be some maids on their way to wake you and your sister."

"Ugh." Antoinette closed her eyes and swallowed, perturbed. "Forgive me, Emery. I wasn't thinking. Yes, they should be on their way in a little while." She sat up, pulling away from him, his hand wanting to linger atop hers for just a moment longer. He was almost sorry he woke her if it meant her leaving his arms so quickly.

Antoinette stifled a yawn as she sat up, stretching her legs. "For once I wish they'd let me sleep in." Emmerich wondered if she noticed him pout, for as soon as she was done stretching, she placed herself back in his arms and snuggled against him more.

He didn't object. If it meant her touch, he'd gladly face those maids. "It is still early. Perhaps they'll be lenient."

"Mother is planning a wedding. As long as the sun is up, there is time for work."

"True." Emmerich smirked. "But in our defense, we were up all night planning a wedding, too - one that is actually going to take place."

She smiled as she closed her eyes, resting her head on his shoulder. "Today is the day, then."

He hugged her gently. "Today is the day."

"Are you sure the plan will work?"

"Yes," Emmerich began. "You will tell your mother you are going to spend a day with Bernette to enjoy each other's company before your marriage. I will meet you at the minister's at noon. From there, we will have the wedding at the church and go to the inn to…uhm…"

He paused, his face blushing red. It was a general rule of marriages that to prevent annulment, it had to be consummated. To make sure the elopement was legal and to prevent Susanna van Echt from fighting it, they had to cover all their bases.

And that meant moving the wedding night up half a day early.

He cleared his throat, trying to cover his embarrassment and the heat that climbed up his gut, and continued. "To go to the inn and...well..."

Antoinette gave a chuckle, making him turn. "You're cute when you're nervous."

"I'm...I'm not nervous."

"Yes you are. You're stuttering and your heart's pounding like your horse chasing after some apples."

He snickered, remembering Waffles being tied up in the stable. He wondered how the horse fared after eating all those jars of apple jam.

"You have nothing to be nervous about," Antoinette said.

"I know. I'm just..." Emmerich looked away, his face flushing again. "I'm just not experienced...I haven't..."

"You know," Antoinette interrupted softly, touching his chin and turning him to face her, "some girls don't mind being the only woman a man has ever been with."

"I never wanted to be with anyone else but you." He kissed her tenderly, enveloping her in his embrace. "It's always been you, and it will always be you."

She could only grin as she wrapped her arms around his neck and kissed him back.

Bernie was never much of a morning person, but when she woke up, she was up.

It was just after dawn when her eyes wanted to open. She kept them closed, fighting the urge to actually stand and start the day, desiring to listen to her surroundings instead as she heard voices coming from the distance.

Apparently she wasn't the only one who woke up. Emmerich was awake, too, and he was just starting to rouse Antoinette.

Bernie barely opened her eyes, the haze of her lashes causing her sight to become blurry but making it seem like she was still sleeping. Not that she was purposely eavesdropping on her sister and her...second...fiancé, but she did find that she overheard the best conversations when the talkers didn't think she was listening.

After a few minutes of hearing their conversation, however, she felt like she wanted to vomit.

Too much cheese, she thought to herself. And when they started kissing and sucking each other's faces off, she wanted to groan in disgust. Did they realize how ridiculous they looked, being so lovey-dovey and hugging each other all the time? If it weren't for them actually getting a room later on, she'd beg them to get a room now and just get the inevitable over with.

She wanted to close her eyes and go back to sleep. Let the maids interrupt their make out session and put an end to her misery for all she cared.

But when she heard Emmerich's words to Antoinette, she kept her eyes peeked. "I love you."

She saw her sister caress his face and he took her hand in his and held it. For a moment they were quiet, just staring at each other, until she heard Antoinette break the silence. "Where do you think we'll go after the marriage?"

A good question, Bernie thought. She wanted to know where she'd be living, too.

"What about Kettensburg?"

Bernie cringed at Emmerich's reply. The capital of Hugellia was so far away and frozen practically half of the year. Antoinette was never one who enjoyed the cold, and Bernie could only imagine how well she'd do living in a land of plains and polar bears.

Okay, maybe not polar bears. But there was a lot of snow. And grass lions. Lots and lots of grass lions who could maul a person just as good as a polar bear.

"That's awfully far away," came Antoinette's reply.

"We'd have a home there."

"I know." Antoinette sighed as she leaned back. "But what about my sister? I don't want to be far from her and leave her with Mother."

Bernie wanted to cheer, but kept her mouth shut. *Please don't leave me here with Mother*, she pleaded in her mind. *I'll clean your house. I'll be your maid. I'll even try to cook for you! I've only caught the kitchen on fire twice...*

She shrugged inwardly at the thought. Two kitchen fires and two attempts at cooking wasn't the best track record. Maybe some things were better left unsaid.

"Of course," Emmerich replied solemnly. "We won't leave your sister. She's done much to support us and I'd feel terrible if we didn't look out for her. We should take her with us."

"How?" Antoinette asked.

"We'll find a way. I'm sure we can think of something."

Bernie wanted to frown. Finally, she found a guy who cared about her well-being! Except it was only because of her sister. It figured.

But did you really expect him to care about you? What do you have that he could possibly want? Or any other guy for that matter?

She ignored the thought, not wanting to answer because she didn't have an answer to give.

"Kettensburg it is, then." Antoinette smiled. "Although I hope I'm not inconveniencing your parents when I show up at their front door."

"They know why I'm here," Emmerich replied. "They'll support us. You needn't worry about anything."

"We may have your parents' support, but what of the rest of your family? I don't think they'll take kindly to our news. I'm not sure they'd want me."

"They will love you," he said firmly. He kissed her cupped hand and held it to his lips. "Never have you been looked down upon by my family, and neither shall they begin now."

"Fair enough. But what about you? You're mocked too much as it is."

"No buts." He smirked. "As long as you are treated well, that's all that matters. I will face every mock and scold for you."

Antoinette laughed. "Even my mother's?"

"Especially your mother's."

Now that is devotion. Bernie imagined what the future would be like during holidays or parties or family gatherings. She wouldn't put it past Mother to poison the tea Emmerich was drinking because she hated the man so much. For him to be willing to deal with the mother-in-law from Hades, he had to love Antoinette more than life itself.

I wish I could have someone like that.

It was nice to wish, but she knew it could never come true. Only pretty girls got the guy - not the big, balding girls who did nothing but read books.

Why can't I be anyone but me?

She closed her eyes, not wanting to see or hear any more. Emmerich was so perfect, so loyal, and it hurt watching him make over her sister. Not that Antoinette didn't deserve someone wonderful. She did, especially after the stunt Prince Eddie the Idiot pulled. And more than anything, Bernie wanted Antoinette to be happy. She just wished she could be happy, too.

You'll always be alone.

She was about to drown herself in pity, to be smothered by her unhappiness and the cloud that always seemed to hang above her head, until the sounds of footsteps from the hallway caught her attention.

"I don't know why the princesses weren't in their chambers this morning," said the one maid.

"Perhaps they've gone to breakfast early," said the other.

Bernie forced her eyes open and quickly sat up. They'd come too far to have their plan fail now because of two nosy maids and two young people who were so busy being smitten that they didn't notice the world around them. She scrambled out of the chair, nearly tripping over her own skirt, yanking the two lovers apart and pulling Emmerich up towards the window.

"The maids!" Bernie hissed in a whisper. "They're on their way here!"

Antoinette nodded, getting up and leading Emmerich to the window as Bernie watched the door. She took the sill and opened it, the rush of cold winter air blowing through. "I'll meet you at the church at noon, just like we planned."

"Sounds good," Emmerich said as he touched her face. He leaned forward, giving her a final kiss, until Bernie had enough and stormed to the window herself. She took him by the arm, yanked him away from her sister, and shoved him out the window.

"Will you two quit smooching? They're almost here!"

Antoinette looked at Emmerich apologetically as he sat in the snow, his cloak being thrown atop his head by a rushing and frantic Bernie.

"Go sit on the couch. Pretend to be asleep," she barked at Antoinette, who hastily complied. Before shutting the sill, Bernie peeked out the window at Emery, who only blinked as he looked at her in surprise. "What are you sitting around for? Go! Get your apple-hogging horse and meet us at the church later! GO!"

He only nodded as he scrambled away.

She quickly shut the sill, trying to be quiet, nearly jumping onto the couch and under the blanket with her sister. The door opened as soon as she shut her eyes, revealing the two maids, and she soon heard a pair of voices ooh-ing and ah-ing as they walked into the room.

"Sisterly love!" the one maid said.

"Reminds me of me and my own sister," said the other.

Bernie slowly sat up as if dazed and just waking from sleep. Antoinette opened her eyes, the poor girl looking wide awake and desperate to hide it. Bernie shrugged. It looked like she would have to do most of the acting.

"I'm so sorry we weren't in our rooms," Bernie said sheepishly as she wrapped her arms around Antoinette. "We were in here talking last night and we fell asleep. Please don't get us in trouble with Mother. My sister's getting married in a few days and I just wanted to spend some time with her before she leaves."

The maids clasped their hands together with quivering lips. "Awe!" said the one.

"Don't you worry, dear," said the other. "We won't say a word! We know how it is with sisters."

Bernie gave a smirk to Antoinette as they were led off the couch and towards the dressing room to get ready for breakfast. The coast was clear, the plan destined for smooth sailing, until they reached the door.

Mother stood there, fully dressed and ready with arms crossed. The maids stopped and bowed as Antoinette's face paled. Bernie gave her sister a nudge. *Get it together. Don't fail us now!*

"Ladies," Susanna replied, her voice low and hallow. "Why were you not in your rooms during waking time?"

Antoinette gulped and opened her mouth to speak until Bernie stepped in. Better her take the fall than the bride-to-be in case she got grounded. "It was my fault, Mother. Antoinette's getting married soon and I just wanted to spend some time with her. That's all."

Mother said nothing as she looked about the room, rubbing her arms after giving a shake. "Why is it cold in here?"

Bernie forgot about opening the window and the cold air it brought in. Antoinette looked to her, her eyes widening. "The fire in the hearth went out during the night," Bernie replied.

"While we were sleeping," Antoinette added. "We didn't notice it until we woke a few minutes ago."

"Oh, I'm sure," Susanna said as she gave a quick glance towards the window, her eyes beading. Bernie held her breath as Mother approached Antoinette. Her quietness was a bad sign. When Mother wasn't nagging, that usually meant she was angry.

Or just bored. Bernie hoped it was the latter.

"Well, child," Susanna said as she put her hand to Bernie's cheek. "It matters not. I'm glad you two could spend such quality time together. I just hope you don't get ill. Your face is so cold!"

Bernie breathed a sigh of relief as Susanna moved to Antoinette and felt her cheek. She paused for a moment, a glare flashing over her eyes before disappearing behind a stony façade. "But I may have to watch you, dear," Susanna replied as she moved her hand away from Antoinette's face. "You're awfully warm. Hot, in fact. I do hope you're not running a fever."

Antoinette lowered her eyes, a look of embarrassment coming across her face. "I stayed warm under the covers. Don't worry - I'm not getting sick."

"Of course not," Susanna said. "I know you'll be well for your wedding to Prince Arnold."

"Yes, Mother," Antoinette muttered, and remained quiet as Susanna walked out of the room.

Bernie watched in silence as Mother left. Antoinette's eyes met hers in a concerned glance, but with the maids still standing there, they kept to themselves. Mother's arrival was close - too close for Bernie's comfort - and she felt in her heart that if Antoinette didn't marry Emmerich before noon that day, there would be no wedding at all.

Mother was a clever woman. It wouldn't take long for her to figure something was amiss.

Chapter 2: Preparations

Over the years, Emmerich would often imagine what his wedding day would be like.

A great celebration. Guests gathered round in the church. His father and mother, beaming with pride over their only child. His extended family either skipping the event or sitting in the back, mocking and jeering with their arms crossed.

All of that would pale once his bride walked down the aisle to him.

He never could imagine it being anyone other than Antoinette. She would look so radiant walking to him. Cheeks flushed pink, hair done up in flowers and a veil, her dress fitted to complement the body that couldn't be any more perfect to him. At the altar they would say their vows and pray to God for His blessing, ending the ceremony with a kiss that sealed their lives together for eternity.

The wedding dinner would be grand with feasts and dancing throughout the night, and after the party...well...he would be lying to himself if he said he'd never imagined the wedding night. Just the mentioning of it made the heat swell up in his gut.

As he entered the stable to retrieve Waffles, he couldn't help but think of how different his actual wedding day would be. Instead of a celebration, it would be secret. Instead of guests, it would be a sister who was their only support. His parents were still in Reigal and wouldn't be there, nor would his extended family even know until he returned to Kettensburg with a new wife.

Antoinette wouldn't have time to choose a wedding dress. Her garb would be classy and tasteful, but nothing fancy. There would be no wedding dinner or a party that lasted into the evening.

But even though what he dreamed wouldn't come to pass, he still had his bride, and she was worth any change of plans.

At least the wedding night stays the same. He smirked to himself as he found Waffles and swung open the door.

The horse neighed groggily as he lifted his head up, still wanting to rest on a floor of hay.

"Wake up, Waffles," Emmerich said quietly as he rubbed the horse's nose. "I need you alert. We have a wedding to go to."

The horse groaned as he lowered his head back down.

"Oh no you don't," Emmerich said as he took the reins and began to nudge the horse out. "I know we aren't doing this all fancy-like, but I'm not about to be late for my own wedding. I've waited too long for this. You've got to get up!"

He tried pulling the horse to its feet to no avail. "Waffles," Emmerich panted as he tried pulling the horse out, "please. The church is a ten minute ride away and I *need* to be there to meet with the priest!"

The horse grunted again, closing his eyes as if wanting to go back to sleep.

"Confound it, horse!" Emmerich muttered underneath his breath as he went to the horse's rear to push the animal out of the stable. "There's no excuse to act like a sloth! I need you up *now!*"

He began to push, barely nudging the horse, as he muttered small vents of frustration. He pushed again, this time making the horse neigh in annoyance. "Don't fail me now, Waffles!" Emmerich huffed as he pushed again, not noticing the faint rumble that rippled through the horse's gut. "This might not be the perfect wedding for me and Antoinette, but I'm going to try and make it as perfect for her as I can!"

As he pushed again, however, Waffles gave a loud grunt, and before Emmerich could back away, he suddenly found himself at the wrong end of a very sick, apple-eating horse.

Within seconds Emmerich went from weathered traveler to horse toilet, covered in droppings and smelling like rotten apple jam.

Bernie's words from the night before came flooding back about how Waffles raided the outdoor pantry and ate every bit of apple jam the royal family had. For a moment Emmerich stood there in silence, unable to say or do anything as the rotten smell seeped into his clothes and skin and hair. Waffles neighed happily, starting to feel so much better, and turned to Emmerich, giving a sneeze as he sniffed the young man.

Emmerich took his hand and wiped the droppings from his face, clearing his throat as his lips and nose scrunched up from the smell.

"*Waffles!*" he yelled, his face turning red as he cringed in disgust. "Out of all the days you decide to take a dump on me, you choose my *WEDDING DAY?*"

Waffles blinked as he took another sniff of Emmerich's tunic.

"No! No more apples, Waffles! You have a problem with them!"

He swore the horse frowned in disapproval as it gave a neigh.

"No arguments," Emmerich said as calmly as he could, trying to regain his composure. "Let's just...let's go to the church."

The horse lifted his head to neigh again, but Emmerich took the reins and held it. "No, no," he said through clenched teeth as he began to lead him out the door. "Not. Another. Word."

They rode in silence to the church, taking the back alleys so as not to attract attention or to smell up the nicer areas of Staalberg. When they arrived, Emmerich unhorsed and approached the side door of the church, knocking. One of the priests answered, holding his nose as he took a look upon the young, dirty man who stood before him.

"Father Thomas? Thomas Meuller?" Emmerich asked.

"Yes," Father Thomas replied. "How may I...*ahem*...help you, my son?"

"I'm here regarding a wedding," Emmerich said quietly, himself starting to feel sick from the smell of his own self. "I believe Princess Bernette informed you of the arrangement with Princess Antoinette."

The priest widened his eyes as he nodded. "Oh yes! Of course, of course! You must be Emmerich van Ketten."

"I am."

"Then good heavens, my son!" The priest waved a hand in front of his nose. "What manner of trouble have you gotten yourself into? The purpose of a secret wedding is to keep it secret! Why on earth did you tell Queen Susanna about the elopement?"

Emmerich lowered his brow in confusion. "I didn't say anything to the queen."

"Then how else do you explain your condition?" The priest stifled a gag as he looked Emmerich up and down, still covered in horse droppings.

"Oh..." Emmerich blushed as he looked at his grimy, smelly clothes. "Well, it's a long story, Father, but you see...my horse really likes apples and..."

"You know what? Never mind," the priest said as he ushered the young man in while directing a boy to take care of the horse. "I think it better I not know what happened between you and the horse. Now before we discuss the elopement, let us first find you a bath! No groom should smell this bad."

Emmerich didn't object as he was led down the hallway to a washroom.

"What of this dress?"

Antoinette twirled around in a blue satin gown she received for Christmas the year before, worn only once to a banquet for the New Year's celebration.

"It looks nice," Bernie answered as she hung a few dresses into the closet.

"Just nice? Bernie, I need your honest opinion."

"I'm giving you my honest opinion," Bernie said, facing her sister. "You've tried on *fifteen* dresses and every one of them looked nice but you've yet to choose one. It's only going to be me, Emmerich, and the priest there, so it's not like you're going to have Mother hounding over you to look perfect."

Antoinette's eyes widened as she glanced back at the mirror. "I look awful."

"You look fine. Will you stop worrying?"

"I know," Antoinette replied as she plopped onto the bed, resting her hands on her lap. "It's just...it's my wedding day, Bernie. I want to look nice for Emery."

Bernie paused from putting away the extra dresses and approached her sister. "You're fretting too much. You could be wearing dented metal armor and the man would still be infatuated with you."

Antoinette smirked, but it quickly faded as she sighed. "I wish we could have a normal wedding where everyone would be happy."

"I know," Bernie said as she sat on the bed beside her sister. "I'm sorry you won't get the fancy wedding, but look on the bright side. You get to marry your best friend. Not many girls get that option."

Antoinette looked up, a flicker of a smile forming. "That's true."

"Besides, if you were having a big fancy wedding, Mother would be making all the choices for you. With an elopement, it's all in your hands."

Whatever smile that was beginning to form on Antoinette's face suddenly faded, making Bernie's heart sink. She cursed to herself as she watched Antoinette's gaze fall to the floor, her lips lowering into a frown.

It wasn't even an hour before when Antoinette was excited and happy about the elopement. Was it nerves suddenly weighing her down? Or was she having doubts about wanting to go through with the marriage at all?

Bernie hoped it wasn't the latter. As confident and strong of a man as Emmerich was, she didn't know how well he'd take losing Antoinette. The man loved her deeply, so deeply he risked drowning himself.

"Are you not wanting to go through with this?" Bernie asked quietly. "With the elopement, I mean?"

"What?" Antoinette lifted her head.

"You know, the marriage. Are you down because you're having doubts about marrying Emmerich?"

Antoinette furrowed her brows, looking almost insulted. "Why would you think that? I want to marry Emery."

"Are you sure?"

"If I didn't, I wouldn't be putting on all these dresses trying to impress him!"

Bernie snickered. Her sister had a point in that one. "Then why so gloomy all of a sudden? You seemed happier an hour ago."

Antoinette lowered her head. "I don't know...I wished we had more time. I still feel like I'm forcing Emery into this and he's only doing it because I've asked him to."

"Trust me, Antoinette. The man's wanted to marry you since he could walk. I highly doubt he's feeling forced into marriage."

"Maybe," Antoinette said. "I just...I don't know..."

Antoinette stopped as the sounds of a carriage suddenly pricked her ear. She heard a guard call out as the carriage stopped, noticing the man sounded excited.

"Hold on," Bernie muttered as she approached the window. No guests were expected today, but there was one who was expected tomorrow.

As she peeked out the window, her fears were confirmed. Prince Arnold of Liegen had arrived early, stepping out of his carriage and greeting the party that met him at the door.

"Oh no," Bernie said.

"What is it?" Antoinette stood to her feet and headed to the window.

"Arnold's here."

"What?"

"He's getting out of the carriage now. And *what is that?* Oh my word, he's flirting with one of the servants."

"What do you mean Arnold's here?"

Bernie whistled. "Never mind. He's not *flirting* with her. He's groping her. What a pervert! Why isn't she slapping him?"

"ARNOLD'S HERE?"

"Oh wait, now she's slapping him...just not on the cheek that *should* be slapped." Bernie slowly exhaled. "Well, this makes things interesting."

But Antoinette didn't share her sister's calmness. She nudged her way to the window, her face pressing against the glass and her heart suddenly feeling like stopping. "No, no, no, no!" Antoinette stuttered. "If he's here, Mother's going to expect me to spend the day with him! I can't do that...I can't...I mean, Emery will be at the church and I can't leave him there and..."

"That settles it, then," Bernie said as she pulled Antoinette away from the window and rushed to the closet to get a cloak. "Looks like we'll be going to the church early."

Antoinette's eyes widened and she gave a loud gulp. "But Emmerich might not even be there yet."

"Oh, he'll be there, I'm sure of it," Bernie said as she put the cloak on her sister and threw the hood over her head. "And if he isn't, we'll just hide in the choir loft 'til he gets there."

"*The choir loft?*"

"Yes. Now stop panicking."

"What about the bags we packed?"

Bernie grabbed one of Antoinette's cloaks and put it on herself, not having the time to go to her own room and get one of hers. "Leave them. We can't be seen walking out like we're going on a trip! We'll get them tonight and you can make your way to Kettensburg in the morning."

Bernie threw the bags under the bed to hide them and pulled Antoinette towards the door.

Her sister barely budged. "I haven't done my hair!"

"You look fine," Bernie said.

"But it's all knotted and sticking out everywhere!"

"Well if you didn't spend so much time with your bath and then trying on dresses..."

Bernie shoved Antoinette out the door, paying no heed that the bride hadn't changed her socks and shoes yet after trying on dress number fourteen.

"I'm mismatched."

"No time to change!" Bernie snapped.

"Wait! STOP!" Antoinette pulled her sister to a halt. "I can't go yet. I don't have any makeup on!"

"Then it's a good thing men like the natural look!" Bernie pushed her back towards the hall, Antoinette giving a quivering pout as she looked back.

"I look like a clown," Antoinette mumbled as they rushed down the stairs.

"Clowns wear makeup, actually.   Besides, you look presentable. That's good enough."

"But Emery's going to look nice."

"It's either you go back and don't get married or look like this and get married. Take your pick!"

Antoinette sighed, following her sister out the door.

When they reached the winter air, the girls shivered in the cold, but Bernie found herself shivering more once she saw Prince Arnold and Mother lock eyes with them.

She muttered her disappointment under her breath. She was hoping they could sneak out unnoticed.

"Ladies," Mother called out as she approached them. Bernie and Antoinette stopped, their hearts nearly beating out of their chests. "Prince Arnold has arrived a day early! Shouldn't you go and greet him? Especially you, Ant-AHHHHH!"

Susanna stopped and covered her mouth with her hands as she beheld her eldest daughter with unkempt hair and mismatched attire. "My word, child," Susanna muttered as Arnold approached them with his own surprised look. "I daren't say I've ever seen you walk out the door without your makeup! What devilry is this?"

"Uhm...I can explain..." Antoinette stuttered as she began to sweat.

"I'm taking her out for a beauty day," Bernie interrupted, making Susanna look at her with brows raised. "I mean, she's getting married and she needs to look her best, right? She can't wear makeup because she's getting a skin treatment and she hasn't done her hair because she's getting it done too!"

"And the mismatched socks and shoes?" Susanna asked.

"My fault, completely," Bernie replied sheepishly. "I lost track of time for our appointment. We're late, so we were hurrying and I rushed her out before she could plan the perfect outfit."

Susanna frowned as she crossed her arms, looking at Antoinette as she gave a nervous laugh.

"Is this true?" Susanna asked.

"I need to look my best for the wedding, Mother," Antoinette said.

"And what an improvement it shall be, oh Queen," Arnold chimed in as he took Antoinette's hand in his and caressed it. "Spare no expense, my dear, as you opt to look your best. I look forward to seeing the results!"

"Of course," Antoinette said through clenched teeth as she noticed his eyes met her chest instead of her face.

"So may we go now?" Bernie asked as she looked towards Mother. "I don't want to miss our appointment."

"Where are you going to?"

"Sternberg Street."

Susanna frowned. "That's on the other side of town."

"Hence why we need to hurry." Bernie paused, waiting, hoping that Mother would take the bait.

A few seconds passed before Mother's face brightened and she nodded with a smile. "Very well, child. Off you go. I shan't keep you from beauty treatments. But do hurry back when you're finished so that Arnold may spend some time with his bride-to-be."

"Of course, Mother," Antoinette replied.

"We won't be long," Bernie added.

"See that you aren't late. Farewell," Susanna said as Bernie and Antoinette hurried towards their carriage.

They rushed inside and Bernie whispered to the driver. "To Father Thomas' church, and say not a word!"

"Of course, Princess Bernette," the driver replied.

Antoinette leaned back as the carriage drove on. Bernie looked out the window, watching as Mother and Arnold stood staring back.

"That was close," Bernie whispered.

"Too close," Antoinette said. "I...I just lied to my own mother..."

"You didn't lie," Bernie replied. "I did."

Chapter 2 – Preparations

"And that makes it any better?" Antoinette asked. "We're going to a *church*, Bernie! I feel like a wolf in sheep's clothing."

"You're fine, Antoinette."

"I don't like lying," she muttered as she looked away.

"I don't like it either, but we have to do what we have to do."

"All this deception…" Antoinette paused, shaking her head. "It's going to come back and bite us, you know."

"It won't," Bernie replied. "You'll see."

Chapter 3: Longing for a Broken Dream

Edward awoke to the sound of church bells in the distance. He stirred, careful not to wake the woman sleeping beside him, and opened his eyes. The room was barely lit with the sunlight seeping through the windows, but his vision was clear enough to see that he faced the back of his wife, her features and body turned away from him as if wanting to scorn, a great distance between them in the sheets.

He fingered the fabric between them, wishing more than ever there was the softness of skin keeping him warm instead of scratchy wool.

His body turned and he soon faced the window, away from his still-sleeping wife, doubtlessly tired from all the mingling she'd done during the past few days with visiting nobles sent to congratulate her on the birthing of a new prince. He was fooling himself thinking he would ever have the intimacy he could have had with Antoinette. Malina was not his lover, nor was she his friend, and he felt like he was only an empty vessel she occasionally needed to control and get what she wanted.

He never realized how fortunate he was to have fallen in love once. It was something he thought was so common when he was with Antoinette, but now that she was gone and they were living their own separate lives, he suddenly realized just how unusual true love was amongst the powerful. His own parents were part of an arranged marriage, just as Antoinette's were. How could he have been so stupid to throw something so precious and rare away?

The thought plagued him as he got up from the bed, not caring anymore if he woke Malina or not. He gathered some fresh clothes and changed as the bells continued to sound, stopping as he pulled out a tunic from his dresser.

It was a soft, warm material made from cotton in the fields near Circh. He felt the fabric between his fingers before donning it over his chest, and as he looked at himself in the mirror, he felt a tinge of emotion. Antoinette had given him that same tunic two years before when he was recovering from a nasty head cold.

He remembered lying on the couch, still congested and aching when she stepped into the room. Her face showed such concern when she touched him, kissing his flushed cheeks as she tucked the blankets around him tighter across his chest. When she finished, she pulled out a box and opened it for him, revealing a warm tunic for him to wear.

"You'll never be cold again," she said.

Even now the memory warmed him more than the fabric ever did.

The song from the church ended and he approached the window, looking out upon the snowy cityscape of the capital. Only a few merchants and paupers dared to venture out into the cold this early, but there were some busily clearing the streets and making a way for what was going to be a big day. A wedding, arranged for two young nobles in Reigal. Edward smiled at seeing so many hard at work, braving the elements to make sure everyone had a happy day despite the uncouth weather.

As he watched them work, his mind began to drift back to Antoinette. Susanna had mentioned her daughter was marrying soon and Edward couldn't help but wonder if today was her wedding day. Emmerich had gone, as did Aldaric, so it was safe to assume if the wedding wasn't today, it wouldn't be far off.

The thought of Antoinette marrying his cousin brought a pang to his heart, but even though it hurt him to be separated from his truest love, he couldn't help but be glad she was going to the best man he knew.

Antoinette would finally be happy, and so would Emmerich.

He could only imagine just how beautiful she would be.

"She fills my heart with such life!" he remembered Emmerich saying when they were young, before they were enemies. *"I'm going to marry her one day, Ed. I know it!"*

That dream was finally coming true, but how he wished it was his dream instead of his cousin's.

"How could you do this to me?" He remembered the moment Emmerich learned of Edward's betrayal, how Edward stole the letter and forged it in his own handwriting, giving it to Antoinette and winning her hand with the flowery words. He never heard Emmerich's voice be filled with such anger. *"I trusted you! I trusted you with the one thing I cared about the most, and you stabbed me in the back just like everyone else in this family!"*

Memories of Emmerich's shock and anger after Edward returned from Veloris suddenly filled his mind. The way his cousin held her close in a protective gesture, the way he defended her with every fiber of his being when her honor was insulted, the way he followed her home to make sure she had a shoulder to cry on.

Love is for those that deserve it, he thought bitterly as he turned away from the window. *Emmerich and Antoinette deserve each other. They always have.*

And that was why fate bound him to Malina.

Edward turned away from the window, not even glancing at his sleeping wife as he left the room, heading across the hall to Calimus' nursery where the baby was being taken care of. Though he didn't have a loving wife, he at least had his son, and more than anything, Calimus was the one who had brought him the most joy since the days of the birth. He opened the door slowly, seeing one of the wet nurses burping the baby after his early morning feeding, and walked in.

"Good morning, Your Majesty," the young woman said as she turned to the king. "Your son has been fed already. Would you like to see him?"

"I would," Edward said as he held out his hands. The nurse took Calimus and placed him in his father's arms, making the baby coo as he clutched Edward's tunic with his tiny fist.

"He's happy to see you," the nurse said as Edward gently rocked his son.

"As I am to see him," Edward replied warmly as his eyes met with the bundle of joy in his arms. Already the despair of the morning was starting to leave. "Tell me - has his mother come to see him?"

"Rarely." The nurse shrugged. "The queen is probably tired from the birthing, though. Some women take longer to recover."

Edward stifled a snort as he shook his head. It didn't surprise him that Malina kept her distance from Calimus since his birth a week before. Caring for a baby was probably the least of her priorities now that she had a crown on her head.

It didn't matter. Edward planned on being in Calimus' life more, anyways. He refused to be a distant father.

"May I spend some time alone with him?" Edward asked as he turned back to the nurse. "Not that I don't enjoy your company, but I'd like to take him for a walk about the palace."

"Of course, Your Majesty," the nurse replied with a smile. "Take all the time you wish. If you need me or any of the other nurses, we will be here."

"Thank you."

Edward walked out of the room, holding Calimus close as he went down the hallway slowly, approaching another large set of windows across from him. He stopped, enjoying the peace save the occasional grunts of the baby, and kissed the top of his son's head. Calimus held out his hand, which Edward gladly took hold of, feeling his heart melt.

There had been so much loss in the past year. Antoinette, his father, his dignity. And yet despite all the heartache and guilt, he held something of joy in his hands. His son was so tiny, so full of hope that the future wasn't all bad, and he couldn't help but think that despite getting all that he deserved, somehow he got something he didn't.

He didn't deserve such a wonderful, healthy son. He didn't deserve every look of affection and every grasp of a hand around his finger. He didn't deserve every joy Calimus was going to bring.

He remembered seeing the warrior from his dream threatening his son. Was the boy on the ground Calimus? He didn't know, but it had to be, and he wasn't about to let anything bring him harm.

"You know I haven't done much good in my life," Edward said quietly as Calimus looked at him in the eyes. "If anything,

I've made people more unhappy than glad and I've done more hurt than help."

Calimus only cooed as he began to shut his eyes, feeling sleepy.

"I've asked God to forgive me, and I know He has," Edward continued as he gently rocked his son. "But I know that despite His forgiveness, there are still consequences to what I've done. I don't think I'll ever be truly happy, and I don't think I'll ever be loved."

Calimus' grip on his finger loosened and he started to doze.

Edward kept his hand on his son's, never wanting to let go. "I may not be the perfect father to you, Calimus, but I want to try. I want to be there for you, teach you, love you. I want you to grow up and be the man I couldn't be. I don't want you to make the same mistakes I've made. I don't want you to be like me."

He paused for a moment, swallowing hard. "Will you promise me, Calimus, that you won't be like your mother, either?"

Calimus remained quiet.

"Please don't be like your mother," he repeated quietly as he kissed the baby's forehead. "Be nothing like the people who have brought you life. Instead, be the good man that I know you can become."

Calimus' head turned to the side as he gently breathed, fast asleep.

Edward smiled sadly as he held him close to his heart. "Please don't repeat my mistakes."

He held his son in silence, not noticing the shadow watching him from a distance.

Chapter 4: The Humbled King

Edward knew as soon as he stepped outside that he had picked a terrible day for a stroll in the city.

Snow gently fell from the sky and an icy wind blew from the west, chilling his bones through cloth and skin. He pulled his woolen cloak, covered in furs for extra warmth, tighter across his chest as he walked across the streets of Reigal following some nobles in a tour of the market places.

"We are pleased to hear you are taking an interest in our trade, Your Majesty," a large, burly nobleman by the name of Claus said as he walked alongside the king. "Stone is the element of the future and the metals we mine from the mountains will doubtless provide us with a sizeable profit come the summer. Tools, weapons, armor...the possibilities are endless!"

"Not to mention furniture and homes, oh king," another nobleman by the name of Winston added, his thin and lanky figure making Edward think the man would blow away if a strong enough wind blew. "Already we're receiving requests for fences to be built around homes in the outskirts of the mountains, not to mention a few castles have been commissioned near the borders of Braiden."

Edward nodded, pretending to be interested for their sake about all the money they would be making. A year ago he probably would've been interested more in trade, but after such loss and heartache in his own life, money proved to be little help or comfort.

"I'm pleased to hear of your progress, gentlemen," Edward said as they walked past a butcher's stand, the eyes of a few customers glaring untrustingly his way. He ignored their stares and continued on his walk. "Please know that whatever it is you need, I'm willing to provide or at least listen. I wish to extend your trade and make it flourish more than ever before."

"Your wife said the same when I spoke to her at the palace, Your Majesty!" Claus replied with a laugh. "My, what a wonderful woman Queen Malina is. So polite, so charming, so full of joy!"

And so full of horse droppings, Edward thought to himself, but remained silent. His father always said the key to keeping the throne was keeping the nobility, and if it meant appeasing their fancies, he would have to oblige.

"So I hear," Edward began carefully as he gave a quick glance to Sir Peterson who followed him silently behind. Peterson nodded as if understanding his discomfort. "My wife seems quite interested in the affairs of our nobles - much more interested than her own household, I'm afraid."

"She is such a compassionate woman." Sir Winston sighed.

"Compassionate, perhaps, but I'm afraid she overdoes it." Edward shook his head, hoping the nobles would take a hint of displeasure. "Neither I nor my son see her much. This worries me. I do hope you both will help me lighten her burdened…heart. If you have concerns or needs that must be addressed, come to me and I shall see them through."

Edward watched as Claus and Winston looked at each other with confusion, almost as if they were unsure how to feel about Edward's request. "Of…of course, Your Majesty," Claus stammered, wiping his brow. "We will always come to you for anything we need."

"Then tell me, my friends," Edward said as he stepped forward and faced them, his features firm. "How may I assist you now? Do you need more workers? More support? More financing?"

Winston gave a gulp as he fumbled his hands. "We are perfectly fine now, Your Majesty. There is little mining to be done with all of this snow about."

"Then perhaps in the spring, when the snow is melted."

"If we have need of anything, we shall tell you."

Edward felt like cursing after seeing the noblemen's uneasiness with him. Whatever Malina had promised them, whatever she had said the days before had to have been more powerful and more coercing than anything Edward could have said or done. He bit his lip hard despite the numbness of the cold, and feigned indifference at the men's lack of cooperation. "I thank you for your trust, gentlemen," he said through clenched teeth. "Now let us continue with our tour of the market, shall we? I wish to see more of our trade and perhaps meet some of our traders."

Claus smiled, the nervousness of his face fading. "Of course, Your Majesty! Please, follow me."

Edward allowed the noblemen to pass him and he lingered slowly behind, walking beside Sir Peterson.

"I take it Malina spoke with them when they visited her about the prince?" Marcus whispered quietly.

"It seems so," Edward answered, his voice distraught. "What enchantment does she have over men that she can make them do her bidding without question?"

"She is a clever woman."

"Unfortunately true," Edward said. "If the rest of the nobility is like this, then my reign is doomed for sure."

"Do not give up hope so quickly, my friend."

"I'm afraid it's already slipping. My father favored the nobility to keep the peace. They provide the money for the economy, the protection in the knighthood and military, and the support for all our policies. If I lose their favor, Malina has the power to do anything to me."

"Then you should be one step ahead of her."

"I try, but then she is one step ahead of me on that."

Marcus pursed his lips in thought. "Then perhaps you should try a different strategy."

Edward's brow went up. "How so?"

"I'm unsure," Marcus replied. "But I think it will come to you in time. It's like military strategy, I think. Not all battles are won by repeating the same plan over and over, right?"

Edward nodded. "Sometimes you have to think of another way."

"Indeed. But fear not, Ed. You are their king now, and if the people see what I see, they will follow you regardless of what your wife does. Just be yourself and show the integrity that is in your heart. That will gain you respect and loyalty, something Malina will never have."

They walked on past the butchering stations and towards the richer markets where jewelry and cloth were sold. The streets were bustling with customers, many who stopped by to get a glance of their new king. Their stares had barely changed over the months since Edward returned from Verloris.

Though he wasn't being pelted with rotten food and cabbage any longer, most still looked angrily upon him as if he was their greatest regret. He could only lower his head, not meeting their gaze, as he followed the noblemen down the street.

It was towards the end of the market when the noblemen gave a sudden stop, Claus' face turning red in embarrassment and anger as he turned to one of his guards.

"Get that rabble off my street corner! I thought you said you chased him away last week!"

Edward's brow lowered in concern as he stepped forward towards the noblemen and whatever commotion was ahead. The market looked the same as it did before - customers were busy shopping and sellers were busy selling. It was nothing out of the ordinary.

But then his eyes took to the corner and saw a man sitting in the snow, his feet covered with a thin leathery sole and his clothes full of rags and tatters. He was shivering in the winds that cut him from all sides, and he shakily held his hands out, begging for money. His appearance, and undoubtedly his smell, told the tale of a homeless man in desperate need of aid.

"Who is he?" Edward asked as Claus was ready to shove his guard towards the man. The beggar met the king's gaze and Edward saw something in his eyes that was all too familiar. Regret. Pain. A life longing to be started over.

"He's an old piece of filth who chases my customers away!" Claus spat. He rubbed his forehead nervously, facing Edward with an apologetic glance. "Forgive me, Your Majesty, for this inconvenience! The market is typically clear of any beggars but somehow this one managed to straggle back." He turned to the guard and shoved him forward. "Go and arrest that man and get him off of my street!"

The guard was ready to move until Edward held a hand out, steadying him. "Wait," he said quietly. The guard stopped, turning to the king. "I'll take care of this."

"Sire, you needn't concern yourself over such a petty matter as a pauper," Claus mumbled, but Edward shook his head.

"I insist." Edward approached the beggar, causing many of the shoppers to stop from their buying and watch, waiting to see how the king would handle the man.

The beggar turned to see the king approaching and quickly began to scoot away, his face showing fright and concern. Almsgivers standing around soon backed up, and though Edward didn't acknowledge it, his audience began to observe from a distance as if watching a scene from a play.

The beggar sat still upon the curb of the street, gathering his legs to his chest and stuffing whatever coin he was able to gather into a pocket on his tunic. Edward stood in front of him, his head lowering to look upon the beggar, and spoke.

"What is your name?"

The beggar looked around as if expecting a guard to drag him away to prison. He shook out of fear and the cold. "Donald Landen, Your Majesty."

Edward kept his eyes on the beggar, his face showing no emotion but his heart feeling as if it were to weep. The poor man looked starved as if he never had a decent meal before. Even the lanky nobleman, Winston, was big compared to Landen.

"Why are you out begging, Mr. Landen?" Edward asked.

"I'm sorry, sir, *ahem*, I mean...Your Majesty." Landen's eyes danced around, trying to find something else to watch instead of the king's piercing gaze. "I had a job working the fields, but the winter months make it difficult to support my family without a crop. I don't have many skills..."

"There are farmers not working the fields this winter who busy themselves with other things," Edward continued. "What are you not telling me?"

"He's a drunkard and thief, Sire!" Claus muttered as he stepped forward. "The rat was once a serf on my lands and stole crops and drink from my barns. I had him in the stocks for weeks and then removed him from my service. If I knew he'd be such a bother, I'd have had him thrown in jail!"

Edward looked at the beggar with raised brow. "Is this true, what Sir Claus says?"

Landen's eyes finally settled on the king's as he lowered his head in shame. "Forgive me, sir. It is. I'm ashamed of it, but it's true. I lost my daughter and couldn't cope with it. I took to drinking and stealing to block out the pain. I'm sorry for it, and being in the stocks taught me my lessons, but no one will trust me to work for them anymore."

"Your Majesty, allow me to have the guards arrest this man for being a disturbance," Claus interrupted, but Edward held his hand up for silence.

"You look cold, Mr. Landen," Edward said. "Are these the only clothes you have?" He pointed to the rags upon Landen's bones, and the beggar nodded.

"All I have to my name, sir," Landen continued. "Any money I can get goes to my wife and other children for food."

"I see," Edward said quietly. He paused for a moment, watching the beggar in silence, until he took his hands and undid the tie of his woolen cloak. His heart surged with pity towards the man, and in some ways, Edward saw himself upon the beggar's face.

It was our sins that destroyed both of our lives.

Edward took off his woolen cloak, the frigidness of the cold chilling his skin underneath the tunic and pants he wore. It didn't matter - whatever effect the cold had on him was nothing compared to the warmth he was feeling towards helping the beggar. The cloak off his shoulders, he bent down and placed it upon Landen's back, wrapping him in the cloak of a king.

It was immediate when Claus and Winston objected. "Your Majesty, he is a beggar! Do not condone his foolish behavior by rewarding him with such luxuries!"

"I do not condone the acts of a drunkard or a thief," Edward began as he noticed tears well up in the beggar's eyes as he fingered the soft fur and thick wool now warming his body. Edward gave him a smile as he turned back to the noblemen. "Yet I also do not condone any citizen of Audlin suffering."

"Your Majesty, the nobles are right," Landen muttered as he tried to take the cloak off and hand it back to Edward. "This is a king's cloak! I...I don't deserve this..."

"Neither do I," Edward said quietly as he placed the cloak back into the beggar's hands. Landen and the noblemen stood silent, dumbfounded, as Edward turned to Claus' guards. "Take this man and feed him and his family a hot meal. If there is work available, give it to him, so that he may provide for them in the future."

"But Your Majesty!" Claus said amidst a few gasps from the crowd. "This is uncanny! Let the church and others take care of our poor...you needn't concern yourself with them!"

"The poor are my people just as much as the rich," Edward replied, giving Claus a harsh glare. "And if you will not provide for them, then I shall."

"But he is a drunkard and a thief!"

"*Was* a drunkard and a thief, Mr. Claus. Now he is a poor man restricted to begging because no one can forgive the past."

"We don't disagree with Your Majesty, of course," Winston muttered as he approached the now-fuming nobleman and king. "We all like to help as much as we can. Financially speaking, however, it's next to impossible to come up with the resources to provide for every pauper that comes to our door."

Edward lowered his brow, his voice nearing a rumble. "Did you not just tell me that castles were being commissioned to be built? And did you also not tell me that the ore trade is flourishing? It takes workers to mine the ore and break the stone and it takes workers to smithy the metal into armor and goods. If you are unable to find work for a man who needs it, then send him to the palace where I shall provide a job for him!"

Both Winston and Claus remained silent as the king glared them down. Claus shook his head, muttering, "Fine. He can work for me."

Edward's face softened as he motioned for Sir Peterson to come forward. "Take Mr. Landen back to his family and escort them all to the palace. Provide them with food and drink, and afterwards Mr. Claus will discuss proper employment for him."

Peterson nodded, the hint of a smile barely contained in him. "Yes, Your Majesty."

The knight ran to the beggar, helping him to his feet, and escorted him to a carriage down the road. Edward stood there, watching as they left, until Winston interrupted his thoughts.

"Shall we continue on our tour of the markets, Your Majesty?"

Edward nodded, crossing his arms after he was handed another coat from one of the guards. "Lead the way, Mr. Winston."

Winston scrambled away, Claus stomping behind as he ignored the king, heading down the street. Edward followed them, his head lowered, hoping whatever stares he received from any onlookers would go away soon. He didn't want to be yelled at or hit with items thrown at his head.

But the crowds stopped and stared until he was no longer in sight, their hands and voices still.

Malina rubbed the ache in her neck as she was refixing her hair. She was to meet more nobles for tea while Edward walked the city and she had to make sure she looked presentable. Vacius was a lover who was wild as he was efficient, and though she hated to part with him, she knew duty had to come before pleasure.

But then again, duty didn't last forever. She could still see him later in the night while Edward slept.

She straightened her dress and touched up her makeup, eyeing herself one last time at the perfection she saw in the mirror. She turned, about to head out towards the tea room, but gave a startled jump as she saw a man dressed in black and gray leaning against the wall with his arms crossed.

She put her hand to her chest playfully to try and hide her embarrassing jump, feeling the pounding of her heart starting to steady as she forced a smile. "Malum," she said as she paused in her walking. "I did not expect to see you here."

Malum, the leader of the Velori. Vacius' boss and probably the most powerful man in Verloris besides her father, the king.

His face remained stoic, neither showing approval nor disapproval as he met her gaze. She had thought he would have stayed in Cathal, gaining favor with her father and sister. She couldn't deny that even though his presence startled her, his unexpected visit gave her a thrill that set her heart aflutter.

Vacius may have been a wild man, but Malum was a hurricane - and she longed to be swept up in it.

He slowly approached her, never breaking eye contact. His silence made her wonder what was going on in that mind of his, but she kept her cool. Malum was not a man for the faint of heart, and she was one of the lucky few he tolerated with his presence.

"Is everything well in Cathal?" she asked, hoping to start a conversation, or at least pick his brain as to why he arrived.

"Everything is as planned. You needn't concern yourself with it." His voice was soft, calm, reminding her of a breeze in summer. He stopped, facing her. "I hear King Arden is dead."

She frowned a little, unsure of how he would take the news. Malum was unpredictable - what others saw as a victory would easily be seen as a loss in his eyes. Regardless, it was best not to lie with him if it could be helped. He did not take kindly to manipulation. "It's true. The king is dead."

Malum looked away and circled the room, inspecting every item before him. "That was not the plan, Malina."

Had the king's death brought him all the way from Cathal? Surely such a trifle would not alter the grand scheme of things. "I know," Malina said, turning and following him with her gaze. "But there was little choice in the matter. Arden was about to remove Edward and I from the throne and..."

"It doesn't matter," Malum interrupted, acting as if he didn't care. "I can work around this failure."

Malina gathered her hands to her stomach, trying to hide the disappointment her face wanted to give. At least he was taking it well...maybe. "The king was going to die eventually, Malum."

Her comment made him bead his eyes at first, but he looked away, picking up a trinket from her dresser and observing it. "Is Edward king now?"

"Yes."

"Then at least you've done something right."

She frowned, about to say something in return before he interrupted her again.

He set the trinket down on the dresser and looked around the room. "Everything looks different since I was here last."

Malina's eyes widened. "You've been here before?"

"There are many places I have been. This is but one."

Malina watched as he continued to study the furniture. "I did some redecorating. Maria has terrible taste."

"But there are other matters more important than style." Malum returned his sight to Malina. "Are you winning the nobility?"

"Yes. I'm about to meet some more of them for tea. I make sure I meet them every day to get them on our side."

"Good. Continue to whet their appetites and you will keep your throne. You mustn't let Edward gain any ground while you walk on it."

"I won't. I'm watching everything carefully."

"What of Vacius?"

Malina rose her brow. Dared she hope this was a sign of jealousy? Malum was not one to have lovers, but there were exceptions. He was human. He had the same desires as other men.

She saw just how wild he could be. Any man who could leave her with such a memory had the ravenousness of a beast.

"What would you like to know about Vacius?" she cooed.

He gave her no hint of pleasure. "Is he doing his job?"

"If you mean that he is breaking his vows to the Velori by loving on me, then yes...he is doing his job daily."

He remained still, his emotions hidden. If only she could gather a hint of approval. She tried to bait him with flirting, hoping he would take a bite. "Does this displease you? Shall I have Vacius be busy with other matters? I would be happy to please myself with someone who is clearly more...experienced."

She batted her eyes at Malum to no avail. Heavens, the man frustrated her as much as he drove her insane with fantasy! There was never a man she couldn't conquer, but Malum was proving difficult. It made her want him all the more.

"Who you whore with is not my concern." His words stuck her in the gut, and she couldn't help but admit disappointment. She lowered her grin and tensed her hands in frustration. "Only watch Vacius. His jealousy grows easily, and we wouldn't want another premature death on our hands. He is supposed to watch Edward and make sure we are not surprised."

"I've told him to not be jealous. What more do you want?" She no longer cared if her voice sounded irked. Let him be angry and feel the ache she felt.

"I want..." he began with lowered voice, inching closer to her face so she could feel the heat of his rage, "everything to go according to plan. Not another mishap, Malina. The king's death has come too soon and it was *needless*. If you can't handle your task, I will find someone else who will."

She narrowed her eyes, her confidence glowing, and she faced the man who was the only one worthy enough to be her equal. "Darling, you know I am capable. I control every person in this city. I am their puppet master. Everything they do or say is because I tell them to!"

Malum smirked, almost as if he was laughing, and he put his hand to her shoulder, brushing it with his fingers.

His touch sent a ripple through her arm and her anger subsided. If standing up to him was what it took to bring him to her bed, she would've tried it a long time ago. She watched him, impatient with hunger, for his response.

A laugh, light and barely noticeable, came from his lips. "The puppet master."

His touch left her shoulder and she couldn't help but pout. Was he only grooming her for her meeting with the nobles? She was overcome with disappointment. "Sorry," he muttered as he lifted a tiny thread between his fingers. "You had a string."

She said nothing as he stared at her with a smirk.

The moment passed quickly and he turned towards the door. "I have the other Velori monitoring the situation in Cathal. I shall stay here a little while to make sure Edward's transition to power goes smoothly."

Malina gave a scowl. "I have it under control."

"Of course you do," Malum replied softly. He turned to the door and opened it, giving a quick glance into the hallway. It was clear. "One last piece of advice, Malina. Don't ignore Edward too much. Your flings with Vacius may give you more trouble than what you can afford."

She clenched her fists. For that comment, she would spend even more time with her lover!

Malum gave her one last glare before leaving the room.

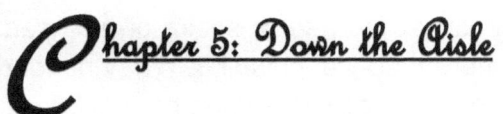

"Is this all you have?"

Emmerich looked into the mirror as the priest shrugged in embarrassment. The clothes were too big, too baggy, and if Emmerich was being honest, too itchy for proper groomsman attire. He rubbed the back of his neck, looking at himself from head to toe, and grunted.

"I look like a monk."

"Nonsense! You're wearing a cleaning robe. You look much more like a janitor."

Emmerich bit his lip as he didn't know whether to laugh or cry. When he imagined his wedding day, he figured he'd wear something that would show him bound to his bride, not a holy and celibate order.

"Please don't tell me I'm going to be chastised for breaking vows I didn't make."

"Of course not!" Father Thomas laughed as he clasped Emmerich on the shoulder. "I'll just explain that your original clothes weren't presentable for church."

Emmerich turned away from the mirror. "They only needed cleaning."

"My dear boy," the priest replied after a shake of his head. "Those clothes needed more than just cleaning. They needed to be burned and the ashes dumped into a chamber pot!"

Emmerich frowned. "Was it that bad?"

The priest nodded, his face in a daze. "I've never seen such horror come from a horse's behind. I recommend you have it see a doctor before taking it home. What comes from its bowels is...unnatural!"

Emmerich sighed as he looked back to the mirror. Antoinette would be beautiful, her dress proper and rich and her features done to flawlessness. She would be the perfect bride, ready for her groom and her special day, and he would meet her down the aisle, dressed as a poor man in a simple brown tunic that had too much wool for comfort.

He bowed his head in frustration. Only to him would such a ludicrous event happen. The day could not get worse.

"Thank you, Father, for your hospitality," Emmerich said as he forced the words from his lips, desperate to sound polite. "This day hasn't gone according to plan, but...I am grateful. Thank you for the clothes you've provided."

"I know it isn't perfect, but at least you'll be warm! And smell better, to be honest." Father Thomas grinned.

Emmerich smiled. At least there was a bright side to the oversized fabric.

"You know what I think?" a voice from behind asked with a chuckle. Emmerich turned, his eyes widening. He knew that voice, and he was both happy and surprised to hear it.

"Bernie?"

His future sister-in-law grinned as she approached him, the priest excusing himself to give them privacy. She looked him up and down and shook her head. "I think Antoinette isn't the only one having a bad hair day. Or fashion day, for that matter."

"She's here? Already?" Whatever calmness Emmerich had now turned to panic. He looked horrendous. He smelled even worse. Anything that could go wrong was going terrible. Had he lost track of time?

"We got here early," Bernie cleared. "Arnold's at the palace. We figured not to chance it and came to the church." She paused, looking unsure. "You don't mind moving up the wedding time, do you?"

That was one request he would be happy to grant. "I wouldn't mind it at all…as long as she's comfortable with it, of course."

"Well, she's a bit frustrated she hasn't had more time to prepare, but otherwise she's fine."

Emmerich nodded. As long as Antoinette was happy, he was happy, though he wished he was more presentable in his appearance. "You don't think she'd mind me looking like I've just joined a monastic order, do you? I don't smell like rotten apples thanks to Waffles and his uncontrollable bowel movements, but still…"

"As long as you don't mind her having tangled hair, no makeup, and mismatched attire."

Emmerich let out a laugh, rubbing his brow. "I didn't think getting married would be this complicated."

Bernie gave a smile, shrugging. "At least you'll have a story to tell, right? I mean, it's pretty funny."

"Yeah," Emmerich replied. "It is."

"But don't worry about how you look," she continued, her voice suddenly quieting. "I think you look pretty handsome as a monk." She paused, her face slightly blushing. "I mean, I think that's what Antoinette would think, because...you know...you two are getting married and all of that."

There was an awkward moment of silence and he noticed Bernie had looked away, playing with the sleeve of her dress as if wanting to pass the time. She looked tired, worn out. No wonder she stumbled over her words. He could only imagine the worry going through her mind about what all Antoinette had been through during the last year.

He couldn't help but be thankful for her, for being so faithful to her sister. "Is Antoinette out there waiting for me?"

"Yep. She's in the sanctuary."

"Okay," he said, pursing his lips. That awkward silence threatened to continue and she looked away again. Instead of saying nothing, however, she spoke.

"We...uhm...should get going. Don't want her thinking we left her." She paused, looking as if she wanted to smack herself. "I mean..."

He'd save her the trouble of fixing her words. He wouldn't have much time to thank her later for all that she did for him and Antoinette, finding the church and a priest who would keep quiet and going the extra distance to keep everything hidden from Queen Susanna. While he and Antoinette went to the inn, it would be Bernie who would bear the brutality of her mother first. That alone was worth the praise of a king.

But he was no king, nor would he ever be. He would, however, be her brother-in-law, and he vowed to always care for her if no one else did.

"Thank you, Lady Bernette." His arms wrapped around her in an embrace, and for a moment he worried about the stench that might still be there from his horse's sickness, but she didn't say anything in protest. Rather, she seemed shocked he would bother to embrace her, family or not. It was an all too familiar scene.

"Uhm...why are you hugging me?" she asked through muffled voice.

"Because you deserve it," he said as he pulled away. She looked confused, almost bewildered, and he kept his hands on her shoulders. "You have done so much for your sister and I. From the bottom of my heart, I thank you. You have no idea how grateful I am that you've supported us in this."

"Well, I'd be kind of rude if I didn't."

Emmerich smiled, her modesty warming him. "I know how much blame you are going to take from your mother for us, Bernie. That alone would make any man or woman tremble and turn."

Bernie shrugged, giving a smirk. "Wouldn't be the first time I angered her. Certainly won't be the last."

"She may see you as a troublemaker, but I don't care what she says." He paused, looking her in the eyes. "You are a treasure, Bernie. Never forget that. Anyone who is as selfless as you is a treasure the world does not have enough of."

She smiled, a genuine look of appreciation coming upon her face. "Thank you for that. It's a little over the top, but I don't mind hearing it."

He smiled back. "It's a shame more people don't tell you."

"And it's a shame you're keeping your wife-to-be waiting." Bernie took him by the arm, playfully shoving him towards the door. "Now hurry up! Get out there and marry her. Not like we have much time, you know."

He happily obliged, making his way to the sanctuary of the church.

Antoinette stood near the front pew, her hands together in a nervous clasp as she paced the floor, waiting for her future husband to arrive.

Bernie had left only seconds before to fetch him and the priest, and as she stood alone in the church, she couldn't help but feel a mixture of nerves, excitement, dread, and happiness all rolled into one.

Her emotions were so mixed, and yet she knew she had to calm herself. She couldn't go into her marriage unsure or full of false expectations. She also couldn't dwell on what could have been instead of what was standing right before her.

Only months ago she was planning a wedding to Edward. Now, she was seconds away from marrying his cousin.

It was funny how life had a habit of changing things so quickly. She had thought for so long she and Edward would be together forever, that he was her soulmate and he was "the one" destined for her. She'd spent countless nights awake and unable to sleep, thinking and dreaming of the life she'd get to live with Edward. So romantic, so lovely, so pure. But that dream was broken when he chose another woman.

And yet even though her dreams shattered, someone was there to pick up the pieces. Emmerich, the boy who loved her since childhood. Her best friend and confidante for most of her life.

Now, he would be not just her friend, but her lover. The father of her children. Her partner in life for the rest of her days.

Her dream with Edward may not have come true, but she was still marrying a good man that would undoubtedly make her happy.

Did she love him? She was still unsure. Emmerich van Ketten had always been a friend to her and they hadn't been given enough time to let that friendship grow into love. There was something there, though. A spark, a flicker of a flame. Certainly not what she had with Edward, because it felt different, but it was there. And there would be no hurt with Emmerich. He would be loyal and faithful.

He always had been.

The door opened and in walked Bernie, telling them to wait in the sanctuary as she got the priest. Following behind was Emmerich, and to her surprise, he was dressed like a monk. She stifled a laugh behind her hand and wondered if his morning had been as interesting as hers, and as they approached each other, they both grinned sheepishly.

"You look lovely," he said as he stared at her in awe.

"I look terrible." Antoinette tried to flatten her frizzy hair, probably still tangled when she remembered she hadn't brushed it yet. "I don't match and I didn't have time to put on my makeup and..."

"You look lovely," he repeated, his hand clasping hers gently and putting it to his lips. "Though I think I've got you beat in costume. At least you are not dressed like a monk."

"I thought what you had on this morning was fine," Antoinette said. "You could always put that back on if you want."

"It's currently nothing but ash. The priest burned it."

Antoinette's eyes widened. "Why on earth would they do that?"

"Remember Waffles got into the apple jam last night?"

Antoinette tried hard not to laugh. "Oh dear."

"I've learned a valuable lesson in that you should never push a sick horse from behind."

She snickered. "I thought I smelled something funny."

His face went from pleased to mortified as he took a step back. "I promised I bathed. Is the stench really that bad?"

She felt a little guilty implying he stunk. She took him gently by the collar and pulled him back towards her, giving him a gentle peck on the lips. "Nonsense. You smell fine."

He smiled as she brushed a few wet strands of hair off of his brow. He was probably cold with his head still having water on it, not having enough time for his hair to dry. She pulled him closer into an embrace, hoping it would keep him warm.

She found his touch to be more welcoming than a fire in a hearth, and she snuggled close to him, their foreheads touching together. His fingers caressed her face, and she could only imagine what he had in store for her once the wedding was over and they went to the inn.

"Do you remember, when we were kids, how we used to talk about the future?" he asked in a whisper.

She smiled at the memory. "I do. Weren't we planning on sailing around the world right now?"

Emmerich laughed. "We'll eventually get to it." He gave her a gentle kiss that made her heart flutter. "It's funny, though, how things change over time, and yet some things stay the same. If I recall, didn't we say we'd get married one day?"

She grinned. "We were children, but yes…I think we did say we were going to get married."

He closed his eyes as if he were dreaming. "You wanted pink dresses for your bridesmaids."

"And you wanted to make sure there was turkey pot pie at the reception."

He chuckled at the thought. "And your doll was going to be the maid of honor."

"And your stuffed horse was going to be the best man."

He held her close as he opened his eyes back up. "It's not quite what we imagined it would be, was it?"

"No. But I'm sort of glad, though. Bernie would throw that poor doll out the window if she knew it was the maid of honor."

"You have to admit turkey pot pie sounds good, though."

She smiled, noticing she was starting to feel hungry. "It does, actually."

"Maybe dinner in bed for later, then?" He rose his brow playfully at her.

"It's a date."

He kissed her again, longer this time as if not wanting to part. "What a story we'll have to tell one day. A secret wedding and how you married a monk."

She kissed him back. "And what a story it will be."

They held each other for a moment in silence, and for the first time in a long while, Antoinette felt like the future was finally starting to look bright. In the end, she would be happy.

They turned as the priest and Bernie walked into the room, ready to begin the ceremony.

$\mathscr{C}$hapter 6: The Wedding

"Aldaric," Anna whispered softly as she sat up on the bed, putting a hand on her husband's shoulder. Aldaric remained silent as his back was against the headboard, his eyes deep in thought and his face crinkled in worry. When he didn't stir at her touch, she gave a sigh and rested her head on his shoulder. "Can't sleep?"

He shook his head. Perhaps the loss of his brother-in-law, King Arden, went deeper than what she thought. Or maybe it was their son. He was, after all, on his way to elope. She gently caressed his hand, hoping it would comfort him to rest. "Something on your mind?"

"I'm worried about Emery," he answered quietly.

Not that she didn't share his concern. In a way, she wanted to sneak and follow their son to Edeland just so she could witness him get married. "What worries you?" she asked. "Do you think we should've followed him?"

He shrugged as his eyes went to the window, the mountains of Reigal in the distance. "No. I trust him to find his way there."

"Then what is it? Do you not want him to marry Antoinette?"

"It's not that, either," he said as he turned back to her. "I know Antoinette will be a lovely wife for him. I'm just concerned about what will happen after the wedding."

She frowned as she remained at his side. "What do you mean?"

"You and I both know when word of this comes out that there'll be controversy."

"Of course. But we're going to stand by Emery, aren't we? It's not like he's doing anything wrong."

Aldaric let out a sigh. "Tell that to the queen."

"You're worried over Susanna?"

"I'm worried about her reaction." Aldaric rubbed his eyes, eyes that were weary and longed for sleep but refused to rest. "She won't take this kindly."

Anna could agree with him on that one, but when did Susanna ever take anything kindly? She was never an easy one to please, especially when Anna spoke to her. She eventually gave up trying.

"We'll just have to trust she'll support the marriage," Anna replied as she brushed Aldaric's hair with her fingers. "And if she doesn't support it, we'll stand by Emmerich and Antoinette."

"It's easier said than done," Aldaric said. "Susanna will go to Erick if she doesn't get her way. She'll make it bigger than what it actually is and I fear Emery's reputation will be tarnished."

"Erick wouldn't be that cruel. He may be a foolish king, but he knows he will lose you as an ambassador if he did anything to hurt Emery."

"Erick wouldn't be cruel, but Susanna would." Aldaric clasped his hands together and rested his chin atop them. "I fear what she would do to him, Anna. Once she's angered, there's no quenching it."

Anna sat up, her eyes widening in concern. "What are you trying to say?"

"I'm saying I know from experience how difficult it is to deal with her when she's caught unawares. I need to be there and make sure this doesn't blow up into something worse." He got up from his bed and headed towards the armoire to dress.

Anna stood and followed him. "I'll go with you. I don't want her hurting my baby!"

"No. I need you to stay here." Aldaric held her hands and put them to his lips, kissing them. Anna frowned as she faced him. If her son, *her only child*, was in danger of a maddening queen, then she wanted to be there to protect him!

"Aldaric, if Emery's going to be in trouble, I should be there."

"I know; trust me when I say your being there will only make things worse."

Anna's eyes flared with anger. "What's that supposed to mean? I'm not afraid of her royal high and mightiness!"

"I know you aren't. But Susanna will be more apt to reason if you aren't there. You're a threat to her, my love, and she will only be intimidated by your presence if she sees you."

She gave a huff as she looked away. She could care less what Susanna thought of her as long as Emery was alright. "If Emery needs me, though…"

"I'll only be going to make sure Emmerich and Antoinette make it back here. If I can keep Susanna calm, perhaps we can prevent anything bad happening." He paused, watching her disapproval, and pouted. "Please, Anna. Trust me."

She gave him a perturbed look. "I trust you, but I don't like you being alone. I don't trust her."

"I know. I'm not exactly fond of it, either. But Emmerich isn't going to be thinking of her reaction. His mind is on his bride, not on his mother-in-law." He kissed her gently, the touch of his lips lasting longer than what it typically did. His forehead pressed against hers and he caressed her cheek. "I'll be back soon. Go back to Hugellia with the rest of the family. I'll meet you at home with Emery and Antoinette."

Anna held him close, not wanting to let go. "You don't have to leave now. Wait until you hear from Emery that the wedding has happened and then see if he needs you there."

"He's going to need me now, Anna."

"But maybe not yet."

"I have a feeling he will, my love, and I can't ignore it." He kissed her again one last time before grabbing his cloak and heading to the door. "Tell my sister that I'm following Emmerich on an errand for King Erick. If she asks questions, tell her we'll be fine. I'm sure she'll be the first to find out the truth."

He hurried away, leaving Anna alone in the room.

Emmerich watched as Antoinette faced him, their hands held and their bodies close enough that they could feel each other's breath as they spoke their vows in front of the priest.

"I, Emmerich Matthias van Ketten, take you to be my lawfully wedded wife."

His voice was shaking as he put his grandmother's ring back on Antoinette's finger. They didn't have time to get wedding rings - yet another thing they'd have to do when they got back to Hugellia. But a lack of rings didn't matter. He watched as Antoinette smiled back up at him, her fingers giving his a gentle squeeze.

I've waited so long for this. If time could stop, it happened at the altar as the priest stood before them, turning to Antoinette to say her vows.

She looked just as nervous as him to be put on the spot, every eye on her, but never had he loved her any more than when he saw her standing before him. Her face was radiant, her eyes shining like the glistening snow outside. This was the beginning of forever, and never had he wanted to take the journey more than what he did now.

"I, Antoinette Maria van Echt, take you as my lawfully wedded husband."

Husband. Hearing their new titles filled him with such passion and love as he had never felt it. He didn't know much about what his purpose in life was, but he knew it was something big. It suddenly dawned on him that maybe he was looking at his purpose now. A young Edelandian girl that deserved love and loyalty from someone who could give her both.

It was a purpose he would gladly accept, and he vowed in his heart to care and adore her every day for the rest of his life.

"I now pronounce you husband and wife."

My wife…

The priest's words were like a dream as his gaze rested on Antoinette. "You may now kiss the bride."

The world around him stopped, every sound gone silent and every movement ignored like a distant fog.

Antoinette inched closer, unsure if she should make the first move or not. It didn't matter as Emmerich leaned forward, his hands cupping her face and his lips gently brushing against her own. The night before, his first kiss with Antoinette sent a fire that rippled through him that was like lightning striking his very soul with passion. That same ripple went through again, but this time there was a peace, a serenity that he couldn't explain, entering his heart. Their love was perfect...it was right.

And now it was forever.

I'll always love you...even into eternity.

He didn't know how long he had kissed her. Didn't know how long the priest had been watching, smiling to himself, or how long Bernie had been clearing her throat, tilting her head as if to hurry them. It didn't matter. He was going to enjoy every moment. As crazy as it had been, this was the happiest day of his life. Nothing could ruin it. Nothing could quench the blaze that fired in his spirit.

He was a married man now, and he was forever bound to the only woman he had ever wanted.

When he pulled away, he still held her close, gazing into the eyes that looked calmly back at him. He gently clasped her hands with his and held them close to his chest.

"I hate to break up the moment, but if you both want this marriage to be legitimate, you need to get busy." Bernie stepped in front of them and they looked at her, eyes widened and the priest starting to blush. Bernie sighed as she rubbed her brow, muttering, "Get busy...going...*out there*...at the inn...uhm... not here..."

Emmerich grinned. "We'll go."

"It's the inn down the street, room four," Bernie said as she handed them the key. "I'll wait a bit before going back to the palace so you'll have some time. If you're not back before me, I'll stall."

"And then what?" Whatever joy was in Antoinette's face suddenly turned to concern. The night before only included discussions on the wedding and the inn. What happened after was anyone's guess. Antoinette looked to Emmerich and he frowned. Her look of uncertainty saddened him, and he gave a gentle squeeze to her hands and put them to his lips, kissing them.

"Don't worry. We'll play this by moment," he said. "We can go to your mother together - the two of us - and I will tell her what happened."

"And what if she doesn't listen?" Antoinette asked.

"I can fake the stomach flu again as a distraction," Bernie chimed in.

Emmerich faced his wife, his voice lowering into seriousness. "If she doesn't listen, then we can leave. As long as we are married and united as husband and wife, then there is nothing she can say to you, nothing she can make you do without your consent." He paused as he lifted her lowering chin. "I promise I'll take care of you, Antoinette. You will not be forced into anything you don't want to do."

She nodded slowly, swallowing hard as she buried her worries beneath a brave face. "Alright. Let us go, then."

They thanked the priest, appreciative of his secrecy, and before leaving out the back of the church, he watched as Antoinette turned to Bernie one last time. "I'll see you soon. Be careful if you get back home before I do."

Bernie nodded. "You too."

Hoods covering their heads and cloaks covering their bodies, Emmerich and Antoinette headed out into the snowy streets, careful to not be seen as they rushed to the inn.

Chapter 7: The Wedding Afternoon

The inn room wasn't as Antoinette expected it would be. Dark, cold, dusty enough to warrant a sneeze or two as she entered through the door. When she imagined her wedding night (or, in this case, afternoon), it would have at least been in a place with color and a fire. The hearth remained empty and unused, however, and the grayness of the room matched the gloominess of outside.

"It's...cozy..." Emmerich shrugged as he looked at her, trying to make the best of things. She could only laugh as she looked at the nervous grin he gave back. "I mean, I've seen worse, but...uhm..."

His voice trailed off into silence and they stepped further into the room, Antoinette rubbing her arms as she shivered.

Emmerich looked at her in concern, putting a hand to her elbow. "Are you cold?"

"A little," she replied, and she watched as he took his cloak off and put it over her shoulders and across her chest.

"I'll get a fire going," he said as he smiled at her.

She smiled back as she clasped the cloak's collar closer together. "Thank you."

He quietly went to work at the hearth as she sat upon the bed and watched.

He got on his knees, arranging the wood pieces before a fire was kindled, bringing warmth to the room. As she watched him work in growing the fire, she began to think of the day's events.

Was her wedding as expected? Certainly not. When she was a girl, she dreamed of a big party and frilly dresses and a dashing prince on a horse. What she got was more of the opposite of her dreams. Instead of a party, she got secrecy. Instead of a beautiful gown, she got a mismatched outfit from the back of her closet. Instead of a prince, she got a dishonored ambassador's son whose only horse had a bowel problem.

But as she watched her husband work, she realized what stood before her was much better than any dream she ever had.

He was loving. He was loyal. He was kind. In his eyes were devotion and care, not carnal desire that needed quenching. She remembered him saying he loved her, and his promises to care for her were more than proved by past experience.

Out of everyone, he had always been there for her. To laugh, to cry, to listen. And now she had forever to give all of that to him.

"Thank you," she said as he stood, the hearth now blazing.

"For what?"

"For being so good to me." She looked at him lovingly, noticing his features in the light from the hearth. Goofy grin, wavy locks of hair, an honest face that promised happiness to make up for all her past hurts.

He leaned forward, caressing her cheek. His touch warmed her, expelling any cold from the icy winds outside.

"You've been even better to me," he said lovingly. A lie, to be sure, but one she could see he believed with all his heart.

She took his hand away from her cheek and kissed his palm. She didn't know much about how to physically please a man since she'd never tried it before, but she hoped she could please him. She felt so nervous as her heart fluttered inside her chest, not knowing what to do, not knowing what was going to happen after their moment and her mother would find out the truth. She didn't want anything to happen to him. Didn't want Emery to pay for helping her escape a marriage to Arnold.

She kissed his palm again, her lips lingering on his skin a little longer as she forced the worries from her mind. No - she wouldn't let her fears take away this moment. Emmerich had waited so long for her love, and she had waited too.

Her eyes closed as she felt his fingers graze through her hair; never had she felt so nervous and excited at the same time. He inched closer to her and her arms went around his waist, and as he stroked her head, he asked, "Are you comfortable with this? I don't want you to think I would ever force myself on you..."

His concern melted her heart. Though attraction was there and growing, he was gentlemanly enough to make sure she was ready. They had been close for such a short while, and she wondered if he noticed her anxiety. His kindness made her want him more.

She stood to her feet and faced him, kissing his lips. "I'm ready if you are, Emery."

He gave a slow breath as he grinned. "I'm more than ready."

She smiled as she moved her hands away from his waist and back towards herself. She removed her dress, leaving only her chemise and corset, as he removed his monk's robe, leaving only his trousers. Her heart skipped a beat when she saw his chest and arms, and she couldn't wait to feel the warmth of his skin against her own.

But she needed a little help first. Unable to undo the corset from behind, she turned to her husband. "Can you get my corset?"

He gulped, but nodded, as his hands fumbled for the string.

Poor man; if she was nervous, he had to have been terrified. She could feel his heart pound just by standing in front of him, and she could only imagine what was going through his mind as his greatest desire was suddenly turning into a reality.

"Let's see...uhm..." She could feel him trying to undo the knot, but to her surprise, her corset remained tight.

"Can you get it?" she asked, wondering if he needed help in undoing a tie.

"There's...well, there's a few knots in this thing."

"How many knots?"

"About seven."

She gave a giggle as she rubbed her brow. Bernie. She should've known better than to entrust her in tying her corset.

"Remind me to have a talk with my sister when we get back," Antoinette said as she felt a small pull.

Emmerich gave a huff as he tried pulling the knots apart. "Don't worry - I will."

"If you try loosening the first knot it might..." Before Antoinette could finish, she suddenly felt a tightness come across her chest and she had trouble breathing.

"Wait! Too...tight..." she gasped, and suddenly Emmerich began to panic.

"I'm sorry...I'm sorry...I've never done this before!" His hands were shaking harder now as he tried to loosen the corset, and after a few seconds of panic, Antoinette began to wave her arms to get his attention.

"Just...break...it..." she coughed out. As soon as the words left her lips, she felt a great tug and heard a ripping sound, and she watched as Emmerich tossed the torn corset to the floor.

"Are you alright? I'm so sorry, my love...are you hurt? I didn't hurt you, did I? I'm so sorry..." She felt gentle arms wrap around her and his hands stroked her stomach, and as she caught her breath, she playfully fell back in his arms and laughed.

"Next time, I'll get the corset," she said with a snicker, and he breathed a sigh of relief as he lowered his lips to the crook of her neck.

"And now you have proof I know nothing of women's clothing," he mumbled through her shoulder.

She laughed again, turning around and tugging him towards the bed. He followed, his hands clasped with hers.

"Seriously, though - you're not hurt, are you?" His worry never ceased.

"I'm fine, silly." She pulled him atop of her as they both fell upon the bed. "Now stop fretting and kiss me."

"Yes, my wife," he cooed as his lips pressed against her own.

It didn't take long for their passion to resume. His lips remained on hers for a moment before moving across to her neck, and her hands followed his lead as they began to massage each other's backs. Even with Edward she had never went this far, but she was happy she had saved her passions for Emery. Everything now felt so perfect, so right, and as they rolled on the bed, she could feel her soul connecting with his at that very moment.

She was atop of him now, her lips aching to kiss the skin above his pounding heart. But before she could move, she felt him roll to move back atop of her, and instead of ending on top, she felt him going away.

She heard a loud *thunk* and a pained moan, and as she sat up, she realized Emmerich had fallen off the bed and landed right on the hard, wooden floors in front of the hearth.

"Ow…" he muttered as he scrunched his eyes closed for a moment before opening them back up and looking at her.

She tried not to laugh as she looked at his embarrassed state. "Are you alright? You didn't hit your head, did you?"

"My rear took the blunt of it," he muttered as he sat up. "I hope I didn't break my tailbone. I'd hate to try and explain this one to the doctor."

She smiled as she got off the bed and went to him. "Are you hurt?"

"Just whatever manly pride I had left," he said with a smirk. "Otherwise, I'm fine." His hand went back to her cheek and cupped it, and she leaned into him.

"I'm sorry," he said quietly as his fingers stroked her skin. "I'm not a very savvy lover, am I?"

"You're a bit klutzy, but that's okay," Antoinette replied. "It's one of the things I like best about you."

"You like it when I make a fool out of myself?" He chuckled.

"I like it when you're comfortable enough that you can be real around me," Antoinette clarified. "And I can be real around you."

Emmerich leaned forward and pressed his forehead against hers, the fire warming them and illuminating them in light. "That, my beautiful wife, is one of the many reasons I chose you. You're the only one to ever accept me for who I am, lack of good fortune and all."

He kissed her, their passion nearly taking her breath away, and then she stopped when she felt his hands gather the fabric of her undergarments.

This was it, then. The moment when they would become one - husband and wife, one flesh, a family.

He pulled the blanket from the bed towards them, making the floor more comfortable. Her hands undid the tie of his waist cord, and as he held the gathered fabric of her chemise at her hips, they could only look at each other's eyes.

The man who waited didn't have to wait any longer, and before he offered himself, he whispered in her ear.

"I love you."

His words were about to become action before voices were heard outside the door. They both paused, Emmerich's eyes looking ahead in concern, and as Antoinette turned to look, a loud bang sounded, making her jump in fright.

Another noise followed, and soon the door was kicked open, letting in three Edelandian guards who rushed towards them.

Emmerich stood, demanding to know what they were doing, but after one tried to grab Antoinette to pull her away, it became clear the guards weren't there for conversation. Antoinette jerked herself away as Emmerich gave a swing of his fist and knocked the guard in the jaw, pushing the others.

A scuffle began that didn't last long. The guards pulled their weapons and there wasn't much a man could do with hands against metal. Emmerich tried his best to protect his wife, but he was soon overpowered as he was pushed against the wall, one of the guards ramming the hilt of his sword against Emmerich's stomach. He doubled over in pain, and as Antoinette screamed for them to stop, their beatings worsened.

"GET AWAY FROM HIM!" She saw him crumple to the floor, struggling to get up and return to her, and when she stood to run to him, she was suddenly pulled back by a familiar grip.

"*Be still, child!*" Mother's voice, full of fury, made her blood run cold.

"No...please, Lord in Heaven, no..." Antoinette's prayers caught in her throat as she turned to her mother, who only glared back.

"*Did you really think you could hide this from me?*" she seethed in her daughter's ear. Antoinette's heart pounded inside her chest, her mind racing as to how Mother could have known. Was Bernie caught and did she reveal the truth? No, Bernie was more loyal than that. Perhaps it was the priest? Or were they followed?

Or maybe fate was out to crush her dreams once more.

The sound of another hit against her husband brought her back to reality. "Don't hurt him! I beg of you, please!"

"Have no mercy on that boy!" Susanna ordered as she pulled her daughter back. "He is a kidnapper and you have seen it yourself how he has mistreated my daughter! Bind him and put him in the carriage. I will not wait a second before justice is done!"

Emmerich tried to move once more only to be beaten down. He struggled with consciousness, and he called Antoinette's name.

"Emery..." Antoinette's eyes filled with tears as she watched blood trickle down his face from a gash near the forehead.

"No...Antoinette..." Before he could say any more, he was silenced with a blow to the temple. His body went limp as he was knocked unconscious, and the guards drug him out of the room and into the snow where a carriage waited.

"*NO!*" Antoinette screamed, shouted, thrashed about as much as her body allowed her, but as soon as the guards left, she was thrown back down onto the bed, her mother facing her.

Antoinette could only weep as the interrogation began.

"How long have you been with him?"

She said nothing as she cried softly to herself, her eyes on the small trail of blood that led out the door.

Susanna's eyes were lit with a fire that burned brighter than the hearth. "ANSWER ME!"

Antoinette's voice cracked as she sniffled. "Not long."

"Did you go anywhere else besides this inn?"

"We were at the church."

"And what did you do there?"

Antoinette's cries softened as she looked at her mother, glaring. "I married him."

Susanna said nothing as her lips pressed so hard together they began to pale. "Did you sleep with him?"

"I..." She almost did, and her heart ached at the thought of it. They were so close to becoming one. So close to sealing their marriage with the love and loyalty that bound them.

"I AM SPEAKING TO YOU, CHILD!" Susanna's voice boomed in the room.

"YES!" She hated to lie, but her anger was boiling so furiously hot that she wouldn't give her mother the satisfaction of defeat. She wasn't going to lose Emmerich to an annulment. Not if she could help it. "Isn't that what married people do, *Mother*? Express their love *physically*?" She paused, narrowing her eyes in defiance.

Susanna huffed as she took Antoinette's dress from the floor and threw it at her. "Put this back on," she seethed. "You will be taken back to the palace and we shall speak to Arnold about this little matter."

"Tell him what you want," Antoinette replied with a sneer. "I'm married to Emmerich now, Mother. Arnold can't marry me. It's against the law."

Susanna gave a smile that showed more anger than pleasure. "I am a queen, Antoinette. I am the law. I control anything and everything that happens in this land!"

Antoinette stood after she hurried the dress back on. "Well you don't control me! I've made my choice, and I'm going with my husband!"

With a stomp of her feet, she shoved her way out of the room and followed the guards into the carriage.

Chapter 8: Wrath of the Queen

Bernie didn't know how long she was to wait in the church sanctuary before returning back home. She sat on the pew, glancing at the hymnal for something to do while her sister did the nasty with her new man, and waited. Her mind drifted and she started to wonder when she should return to the palace, and when she did return, what would her excuse be for why her sister wasn't there?

She gave a huff as she put the hymnal back on the pew and leaned back. Emmerich and Antoinette should have planned the day better. Why was it always up to her to come up with the excuses to stall so everyone else could have their moment?

Then again, she could only imagine if Emmerich and Antoinette were given her role in the plan. Antoinette would crack at the first lie and Emmerich would attempt the truth just for the sake of proving himself right.

Maybe it was better she was left to deal with the cleanup, after all.

She sat in silence, swinging her legs out of boredom, until the sound of carriages caught her attention. They sounded large, going almost too fast on a side street, and it pricked her interest. She got up from the pew and headed towards the door, giving it a crack so she could peek outside. She saw a few people start to look and mutter about, glancing down the street towards a building the two carriages stopped at. At first Bernie didn't think much of it until she realized the carriages down the road looked an awful lot like the one she and Antoinette had ridden to the church.

Her heart felt like stopping as she suddenly realized what was happening. *Mother...*

She bolted out of the church, not caring if she left her coat on the pew. The icy winds of winter stung her skin, but she ignored the pain and cold as she rushed towards the inn. A crowd was starting to gather, and she could hear the noise of a fight and a familiar scream. Her hands began to push and shove people out of the way as she made her way to the door, suddenly stopping as she saw three guards drag an unconscious and half-dressed Emmerich van Ketten out into the snow, followed by trickles of blood.

Oh no... Her voice caught within her and she froze in place. Caught. It was the only word she could think of at that moment. And when she heard her mother yell from inside the inn room, her mind went through every step she took in covering the elopement. She told no one save the priest and the carriage driver. The priest was still at the church and the carriage driver was still down the street waiting to take her back home.

How did Mother find out? How did Mother know where they were?

Her thoughts were interrupted as she saw Antoinette storm out of the inn room, her face looking flushed and livid like Bernie had never seen. Her sister swung open the doors of the carriage Emmerich had been dragged into, yelling at a few of the guards to "GET OUT!"

Susanna arrived as one of the guards was pushed out of the carriage, and with a sneer she went to where Antoinette was, ordering her to come out of the carriage and leave Emmerich alone.

"No!" Antoinette's voice seethed.

Bernie blinked in surprise. She'd known her sister for her entire life, but it was the first time she'd ever seen Antoinette stand up and rebel against Mother.

She couldn't help but be proud of her, despite the circumstances.

Mother, however, would have none of it, and in her anger she forced herself into the carriage, pulling another guard out. "Meet us at the palace," she said. "I shall watch over my daughter. The poor dear is hurt and I will stay in the carriage to make sure that wretched boy doesn't touch her again."

"Yes, Your Majesty."

"And find Bernie. I know that girl is here somewhere. Find her and bring her back to the palace at once!"

Bernie gulped as she stepped further back into the crowd, hoping to stay hidden.

Susanna slammed the door shut, motioning for the driver to go, and they rode on towards the palace. At first Bernie wondered if she should run and try to think of a new plan to help them escape, but without being at the palace, she wouldn't know where to look and find them. Besides, she needed to know what Susanna was planning on doing. If Emmerich and Antoinette didn't...well, do what married people do...then Susanna had grounds to annul the marriage.

But Bernie knew in the back of her mind that even the law wouldn't stop Susanna from trying to split them apart.

She knew what she had to do. She had to get to the palace and find another plan to save her sister.

She forced her way forward as she approached the two guards, getting up into their faces. There was no need for pleasantries and she wanted to cut to the point, anyways. "How did you find us?"

The guards stood at attention and looked surprised to see her so soon. "Your Majesty?"

"I said *how did you find us?*" If they wouldn't answer her, she'd cause a scene that would make them reply.

"I can't say, Your Majesty, as the queen told me to remain silent," the one guard answered. "But it matters not. Come, I shall escort you back to the palace..."

"I'M NOT GOING ANYWHERE, MR. METAL PANTS, UNTIL YOU TELL ME HOW YOU FOUND US!"

The crowd that had started to disperse suddenly started to gather again.

The other guard gulped as he gently tugged the princess towards him. "Your Majesty..." He paused, swallowing hard. "The queen was suspicious and she had some guards follow you. When you stopped at the church, one guard went back to the queen to warn her while the others watched where Princess Antoinette went. That's all I know. Now please, stop making a scene and come back to the palace with us."

Bernie felt like cursing her rotten luck. Mother was clever - that much she knew - but she wished Susanna would have ignored her instincts so they could escape.

"Fine. I'll go," Bernie replied. "But you better get me there fast if you know what's good for you."

Emmerich was woken by a jolt that sent pain radiating through his head. He groaned, not wanting to wake, but at the sound of Antoinette's voice, he forced his eyes open.

The memories of before he blacked out suddenly surfaced. Susanna. The guards. Pain and fear tearing through his body. His wife being attacked.

"Antoinette?" Her name sounded muffled to him, and he realized just how dazed he was. He could tell he was in a moving carriage, and he felt a burning cold as the air met his bare chest. His vision was blurry, a hazy swirl of colors that tinted red, and he felt dizzy. His head ached so badly.

"Don't worry, Emery," Antoinette's voice whispered. "I'm here."

"Are you alright?" He tried to sit up only to nearly fall off of the seat he was laying on. His vision was starting to clear and he could see he was in a carriage car, Antoinette kneeling on the floor and holding a ripped piece of her dress to his forehead while Susanna and a guard sat across from him.

"I'm fine," Antoinette answered as she helped him lie back down. Her hand grazed his chest and then felt his face. "You're freezing. I'll get you warmed up."

He watched her turn to the guard and demand his cloak. The guard looked uneasy, and he turned to the queen, who shook her head.

"I'm sorry, Princess. I can't give you my cloak."

Antoinette huffed as she looked to her mother, giving her a nasty glare. "*Fine*," she muttered, and she pulled her dress off, leaving only her chemise as her covering. Susanna gave a gasp, followed by a growl, but her daughter ignored her as she placed the dress atop Emmerich to keep him warm.

"Child, have you no decency?" Susanna shouted as she tried to grab Antoinette's arm. Antoinette pulled her arm away and scooted closer to her husband.

"I don't want him getting hypothermia, Mother, so if you won't let me have a cloak, then I'll give him whatever I have!"

As much as he appreciated her thoughtfulness, he worried more over her than himself. "Darling, you'll get cold," he said as he tried putting the dress around her shoulders. "Please. I'll be fine."

"If I recall, I promised to take care of you," Antoinette said, draping the dress back over him. "Let me keep my promise, Emery."

Susanna gave a scowl as she ordered the guard to give Antoinette his cloak. Antoinette took the cloak and put it on her shoulders, draping half of it over her husband.

The warmth didn't help his aching head, but it did stop the shaking from the cold. And as long as Antoinette was there, unhurt and with him, his mind was more focused. It was all about protecting her now. Nothing - not even injury - would stop him from keeping her safe.

He forced himself up, fighting the dizziness that wanted to overtake him. At first Antoinette tried to keep him down, but after a gentle caress of her cheek, he sat straighter in the seat, helping her off the floor to sit beside him. His arm went around her in a protective gesture as he faced Susanna, his free hand taking hold of his wife's and keeping it close to his chest.

Susanna's reaction reminded him of a grass lion finding prey that dared to encroach on her territory. She was at her most irrational and most dangerous at that moment, but there was no time for fear and intimidation. He wouldn't give her the pleasure of controlling him like she tried to control her daughters.

He was the first to speak, and he forced the words from his lips as his aching head tried to slow his speech. "What...madness...has overcome you, Susanna...to make you treat your eldest with such disdain?"

"I should ask you the same, *Emmerich*." Saying his name made her face scrunch up like she had tasted poison. "My daughter is pledged to marry Arnold von Liegen and right before her wedding, you kidnap and force her to marry you!"

Emmerich narrowed his eyes, the heat of anger rising in his heart. To think that she would *dare* suggest him capable of such a monstrous act burned him to the core. "We both know I would never do such a thing, and I'm offended that you'd even suggest it! Your daughter is here on her own free will - I have committed no such crimes against her! It is *you* who have forced your will upon her, arranging this marriage with Arnold when you *knew* she did not wish to partake in it!"

"She is a royal, Emmerich! Such things are too above you to understand."

Emmerich lowered his brow. "And she is also a human being who deserves respect and love. I'm sorry that is too great for your understanding!"

"You insolent boy! How dare you speak to me in such a manner! I am a queen!"

"And I am a man who doesn't care who you are in this life. I love your daughter, and if you will not give her the love and respect she deserves, then I will!"

Susanna's face reddened as she matched Emmerich's anger with her own. "You beast! You aren't capable of such decency that you could ever please her. She is a princess and deserves the highest ranking of birth and nobility, not some son of a royal-want-to-be and a filthy pauper! Arnold is of noble breeding and royal blood! He is more her equal than you could ever be!"

"I may never be her equal, but at least I am loyal. Arnold is nothing but a man who is known for his many lovers and crude character."

"Better a man with experience than a boy who knows nothing."

"Mother!" Emmerich was about to offer his own retaliation to Susanna's attack on his manhood, but seeing his wife so livid made him step back. This was a different side to her, one he hadn't seen, and he began to realize that though Antoinette was never one to argue or fight, if someone she cared about was being threatened, she would lash out.

Seeing her strength come to the surface made his heart swell with pride.

"You're acting like I am nothing but an object you can give away to the highest bidder!" Antoinette seethed, her grip clasping hard on Emmerich's hand. "I told you I didn't want to marry Arnold and yet you went along with the arrangements anyway. I'm nineteen years old, Mother, and I'm old enough to make my own decisions! I'm choosing love over prestige and I want loyalty over power, so you need to understand that I married Emmerich because I wanted to. I made love to him because I wanted to. And now I'm going to spend the rest of my life with him because I want to. You can't change that!"

Emmerich looked at her, somewhat perplexed at the mention of them sleeping together. She gave him a glance, almost as if saying, *Play along*, and he squeezed her hand in agreement. It was a smart move on her part, pretending they actually consummated the marriage when they hadn't. An annulment would be an impossibility now.

A small chuckle was heard, and Emmerich and Antoinette both looked to Susanna to see her trying to stifle a laugh by putting a hand over her mouth. She shook her head, giving a wave of her hand, as she turned back to Antoinette. "Oh child, do you not hear how silly you talk? You are young and naïve and do not know what you yet want. I have lived much longer than you and have seen the world how it really is. If I recall, the last time you chose love, it left you wanting and broken because it chose another woman."

Emmerich snarled at the thought. *Edward*. "I am not my cousin, Susanna. Edward has always been a fool and I'm offended that you'd even compare us."

Susanna ignored him as she kept her eyes on her daughter. "My child, I must warn you that your choices will bring you much harm in the future if you don't listen to me. You think I'm trying to control you, but I'm only looking out for your heart and do not wish it to be broken again. You sit next to a man who has an adulterer's blood flowing through his veins."

Emmerich sneered. "I am *not* Edward, Susanna!"

"I wasn't speaking of your cousin, you daft boy."

Antoinette blinked in confusion and Emmerich lowered his brow as Susanna continued, her eyes remaining on her daughter. "You want to know why I am so against this little relationship? It is because I know it all too well. I know how loyal a van Ketten can be because I was once pledged to be married to one."

"What do you mean?" Emmerich asked. What madness was this? He knew nothing of an engagement or even a relationship between Susanna and any of his kin.

"Did your father not tell you, little Emery? Or was he too ashamed to admit he broke his promises with me to be with your mother?"

Emmerich felt Antoinette's grip on his hand loosen, and the look on her face showed doubt, confusion…even a tint of fear. His anger burned as he faced Susanna, leaning forward. "You are a liar and you are full of wickedness to bring my father into this!"

"I assure you, Emmerich, that I would not lie on such a matter. Ask him yourself if you don't believe me. Your father and I were in love and pledged to be married and then he broke my heart and left me for Anna." Susanna turned back to Antoinette, leaning forward and putting her hand atop her daughter's. "You wonder why I have tried to keep you away from Emmerich? It is because I wanted to prevent my past in becoming your future."

Antoinette looked to Emmerich, her eyes widened. "Is this true? Did your father ever tell you of my mother?"

Emmerich shook his head. "He never said a word about her. I only knew…" He paused, seeing the sudden change of expression on Antoinette's face as that familiar look of hurt came across her eyes. It was the same look she had when Edward returned to Reigal with Malina, that same look of being betrayed.

"I…only knew…" He had to choose his words carefully. He couldn't lose Antoinette to Susanna's cunning. "…that he was engaged. My father told me that he was engaged to marry a woman and that he broke the engagement to pursue a relationship with my mother. There was no affair and no betrayal. It was simply a broken engagement."

"That he told you about," Susanna interrupted. "And yet why did he keep it secret that it was I who was his fiancée? I find it strange that your father would keep such a thing quiet when it was supposedly no big deal. But you are daft to think there was nothing going on between him and Anna while he was with me. You did, after all, say he left me to pursue her."

Emmerich beaded his eyes. "What point are you trying to make?"

"The point, *little Emery*, is that your father had more going on with Anna than what he told you. Why else would he risk losing me to pursue a commoner whom he had no guarantee would love him back? It is a foolish move indeed to leave a lover who was loyal to chase a fantasy that just so happened to work out."

Antoinette's hand was barely clasped around his own now. She was beginning to doubt, and her mother's words were clouding her thinking. "My father said you gave him reason to leave." He was desperate for any excuse to win Antoinette back. She was slipping, and he was trying so hard to hold on.

"And what reason would that be? Had I any affairs on him? Was I ever disloyal?"

Emmerich turned away, his head pounding so hard now. What could he say in answer? His only choice left was to lie, and that would only prove Susanna's point.

"No, you had no affairs to my knowledge," Emmerich began with a sigh. "And I don't know the situation or events that drove my father and you apart. What I do know, however, is that you are comparing the present to something that happened in the past. I have always been and always will be loyal to your daughter, Susanna." He paused, turning to Antoinette and facing her. "And I promise that no other woman will ever hold my heart except her."

Antoinette's lips turned up in a trembling smile until Susanna gave another chuckle. "Funny. Your father told me the same thing."

Antoinette's smile faded as she looked to her mother. The carriage stopped and the palace was before them.

"I cannot make you listen to reason, child," Susanna said to her daughter. "I can only hope that you will let my experience teach you. You've already witnessed a great hurt when Edward left you for Malina. Are you willing to risk that hurt again with a man who has an adulterous lineage?"

"I *would never, ever leave her*!" Emmerich seethed.

"Says any man who's ever loved a woman," Susanna replied. "But that is the beauty of entering a marriage not based on love. You enter with responsibility and grow into loving each other. Childishness is put into the past."

Emmerich put Antoinette's hand closer to his heart. "Arnold is a lover of many women. You are blind if you think he would stay loyal to her."

"My husband the king was once a lover of many women as well, little Emery, but marriage forced him to be faithful. You are not royal and are therefore not under the public eye. No one is watching when you take a mistress. Arnold is a prince, however. He is subject to scandal and disgrace if he leaves his wife for another." Susanna looked to Antoinette with a confident gleam. "I speak of this from experience, child, and no decision of yours will keep me from being your mother. If you will not save yourself from this terrible future, I will." She swung the door open and tilted her head to the side. "Now both of you - out of the carriage."

They complied, but Emmerich refused to let go of his wife's hand. Susanna may have doubted his loyalty to Antoinette, but he would prove her wrong.

He just hoped Antoinette would believe him.

Chapter 9: A Common Heart

Aldaric pulled his cloak closer to his chest as the wind picked up. Though a cold winter was nothing out of the ordinary, he still disliked the chill that ached his aging bones, and for a moment he wished that if he were to have to chase his son through the forests of Edeland, it would have been during the spring. It didn't matter, though. What was done was done and he'd brave ice or heat or any of the elements if it meant keeping his only child out of harm.

He trotted on his horse past the gates of Staalberg, still familiar territory though he visited less and less as the years passed by. The small city was once a second home to him, but time changed things. Life changed things.

When he passed the gates as a young man, his heart was always filled with hope. Now as he passed the gates, though, his heart was filled with dread. He knew what was coming, knew what he was about to face once he reached the palace.

Susanna van Echt, a woman once his lover who turned into an enemy, and she would have no mercy once she found out his son and her daughter were getting married.

Aldaric dreaded the meeting more than any other he had in his life.

The trot became a gallop once he reached the side alleys that held few pedestrians roaming the sides or carriages taking up the main road. Speed was his ally and time was not on his side. His concern grew over every passing moment, and in his heart he knew his son's plan was now known. Doubtless Emery and Antoinette had been married quickly and Susanna was learning of the deception.

And Aldaric knew how the queen would handle that.

"Suzy, we need to talk." He remembered their breakup so vividly, though it was many years ago. They were young, their wedding just a few months away, and whatever giddiness his bride-to-be had suddenly faded from her face when she saw the seriousness in his eyes as he approached her in her family's parlor room.

"What is it? Is everything alright?" It was the first time she showed concern since he could remember. She was always so carefree when it came to things, but even she could tell that this time something was different.

"Will you walk with me in the garden?" He evaded her question, but she nodded anyways. He took her hand in his and held it close, the guilt rising over what he was going to do. But his heart hoped more than it ached, and he knew it had to be done.

They walked outside, the sun of summer's day glistening through the plants and trees. It was a beautiful setting, fit more for romance than hurt. As they walked, he held her hand, keeping his eyes ahead. The grass seemed so much greener in the distance, he remembered.

"What is it you want to talk to me about?" she asked, breaking their silence. "You look troubled. Is there a snag in the wedding plans? If that tailor is unable to get the silk I've requested, I know a better one that can make you a finer suit."

He shook his head, ignoring her constant complaints over their nuptials. It was so pointless fretting over frivolous things.

"No, the tailor is fine. It has nothing to do with him, but…it is related to the wedding."

"Say no more." She gave him a playful wink as she drew closer. *"I understand what it is that bothers you. You wish the wedding to be sooner. I promise, my handsome Daric, that I share the same sentiment. When I think of waking in your arms every morning, my heart flutters in delight!"*

"Suzy, that's not what I mean…"

His words went ignored like they usually did, and it made him think of Anna. The simple Hugellian girl he met walking the roads of Kettensburg one day, helping her up after a nobleman knocked her down passing by. She was so kind and willing to listen when he spoke, and though they were only friends, his heart ached to be with her. She was the one he loved so ardently. Even if it meant never marrying, he always wanted Anna. Whether she was a friend or a lover, it didn't matter to him, as long as she was in his life.

"Prince John will let us use the palace, I'm sure. He's very fond of me, you know. Always sending me letters. Had I not told him I was marrying you, I'm sure he would've snatched me up!" Susanna stopped, pulling Aldaric with her as she kissed him tenderly. Her lips sent no passion through him like it once did, and her mentioning of Prince John only killed whatever feeling he had for her. *"It just shows how much I adore you, my handsome Daric. I could have any man I want - even the future king - and I chose you."*

She kissed him again, her arms wrapping around his waist, but before she could go any further, he pulled away.

"Daric, what's wrong?" she asked, perturbed. *"Don't tell me you're not in the mood for this, because I know better."*

"I'm not in the mood right now, Suzy. I came out here to talk. Nothing more." He removed her hands from his waist

and held them to his chest. Her brows lowered, half in concern and half in frustration, and she gave a low huff.

"What is it then?"

He exhaled slowly, hoping and praying for the right words to make the moment go easier. He was never one who wanted to hurt someone, especially one he cared about, but things had gone too long with her. As much as he tried to convince himself that he had a happy life with her, he didn't, and his future would be no different.

He couldn't change her to be the woman he wanted her to be and he wasn't about to spend his life in regret. He saw with his own mother and stepfather how a marriage built on prestige and lack of intimacy worked. All they had was physical attraction, but that faded quickly in time. Now the only thing that held them together was their wedding vows and the hope of preventing divorce.

And if he stayed with Susanna, he knew they would head down the same path. Was he attracted to his fiancée? Certainly. She was even more beautiful than Anna. But there was nothing else. There was no friendship and deep bond where he could talk about anything with her. There was no give and take. There was no shared purpose or deep understanding between them.

With Anna, he had all of that, but with Susanna, he didn't.

"I want to let you know, Suzy, that I care for you very much." His words started off flowery, and she smiled when she heard them.

"I care for you very much, too."

"And because I care for you, I know that it would be unfair to you by keeping my thoughts bottled up."

Susanna's smile widened, and it pained him to see it. She wasn't understanding that what he was about to say would hurt her. It was time to stop playing with words and just tell her what was on his mind.

"I'm in love, Susanna, but…it's not with you."

At first she gave a laugh, as if she didn't believe him, but after seeing the seriousness on his face, her lip quivered, and whatever joy was in her eyes suddenly flashed with fury. She didn't cry - no, she was too proud for that - but she did slap him in the face, and it stung.

"Who is the other woman?" she demanded. "How long have you been with her? How far have you gone?"

He rubbed the reddening area of his cheek, feeling the burn. Before he could say anything, she slapped the other side and yelled, "ANSWER ME! If you are having an affair, then I want the details!"

"I haven't had an affair," Aldaric replied calmly, keeping his voice in check to prevent the conversation from going into a fight. "I have always been faithful to you, Susanna. That hasn't changed."

"Then how can you be in love if you haven't done anything? I know you're lying, Aldaric. Who is the woman?"

He sighed, frustrated she didn't believe him, though he was telling the truth. Even Anna didn't know his feelings for her. "I'm not lying, Susanna. I've been faithful to you."

"Clearly you haven't, if you're in love with someone else! Now stop changing the subject and TELL ME WHO THE WOMAN IS!"

He paused, unsure if he should say anything, yet knowing Susanna wouldn't let it go until he did. "It's Anna."

"Anna? That street-sweeper from Kettensburg?"

"Yes."

"But she's nothing but a filthy peasant!"

Aldaric beaded his eyes; he wouldn't take the bait. She was itching for a fight, but he wasn't about to give her one. "I'm sorry. I know this hurts you, but…"

"Hurts me? Let me tell you something, Aldaric! This doesn't hurt me. I can have any man I want! It's you who's going to be hurt! She'll never please you. She'll be nothing more than a common dog!"

Aldaric bit his tongue to keep it from lashing out. "Susanna, please…"

"No! I'm not done speaking, Aldaric, and you will not interrupt! Do you realize you are NOTHING without me? I'm the one who gives you favor with King Erick. I'm the one who could get you the throne of Hugellia instead of that pathetic ambassador job. I'm the one who gives you connection and style and prestige in the people's eyes! I'm the one who gives you even a chance of having money!"

"Do you not get it, Susanna," Aldaric interrupted, his voice finally starting to raise, "that those things mean nothing to me? I don't care about the power and wealth and how I look to the people! Do you want to know why I fell in love with Anna? It's because she understands what's more important in life!"

"Money and power get you ahead in the world, Aldaric! Sweeping streets is useless once a horse tramples through."

"But this is why it isn't working with us. I don't want to take Erick's place as king! I don't want more money so I can flaunt it in front of others. I don't care about popularity. I wanted that ambassador position so I could help my nation without Erick's

meddling. I wanted to connect with people so I could hear their concerns and help them, not make myself look better! And if I do have money, I want to give it away to people who need it. Anna understands these things. That's why I'm in love with her; we share a common heart!"

An awkward silence passed save the heaving of Aldaric catching his breath. Susanna only stood there, shocked and looking hurt, saying nothing, and it made him feel terrible.

"Suzy...I'm sorry." He tried kissing her cheek to see if that would help, but she didn't stir. He tried taking her in his arms and holding her like she always enjoyed, but her hands remained at her side. "Suzy, if you and I could share those ideas, then I would be at your side for all eternity. But I know how this works. If all we have is physical attraction, our relationship will fall apart."

"It's already falling apart," Susanna said quietly, her eyes on the ground. "It fell apart when you said you loved her."

Guilt crept into Aldaric's heart, and for a moment he wished he never said anything. To see his fiancée's face so downcast and sad...it made his heart ache.

"I still love you, Susanna. I'll go to my grave loving you. But I can't keep pretending that our relationship is perfect when it isn't. I've been willing to work and make it better, but you never listen..."

She pushed him away at that comment, and her eyes flared with anger again. "I always listen, Aldaric! It's you who never listens! We never had any problems between us, and I have been faithful to you when I had so many chances to leave. It's you who's the problem! YOU!"

She gave him another smack before stomping off towards her home. He thought of following her back to see if she was alright, but then thought against it. She was in no mood for reconciliation, and what could he say to make her feel better?

"GO BACK TO YOUR PEASANT WHORE!" he heard Susanna shout, making a few of the workers in the distance suddenly look up in concern. "I DON'T NEED YOU AND CAN HAVE ANYONE I WANT! I PROMISE YOU, ALDARIC, THAT YOU'LL REGRET LEAVING ME, BUT I'LL NEVER REGRET YOU!"

Their engagement was broken after that. They never spoke of the relationship again until years later when he and Anna visited Edeland when Emery was a child. Even then, the conversation was unpleasant. But the past was the past, and he refused to dwell on it. He returned home and confessed his love to Anna while Susanna married Prince John. They made their homes and had their children.

But then their children just had to fall in love with each other. It was an awkward inconvenience, to be sure.

Staalberg palace was ahead and Aldaric approached the front gate, removing his hood as a royal guard came before him.

"State your business," the guard said.

"My name is Aldaric van Ketten of Hugellia," he began, his accent clear and thick. "I am here on a matter regarding my son, Emmerich, and must speak with Her Majesty, the queen."

"Queen Susanna is busy at the moment dealing with a personal matter."

Aldaric frowned. Already he had lost too much time. "And I assure you, sir, that personal matter is related to me. Please, tell her I have arrived and request an audience. I am sure she'll let me in."

The guard nodded, sending a messenger to the throne room.

It didn't take long for Aldaric to be admitted. He was quickly ushered through, being led by a few guards straight to the throne room. Their quietness concerned him, and he knew it had to be serious for him to be given such easy passage. As they walked down the hall, he could hear the conversation boom in the distance.

"I don't care who he is, Your Majesty! If he took my bride, then I want him hanged immediately!" A Liegen accent, clearly the supposed groom Antoinette had left for Emery. He sounded angry and his voice was laced with fire.

"Justice will be served, my prince, I assure you!" Susanna's voice sounded grating to Aldaric's ears, and he could only imagine the venom she spewed at his son. It burned his heart hearing it.

"You beast! Do you deny you have forced my fiancée into marriage and into the marriage bed?"

"As I have told the queen, I will tell you...Antoinette and I married on our own free will and our relations were consensual. You have no proof that it was forced and therefore cannot arrest me!"

Emmerich's defense of himself made Aldaric hurry his steps. Susanna would not take kindly to his words, true or not.

"Then let Lady Antoinette speak for herself!" Prince Arnold replied, but the opening of the throne room door kept anyone from saying another word.

"Forgive us for the interruption, my queen," the head guard said. "Aldaric van Ketten of Hugellia has arrived and requests an audience with you."

Aldaric watched as Emmerich turned in surprise, his face full of mixed emotion as their eyes met. He looked hurt, beaten, and that angered him. And yet something else bothered him in what he saw. He thought his son would be filled with relief at seeing him, but there was too much confusion...even a hint of anger...in his face. That could only mean one thing.

He knows of Susanna and me.

"I see you waste no time in getting here, Aldaric," Susanna said with a scoff. "It makes me wonder if you knew about this little situation between your son and my daughter ahead of time." Aldaric looked around, noticing the others. Arnold had his fists clenched and Antoinette had her head down, looking away and saying nothing. Emmerich just looked at him.

"I only learned of my son's intentions as he left Reigal, Your Majesty."

"And yet you are here, requesting an audience with me. Do you not trust our children to handle their own affairs?"

"Clearly you don't, seeing as you got to them before I did."

Susanna frowned, resting her chin on her palm. "What is it you want, Aldaric? Are you here to reason with me or are we on the same side for once?"

"It depends. Though seeing my son bloodied and bruised makes me think we're about to have a disagreement."

Susanna narrowed her eyes. "He deserved it. He was caught kidnapping my daughter and forcing her into marriage."

"That is an awfully big statement to back up without much proof."

"It was consensual, Dad," Emmerich muttered. "I didn't force Antoinette to do anything."

Of course he didn't. Aldaric knew his son better than that. He raised him to treat women with the utmost respect. But his eyes went to Antoinette, and his brow lowered in concern. She wasn't saying much, and that made him wonder. "What of you, Princess Antoinette? What say you on this matter?"

She looked up, her face firm. "I've told my mother that I married him on my own free will. Our relations were consensual."

He turned back to Susanna. "There you have it. No proof."

"I am not convinced, Aldaric. I know how conniving and deceptive a van Ketten boy can be. Was I not misled by you as well at their age?"

Aldaric turned and saw Emmerich cross his arms. So he knew, then... as did Antoinette. He could only imagine the lies Susanna spread to turn his child against him.

"Susanna, you are misleading the conversation. This is not about us. It is about them."

She leaned forward. "I never said it was about us, Aldaric. Your boy has done a very grave thing in Edeland and justice is being demanded by Prince Arnold. I do not take this lightly."

"And neither do I," Aldaric answered. "Which is why I requested an audience with you. Speak with me, Susanna, so that we may discuss this matter."

"Anything you wish to discuss can be discussed now."

"Everything we say will be interrupted by others. For now, I ask that you give me a private audience. Then we can speak with the others."

His eyes met Susanna's and he held her gaze. For a moment he saw a hint of the young girl he was once betrothed to, but it quickly passed and he was left with the hardened woman he left. "Very well," she replied with a sneer. "But it will not be long." She turned to the guards. "Take my daughter to her room so she may clean herself up. Prince Arnold and the van Ketten boy can be outside the door."

"Emery goes with me, Mother," Antoinette said as she took Emmerich's hand in hers. "I want to talk privately with him, too."

Susanna frowned. "But..."

"*I said he goes with me.*"

Aldaric watched as they were led out of the room. For Susanna to allow Emmerich to go with Antoinette, something had to be wrong. He was sure of it.

The door shut, interrupting his thoughts, and soon only the guards were left. After a moment of quiet, Susanna turned to them. "Leave us."

"But...Your Majesty..."

"I said leave us."

They hesitated at first, but after a firm glare, they bowed, exiting the room. Aldaric watched as the last of them left, and before long, he was alone with Susanna in the throne room.

"Well, my sweet Daric," she said with feigned pleasantry. "Pray, what is it you wanted to tell me?"

Chapter 10: Curse of the Bitter Heart

Antoinette shivered as she hurried down the hallway. Though her dress was back on and she had been given another cloak to be warm, she still felt a chill plague her. She hadn't the heart to say it wasn't from the weather, but from her own anxiety, and she crossed her arms tight to keep her body from shaking.

Emmerich seemed to notice she was bothered, and he kept a steady hand on her back, staying close.

"Are you alright?" he asked as they entered her room. The guards remained at the door, not leaving their sight and giving them little time alone.

She ignored Emmerich for a moment and turned to the guards. "May I have a little privacy? I'd rather not change my clothes in front of you."

The head guard turned to Emmerich, expecting to take him out of the room, too. Antoinette shook her head as she pulled Emmerich towards her. "I need Emery here. You go. That's an order."

The guards shrugged, stepping outside and closing the door. "We're right here in case you need us."

"Thank you," Antoinette answered, and she turned to Emmerich.

He stayed close, watching for any clue to what she was thinking. "Are you alright?" he repeated.

She left his presence and sat on the bed with a huff. "What do you think?"

He blinked, almost as if he was confused. Typical, clueless male. "I don't understand."

"What's there not to understand?" Antoinette asked, her brow scrunching. "You lied to me, Emery!"

His eyes widened. "What did I lie about?"

"You never told me your father had an affair on my mother!"

He looked shocked, almost appalled, as if she hadn't seen that reaction before. "He didn't have an affair!"

From what her mother said, the story was much different. "They were engaged. He met another woman. He then left my mother and married the other woman. You honestly think that doesn't ring familiar to me?"

Emmerich's mouth dropped agape, and at first he was quiet. "Antoinette...my father and Edward were two different people in two different situations..."

"How is it different?"

"Because for one, Dad ended the engagement before he even got involved with my mom!"

Antoinette's voice rose. "Oh? So you *do* know the story?"

"Look..." Emmerich sighed, rubbing his brow, his head still aching from the hit he received earlier. "You want to know what I know? Fine. I'll tell you. My father told me he was engaged once and that he ended it. He didn't tell me who he was engaged to. All he said was that he and she were different people and going down different paths. He felt bad about ending it so late with her, but he knew they weren't meant to be. He broke the engagement and went back to Hugellia and then told my mother he was in love with her."

"And that's all you know?" Antoinette asked, still not believing him.

"That's all I know. Anything else is what I found out with you."

A moment of silence followed, and Antoinette watched as Emmerich's face softened. He approached her, taking her hand in his and pressing it to his lips. "Antoinette, let's not fight." He kissed her fingers again, closing his eyes with the tenderness a husband would use. When he opened his eyes again, he met her gaze. "I know today hasn't been ideal, but it's a special day for us. We're married now. It's the first day of forever. Instead of fighting, we should be standing by each other."

"Emery, I'm standing by you. I even lied for you. But I don't appreciate being in the dark over something this big!"

"But it's in the past. What happened with our parents won't happen to us."

Antoinette looked away, her eyes watering. How blind did Emery think she was? He believed in fairy tales, that there was such a thing as happily ever after, but she knew better. She saw that fairy tales were just stories and that happily ever after was a product of imagination, not truth. She believed with all her heart that Edward would be faithful, and he proved her wrong.

"Emery, nothing's a guarantee," she whispered.

"How can you say that?" he asked, his face showing hurt. "Have I ever, *ever* shown myself as unfaithful?"

"Edward never did until he came back with Malina."

He let go of her hand, moving so he could be in her line of sight. "I'm not Edward, Antoinette. I never have been and never will be. I made a vow before God that I would always be faithful to you and I will *never* break that promise. How can you even think that I would?"

"Because you weren't honest with me."

"I am being honest with you. When have I not?"

"You weren't honest with me about the letter."

Emmerich blinked, shaking his head. "What?"

"The letter that you wrote to me confessing your feelings; the one that Edward stole," Antoinette reminded him. "You weren't honest with me about that. I didn't know how you felt for *years* until I confronted you about it. You kept that a secret too!"

"Antoinette, you know why I didn't tell you about that!"

"And yet you know I would've wanted to know anyways, but you still kept me in the dark!"

"How is that even lying?"

Before she could answer, there was a swing of the door, and in walked her sister. "What do you mean I can't go in? It's not like I haven't helped my sister with her corset before!" But after shutting the door and seeing Antoinette sitting on the bed and Emmerich standing in front of her, she whistled and put her hand back on the knob.

"Oh...uhm...well, this is awkward..." Bernie stammered as she looked around the room. "Didn't think that you were in here, Emmerich."

"Where else would I be?" he asked, perturbed, as he crossed his arms.

"The stocks were my first thought, to be honest." Bernie smirked. "I take it Mother knows of our little plan and is taking it better than we thought?"

Emmerich lowered his head, rubbing his brow. "If you call knocking me unconscious and spreading lies as taking things well, I'd hate to see her cross."

Antoinette's eyes flared at Emmerich's remark, and she stood to her feet. "My mother is not lying! If anything, she's the only one being honest!"

"How is she being honest when she kept quiet, too? You were in the dark just like I was. Why didn't your mother tell you about the relationship?"

Antoinette's anger subsided for a moment as she listened to Emery's words. As much as she hated to admit it, he was right. Why *didn't* Mother tell her about Aldaric? "I...I don't know..."

"How is she any different from my dad, then?" he continued. "We've both been kept from the truth, Antoinette. I'm just as surprised as you are!"

It was true, but there was still a major difference, and that was what made Antoinette hurt the most. "You're right, but that doesn't change the fact that your father left her."

"Uh...I take it I missed something." Bernie stepped forward in between the two. "Who said what, now?"

"Apparently Emmerich's father and our mother were once engaged, Bernie," Antoinette began. "Then he left her for another woman. Sound familiar?"

Bernie's eyes widened as she looked to Emmerich. "Wait - *what?*"

"I didn't know he was engaged to your mother," Emmerich replied to Bernie, his face stern. "I knew he had a prior relationship, *but that was it.*" He looked back to Antoinette, frowning. "Just because my father and Susanna's relationship ended doesn't mean history is going to repeat itself."

"Well...that explains Mother's constant crankiness and why she hates you so much," Bernie said, giving an exhale.

"You don't know the half of it," Emmerich muttered.

"She's only looking out for me. You can't blame her for that!" Antoinette said as she edged closer to him.

"She's trying to turn you against me, but you're not seeing it!" Emmerich argued back. "She's putting doubts into your head and she's trying to break us up!"

"Or maybe she's trying to warn me because she doesn't want another man leaving!"

"I'm not going to leave you, Antoinette!" Emmerich's voice sounded like a plea, and she turned her back on him, not wanting to hear his excuses anymore. Emmerich muttered a curse, throwing himself onto the bed and burying his face into his hands.

"Have I ever given you a reason not to trust me?" His voice was cracked, almost as if holding back tears. She didn't care. Even Edward sounded hoarse when he told her he loved Malina.

"I'm not saying you have. But I'm in a difficult place, Emmerich." She turned back around to face him. "You don't understand because you've never had anyone you loved walk out on you. I have." She paused, her lip quivering again, and she couldn't help but let a few tears fall. She thought she was over the hurt Edward had caused, but now, as she stood in her room, she realized it was still there. She was still angry. She was still hurt. She was still so bitter Edward chose Malina over her. "I can't...I can't go through that. My heart was ripped out of me and I refuse to let anyone else do that again!"

"And I won't," Emmerich said as he looked back up, meeting her teary gaze.

"But I don't know that," Antoinette choked. "Your father left my mother. Your cousin left me. Unfaithfulness seems to run in your family."

She let out a quick sob as Bernie came around and put a hand on her shoulder, but she got it under control. She was so tired of crying and she wanted to be strong. Emmerich watched from the bed, his own eyes teary, but he didn't move. He only looked at her as she looked at him.

"Antoinette, I can't make you trust me," he began softly. "I can't undo what's happened in the past. I can't guarantee what's going to happen in the future. What I can guarantee is that I love you. I have told you that so...many...times...and not once have you ever said you loved me back."

"So what are you trying to say?"

"All I'm saying is that I love you. I always will." He sighed, his expression looking suddenly weary. "And I trust you with my heart. I just hope you can trust yours with me."

Antoinette looked away, unsure of what else to say.

It had been a long time since she had seen Aldaric last.

His appearance changed little. His dark hair had been sprinkled with gray and his eyes were wearier than before, but otherwise he stayed the same. His weight hadn't changed and his face remained handsome. His posture was still firm and straight and he carried himself like a nobleman should.

But that didn't mean Susanna was happy to see him. She knew why he was there, and for that reason alone, she wanted him to leave.

He was the first to speak. "Where's John?"

His inquiry of her husband brought some pleasure to her heart. She made sure that her beauty only improved with age, and she was certain Aldaric was admiring what he could have had from behind seemingly disinterested eyes. "My husband is out of town with the boys, hunting. They will return tomorrow." She paused, eyeing him curiously. "What of Anna?"

"She is with my family."

"How quaint. I suppose it is just the two of us then."

He nodded. "We can speak honestly with each other."

"Don't we always?" she began with her typical confident gaze. "My guard tells me you wished a private audience with me, so here I am. What have you to say?"

"I think you know the topic of conversation," Aldaric replied as he stepped forward, stopping before he got to the throne. "I'm here for my son."

"Here to defend him, or here to take him away?"

Aldaric tilted his head. "That depends on you."

"Hmph." She leaned back in her seat, looking at him with a pout. "I should say it depends on your son and his actions. These charges are serious matters."

Aldaric's eyes narrowed. "You and I know Arnold's accusations are overwhelmed with falsehood."

"You know me so little, Aldaric, if you think I take this lightly. My daughter acts strangely, and when I follow her, I find her in a bedroom with a man who is not her fiancé and in the most indecent of situations. Forgive me if I consider Antoinette's honor a serious matter."

Aldaric never did respond well to sarcasm, and he crossed his arms. His face remained firm, and Susanna felt a thrill in seeing his typically hidden temper rising. Good. She hoped to anger him so much that he'd get a glimpse of how angry she felt when he left her.

"I take this very seriously, Susanna. Why else do you think I followed him here?"

"So you admit you knew something of the matter, then?"

"I admit I knew of my son speaking with your daughter and her saying she was being forced into a marriage with a prince she wanted nothing to do with. It's a shame that you were in the dark about it."

Susanna clenched the arm rests of her seat as she faced him. "My daughter has said nothing to me in objection to her engagement!"

"I doubt that," he said, his voice low. "You never were a good listener, Suzy. You only hear what you want to hear."

Her anger flared, and she didn't know what infuriated her more - the fact that he brought up a flaw he had always accused her of, or the pet name he called her when they were together.

Either way, she was livid.

"Be careful how you tread here, Aldaric," she began, her voice low. "I am not the young maiden you once knew. I am a queen; though my husband is Edeland's leader by name, it is I who runs this country and its affairs. If you seek to insult me in my very throne room, Emmerich's fate will become the least of your worries."

"I'm not here for insults, nor am I here to bring up old wounds," he said, his voice softening. It was pathetic how easily he was reined in. "I am only here for my son to make sure he gets back home."

"And that is where the problem lies," Susanna said. "Your son is now married to my daughter and the marriage has been consummated. I am not willing to part with my daughter, and I am especially not willing to give her up to a criminal."

Aldaric clenched his fists. "He is *not* a criminal. It is a mockery of justice to charge him with no proof or accusation from Antoinette!"

There was a moment of tense silence, and the two only stared at each other, both trying to keep tempers in check. Susanna watched as Aldaric's eyes never left hers, and she waited. He was never one to stay angry for long, and if there was ever a person that was more stubborn, it was her. She would never concede defeat.

He finally turned away with a huff, crossing his arms. "Hugellia will consider this an international incident knowing you are holding a member of the royal family and charging him with crimes he didn't commit."

"You act as if your son is a prince. Ha! Erick will not care. Besides, the situation favors me more than it favors you. He will want to know why your son hurried off to Edeland when he wasn't supposed to be here. He will also want to know why he meddled in an arranged alliance between us and Liegen. Lies, deceit, tampering with international relations...it doesn't look good, Aldaric. You know this. Erick will not side with you."

"You portray this completely one-sided. Antoinette wanted Emery to be here and save her from a forced union. Even Erick cannot deny this," Aldaric said.

Susanna stifled a laugh. "Perhaps not. But you are still in a bind. A member of his family secretly married a princess in another country. You saw what happened with Edward's scandal. Do you think your son will fare better than him in the same situation?"

Aldaric frowned, knowing he was caught. Susanna couldn't help but feel a rush of pride go through her heart in seeing him so cornered.

"I won't deny the scandal that may ensue," Aldaric began with a sigh. "But as Edward has weathered his storm, so can our children...as long as we support them."

"You ask me to support such a marriage? How dare you, Aldaric!" Susanna snarled. "You forget the charges brought up against your son! Would you really think I would support someone like that?"

"Emery is innocent. You forget that Antoinette has brought up no charges against him and has said her relations with him were consensual."

"In front of her 'husband', she says this," Susanna scoffed. "But she could be saying such things under pressure. I would not take her words at heart unless she said them in confidence."

"Then our talk is wasted when the decision should be hers. If she wishes to be married with my son, then there should be no issue."

"But the question lies in whether she wishes to be married to him." Susanna paused, straightening herself up in her seat. "If this is a forced marriage on your son's part, rest assured I will have no mercy on him."

"Then bring Antoinette here without Emery and without Arnold. Ask her yourself if she was forced into this marriage."

"I can agree to that."

Aldaric pressed his lips together and nodded. "Good. I have faith that Antoinette will speak the truth and settle this matter for us."

Of course she would, but not in the way he suspected. The thought made Susanna laugh internally. She got up and strolled to the doorway, calling one of the guards. "Bring my eldest daughter here to me," she said. "I wish to speak with her alone."

"Yes, Your Majesty."

The guard scurried off and Susanna turned back to Aldaric and went to him. He stood stiffly as she circled him, obviously nervous in her presence. She couldn't help but find pleasure in his being so uncomfortable.

"If you don't mind stepping away as I speak with her, I would be appreciative," she said as she stopped in front of him. "I don't want her being pressured by your words."

Aldaric narrowed his eyes. "Very well."

She turned away and sat back on the throne, waiting for Antoinette to arrive. As she watched Aldaric stand in silence, she couldn't help but feel confident. The look on his face showed worry, fear…but the look on her face showed triumph.

He was about to lose the most precious thing to him, and his heart would soon be shattered. She hid a smile behind her hand as she rested in her seat.

Revenge had never felt so wonderful, and she couldn't wait to see Aldaric suffer.

$\mathcal{C}$hapter 11: The Choice of Faith

"I'm sorry."

Antoinette looked up from where she stood, noticing Emmerich had gotten up from the bed and approached her. He exhaled slowly as he took her hand in his and held it to his heart.

"Sorry for what?" she asked, meeting his soft gaze.

"For not telling you about my father's engagement." He took her hand and caressed it, the gentleness of his touch feeling light on her skin. "I did not think it relevant before, but now I know better. Forgive me. There should be no secrets between us and I am sorry for causing you distress on what should have been our happiest day."

He lowered her hand back to his waist, gazing into her eyes. He looked sorrowful, like a scolded puppy, but the truth still hid behind his eyes. He firmly believed her mother wished to separate them, and the story of Aldaric was only a way of pushing her back towards Arnold. Truth or not, it was certainly a possibility, and more than ever she wished things were more clear.

"You don't have to apologize," she said quietly.

"If it reconciles us and keeps us together, then I will apologize as much as I can," he said. "No matter what, I'm going to stand by you and make this marriage work."

She gave a small smile. Doubts remained, but she couldn't deny Emery's persistence.

He leaned forward, gently touching his forehead to hers. "I have faith in us," he whispered. "And I have faith in you."

But did she have faith in him? It was a question she couldn't help but wonder.

Her thoughts were interrupted as the door swung open, revealing two guards from the throne room. Bernie stood at attention, crossing her arms in a huff as she glared the men down. "Not much for privacy, are you?"

The guards ignored her as they approached Antoinette, motioning for Emmerich to move. He kept a hand around her in a protective gesture, standing beside.

"The queen requests your presence, Princess Antoinette," the first guard said. He turned to Emmerich. "Alone."

"Very well." Antoinette moved away from her husband, giving him a quick glance as he hesitated to let her go. "I'll be back soon."

His hand dropped away from her waist slowly and he watched her leave.

She was led down the hallway towards the throne room, her mind racing and her emotions a wreck. She knew it was only a matter of time before Mother would want to speak with her regarding the day's incident, but she felt unprepared for what she was about to face. Mother's earlier conversation regarding Aldaric was jarring, filling her once-made-up-mind with doubts. But then there was Emmerich's pleading of trust to her. She made a vow before God and man only hours earlier to be faithful and trust him with her life. Could she really run at the first test of their relationship?

I trust you with my heart. Will you trust yours with me?

Faith was something she should have in her husband, but with a whirlwind of a romance and a hurtful past, doubting was much easier and made her feel secure.

She wanted to cry as she entered the throne room. Never had she felt so torn in all her life.

Aldaric stood to the side as Susanna sat on the throne, and the guards led Antoinette to her mother before returning to the Hugellian ambassador. Aldaric remained silent, giving her a kind nod as she met his gaze, and her heart sunk as he was taken out of the room. Aldaric remaining silent meant that her future was in the hands of herself...or her mother.

Either way, the outlook seemed grim.

"Step forward, child. No one will hear us speak when it is the two of us," Susanna began as she beckoned Antoinette to approach the throne. "We have much to discuss."

"About my relationship with Emmerich?"

"Yes."

"What is it you wish to know?"

Susanna's face was warm yet firm, and it made Antoinette uneasy seeing her mother so calm. "Are you two romantically involved?"

"Yes."

"For how long?"

Antoinette pursed her lips. "A...few days..."

Susanna's eyes widened and she let out a laugh. "Are you serious, child? What foolishness is this?"

"We rekindled our friendship after Edward and I broke up," Antoinette began. "Emery was there for comfort and support. He revealed he had feelings for me, but I insisted we wait until I was ready to pursue a relationship. When I became engaged to Arnold, however, we spoke once more and he proposed. I accepted."

"And so you eloped?"

"Yes."

"Tell me, child," Susanna said as she rubbed her brow. "Why did you accept his proposal without being in a relationship?"

Antoinette felt her heart rate go faster in nervousness. She knew where this was leading. "I didn't want to marry Arnold."

"Oh. I see." Susanna gave a pout. "Why did you not wish to marry him?"

"Because I don't love him."

"And you love Emmerich?"

Antoinette opened her mouth to speak, but nothing came out. She closed it quickly, letting out a sigh. Did she love Emmerich?

"I've asked you a question, child. Do you love Emmerich?"

"I..." Antoinette's voice caught in her throat, and her heart felt heavy. Emotions were swirling and her feelings were a mixture of both love and anger, faith and doubt. But as she looked deeper, asking herself what she really thought of him, questionable family past or not, the truth became clear.

Out of every man, he never abandoned her.

Out of every man, he never forced his wants.

Out of every man, he put her needs above his own.

Out of every man, he was willing to sacrifice his own happiness just to see her happy.

Out of every man, he didn't just say he loved her. He proved it with every fiber of his being.

She had no guarantee of the future, but she could look at the past and present, and aside from her sister, Emmerich van Ketten was the only faithful person she had in her life.

That was proof enough to show what she thought of him.

"Yes," Antoinette replied confidently as she met her mother's curious gaze. "I do love him. Very much, actually."

Mother made no frown, had no change in facial expressions to show what she really thought. She only nodded, as if listening to the conversations of a fool, and folded her hands to her chin.

"Emery is a good man," Antoinette continued, her voice barely above a squeak. She hadn't seen Mother this calm. As strange as it sounded, it worried her. Mother was trying too much to remain in control. "I have known him nearly my entire life and he has been my greatest friend. Once Edward left, though, I realized...Emery was more. When I'm with him, I feel so loved and cared for."

"You sound conflicted, though," Susanna replied softly. "When I found you at the inn, you were much different and more...infatuated...with him. What has changed, aside from him being fully clothed now?"

Antoinette scoffed. Did Mother not listen when she said she loved her husband? Or was it that Mother did not want to hear her words?

"I see my story has been taken to heart." Susanna leaned forward, oblivious to her daughter's lowering brow. "Antoinette, I know this is difficult for you. You play with love because you want it so badly, but you know I only tell you of Aldaric and I to prevent you from suffering as I did."

"This is a different situation, Mother."

"But it is the same feeling. I understand your desire to love and be loved, yet I also understand your heart. Aldaric broke mine, my darling, and I thought I'd never recover until I married your father."

Susanna paused, bowing her head. "Your father picked up the pieces of my broken heart. Though I did not love him as I loved Aldaric when we first married, I grew to love him. And as you see, I am very happy."

"So you married Father after Aldaric left you?" Antoinette asked, her heart starting to fill with fire.

"Yes, child. He proposed very soon after Aldaric left."

"What made him propose to you?"

"Oh, it's a wonderful tale!" Susanna said as she leaned back dreamily. "We had been friends for some time and he had always been in love with me. When Aldaric left, he made arrangements with my parents for me to marry him..." Suddenly she paused, her eyes widening.

Antoinette could only look at her mother as her face hardened. They did not have to say a word to each other, but they understood, and Susanna's once calm demeanor soon turned to a stifling rage. She knew she had slipped up.

"Your marriage to Father sounds awfully similar to mine, Mother. The only difference is I eloped while your parents gave your union their blessing." Antoinette narrowed her eyes, her jaw still clenched tight.

"It is still different, child," Mother said, her voice low. "Your father did not come from a family of adulterers. His lineage is pure and spotless."

Antoinette looked away, unable to speak. What could she say in retaliation?

"Nothing to say on that one?" Susanna gave a smirk. "It seems that your doubts in this marriage are already stronger than your faith."

Antoinette's voice rose. "*No.* Emery won't leave me. I have faith that our marriage *will* work!"

"Hmph. So you wish to stay with him?"

Antoinette nodded. "I do."

"Well I cannot force you to listen to reason," the queen said. "But I can take steps to make sure you are looked after and are given a life that you need."

Antoinette's face paled as she looked to her mother, her features firm and serious and, if she was willing to admit, frightening. Eyes fiery, fists clenched, jaw tense and a body no longer casual, but confident...Mother meant business when she spoke this time, and things could only get worse.

"What sort of steps, Mother?"

"I cannot have a scandal with you marrying that worthless son of the Hugellian ambassador. A princess is not meant to marry someone with the taint of the peasant class. It is beneath you and it is beneath your family that you would even enter such a union."

"But I am married to Emery. That can't be changed!"

"Your marriage can be easily annulled," Susanna replied with a scoff. "I am queen. Anything I say can be made law. But I am not a harsh woman. I shall leave the choice up to you on what happens next."

Antoinette blinked. "What are the choices?"

"Either leave Emmerich and marry Arnold on your own accord, or I shall dispose of Emmerich myself so you can marry Arnold."

Antoinette's eyes flared with fury. "That is no choice, Mother! Either way you are forcing me to marry Arnold!"

"There is no questioning this, Antoinette. If you wish to behave like an adult and make your own decisions, then you must accept one of the choices! I will have it no other way."

"That isn't fair, Mother, and it isn't right! What has Emery ever done to you to make you hate him so?"

"His only fault was being born. Such an abomination of the nobility should not even be allowed inside our presence! The stain of the peasants will forever be on him, and by marrying him, it stains you. But I can fix that. I can wash away that stain. I can help you overcome your gullibility and provide for you a stable and prosperous future like what I've achieved."

"But I don't want *your* life! I want a life of my own!" Antoinette's voice neared a yell and for once, she didn't care. Doubts were one thing, but marrying Emmerich was *her* choice. If it was the wrong decision, then she was willing to live with the consequences. But no matter what she chose, Mother would not have it. No matter what, she wanted Arnold in the family. "You can't make me marry Arnold, Mother! I'm staying with Emery whether you like it or not!"

"Impossible child!" Susanna spat. "I refuse to have such a taint upon my household!"

"You can't make me leave him, Mother. Not if I want to stay."

"Silly girl, do you not see how this works? I may not be able to physically pry you away from him, but I can *make* you leave him. Know this: I am the least of your concerns. Arnold is demanding justice in his unfair treatment, and I have no choice but to give it. If you wish to stay with Emmerich, then Arnold has a right to make claims against him."

"What do you mean?"

"I mean you're about to see the first ripple of the wave you just made." Susanna stood to her feet. "Arnold has brought charges against him, child. I cannot let such claims go unheeded, and I have no choice but to arrest Emmerich!"

Antoinette's eyes widened in horror. "But...Mother, I told you everything was consensual! Emery and I have done nothing wrong!"

"I doubt you, child. I don't know how that boy is controlling you or how he has tainted your mind, but I will not let more harm come to you. I will allow Arnold to speak and we will try Emmerich when your father returns tomorrow."

"But Mother!"

"Fear not, my daughter, as I will fix things in time. I will not let the loss of your chastity go unpunished and will make sure your dignity is restored."

Antoinette moved forward, her voice shaking in panic. "Mother, listen to me! The charges are false. I didn't consummate the marriage with Emery. We never slept together!"

"That would certainly change things, if it were true," Susanna replied. "But how can I believe you? You already said you slept with the man."

"I lied to you to make sure the marriage couldn't be annulled. I swear by my heart that I did not have relations with him!" Antoinette got on her knees to beg. Despite her doubts and stubbornness to stay, she couldn't let Emmerich pay for coming to her aid. He couldn't rot in a jail just because he loved her and Mother wouldn't allow it.

"Get up child! Your begging is an insult as a princess!" Susanna said as she pulled her daughter to her feet. "Besides, this matter is out of my hands. It is Arnold who is being denied his bride. If he could be appeased, however, then perhaps the charges would be dropped."

Antoinette felt a lump come in her throat. "What are you saying?"

"I'm saying Arnold must have his way or else."

Antoinette lowered her head, her eyes filling with tears. This wasn't supposed to happen. Her doomed-from-the-start marriage, her troubled mind, her being hurled into a future of uncertainty and control.

She thought she had a new dream with Emmerich, but even that was starting to shatter.

"How can you allow this, Mother? Does what I want mean nothing to you?"

"You are young, child. You do not yet know what you want."

Antoinette narrowed her eyes, tears suddenly streaming down her face.

"Now make your choice, Antoinette. If you have not consummated your marriage to Emmerich, it will be annulled, and if you marry Arnold, I am sure the prince will be happy to drop the charges and we can put all of this unpleasantness behind us." The queen paused, her voice becoming firm. "But if you choose to stay, there is nothing you can do to save him, and you guarantee him at least imprisonment. But even that would be too easy a punishment."

Antoinette felt her world stop. No matter what, she would lose. Her only choice now was how much she was willing to give up.

"So make your choice, Antoinette: a pleasant life with Arnold or a doomed one with Emmerich."

Antoinette prayed for strength as she lifted her head, the answer uncertain. *Guide me*, she muttered in her spirit as she met her mother's piercing gaze. *Lord, show me the way...I don't know where to go...*

It entered her mind on the route she could take, and she prayed the road would become clear. Her eyes drying, she stood tall and faced her mother. "Where can I get annulment papers?"

The queen smiled, victory etched on her face.

Chapter 12: The Dream Breaks

Emmerich sat in Antoinette's room, saying nothing. Bernie had already gone to spy on the queen's conversation and Aldaric had taken her place. At first, father and son were met with an uncomfortable silence, unsure of what to say to each other, until Emmerich blurted out what was probably on both of their minds: why Aldaric kept quiet about Susanna.

"It wasn't important. My past with Susanna made your mother feel uncomfortable, so I kept silent."

"You should have told me, though," Emmerich had replied. "I just married her daughter. If there was a past between our parents, don't you think I should've known, especially if there were problems between you two?"

"I already told you of my past relationship before your mother. I just didn't say who it was."

"But you should've."

"I was going to tell you in time if your relationship with her got serious. How was I supposed to know this was going to happen so fast?"

Emmerich never scoffed so hard in his life. "You knew I was going to marry her when I left for Reigal. Why didn't you say anything then?"

"I tried to tell you. But even if you did know, would it have stopped you?"

The conversation only got more heated. Once Emmerich was through with his father's excuses, Aldaric then started sounding like Susanna. The marriage wasn't a good idea, the marriage could only lead to trouble...

"It's not that Antoinette isn't a lovely woman," Aldaric continued. "It's just that your relationship with her causes more trouble than you think. The elopement doesn't just affect you, but everyone. Arnold is denied a bride and that angers the royal family in Liegen. Susanna is lied to and that angers the royal family in Edeland. And with you running off and eloping with a foreign princess, that angers our own nation. Your marriage, like it or not, is a scandal similar to Edward's. Everyone will be caught up in it and you'll be shamed for life."

"I'm not Edward. This is different."

"I know. But nations are never fond of surprises, and you just gave them a big one."

Emmerich rolled his eyes. "I don't care what they think. All that matters is that I take care of my wife."

"And what of you? Do you think Susanna will just let you walk out of here with her daughter?" Aldaric's face hinted fear when he spoke, making Emmerich feel a tinge of guilt. "You want the truth of the consequences you're facing with this marriage? If you're lucky, you'll just be thrown in jail. But if we're being realistic, you're facing the hangman's noose. Arnold is already threatening charges on you and he is being encouraged by Susanna."

"Then do what you do best. You're the ambassador. Tell Edeland I'm a Hugellian citizen and that we can make a deal."

"Emery, King Erick will not side with us. He was always fond of Susanna and it was he who originally made the arrangement that I should marry her. I'm sorry that my past is affecting you're future, but there is little I can do here. Unless your marriage with Antoinette ends, you are dooming yourself."

"Then so be it."

Aldaric's face had scrunched in concern, hints of fear and sadness etching on his face. At first he opened his mouth to speak, but after seeing his son's refusal to give up, he pressed his lips together and looked away.

The conversation had ended there. Emmerich was unwilling to listen to any more and Aldaric knew his words were going unheeded. The two men remained in silence, not even looking at each other, and for what seemed like an eternity, they simply existed in each other's presence.

Never before had Emmerich been in such a fight with his father, but he wasn't going to give up on Antoinette. He was an adult now, old enough to make his own decisions, and he was going to trust her.

He waited patiently for her return, and after a while, the silence suddenly ended and voices were heard from the halls.

"I can't believe you're listening to her!" Bernie. He recognized the girl's seething vocals despite the distance. It didn't bode well from how she sounded.

"I don't have a choice, Bernie."

"You *do* have a choice, but you're letting her make it! The least you could do is fight this! Aldaric will help."

"He can't do anything this time. I'm the only one who can."

"But..."

The door opened and Emmerich stood to his feet. Looking at the girls' faces, he could tell they had been under stress. Bernie's face was red and fuming, her brows lowered, while Antoinette's face was pale and tired. His wife looked as if she had been through a strenuous battle, and he didn't doubt that her mother held no mercy for her.

The thought burned his heart, and he wanted nothing more than to run to Antoinette, take her in his arms, and hold her so she could find rest.

He attempted to approach, but her words stopped him in his tracks. "I need to speak with Emery alone."

Aldaric looked to his son with a sad expression, but complied after a nod from Emmerich.

Antoinette turned to Bernie to follow, but her sister only crossed her arms. "No. I'm not going."

"It's my life and you can't make my choices. I'll speak to you later, Bernie. Please. Just go."

Antoinette gave her a look, and after a grunt and a stomp of her foot, Bernie complied, going out of the room. Aldaric was the last to go, leaving Antoinette and Emmerich alone with the guards standing watch at the door.

"I take it the conversation with your mother didn't go well," Emmerich began. Antoinette shrugged, looking away.

"I think we both knew that it wouldn't."

"What did she say?"

"She's not happy. She wants the marriage ended. You...probably already know of the reasons why."

Emmerich let out a sigh. "Of course. So what do we do now?"

Antoinette frowned, her eyes still not on him. "Emery, there isn't much we can do. We were caught. It was silly to think that we could..." She paused, lowering her head even further. Was she crying? Or was she simply not wanting to tell him what was going to happen?

He went to her regardless, wrapping his arms around her and pulling her close. "We'll make this marriage work, Antoinette. I promise."

Her arms remained at her side and she didn't embrace him back. He thought it strange that she was still, and he pulled away to face her. She couldn't look at him.

"We'll make it work," he repeated, but then she shook her head.

"No, we won't."

If he could describe his feelings at that moment, it was as if everything within him suddenly fell into a pit. Heaviness weighed him down and worry consumed his mind. What was she trying to say? Was she giving up? Was she walking away?

"Antoinette, whatever your mother said to you..."

"She didn't say anything new you didn't already hear," Antoinette replied. "I just...I've been thinking...and...I don't see how this is going to work between us."

"But..." He paused, his voice catching in his throat. "Why? This morning you were...we were..."

"I was caught up in the moment," Antoinette replied. "I'm sorry, Emery. I didn't want to hurt you. I was just scared over this marriage with Arnold and it made me panic. When you came in offering me a way out, I was desperate. You gave me a chance to escape and I took it."

"But...our vows..." Emmerich felt the tears coming but he wouldn't let them fall. Not in front of her. She couldn't think of him as a weakling seeing him sob. "I thought...I thought you wanted to marry me. You said yes and..." He turned away, shutting his eyes. Holding back was proving difficult.

Her gaze still focused on the ground as she crossed her arms. "I'm sorry, Emery. I've just been through so much this past year and I'm afraid of getting hurt."

"Antoinette, I would never hurt you!" His voice rose, not in anger but in desperation. How was it that moments before he was in the passions of making love to her only to find himself facing annulment?

"I...I'm sorry, Emery. I don't know what else to say. You shouldn't have been caught up in this and I feel terrible that you have."

He watched her as her head remained down. It was strange to him that she couldn't look him in the eye when speaking. Had she not the strength? Or was it all a lie? Antoinette was never a good liar, and her inability to face him only made him wonder more.

"Antoinette, look at me." He tried to gently push her chin up, but she refused, keeping it back down.

"I don't want to," she muttered in a whisper.

There. That proved there was something amiss. "Antoinette, the least you can do is look at me when saying you want to leave." He paused, noticing her lip starting to quiver. "Please."

She looked up, and he noticed there were tears swelling up in her eyes, too. And when their eyes met, she gave a sniffle, desperate to try and hide her emotions, but failing. The sight gave him a small flicker of hope, and he held on to it tight.

He moved forward and kissed her, and to his joy, she didn't reject it. Rather, she embraced it, and for a few precious seconds he felt the connection that bound his soul to hers when they were being intimate in the inn. Heavens, how he missed her touch, even though it had only been a little while! But the moment didn't last long as she quickly pulled away from him, her hands clutching his arms.

"Emery, don't make this difficult. This is hard enough as it is," she said, looking away. "I've made my choice and you need to trust me that it's the best for both of us."

Emmerich felt her slipping once more, and he felt his heart sink. "Antoinette, you can't speak for me. What is my life without you?"

She looked at him sadly, her pouting lips making him want to kiss them once more. "It'll be happier."

If only it were true. But he knew better. Losing her once was bearable, but a second time? He didn't know if he could handle it. "Don't...don't say that..."

"You'll be glad of this, Emery. You don't understand it now, but you will soon." She pulled out a piece of paper she had folded in her hand, putting it forward for him to take. He opened it, glancing at the contents, and the wording nearly stopped his heart.

Notice of Annulment.

His face lowered and shook, tears entering his eyes again. This time he hadn't the strength to hold them back. "Antoinette..." Even saying her name brought pain. He felt the cracks in his heart forming and it was starting to break...

"I told Mother the truth, that we didn't sleep together. She provided me with the papers. After you sign them, I'll sign them, and then present them to Arnold. After that we're going to get married."

God, no...not this... His prayers felt like they hit a wall and went unheeded, and he was desperate for a glimpse of hope. "You...you want to separate?"

"This is the better choice, Emery. It keeps us both from getting hurt any further."

If only she knew the truth, how he was being hurt deeper now than any other moment he could remember. But his feelings were pushed to the back of his mind as he looked to his...wife. He had to know the truth and she had to tell him to his face.

"Antoinette, is this what you want?"

There was a moment of silence that passed between them and they only looked at each other. She looked away when she finally spoke. "Yes."

He bent forward to meet her gaze. "Antoinette, please look at me when you say it."

She faced him, her voice clear after glancing back to the guards listening at the door. "Yes, this is what I want. Please don't ask me again."

Everything around him blurred at that moment save the feel of his heart shattering. Never had he felt such despair and never had he felt such an ache in his soul. But if Antoinette wanted to walk away, who was he to hold on to her? Her happiness was everything.

"Will this make you happy?" he asked quietly.

"Yes," she replied. "It will."

He nodded slowly, a few tears slipping down his face. "Ok. I'll...I'll sign it...I don't want to, but..." He stopped, his voice catching.

He headed to the nearest desk and took a quill from the corner in his hand, hesitating at first and unwilling to sign. But after a hard swallow and a hold of his breath to keep down the tears, he quickly wrote his name on the end of the paper.

He put down the quill and forced the paper forward. "Here. It's signed."

Antoinette took the paper and held it close. "Thank you."

She wasn't welcome, and Emmerich could only lean forward with his hands against the desk and his head bent down, defeated.

She held her hand forward, a small trinket in her palm. He looked and found his grandmother's ring being given back to him. The sight of it made his soul ache.

"Here," she said quietly. "I don't want anything happening to it. It's in better hands with you."

"It was yours, Antoinette. Not mine."

"Then keep it safe," she said quietly. "For me."

He shook his head, refusing it. "It was always meant for you. I'm not taking it back."

She nodded, clasping it in her palm and bringing it to her chest.

There was a pause before Antoinette broke it. "I'll let your father know what's happening."

"Don't worry. I can tell him."

There was another pause, and he felt a small hand grace his back. "I...I guess this is good-bye, then. The annulment will be final once I sign it, so...you're free to marry someone else."

"I don't want anyone else," he muttered, his eyes too sore for comfort. "I only wanted you."

He stood to his feet and turned to face her. There were a thousand emotions swirling about in him, but as he looked at her, whatever rage or hurt or despair he felt calmed, and the sight of Antoinette...the sight of his wife, no matter what a piece of paper said...was still dear to him. He didn't care if the marriage was annulled. He would still be faithful to her, heart, soul, and body. He bent forward and kissed her cheek, saying, "As long as you're happy."

To his surprise, she hugged him tightly, tears streaming down her face.

But before she pulled away, he heard her whisper in his ear. "I trust you, Emery. Now please trust me." She graced his chin with her fingers, her touch lingering for a moment before she walked away.

He watched her leave, and she didn't look back as she hurried out the door. When she was out of sight, he finally sunk to his knees in his despair.

Antoinette headed down the hallway of the palace towards a small room near the back. It was newly furnished and decorated, its tenant still moving his things in from his home back in Liegen. Arnold's office and personal quarters were only a reminder of what was to become part of her new life, and Antoinette could only feel dread.

Chapter 12 – The Dream Breaks

The look on Emery's face was…disappointing. And why wouldn't it be? She had just broken his heart and told him that the love she promised would be his was going to be taken away and given to another man. She was surprised he took it as well as he did - with a grace and nobility that Arnold couldn't dream of having - and that was what made her sick to the core. Out of the many times he had proven his love to her, perhaps this last time was when he proved it the most.

He was willing to let her go if that was what she wanted. Sure, he was upset. His heart was shattering by the look his watery eyes gave. But her choice mattered above all else. What other man on the earth would give her such control over her own life?

She swallowed the lump that wanted to stay in her throat. The next moment was crucial in saving Emery from a cell or the hangman's noose. She hated to do it, but there was no other way. In order to appease Mother, save Emery, and get Arnold's charges dropped, she had to marry again.

As she headed towards the office, the sound of Bernie's voice caught her off guard.

"Where are you going?"

Antoinette didn't face her sister as she continued to walk, the annulment paper in her hand. "Arnold's office. Mother said he would be there so I could speak to him."

"And what are you going to say?" Bernie asked.

"That the annulment is signed by Emery and that the marriage is over."

Bernie sped up and stepped in front, eyes wide. "*You didn't…*"

"I did," Antoinette answered, going around her sister and continuing her walk.

"How...how could you?" Bernie asked, shaking her head in disbelief. "I mean, I get that you're scared and stuff, but you've seen how Mother is. She's trying to force you into marrying Arnold and you're walking right into it!"

"I know what I'm doing, Bernie. I'm saving Emery's life and appeasing an angry woman."

"But...you're letting her control you! Antoinette, I'm all for obeying your parents, but when you know it's not a good decision..."

"Bernie, trust me," Antoinette interrupted, her voice firm.

"I trust you, Antoinette, but so did Emmerich. He trusted you to be faithful to him and not stab him in the back like this! Here you've been going on and on about being scared of rejection and hurt, but you've gone and done the same thing to him!"

Antoinette's speed slowed, and she felt the sting of truth on her heart. Visions of Emery's hurt face and trembling lip nearly overwhelmed her. Hadn't she looked the same when she learned of Edward's betrayal? She forced herself to remember that the circumstances were different. Edward left on his own accord. She left to save a life.

"He's strong, Bernie."

"I don't think he is," Bernie replied. "Antoinette, I'm begging you. Please think this through. You're helping the people who want to hurt you and are hurting the people who want to help you!"

They approached the office, and Antoinette saw Arnold busy sitting at his desk, rearranging some items. It was now or never. She didn't want to do what she was about to do, but there was no other way.

"Bernie, I'm sorry. I have to do this." She stopped at the door as Arnold looked up, a hungry look on his face. She took hold of the door handle and began to close it, leaving Bernie outside in the hallway. "Now I'm going to speak to Arnold alone. I'll let you know what's going to happen after I'm through, alright?"

"I can come up with another plan, though!"

"No more plans, Bernie. This is my decision."

"But…"

Before anything else could be said, Antoinette shut the door.

She stood before the prince and approached him, the paper being unfolded. "I'm surprised to see you here so soon," Arnold said as he looked her up and down.

"Don't be. You knew I'd be here."

He smirked. "Indeed. So what are you here for?"

She placed the annulment onto his desk, sliding it forward for him to see. "I'm here to make a deal."

He leaned back in his chair and put his fingers to his lips. "Well…" he began as he faced her. "Let's hear the terms."

Antoinette let out a sigh before speaking, changing her life forever.

Chapter 13: The Learning King

Edward had barely shaken the snow from his head when he heard his wife's voice down the hall.

"You *stupid* piece of filth! Can you not see that I'm a woman and not a pincushion? Poke me one more time and I shall send you to the stocks!"

A faint and shaking voice followed. "Forgive me, Your Majesty."

Edward recognized the voice immediately. Margaretha, the elderly seamstress who worked on the linens for his wedding to Antoinette.

There was a pause followed by another unearthly yell from Malina. "Bah! You *idiot!*" The sound of a smack was heard and Margaretha whimpered in apology. Edward tensed, listening as the woman's elderly voice rose in defense.

"Your Majesty, I don't mean to shake and I didn't mean to hurt you. If you wish, I could have one of my apprentices continue for me..."

"No!" Malina answered. "I only want people of experience working on this. I'm not about to look like a peasant when I walk about the palace. Either you do your job or you feel my wrath!"

Another smack was heard, making Edward's blood boil.

He didn't take the time to clean off the snow and mud from his boots as he hurried down the hall. The sound of a hit sent him barging into the room, not caring to knock, as he was met with the sight of Margaretha rubbing her reddened cheek. Malina towered above her victim, a dress too big draped over her, and she met Edward's gaze with a perturbed look.

She quickly changed it once she saw his lowered brow. "Darling!" she began with a sing-song cheerfulness. "How was your walk with the nobles? I trust their concerns will be met?"

"It was adequate," Edward replied, his voice low. "But that is not what I wish to speak of. I heard yelling. Is there a problem here?"

Malina's eyes gleamed with confidence as she strolled over to him. "Nothing I can't already handle," she cooed, "but I'll admit the hired help isn't being very helpful."

Edward turned to Margaretha. She remained quiet, seeming frightened. *I meant no harm,* her eyes spoke to him as he met her gaze. *I am innocent. Please believe me.*

"What has she done?" he asked.

"Poked me and proven her incompetence."

He looked and noticed the woman's cheek had a small cut. Apparently Malina had hit her even harder than he thought. Edward clenched his jaw. "And so you struck her for it?"

"Darling, that is what the farmer does to the cattle so they learn their place."

"Your Majesty, forgive me," Margaretha interrupted, straightening up. "If you wish for another tailor or seamstress to finish the dress for you, I can arrange…"

"Silence!" Malina reached her hand back to strike the woman once more. "How dare you interrupt me when I…"

But her words were cut short as she felt a strong hand grip her arm, keeping it steady. Edward held her arm back as she tried to pull it away, and he remained firm, his eyes never leaving his wife.

"Do not hit her again," he seethed.

"And why not?"

"Because I will not tolerate abuse in my kingdom."

"Hmph." Malina gave a small laugh. "And I will not tolerate weakness, Edward. You are a king and must show your authority. Even your father knew this. This is how the people respect us."

"I don't care. Respect is never earned through arrogance and cruelty. You only get fear."

"And is that a bad thing?"

"Here, it is."

Malina smiled as she pulled her arm away with a quick jerk. "Be careful, Edward. You have been given a throne by fate and are already wasting the opportunity."

He remained quiet, saying nothing.

"You pathetic boy," she muttered with a roll of her eyes. "You'll lose your kingdom quickly with the foolishness you rule it with." The queen turned back to Margaretha with a snarl. "You're fired. You shall never work for me again. Now be gone with you!"

Margaretha's eyes widened, filling with tears, but she quickly gained her composure and bowed her head in compliance. "Yes, Your Majesty."

The elderly woman stood, ready to leave the room, until Edward held out his hand. "Wait."

The woman stopped, looking at the king quizzically.

"Stay. You will not lose your job over this." He turned to Malina, his face stern. "And you will not dismiss her. Go and find yourself another seamstress if that is your wish. I will find this one other employment."

"But *I* dismissed her, Edward. She should learn to respect *her queen,*" Malina seethed.

"Then maybe you should start respecting her," Edward replied. "People do often learn by example."

Malina's smile appeared as she approached him. "People also learn by not listening," she said quietly to him. "I warned you, *Your Majesty.* You're being a *bad boy.*"

She turned back to the seamstress and smirked. "Do with her what you will. I'm done with worthless chatter." She walked out of the room, clipping Edward in the shoulder, the sounds of her heels clicking on the floor and echoing in the silence.

When she was gone, Edward turned to Margaretha. "I would ask my wife to offer you an apology, but know she will not give it. I will offer it in her place." He approached her, bowing humbly. "Forgive me for the rudeness that was displayed. I promise - it will not happen to you again."

He lifted his head only to find Margaretha giving a blink followed by a dazed look. Did he do something wrong?

He cleared his throat, unsure of what to make of her reaction, and spoke to hide the awkwardness rising. "I...uhm...want to offer you other jobs in the palace, if you wish to take them."

The woman nodded slowly. "Okay," she said.

"First, the queen mother is having a birthday within the month. I'd like to have her a dress made as a present. It is early, I know, but it will give you plenty of time to work on it. Also, I could use a new suit or two. That should provide you with some work until I can find you more."

Margaretha's brows rose in surprise. "Thank you, Your Majesty!"

"And don't worry about the queen's dress. I will pay you what she owes for your work," Edward replied.

"That is much appreciated."

"Of course." Edward offered her a smile. "I will make arrangements for your return so we can discuss business. Until then, I offer my physician to look at you for any injuries if you have them."

"I'm fine," Margaretha replied. "But thank you."

"Are you sure?"

"Yes. Thank you."

Edward nodded, shifting in where he stood. "Very well. Again, forgive me for the way my wife treated you." He bowed, standing still for a moment as the seamstress watched him curiously. "Good day to you, Margaretha." Then he turned and left the room, the seamstress staying put as she watched him leave, a curious look upon her face.

"Oh look! It's my son!"

Edward glanced up from his paperwork, the study he once abandoned now being put to good use as kingly duties kept him busy morning through night. He watched as his mother gave him a playful smirk, letting herself in as he set his quill back into the ink bottle.

"I know. I'm sorry I missed dinner," he said. "I promise I'll eat later, though. I have much to do."

"Say no more. I understand," Maria began as she sat down on the couch beside him. "When your father became king, I didn't see him for a month. Once you get your rule in order, I expect you to make up for lost time by at least sharing a meal with me."

Edward gave a light smile. "You have my word that I will."

"Good," Maria said. "Tell me - how is everything going?"

"I have visited the nobles and made note of their concerns," Edward began as he rubbed his face, hoping to stay awake despite the desire to sleep. "I have also began scheduling hearings in the throne room. This morning a farmer was quite adamant that his neighbor's pig was somehow cursing his cows because they did not produce as much milk as they did last year."

"Oh my. A terrible thing, indeed." Maria chuckled under her hand.

"The farmer was disturbed to say the least," Edward continued with a shake of his head. "Aside from that, I am working on the list of royal guardsmen. There are none I plan to send away, though there are a few I'd like to give promotions to."

"Oh?"

"Yes. I plan on appointing Sir Fauler as head of training and guard selection."

"A wise choice," Maria said with a nod. "Your father wished he chose Sir Fauler later on. Reginald is a fine teacher."

"I'm also appointing Sir Crane for palace security."

"I don't know him. Is he from one of the outlying towns?"

"The Bear Lands. He has had much success in keeping their villages safe."

"I see. I will trust your judgment on that, then."

"As for my advisor, I'm thinking of appointing Sir Peterson."

Maria's smile faded and she lowered her brow in concern. Edward knew that look well from his childhood - a sort of questioning that proved her disapproval.

"I take it you don't agree?"

"It's not that I don't think Sir Peterson is capable," Maria replied. "It is just that he's so young. He's even younger than you and you want him in an advisory position?"

"He's wise for his age."

"So are many, but that does not make up for a lack of experience." Maria frowned as she watched Edward rub his brow in slight agitation. "Marcus is a man of great skill, and I know you wish to reward him for his loyalty and friendship to you. I think he may be better serving in other positions, however."

"Such as?"

"Keep him where he is. That way he can grow and prepare for a higher position when he is ready."

Edward rested his chin on his palm, looking away for a moment. Back in Cathal, Edward had promised to reward Marcus for his loyalty. Foolish or not, he was determined to have Marcus in his inner circle. No other had proven himself like the young knight had.

"If he will not be my advisor, then he shall be the head of the guard."

Maria's eyes widened in surprise. "Are you serious? That calls for an even more experienced knight!"

"I won't have it any other way. Marcus is either an advisor or head guard. No other knight in Father's service has proven himself in my eyes."

Maria sighed, discontent clear upon her face. "I can't make the decision for you. If you think Sir Peterson a better candidate than the rest, then choose him. Just know it doesn't meet my approval. It may not please others, as well."

Edward nodded. "I will put Marcus as my head guard, then. Skill is more important than experience in that position anyways."

"Fine. So who will be your advisor?"

Edward shrugged. Who indeed?

"I'll have to look over the list again," he replied. "I'm sure a name will come up."

"You will need someone wise for that position," Maria said. "Someone with experience, too."

"Then who do you suggest?" he asked playfully. "Because I can't help but feel you have someone in mind."

"Perhaps," Maria said with a grin. "What of Sir Rikert?"

Whatever playfulness Edward had suddenly faded. Not that he was offended by his mother's choice. It was actually a smart one. Samuel Rikert was one of the older knights who had experience in multiple areas. Battle, training, leadership...even King Arden boasted how the skirmish near Braiden's border was won because of Rikert's changing of the defense plans.

But Samuel was also one that Edward had wronged. He had warned the former prince to not enter Verloris. Edward, in his rashness and foolishness, did not listen. Though Samuel had remained in the guard thanks to Arden, Edward made sure to avoid the man if he could. The guilt was too great being around him.

"No. I don't think Sir Rikert would want to be in my council."

"And how do you know? Have you asked?"

"No, and I don't plan to."

Maria shook her head with a scoff. "That is folly if I've ever heard it! What has Sir Rikert done to earn your disfavor?"

"Nothing. I have done plenty to earn his disfavor, though. I humiliated him in front of the entire guard and proved myself a child to his guidance. I doubt he would wish to serve a king who did not listen to him."

"You don't know that. Sir Rikert has been very forgiving and has not mentioned you in any negative terms. Even after you sent him away, he was still defending you."

Edward frowned. That made him feel even more guilty doing the man so wrong.

Maria's face softened after she recognized his look of guilt. "Your father and I have known Sir Rikert for quite some time. He is not just experienced and faithful. He is also honorable. I think, besides Sir Peterson, you would find no other knight in the kingdom as loyal to you as he."

Edward pressed his lips together, taking her advice to thought. "That may be true, but that doesn't mean he would agree to being in my council. He's probably angry over how I treated him...and rightly so..."

"You don't know unless you ask, Edward. At least consider it. Your safety is of the utmost importance, and I hope you choose only the best for your guard."

Edward nodded again. "I'll consider what you say, Mother. Thank you for your input."

She smiled at his words, but deep down he felt anything but happy. His mother was right - Samuel would be a good choice. He needed someone wise and willing to tell him the truth no matter what he wanted to hear. That was the sign of a good advisor. And who had that experience? Sir Rikert.

But Edward wasn't going to appoint him blindly. If Samuel was going to be his advisor, he'd have to want the job first.

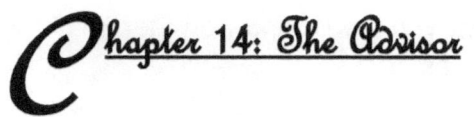

It was unusual for Sir Samuel Rikert to have a day off from the royal guard, but when he did, he made sure he enjoyed it.

He ran through the field outside his home in the outskirts of Reigal, towering, snow-capped mountains rising high all around. His feet crunched the snow beneath him, and he panted for breath as he heard a little boy shout triumphantly in the distance.

"I am the great Sir David Rikert, and I shall not let you pass the palace gates, evil troll!"

Samuel laughed to himself as he leaned against his knees, watching his five-year-old son hold up a wooden sword and shield high in the air like a champion warrior conquering a nation.

Or, in David's case, the back yard.

Samuel wobbled back and forth like the troll he was supposed to be, making growling noises that pulled out a few chuckles from his son who tried desperately to remain serious as he guarded the doors to the horse barn. "I shall smite you, evil troll!" David called out as he rushed forward to his father. "For the glory of the queen!"

He charged forward and swung his sword, pretending to strike his father and slash him in the heart.

"Curses!" Samuel replied in his troll voice as he fell backwards into the snow. "I have failed the king of trolls! Have mercy, Sir David! Have mercy!"

David pointed the toy sword to his father's face as he grinned. "I would like to grant you mercy, troll, but on my honor as a knight, I cannot. The decision lies with the queen."

Both Samuel and David turned to the "queen" of their imaginary world as she stood outside the barn gates. "Lady Goats-beth! What is your decree regarding this knave of the troll kingdom?" David called to the young goat who was quietly chewing on some grass dug up from under the snow. She looked up at the sound of David's voice and gave a disgruntled "meh" before returning to her meal.

Samuel and David paused for a moment until David lifted his sword. "Lady Goats-beth has spoken! The troll is to be executed!"

The sword lowered and David puckered his face. "Any last words, troll?"

"Of course, Sir David," Samuel replied with a smirk as he sat up, his son eyeing him warily. "Long live the troll king!"

And with that he pulled David to the ground and began tickling him with all his might.

David could barely contain his laughter as he turned to the horses grazing to his left. "To aid, my knights! I am in need of you!"

The horses ignored him as grass and snow were clearly more important.

"Ah ha ha!" Samuel said as he lifted his son in his arms and hugged him tight. "Now that I have you, Sir David, I shall take you to the troll king to become his prisoner!"

"Not a chance!" David replied as he laughed. "I shall escape you and your dungeons, but only after dinner. I'm starved! Has Mom finished cooking yet?"

Samuel chuckled as he set David down and ruffled his blonde hair, the remains of snow flying off of his locks. "I'm not sure, but we can go back inside and find out."

"I hope it's ready," David said as he caught his breath. "What I wouldn't give for some chicken right now."

"All those fighting trolls have made you hungry, I take it?"

"Absolutely. A knight has to eat!"

Samuel put his arm around David's shoulder and pulled him close. David snuggled towards him, unashamed he was his father's son and proud of the fact that his father was not only a knight, but of the royal guard. The thought that his son idolized him warmed Samuel's heart, and he vowed to work hard every day to make his son proud.

"Do you think I can be a knight some day?" David asked as they passed some workers feeding the cattle. "Be a swordsman like you and work my way in becoming a royal guard?"

Samuel smiled as they approached the manor. "You already have the speech for it. In time, I think your skills will surpass mine." They stopped as Samuel opened the door, turning to David. "I think you will make an excellent knight one day."

"As good as you?" David grinned.

"Even better than me."

David's eyes widened in surprise as they stepped inside the house.

The smell of roasting chicken and potatoes filled the air as dinner was starting to be set on the table in the dining room. "Go wash up for dinner," Samuel ordered as David rushed down the hall to his room. Samuel headed towards his and did the same, taking off his muddy, snowy tunic and coat and changing into something more formal and dry. He left the room and headed down towards the dining area as his wife and daughter were finishing setting the table.

"I heard you and David laughing outside," Samuel's wife, Katherine, said as she set a loaf of bread on the tablecloth. She approached her husband and kissed his cheek as he kissed her back, his hand lingering on her shoulder.

"Go sit down. You look tired," he said as he followed her into the kitchen and picked up the platter of chicken. "Katie and I can finish setting the table." Samuel looked at his three-year-old daughter, named after her mother. She smiled as she took a handful of napkins and held them close to her chest, eager to help.

"No offense, but you do a terrible job setting the table. You always put the food next to you and David." Katherine smirked as she took the platter from his hands. "If you can get the baby, that would help me more. We'll have the table set by then."

Samuel knew better than to question his wife's orders and made his way towards the baby's room where she quietly slept.

He bent towards the crib and saw his little girl sitting up and chewing on her finger, her hand all slobbery from teething, but her blue eyes were bright and her curly dark hair glistened in the sunlight coming from the window. She was only eight months old, but Samuel enjoyed her nonetheless. The baby stage had always been his favorite with his children and he wanted to make sure he was there for baby Clara as much as possible before she grew up and reality became a memory.

"Your mother said it's time for dinner," Samuel said as he scooped her up in his arms and cradled her to his chest. She cooed softly as she sucked her thumb, muttering "Ma-ma" in between gurgles.

Samuel chuckled as he lifted her up to face him. "Yes, ma-ma." He repeated to her. "But what about me? Can you say daddy?"

She smiled as she said, "Ma-ma."

"But what about daddy?"

"Ma-ma."

Samuel snickered. "Let's try something easier." He said as he walked her out of the room towards the dining area. "How about pa-pa?"

Clara stuck her tongue out and spit. *"Pft!"*

She laughed as Samuel shook his head, hiding a smirk. "Close enough."

He set her in her high chair as the rest of the family gathered at the table. David took the seat closest to the chicken, eyeing it hungrily as he fidgeted, waiting to eat. Katie and Katherine took their seats besides the baby and Samuel sat beside his son, and as they quieted, Samuel bowed his head to lead the family for the meal prayer.

"Heavenly Father, we thank You for this bountiful harvest that You have provided." Samuel paused as he heard a slight noise from beside him, and as he peeked his eye open, he noticed David slipping a quiet hand up towards the chicken. He lifted his hand and took David's gently, pulling it back away from the food and continuing his prayer. "And we ask that You bless this food to our bodies and be with those who have none, that they may be blessed even more than us, and that You would watch over the poor and..."

But before he could finish the prayer, he heard the door to the dining room open and a worker coming in. Samuel stopped and opened his eyes as did the rest of the family, their sights going to the door. The man bowed humbly in apology, his voice low. "Forgive me, sir. I wouldn't interrupt if it wasn't important. The king is here to see you."

Samuel's brows rose and he noticed Katherine looked at him in concern. The last time an interruption took place, there was a war brewing near Braiden's border. He had to leave immediately, not seeing his parents for over a year. He was younger then and wasn't married at the time, but the months away from his family took its toll. He didn't want to miss out on seeing Clara's first steps or hearing Katie read from a book. He especially didn't want to be away from David, who'd undoubtedly go mad being surrounded by nothing but women. The poor boy could only handle so many tea times with his sisters.

But duty called. He was not only a father and husband, but a knight as well, and desperate times called for his country to come first. He stood from the table, turning to the messenger in thanks. "I will meet him. Where is he waiting?"

"In the parlor."

"Then I shall see him there." He turned back to his family. "I'm sorry. I won't be gone long. Go ahead and start dinner without me."

Katherine frowned, but nodded nonetheless. She turned to David, "You can finish the prayer."

"God bless this food. Amen," the boy said quickly, and then reached out to grab a piece of chicken.

Katherine shook her head as Samuel chuckled, walking out the door towards the parlor.

Thoughts ran through his mind as to what the king would want. If it was a battle on the horizon, a worker or fellow guard would arrive to tell him the news. For the king himself to be there, it had to be bad. He couldn't help but wonder if the problems with Edeland after Edward's return had gotten worse. That would possibly explain the king's presence, as Samuel was one of the few knights who had experience in training with Edeland's military.

The door was opened and Samuel stepped in, noticing the king was standing alone, looking over some small pieces of clay artwork that had been sitting on the mantle of the fireplace. The king had been handling one of the pieces, admiring it, and he quickly put it back in its place as he noticed Samuel walk in.

"Your Majesty," Samuel said with a bow. "It is an honor to see you here."

Edward cleared his throat, his face showing hints of anxiety as he looked away. "Forgive me. I was admiring the clay work you have on your fireplace. It is very fine craftsmanship."

"Thank you, Sire. My three-year-old was pleased with her work as well."

Edward blinked in confusion, nodding slowly. "She is a very talented artist."

Samuel had to stifle a laugh. If globs of clay were considered art by the king, perhaps Katie had a future in sculpture after all.

"My doorman says you wished to speak with me," Samuel said, changing the subject. "Is the guard assembling for battle?"

"Uhm...no...there are no threats at the moment," Edward replied as he rubbed the back of his neck. Samuel couldn't help but notice the king still seemed nervous. If it wasn't battle that troubled him, what else could it be?

For a moment the thought came to him that perhaps it wasn't the king's enemies that were troubling him. Perhaps it was his family.

Malina.

"Then how may I be of service to you, Sire? I am at your disposal."

Edward paused, pressing his lips together and holding them shut. For a moment there was silence, and after a heavy sigh, the king faced the knight.

"I'm not here for you to do anything, Sir Rikert. I'm here only to speak with you." Edward paused, swallowing hard. "I...wished to apologize."

"For what?" Samuel asked. "I have no recollection of being offended by you, Sire. No apology seems needed."

"Your humility is admirable, Samuel, but unnecessary. You know I have wronged you, and I am here to address it."

Samuel nodded as he clasped his hands in front of him in a casual stance. Was the king apologizing only to remove him from service? Edward was not one to be very fond of him, that was certain, but then again, Edward could be full of surprises. Had he not heard about the beggar Edward had clothed in the middle of the street with his own cloak? Or even the seamstress he saved from Malina's wrath? Perhaps Edward's mistake in Verloris affected him not just in a negative way, but in a positive way as well.

"If you are speaking of the incident outside Cathal, know that I feel no ill will towards you. I spoke out of turn and did not mean to seem as if I was undermining your authority."

"And yet you were wiser than I in that instance. Had I listened to you, Edeland would still be our allies, Hugellia would not have been angry, and I would be married to a woman who loves me instead of hates me. You were right and I was wrong. I was also wrong to send you away."

Edward stepped closer, bowing his head to the knight. "Forgive me, Sir Rikert, for wronging you. I ignored your counsel and humiliated you in front of the men. I also nearly destroyed your career and honor as a knight. That is a crime not forgivable in my eyes, but I wished to makes amends to you, regardless. You know that I am deciding who to keep in my royal guard, and I want you to know that I consider you a vital part of that. If you are willing, I wish for you to still serve."

Samuel unclasped his hands, his face softening. "I will do as the king commands. If you wish me to remain in the guard, I shall. I am honored to serve."

"Thank you, Sir Rikert," Edward said. "I feel now, more than ever, your counsel will be needed."

"And I will be happy to provide it."

Edward smiled. "Good. And I promise - this time I will heed it."

Samuel smiled back, and another moment of silence followed before Edward broke it.

"That is all I wished to say to you for now. Forgive the interruption, Sir Rikert. I will see you tomorrow night at the banquet when I announce the guard."

"Of course, Your Majesty." Samuel bowed in respect. "I will see you then."

The king gave a final nod before leaving the room and returning to his carriage outside.

After watching him leave, Samuel returned to the dining room as his family continued to eat. Katherine set down her spoon and turned to her husband, eyeing him curiously as he took his place beside David.

"Well?" she asked, leaning forward. "What did the king say?"

"You're not leaving, are you?" David asked with a pout.

"No," Samuel replied warmly. "The king only wished to talk."

"About what?" Katherine asked.

"An apology."

Katherine's eyes widened. "The king apologized? Really?"

"Over the incident in Cathal," Samuel replied as he began to fill his plate. "He said that he was sorry over my mistreatment and regretted not listening to my advice. He also said he wants me to stay in the royal guard." He paused, a gleam in his eye. "He said my counsel would be needed."

"That is curious. I wonder what he means by that?"

"I'm not sure. It's worrisome that he is so concerned he feels he must turn to me. I think there are…some things ahead."

"What kind of things?" David asked, his mouth full.

Samuel couldn't be honest and worry his son over Audlin's troubles or his suspecting of Malina and her husband having a duel of power. If he could guess, Edward came to apologize because he knew he needed people he could trust by his side. And a paranoid king was never a good sign.

"The kinds of things that happen when young boys eat all the chicken and don't save their father any." He gave David a playful pout as he eyed the boy, his plate empty and his belly full. He sunk into his seat with a guilty expression.

"It's Mom's fault. She cooked it too good," David said.

Samuel snickered as he picked up a small plate of ham. "And that's why I cook two meats," Katherine chimed in.

He took the slice of ham and put it on his plate, burying the worries in his mind as he enjoyed the moment with his family while he could.

Chapter 15: The Royal Guard

Marcus was never one for parties.

They were too loud, too busy, too crowded for comfort. Maybe he disliked them because he was in the royal guard and could imagine a thousand different ways a party could go bad and put the king at risk. Or maybe he was just a tad shy. His father was a classic introvert, and he didn't doubt that he inherited his father's tendencies to become exhausted after a late night with the people.

Either way, he couldn't wait to go home and sleep.

But tonight was one of those nights where he wasn't just there for the king's protection. No, tonight was the night where Edward would announce who was to be in the royal guard under his reign. With every king came the decision to choose a new guard or keep the old, and tonight, in front of many guests and nobles, Edward would announce who his guard would be.

"You'd think there'd be more mutton at this party," Sir Ichabod muttered as he browsed the buffet table with a frown. "Chicken, fish, beef, but no lamb? I am insulted!"

"It could be worse," Sir Rikert chimed in, taking a sip of tea. "King Arden's father, King Ethelric, served only cheese and crackers at his ceremony. I remember my father being livid he did not get any wine."

"I remember my father speaking of that party," Ichabod said. "Although he did not mention a lack of wine. Must have snuck it in!"

Rikert shook his head, chuckling to himself as he took another sip.

"So how do these ceremonies work?" Marcus asked, feeling awkward he was still considered "the new kid" even though he had been with the guard for some time. "What do we do?"

"The king will read a list of names on who he has decided to remain in his company," Sir Rikert replied. "If our names are called, we go to the front and stand to receive acknowledgement."

"*If* our names are called?" Marcus asked.

"The king has the right to keep or reject any of us," Ichabod clarified. "Try not to let it worry you, though. I'm sure your inexperience won't go against you."

Marcus rose a brow as he looked to Sir Rikert. The middle-aged knight only shook his head as he rolled his eyes.

"So he just calls our names and that's it?" Marcus asked.

Rikert shrugged. "Well, there will be a change in authority, I'm sure. The head of King Arden's guard, Sir Braun, is retiring, as are many others. And of course, the king will choose a new military counselor."

"And we all know who will be that," Ichabod added.

Rikert lowered his brow playfully. "I highly doubt it."

"Oh come now, Sam! Everyone knows you are the sage of our order! Even King Arden regretted not making you his counselor before."

"With respect, Jacob, my advice is rarely headed," Rikert said. Marcus couldn't help but remember the time they arrived in Cathal where Edward didn't listen to Rikert's warning about the Verloris. "I'm sure someone more qualified will be chosen. Besides, I am getting too old for this life. I'd like to eventually retire and finish raising my children."

At forty-eight, Sir Rikert was certainly one of the older knights, but his stamina reflected the energy of youth. If ever there was a man who would make an excellent advisor to the king, it would be him. At least Marcus thought so.

"Well if Samuel is going to be the king's counselor, who will be the head of the guard, you think?" Marcus asked, making Rikert give a light snort.

"It's obvious, isn't it?" Ichabod gleamed, his eyes brightening.

"It is?"

Ichabod grunted. "Of course! It's me, you idiot!"

"Oh!" Marcus cleared his throat as he watched Rikert stifle another chuckle. It wasn't that Sir Ichabod wasn't experienced in what he did. It was just that he put other things...rather, pleasurable things...over duty a little too often. "Well, being the head guard will be a lot of responsibility, Jacob. Are you sure you really want it?"

"I come from a long line of knights, Marcus, and for seven generations a patriarch from my family has led the royal guard. It is destiny and divine right that gives me this position. I was born for it!"

"Be careful not to be overconfident, though, Jacob," Rikert warned. "The king can still surprise us."

"Ha! As if anyone else is a better choice than me," Ichabod scoffed. "Who else has my talent and skill?"

"Not many," Rikert replied. "Though you are standing in the presence of one who could best you in a duel."

Ichabod laughed. "Only in your dreams could you beat me, Sam."

"I wasn't talking of me."

The men both looked to Marcus, making him gulp. "Uhm...I'm...uhm...I'm sure that I am not experienced enough to do much of anything except follow orders."

"Your modesty suits you, Marcus, but you think too little of yourself. The king holds you in high regard, and do not believe your loyalty to him will go unrewarded," Rikert said.

Ichabod gave a scoff as he lowered his brow. "You can't be serious, Samuel! Marcus is barely out of boyhood and you think the king would have him lead us?"

"I think him very capable," Rikert replied.

"That is insulting to me," Ichabod muttered as he gave Marcus a glare. "The king will never choose someone outside of the nobility, anyways. It has never been done. Though talent may have gotten you into the royal guard, your birth will keep you from leading it!"

Rikert lowered his brow as Marcus frowned. It was true that noblemen typically made up the knighthood and royal guard. Only raw talent drew exceptions, and had it not been for a stroke of grace and skill, he would have remained in Circh as a common soldier.

"Then you should have nothing to worry about, Jacob," Marcus replied, his voice quiet. "I doubt the king would disturb the social order by placing a commoner at his right hand."

Ichabod only snorted as he took a swig of wine.

After the blow of a horn, the crowd soon silenced as the king stepped forward near his throne. Malina sat quietly at his side, clearly bored having to sit there while he read the names, and Marcus watched and waited for his to be called. Edward stood, unrolling the large piece of parchment, as he began reading the names of the thirty individuals who would be assigned to protect him.

As he began to read, many of the names were familiar. Guards who had served under Arden returned to serve under his son, and they were called to stand in front of the king.

A few, however, garnered some reaction from the crowd, and Marcus listened as Ichabod and Rikert began to whisper amongst themselves.

"Who is this Alistair? Or Raymond? Or Lyle?" Ichabod asked.

"They are soldiers from the Bear Lands," Rikert replied.

"I didn't think we had any knights in the Bear Lands," Ichabod said.

"We don't."

Ichabod widened his eyes. "What madness is this? Are they common soldiers?"

"Lyle is a commander of the king's army in charge of the safety of the villages there. He is a great tactician and leader with many years' experience. Raymond and Alistair are…scouts, if I recall. They are experts in wilderness survival and camouflage. They would be vital if the king ever got lost or was kidnapped."

"But they are commoners!"

"They also have much talent and skill," Rikert replied. "The king is wise to have a diverse set of warriors protecting him."

Ichabod only grumbled as he went back to listening to the king.

As the names were read, many more were called up, and Marcus was surprised to see just as many commoners as noblemen were named. Though Rikert did not comment on them all, Marcus could tell by the way the men were dressed who was who. The noblemen typically wore rich silks and colorful fabrics while the commoners stuck with their leather and uniforms. Regardless, Marcus was happy. For once, he wouldn't be the only commoner in the guard.

As the count got closer to thirty, Ichabod, Rikert, and Marcus were all called to the front. Marcus felt a swell of pride knowing Edward trusted him enough to keep him in the guard, and he couldn't help but feel glad that Sir Rikert was allowed to stay, too. Though Edward and Rikert spoke little to each other, Marcus knew Edward respected the man. It was folly to think that Rikert was anything but a wise and loyal knight, and Edward was not one to pass up someone who would aid and protect him in his coming reign.

After the names were read, Edward rolled up the parchment and returned it to a secretary at his side. "I thank you for your past service, noble men, and ask that you swear loyalty to the crown and its protection for the future. For God, for king, for country!"

The knights repeated the oath. "For God, for king, for country!"

"Amen," Edward said as he clasped his hands in front. "And now I shall announce my inner council. For the head of palace security, I appoint Sir Lyle Crane of the Bear Lands."

The man stepped forward and bowed as the sounds of murmuring nobles filled the room. Marcus pressed his lips together as he looked around. Many of them did not look happy.

"For the head of training and selection of guards, I appoint Sir Reginald Fauler of Reigal."

The crowd clapped in delight as a nobleman was appointed. Marcus didn't mind the selection of Sir Fauler. Though quiet, he was a patient and knowledgeable man who would keep the guard well-prepared.

"For the head of military advisory..." Edward paused, looking forward. "I appoint Sir Samuel Rikert of Reigal."

Sir Rikert's eyes widened in surprise as he carefully stepped forward, unsure if what he was hearing was the truth. After a bow, he thanked the king, turning back to Marcus with brows up. Marcus could only smirk back as Ichabod laughed.

"And finally, for the head of the guard." Edward bowed, taking a breath. "I have thought long and hard of who I wish to lead this group of honorable men. This position is one that I do not take lightly as it concerns the protection of myself and my family. I consider the individual I am about to appoint as the most loyal, bravest, and honorable man I know. He has remained at my side through the good and the bad and I can attest to his nobility of heart. For the head of the guard, I appoint Sir Marcus Peterson of Circh."

Gasps were heard around the room, and Marcus could have sworn he saw Ichabod's lips mutter curses underneath his breath as his face reddened. The crowd neither clapped nor cheered as Marcus approached and bowed, thanking the king.

"I told you I would reward you for your faithfulness," Edward replied as Marcus lifted his head. "And I know you will serve your post loyally."

"I will, Your Majesty," Marcus said, and he felt both joy and terror at the responsibility.

"I can think of no better choice," Rikert said with a smile, and Edward had the guard turn to face the crowd.

"Your royal guard," Edward said, and only a few of the nobles clapped.

But Marcus saw, in the back of the room, rows of workers and servants gathering around. Though the nobles barely acknowledged their half-noble, half-common guard, the peasants behind them cheered. Never had Marcus seen a look of elation on their faces as he had seen that night, and for the first time in his life, he could see something different on their faces: hope in the future.

As Edward dismissed the crowd to resume their festivities and party, Marcus could only watch as many of the nobility left in a huff. Their leader, who was the first out of the room, was Sir Ichabod, and before he left, Marcus heard him mutter, "Peasant king…"

It was late in the evening when Vacius entered Calimus' nursery.

The nurse slept on a couch beside him, but noise would not be an issue. He made sure the woman was drugged enough to sleep through Calimus' cries. He reached forward, eyeing the dozing baby lying before him, and touched his head, frowning.

"Admiring your work?"

Malina's voice was light, doubtless from all the excitement of conversing with her nobles during the party that evening. He didn't turn, didn't greet her with his typical hunger that he usually met her with. Instead, he kept his eyes upon the child, his voice lowering. "Why does he not look like me?"

Malina chuckled as she put her hands on his shoulders, embracing him from behind. "Darling, all newborns look alike when they first arrive. They only begin to mimic their parents as they age."

"Then why are his eyes blue and not gray like ours?"

"Some babies have different eyes. Look at my sister – her eyes are brown."

Vacius frowned further, the sounds of Malina's carefree attitude making him burn with desire for truth. "Is the child Edward's?"

Malina faced him, stifling a laugh. "Of course not. Why would you think that?"

He said nothing for a moment, reminding himself of all the reasons. *He does not look like me. He does not wake for me. He does not have my mannerisms.* But the truth was, deep in his heart, he had a feeling that the child was not his, but Edward's.

And that was what made his soul heat with rage.

"Darling, you worry so much," Malina comforted, caressing his cheek. "Fear not for the future. You and I shall take this throne in Audlin and rule as one, our son being your heir and the start of an unending royal line!"

"Do you swear this to me, Malina? That Calimus is mine?"

Malina blinked, almost perturbed that he asked such a question. "Of course. I swear by my blood that he is yours."

"Then why do I not believe you?"

She looked offended by his remark, but he didn't care. He wouldn't deny that his lover was a whore and he was one of many ensnared by her lusts. But though he didn't care about being a number in the past, the present was proving difficult. He wanted her to himself, unwilling to share. He wanted his woman, his child, and his throne *now*. He was tired of waiting.

"I cannot give you proof, Vacius," Malina cooed as she held him. "I can only give you my word and ask that you trust me. Can you do that?"

"I'm risking much, Malina," Vacius replied, his voice quieting. "The Velori are not allowed such pleasures as a woman and children. My life is forfeit if I am caught by my brethren."

"And that is why you and I should remain together," Malina said. "With the power of Audlin, we can protect ourselves. With an army, we can conquer Verloris."

"And when Verloris falls, the Velori will be no more."

"And you shall be free," Malina said, kissing him. "These things take time, my love. We cannot conquer the world in a day."

"But we can conquer a nation." He held her close, his mind going back to the child. "One word, Malina. That is all it takes to allow me to kill Edward."

Her face hardened. "He is not to die yet."

"Why? Calimus would be crowned the heir and you could rule in his place. It is folly to let Edward continue in his life!"

"I told you before, Vacius. If he dies too soon we may become suspect in his death."

Vacius released himself from their embrace and turned away. "Why do you insist on protecting him?"

"I don't," Malina clarified. "But I am thinking rationally about this. Clearly you aren't."

He faced her with a fire in his eyes not easily quenched. "Are you defending him?"

"Of course not! Don't be absurd."

"Then let me be rid of him!"

Malina approached, her eyes in a stare that reminded him too much of her father and his violent temper. "Jealousy does not suit you, Vacius. I chose you out of the Velori because I thought you could handle taking power, but I see it is proving difficult. If you cannot deal with a simple nuisance like Edward, then a nation will overwhelm you. I only want the best and most capable at my side, and I will not hesitate in replacing you."

"I'm the one who brought you here, Malina, lest you forget!"

"And I'm the one keeping you alive, fool. Malum is here and he is watching!"

Vacius paled at hearing his superior's name. He was not one easily made afraid, but there was always an exception. "Malum is here? Why?"

"He comes and goes as he pleases. Who am I to know?" Malina continued. "He has taken an interest in Edward's rise to power. We must tread carefully, lest you and I are caught."

"What has he said to you?" The fear was apparent in his eyes, but Vacius took no shame in showing it. Malum was the

Velori leader. His word was final and his actions were swift. There was no mercy with the man, nor would there ever be.

"He expressed his displeasure at Arden's death," Malina replied. "He thought it unnecessary. Fear not, however – I handled it."

"He had mercy?"

"For now."

"Does he still believe I am here only for your protection?"

"Yes. And as long as you stay quiet and in the shadows, our secret shall remain that way."

She cornered him, running her fingers down his face and towards his chest. "I can protect you, Vacius, but you must not be rash in your jealousy. If you kill Edward, Malum will know, and I cannot protect you from him."

"I do not need protecting from him," Vacius said with a sneer.

"Hide behind your pride if you wish," Malina said with a scoff. "But know that if you allow your heart to rule your mind, we shall both fall."

Vacius beaded his eyes. "I won't let that happen."

"I should hope not." Malina replied. "There is no second plan. Either we succeed or die."

He took her in his arms, holding her close. "And we shall succeed. I promise I will stay my hand for you."

"Good." She kissed him tenderly, the touch of her lips and tongue making him long for more. "I don't wish to part from you, my lover. Be wise in your anger, for losing you is a terrible thought to me."

"You needn't fear it."

"I won't," Malina said, pulling him towards the door, "for I know that you are strong. My brave, *handsome* Velori..." She kissed him again, whispering in his ear. "Release the worries from your mind and let me soothe you."

"Certainly not here," he said.

"Of course not." Malina chuckled. "I have a much better place in mind."

"And that would be...?"

She leaned forward. "Follow me."

He obeyed without question, going back to the shadows as she led him through the halls where no guards could see. But before the nursery was out of sight, he glanced back one last time towards the child, his spirit feeling bitter.

Calimus is mine and not Edward's, he reminded himself. But no matter how hard he wanted to believe his lover, the doubts remained.

He pushed the thoughts to the back of his mind as Malina led him to a spare bedroom, shutting the door and locking it as they fulfilled their lusts in the night.

Chapter 16: Separation

Night had fallen and Aldaric watched as his son lay still on the bed across from him. His back was turned, his eyes faced the wall, his arms were crossed and his knees were bent. All in all, Emery looked as if he was shutting himself off from the world, never wanting to be part of it again.

Aldaric sighed, not able to sleep while his son was like that. They had just crossed the border into Audlin and had stopped at an inn to rest, but he wondered if it would have been better to keep going to Kettensburg. In the city, he could bring his son to Anna for help. If anyone could bring Emery out of his melancholic anger, it was his mother.

But for once Aldaric feared this was one time that would prove difficult. He remembered years ago when his son first lost Antoinette to Edward. They returned to Kettensburg and Emery didn't eat for days. He barely spoke a word for weeks. He shut himself in his room, simply staring at the hearth as it burned quietly. After encouraging him repeatedly, Anna had finally been able to get him out of whatever rut he was stuck in, and life seemingly went back to normal save the chip he wore on his shoulder.

But now, after getting Antoinette and losing her a second time, because of her own choice now, Aldaric was unsure of whether Emery would bounce back so quickly…if at all.

When Aldaric received word that the charges would be dropped by Arnold, he was relieved. Relieved that his son would no longer face jail time and relieved that he was no longer threatened by Susanna's madness. There were, of course, conditions to the charges being dropped. Emmerich and Aldaric had to leave Edeland and Antoinette was set to marry Arnold on their original wedding day. The annulment would be approved by the priest and everything was set to go back to the way it was.

The girls weren't allowed to bid them good-bye as he and Emmerich readied their horses to leave. Looking up, he could see Antoinette watching them from a window, a sad look on her face as she stood beside her embracing sister.

Aldaric frowned as Susanna stood before them, arms crossed and eyes harsh like a parent making sure her children were following the rules. It didn't surprise him that she was there, making sure he would leave with his son. It didn't stop him from speaking his mind to her one last time, however.

"You should have given them more time, Susanna," Aldaric said quietly.

"I've given them more than what you gave me," she sneered.

He frowned, knowing the falsehood in what she suggested. It was she who distanced herself quickly when they broke up. He tried to console her - even reconcile, to an extent - but she wouldn't have it. She was never one to face her problems.

"Will you never let go of the past?" he asked as Emery looked up to the window where Antoinette stood, his eyes never leaving her sight.

"Hmph! As if I hold on to trivial things. If anything, it's you who's not letting go!"

Aldaric sighed, knowing he wasn't going to get anywhere with reason. It didn't matter. His life, his past with her was gone and he wanted to never be part of it again.

But that didn't mean his son should pay for what happened so long ago. "This feud between us…I understand if you wish to hold my decision against me, but Emery and Antoinette shouldn't suffer for it."

"I refuse to have my daughter be treated like I was treated," *she seethed.*

"Susanna, I was always good to you. You can't deny that. I tried to make things work between us, but we were too different and I had to walk away."

"Your petty excuses no longer interest me."

"And your bitterness over something that happened decades ago should be forgotten. Our children are suffering for our mistakes!"

"I am preventing suffering, Aldaric. Antoinette will never be hurt by your spawn again!"

"Emery never hurt her and he never would. You and I both know this." *He paused, his face softening.* "Give them a chance, Suzy. What we had may have faltered, but it can live on in our children."

The queen's eyes burned with rage. "Antoinette has made her choice."

"And her choice was Emery until you spoke with her."

"Am I a monster that I would force my daughter towards a man she does not want?" *Susanna asked.* "Speak with her yourself if you wish to hear it again!"

"I know what she said," Aldaric continued, *"but I also know how this works. You told me the same thing when you married John, and yet that didn't stop you from coming back."*

Her eyes widened, and for a moment he saw the young girl he used to love before he met Anna look back at him until rage overtook her. *"My daughter will never love your son, Aldaric. I'll make sure she will not be as foolish as I once was."*

"Time will tell, though, won't it?" he replied. *"Just like it did with you."*

Her fists tightened as if she wanted to strike him, but he met her stare with his own. They said nothing to each other for a moment, and he gave a bow, turning to leave, until she spoke one last time.

"You think you know everything, Aldaric, but you don't!" she seethed quietly. *"All those years I spent with you...they mean nothing to me! You mean nothing to me! You'll be sorry for what you've done!"*

He turned back to face her, his eyes soft in pity. She had fallen so far since they had broken up, and he wondered if he had stayed, would she be more happy than bitter? It was a question in which he would never know the answer, nor did he want to. He made his choice in life, and he never regretted it.

"I am sorry, Susanna, for all the pain I caused you, and I hope you can find it in your heart to see the truth in why we parted."

"It's because you never loved me, you horrible beast!"

"I loved you more than you'll ever know. Were your heart not consumed with pride and bitterness, I would love you still."

With that, he turned and walked away, leaving the queen in her fury. He led Emery away and towards his horse, both men remaining silent as Emmerich hesitated to go. Aldaric hated to pull his son away, but he had to get him out of the pit that was Staalberg and the pain that lingered there. They rode away, Emmerich glancing back at the palace window one last time, and they began their journey home.

The first hours of the ride had been quiet. Not the kind of quiet experienced when someone is ill or not wanting to speak. Rather, it was the kind of quiet that held an uneasy feeling with it, one of a growing anger ready to explode.

Aldaric could only imagine the emotions swirling within his son, and they were about to come out.

"You're not talking much," Aldaric said quietly as they trotted through the forest trail towards Audlin.

"What's there to talk about?" Emmerich sneered, his eyes set forward on the road.

"From your tone, it sounds like a lot."

Emmerich scoffed. "Forgive me if I'm a little upset right now. I'll try to be perkier later."

"That's not what I meant," Aldaric said. "I know you're hurt and there's a lot going through your mind…"

"I'm not hurt, Dad. I'm livid!" Emmerich pulled Waffles to a halt, much to the horse's dismay, and turned to face his father with an icy glare. "I've only wanted one thing in life. One. And you know what? I just lost it. And do you know why? Because you had some fling with her mother that no one knew about and pulled an Edward! Because of your deceit, my wife thinks I've lied to her and she's afraid to stay with me because she thinks I'm going to leave her just like you left her mother!"

Aldaric stopped and blinked in surprise. "You're blaming me for this?"

"Who else am I to blame? If it wasn't for you and Susanna, I wouldn't be in this mess!"

"Son, I'm not to blame for this. And need I remind you that if I hadn't left Susanna, you wouldn't even be here?"

"That's not the point, Dad. The point is you should've told me about this a long time ago. If I knew, I could've talked to Antoinette or we could've done something different, or…"

"Son, no matter what you knew or what you planned, Susanna was still going to be in the picture. No matter what, she was going to put a stop to your marriage."

"But if Antoinette knew the truth beforehand, she would've stayed. Her mother wouldn't have been able to put all those doubts in her head. Things would be different!"

Aldaric shook his head, rubbing his already aching temple. *"Things wouldn't be different. Susanna may have threatened and used deceit, but if Antoinette truly wanted to be with you no matter what, she would've stayed. She wouldn't have let you go."*

Emmerich lowered his brow, his eyes watering. At first he looked as if he would provide a comeback to Aldaric's remark, but after opening his mouth and closing it back up again, he turned away, his face red and breath heaving. It wasn't anger, however, that now plagued Emmerich. It was the sudden realization that maybe his father was right.

And that made Aldaric feel terrible.

"Son, I didn't mean…"

"I don't want to talk about it," Emmerich muttered as he faced the road once more.

"But…"

"Just leave me alone, Dad. I don't want to talk anymore."

They rode on in silence, not even looking at each other.

That was days ago, but the pain lingered. As much as Aldaric tried to speak to his son, Emmerich would not respond. Whether it was hurt or anger or a mixture of both, he didn't know, but whatever it was, it made him uneasy.

A shift in Emmerich's bed was heard and Aldaric became more alert. He watched as Emmerich sat up and took the covers off, standing to his feet and donning his boots and coat.

Aldaric sat up quickly. "Where are you going?"

"Out," Emmerich replied.

"In the cold?"

"Yeah. I need some air."

It was the longest sentence Aldaric heard him speak. He slid his feet to the floor to put on some boots. "I'll come with you."

"I'd rather be alone."

Aldaric paused. "Are you sure?"

Emmerich never looked up. "Please."

How could he say no? It was best not to push in his experience. "Alright. I'll…be here if you need me."

There was no thank you or acknowledgement. Emmerich walked out the door into the cold night air. The door closed, but Aldaric tiptoed out of bed to follow just in case. He cracked open the door to find Emmerich had only taken a few steps into the snow, sitting quietly on a small bench outside. There were no pedestrians around and the only light that shined was from the moon and stars overhead. And there, in the darkness, his son gathered his knees to his chest and lowered his head, crying softly to himself.

Aldaric pressed his forehead to the door, praying somehow God would help his son.

Susanna looked around the church and breathed a relaxed sigh.

Everything was finally going to plan. Antoinette was marrying Arnold, Arnold was joining the family, and Emmerich van Ketten was far away in Audlin, a near disaster of a marriage prevented by her own cleverness and cunning.

Things could not have been more perfect.

The wedding ceremony had begun and Antoinette walked slowly down the aisle, her face downcast as her husband-to-be awaited her at the altar. Her dress was a shimmering silk of white and her hair was adorned with a diamond crown that shone from the sunlight streaming through the windows. Her green bouquet of winter leaves honored the traditions of her people, and the queen swore she heard every guest gasp in amazement as her daughter walked to the front.

Of course, Bernette followed behind in the green dress that had to be anything but silk. The poor girl's weight demanded elasticity in her costume, and though she tried to find a corset that could somehow make her as thin as Antoinette, no amount of bone and fabric could do the job. The queen gave a roll of her eyes as Bernette's walk seemed too jumpy, void of the grace and elegance that her eldest possessed. She cursed to herself, wondering why the Almighty gave her such an oaf for a daughter after giving her such physical perfection with the first.

Antoinette arrived at the front, facing the prince as Bernette went off to the side. The priest stepped forward, a book in hand, and he adjusted his spectacles as he began to read, beginning the ceremony. Susanna sat proudly at the pew, her back straight and chin up in an elegant pose that showed her pride in the day's events.

The priest began to speak, and Susanna strained to hear the man's words. It sounded mumbled, his accent so thick that he could barely pronounce the words he was reading correctly. Susanna gave a huff to herself, feeling perturbed, but after a glance of approval from Arnold's newly-arrived parents sitting beside her, she faked a smile in appeasement. Susanna had been allowed to plan the entirety of the wedding, but Arnold gave a last minute request. He wished a friend of his, a priest from Liegen, to officiate the ceremony. It was a small price to pay for a man leaving his country and family and culture, so Susanna conceded. After hearing the priest's inaudible mumbles, however, she wished she'd said no.

The price for getting a daughter married off...

She tried her best to hear, but before she could decipher anything the priest said, a great wailing was heard.

Susanna's eyes glared at her youngest, who flung herself forward in a sob that reminded her of a colic-suffering baby who was teething.

"What is that child *doing*?" she seethed as her face burned in fury. The people in the crowd began to turn, their eyes full of concern and their mouths murmuring in surprise.

Her husband gently put his hand atop hers, attempting a console, which she swatted away quickly. "Dear, I'm sure she's only upset..."

"Bernette is doing this on purpose!" Susanna whispered harshly as she avoided a concerned glance from Arnold's mother. "We must do something! She's trying to ruin the wedding!"

"But why would she do that?" the king asked before jumping to the sound of an even louder wail by Bernie. He cleared his throat as the queen of Liegen leaned forward and asked, "Is she alright? Does the girl need a tonic?"

She needed a stern talking to, but Susanna only faked a smile to the queen. "She does this at times. Always crying at weddings because she's so happy."

But at the sound of Bernie shouting out, "*Why, cruel fate?*", Susanna could only rub her aching brow in embarrassment.

"I understand," the queen of Liegen said sweetly. "Our middle son has the same outbursts."

Susanna's mouth went slightly agape at the comment, but she quickly closed it as she motioned for a servant to come forward. "Get my daughter to be quiet or remove her from the church! We cannot hear the vows the priest is saying from all her racket!"

The young man nodded nervously as he tried his best to approach the young princess without getting smacked in the face with her bouquet. The queen watched as the servant tried patting her on the shoulder, speaking quietly near her ear, but Bernette turned around and grabbed the poor servant tight, hugging him and wailing again, shouting, "Bless my wonderful mother for wanting to console me! May I use your sleeve as a handkerchief? Mine is full of snot."

Susanna's face reddened as her hands clutched the pew seat, her nails scratching the wood.

Thankfully, the priest was nearly finished, and before Susanna could get up and drag Bernette out of the church herself, she saw Arnold and Antoinette kiss, the priest lifting his arms to the congregation as the newlywed couple faced them.

Bernie's wails slowly began to quiet as the organ music echoed in the sanctuary, and the couple walked down the aisle towards the door hand in hand. Susanna stood with the crowd, clapping alongside them, and as her daughter passed by, she caught a glimpse of her face.

Antoinette's features remained downcast, and as soon as she met her mother's glance, she looked away towards the floor.

No matter, Susanna thought. *She may not be happy now, but she'll thank me in time.*

Because that's what happened to her after she married the king. Oh, she cried and sobbed for weeks, pining over Aldaric. But time eventually gave her clarity...and a crown. She would not have any of it with Aldaric.

She pushed the thoughts of the Hugellian ambassador to the back of her mind, concentrating on the reception to make sure it was run with perfection.

Antoinette laid quietly in her bed, the festivities of the wedding making her feel tired and drained. The darkness of the night was soothing, the quietness that accompanied it perfect for letting her think. But perhaps thinking wasn't the best thing she could do, for her thoughts had been anything but positive.

She remembered looking at herself in the mirror before walking down the aisle that morning, feeling uglier than ever seeing herself in a silk dress and diamond crown. Physically, she had never looked better - not a hair out of place and not a blemish on her skin or clothes. But emotionally, she felt like a wreck. All she could think of was how unfair life had been and how she wished her wedding with Emery was as beautiful as her day with Arnold. It was Emery that deserved to see his bride in a beautiful dress. It was Emery that deserved the elegant wedding full of family and friends. It was Emery that deserved the party with unending foods and dancing that lasted into the night.

It was Emery that deserved the evening with his wife, to lie there beside her and have her wake in his arms.

She fingered the fabric next to her, feeling the emptiness of the air. Everything had gone so, so wrong…

A knock was heard at the door. She stirred, sitting up and turning. She heard her name being called softly through the wood, and she recognized the voice immediately.

Arnold.

It didn't surprise her, hearing him outside her door. Their newly refurbished rooms in the northern wing of the palace were adjoined and separated by a door. It allowed them privacy when they wanted it, but quick access for…personal matters.

And it was their wedding night, after all. She shouldn't have been surprised he would call.

It perturbed her nonetheless. She wasn't ready to be intimate with him. She never would be. Her feet touched the floor and she approached the door, candle in hand so she could see the knob. The lock remained in place.

"What is it, Arnold?"

His voice sounded muffled from the other side. "Having trouble sleeping?"

She shrugged. "I'm fine."

"I have a remedy for that."

"I'm sure you do."

"It is our wedding night, after all."

She frowned. "And I'd like to go back to sleep."

"You know," Arnold began in a sultry voice, "women often *beg* for my company. Tonight, you can have it for free."

"I don't care."

There was a pause, followed by what sounded like a scoff. "Still thinking about that other guy?"

"I married that other guy," Antoinette replied. "And yes, I am thinking of him."

"You'll never see him again. Why bother?"

"And why are you bothering trying to get something you know you aren't going to get tonight?"

"Ouch," Arnold said with a chuckle. "You know, playing hard to get only makes me want you more."

"You knew what you were getting when you agreed to this marriage, Arnold. I'm not opening this door."

"Your mother is expecting us to consummate this, though."

"I've lied to her before. I can lie to her again."

"But what if I tell the truth?"

"Then I'll tell her why you were in the bathroom for fifteen minutes during the reception."

Arnold paused. "I enjoyed too much quiche."

"I think you were enjoying too much of that noblewoman in the red dress."

"She was much more willing than you, I'll admit." Arnold let out a sigh. "Fine. I know where to find better company for tonight. You can't say I didn't offer, though. You'll never have another chance to spend the night with a man, and I can guarantee that you'd forget all about that Hugellian once you spent a moment with me."

She frowned, thinking of Emery. There was a chance Mother would keep her in the palace for the rest of her life if it meant keeping Emery away. Had the two an opportunity of reuniting, Mother would suspect they would be together.

She shook her head, rubbing her aching temple. She couldn't betray her vows.

"I'm not interested, Arnold. I'm sorry. Please leave me be."

"Can't say I didn't offer," Arnold said. "I'll be back in a few hours, though, if you change your mind. You'll know where to find me."

She kept her mouth shut, listening for his footsteps to lead away from the door.

He walked away, leaving her alone in the room once more. Mother would ask about their wedding night and she would have to appease her with a lie. Doubtless Arnold would go along with it to keep his affair with the noblewoman he met at the wedding a secret. She didn't mind. If he helped her, she would help him. That was what they agreed to, at any rate.

She returned to her bed, setting the candle back on the stand. She closed her eyes, thinking of Emery, clutching the extra pillow she had to her chest and longing for his comfort as her heart ached into the night.

She prayed she made the right decision.

Never had Malina been so perturbed in her life.

That *peasant child* of a knight, now head of the royal guard, had been making her life miserable. Never had he left Edward's side since becoming his own personal guard and never had she seen such an increase in their security. It was inconvenient to say the least. Before, she had the privacy of her own rooms to be with Vacius or any other lover she could get her hands on. Now, she had to worry about noise and alerting the guards stationed by her rooms.

She wanted nothing more than to push that pretty boy's body off the balcony where his physique would no longer be so desirable. Had her charms any influence on him, she would've bedded the boy and controlled him a long time ago, but he was an odd one. So honor-bound and so loyal to the king. It made her sick of his chivalry to the point of vomiting.

If only he were like the rest of Edward's men. So easily swayed and stupid.

But it didn't matter. She was the queen, the most powerful woman in Audlin. It was a trifle to remove a guard that was standing in her way. All it took was talking to the right people.

And thankfully, the right person just happened to be leaving his guard duty for the day.

It didn't take a genius to see the look of disappointment on Sir Ichabod's face when he learned it would be Sir Peterson becoming head of the guard. She'd heard rumors that Ichabod was the most popular choice amongst the nobles, and she could only imagine the fury that engulfed him when he learned his position was given to an archer barely out of boyhood. It was a fool's move on Edward's part, angering one of the richest and most powerful families in the country, but it was perfect for what she needed to complete the next phase of Audlin's conquering.

She made sure she wore her red dress, revealing enough to play with Ichabod's feeble mind and get him to talk. She remembered him well from his stay in Cathal, and unlike Marcus, he enjoyed every bit of his time with the Verloris. It would be a simple task to sway him, and the fun would make up for a lack of seeing Vacius during the day.

He was just walking towards the end of the hallway when Malina finally caught up with him, calling out his name. He turned, confused at first but then smiling and giving a bow when he saw her. Of course, his eyes rarely left her plunging neckline. She couldn't help but snicker at how easily he was reined in.

"My dear Sir Ichabod," Malina began sweetly, "will you join me in my parlor? I wish to speak with you for a moment."

"Of course," Ichabod replied. "Anything for you, my queen."

"Thank you," she said as she reached her hand and linked arms with him, letting him escort her to the parlor.

She had the servants close the door and asked them for privacy. The servants nodded, hastening out, and Malina was left alone with her knight. She could see him watch her curiously, wondering what she was about to do, but she kept her cool. Things couldn't heat up too fast without burning out.

Chapter 17 – Moving the Knight

"Sit with me, Sir Ichabod. I wish to have a word with you." She patted the cushioned seat beside her on the couch, smiling at him.

"I hope I'm not in trouble," he said, sitting.

"Of course not. You are my most noble of knights. Any trouble you would be in with me would only be…a fun kind."

"A fun kind?" Ichabod asked, raising a brow.

"Another conversation for another time," Malina said with a tilt of her head. "But I wish to keep this between us, Jacob. My husband must not know too much of what we speak today."

"Of course. How can I be of service?"

"I'm sure you're aware of Sir Peterson's promotion as head of the royal guard," she replied, noticing Ichabod's frown.

"Yes. I'm aware of it."

"But I don't believe you are aware that I am unhappy with my husband's decision, as are many others."

Ichabod gave a sigh, rubbing the side of his face where stubble was gathering from a lack of shaving. "I was unaware of your thoughts, Majesty, but I'm glad to hear them."

"You are a prominent knight in the order. It is a shame your talents are not more recognized."

"I appreciate it," Ichabod said, his face showing the bitterness he tried to hide behind his eyes. "But alas, nothing can be done of it. A child has been put in charge, and a peasant at that! I only hope the king's decision does not come back to bite him in the rear." The knight paused, his face blushing, as he muttered, "Pardon, Your Majesty. I should have used more proper wording than that."

Malina snickered. "It's alright. I share your fears as well, yet Edward will do what he pleases, even if it is foolish. But you are a wise man, Jacob, and I am a wise woman, and I think you would agree that even though my husband has made a foolish decision, we can make things right."

Ichabod's face brightened in curiosity. He inched closer, a gleam in his smile, as he rested his palms together near his chin. "How so?"

"My son's safety is of the utmost importance. I do not trust a peasant, young or old, to be in charge of his well-being. I will not have my child endangered because of my husband's stupidity. I want only the best knight at my service and you, dearest Jacob, are the best." She paused, leaning forward, watching as his eyes slowly lowered. Good. Let his lust cloud his judgment. "Will you be my personal guard? Will you watch over my son and I? I trust no one else but you." She put her hand atop his knee and felt him tense, but after she smiled at him and he smiled back, she knew she had him. Oh, how simple it was to tame a man!

"Anything for you, my queen," he replied softly. "I'm the best there is and I'll make you proud you chose me."

"Good," Malina purred as her gaze lingered on him a while for added effect. "I'm glad to hear it. I promise your talents will not go wasted. And..." She leaned closer, her lips very close to his ear. "...should you do your duty well, I promise that you will be richly rewarded. I see you can be much more than a knight."

He leaned closer, and she could tell he was wanting something other than words, but she leaned back, not giving in yet. He would prove his worth in due time, and she was just getting started.

He cleared his throat as he went back, watching her confident smirk remain unchanged as she stood to her feet and headed to the door. "What of the king, Your Majesty?" Ichabod muttered as he followed her lead. "He has expressed I remain in the guard as is."

"He will not refuse my request," Malina replied. "You will be my guard, Jacob. Fear not. I take care of those loyal to me."

His lip curled up, and he gave a bow. "Thank you, my queen. I am honored by your grace and wisdom."

"Of course," Malina replied. "Now you may return home. Tomorrow I expect you to be with me. I will show you your new duties."

"Yes, Your Majesty."

"Good," she said, watching him open the door. "Until tomorrow, then."

"Good evening."

She watched him go back out into the hallway, closing the door as he left, feeling quite confident that her new plan was running so smoothly.

Chapter 18: Sins of the Father

Malina paraded Calimus around like a newly-engaged girl showing off her diamond ring.

Edward watched as she cradled his son in her arms, bouncing him and laughing as she showed him to the noblewomen she conversed with at dinner. When no one was around, Malina could care less about taking care of the boy, but when a crowd gathered, her "maternal instincts" just so happened to appear.

It made Edward sick in seeing it. A child should be his mother's pride at all times... not just in public.

By the time dinner had ended and the nobles had gone back home, Malina rushed over to the nurse. The baby had started fussing, probably tired from being at such a long gathering, and squiggled and cried, nearly falling out of her arms.

"Take this child and calm him!" Malina barked as she shoved him towards the nurse. The poor girl nearly dropped him, not used to Malina's strength, and began to try and soothe the child with gentle hushes that went unheeded.

Malina could only rub her brow and close her eyes in frustration. "Do not leave him here to fuss, girl! Take my son to his nursery where we can have some peace. I have had a long day and wish to rest!"

The girl gave a bow of her head and backed away, taking Calimus with her towards the hall. "Yes, Your Majesty."

She scurried off towards the nursery, leaving Edward with his wife.

Malina stormed off towards their room, guards at every corner that undoubtedly perturbed her. Edward followed quietly behind, his mind on his son, not noticing his wife's nagging that echoed as they walked.

"Guards at every corner? Are we at war that we should have such high security?"

Edward kept his head down. Calimus looked so weary, his eyes heavy and puffy from a lack of sleep. Instead of listening to the nobles and their complaints, he should've taken his son himself and put him down for a nap.

"Your guards are overly cautious, if you ask me," Malina continued. "It's not as if this place has had dangers before. The only ones who need protection are the king and his family, anyways. Everything else is expendable."

It was late, certainly, but Edward couldn't help but want to go to the nursery to wish his son a pleasant sleep. Maybe say his bedtime prayers with him, too. He remembered his mother used to do that with him and Stephen when they were young. Surely the tradition could continue on.

"Are you even listening to me, Edward?" Malina stopped, turning towards him, her hands on her hips and her eyes glaring.

Edward paused, looking up. "Yes, yes…I'm listening. What is it?"

Malina huffed as she shook her head. "And you wonder why I tire of you? What a pathetic man you are that you don't even listen to your wife!"

"Perhaps if you gave me something other than a complaint or demand, I would be more attentive," he replied with a sneer, thinking back on the days before when she stormed into the room and demanded Sir Ichabod be Calimus' personal guard. How could he say no when she was so adamant and threatening?

"If you were competent, perhaps I wouldn't have to remind you on how to run a country."

Edward groaned. "I'm not in the mood to argue right now. I'm just worried about Calimus."

"What for? The child is well and in the nurse's care."

"*Calimus* was exhausted. Had you not paraded him all night to make yourself look like Audlin's greatest mother, perhaps he wouldn't have been so ill."

Malina scoffed as she shook her head. "The people wanted to see the future king, Edward. Though he may be young, he still has responsibilities to his people."

"He's a baby, Malina. His only responsibility right now is to be loved and cared for by his parents."

"Hmph," Malina snorted. "And I suppose this is how your father treated you and Stephen, isn't it? Not preparing you for the life of a king. Letting you run around and doing whatever you want. No wonder you're so pathetic at leadership."

Edward frowned at hearing his father being mentioned and the falsehoods that came from her lips. It didn't matter, though. Whatever he said, Malina would have a remark to come back with, and the argument would continue until he was too weary to bother anymore.

"I don't care, Malina. Just do what you want." He stepped past her and went towards the nursery. "But remember he's my son too. I also have a say-so in how he will be raised, and I refuse to put a heavy burden on him. He may have been born into royalty, but it will still be his choice to take the throne."

Malina's eyes flared. "He will have no choice in this matter, Edward! He is the crowned prince!"

"And he is my son first and foremost."

"You stupid man! Do you not care who takes the throne after you in Audlin?"

"I care very much," Edward replied solemnly. "But I care for my son more."

With that, he walked away, leaving Malina in the hallway with a curious look on her face.

He made his way to the nursery, walking past the guards that stood watch during the night. The door to Calimus' room was opened for him, and he entered only to find the nurse still gently bouncing the baby to get him to sleep. He cried and he wailed, the nurse looking more tired than the baby now, and Edward couldn't help but give a sympathetic smile. How many times had he heard his mother talk of how cranky he was as a tired baby?

"He's still not wanting to sleep?" Edward asked as he approached the nurse.

The girl shrugged. "I've tried feeding him and have changed his diaper. He's just not willing to relax yet."

"I'll take him," Edward said, stretching out his arms. The nurse looked at him, confused.

"Are you sure? The queen said that..."

"I'm sure. The queen has her priorities and I have mine. Besides, it's not like I get to see my son often. Here. I will stay with him until he falls asleep."

"Of course, Your Majesty. Thank you." She handed the crying baby to him, curtsying before leaving the room and shutting the door.

Calimus continued to cry as Edward held him in his arms, swaying slowly around the room to see if the motion would relax him. After the baby spit up on his shoulder, however, he learned that perhaps moving around wasn't the best idea. He sighed, taking his sleeve and wiping the baby's mouth off, and tried talking instead.

"Alright, you get motion sickness. Not much of a surprise, I guess," Edward whispered as Calimus continued to cry. "You've been fed, changed, swung around...any other suggestions?"

Calimus only flung his arms and sniffled.

"Alright, how about this?" He hated to do it...knew it would damage his manhood...but since there was no one else around, he figured he might as well try.

"Buckington Bunny went hopping along on a bright and sunny day..." Grant it, Edward wasn't the best singer in the world, but he remembered his mother telling him that lullabies always did the trick when he was cranky as a kid. Surely the cure was passed down the line. He cleared his throat, noticing Calimus suddenly quieting at the sound of his voice, and started over.

"Buckington Bunny went running along
On a bright and sunny day.
He jumped and he hopped,
Then fell and he flopped
And landed in a bunch of hay.
Buckington Bunny was now on a farm.
The animals wanted to play.
The cow said, "Moo!"
And the duck said, "Quack!"
And told the bunny to stay.
Buckington Bunny then packed his bags
To go and move far away.
Now he's on the farm
And having some fun
With his new friends every day."

Edward watched as Calimus slowly started to calm, staring up at him with curious and drooping eyes. Edward smirked to himself, surprised his tone-deaf rendition of the silliest song he knew had enough magic in it to calm his son. "I take it you liked my song," he said quietly as Calimus gave a light coo. "Well I'm glad someone appreciates my talent."

Calimus gave a yawn as he curled his fingers towards his palms and snuggled into his father's chest.

Edward smiled. "Of course, my song *is* putting you to sleep. Maybe it's more boring than I thought." He went to a long chair beside the crib and lounged back on it, placing Calimus upon his chest and shoulder. Then, taking the baby's blanket, he placed it over his son's back and cuddled him close.

"There. Now it'll be nice and quiet for you to go to sleep." He glanced down at his tired son, the baby's eyes closing slowly, yet trying to stay awake. "Now let's say our prayers before bed," he said softly. "God bless Audlin. God bless Grandma. God bless Daddy. God bless me." He paused, giving a smirk. "And God help Mommy because she needs it."

Calimus made a noise that almost sounded like a laugh, at least to Edward.

"Amen," Edward said with a chuckle as he laid there in the silence, watching his son go to sleep. It was a precious moment he had witnessed a few times before, but never got tired of. With his arms wrapped around his son and his own body starting to feel tired, Edward shut his eyes to rest for a moment, waiting until Calimus was fully asleep before putting him in the crib.

As he rested there with his son, his mind started to drift, and he remembered the past.

Stephen and Father had went to the hall of kings behind the throne room, a special place lined with red velvet carpet and marble walls that no one except the king and his heir were allowed to see. In the hallway were portraits of every king in Audlin's history, and towards the end of the hall was Arden's, followed by an empty space that said "Stephen II".

Edward was only seven at the time, but he remembered the hurt of being told to stay behind while Arden and Stephen went down the hall. He remembered walking around the throne room, alone in the silence, and feeling frustrated. He hated being the second son, hated the fact that he felt so useless. Stephen always had Father's attention because they shared a crown and responsibility. What purpose did Edward have? A servant, Father had practically called him. Someone to wait on Stephen for the rest of his days.

He remembered kicking a small stone that made a thunk against the throne's base. Knowing he wasn't supposed to, Edward climbed up the throne and sat on it, pretending he was king of Audlin and was important for once. He waved an imaginary scepter in the air and waved his hand at invisible nobles coming to greet him, smiling at the audience he could see surrounding and hailing him as their greatest leader.

But then a voice from behind interrupted his dreams.

"Get off of that! It's mine!"

He turned to see Stephen coming out of the hallway, their father further behind and unaware of the brothers' bickering. Edward gave a huff as he glared his brother down. "It's just a chair. I can sit on it if I want to!"

"No you can't!" Stephen said as he approached the throne. "That's the king's chair. Only the king can sit on it!"

"Well I'm the king's son."

"Well I'm the king's heir!"

"Only because you were born first," Edward mocked as Stephen's expression sunk. "What did you do to earn it?"

Edward paused from his reminiscence, his heart paining at the memory. He remembered Stephen running back to their father and telling on him. The king had surprised him and told Stephen to make Edward get off the chair because he was the future king, and that position demanded respect. If respect wasn't earned now, it would never be earned.

Stephen never could make Edward get out of the chair, and even Arden had shaken his head in disappointment.

But Edward's hurtful words echoed in his mind. "What did you do to earn it?" They were only children, fools pretending to be wise. And as Edward felt his son sleeping softly on his shoulder, he asked himself the same question he asked Stephen so long ago.

What did you do to earn it?

Lies. Thievery. Adultery. Murder. He did so many terrible things to earn his throne that he was surprised God had even allowed him to have it.

Mercy. That was what really gave him his kingdom, his son. Guilt turned to sorrow that begged for forgiveness in an empty chapel not long ago. He was given what very few in life were given: a second chance to make his wrongs right, another opportunity to earn the throne he sat on every single day.

And as he held Calimus, his son and heir, in his arms, he made a vow then and there to not repeat what his father had done to him.

I will be your father and friend. I will not be your enemy. You will choose your own path in this life, be it a king or something else, but I will teach you that you always have a purpose. No matter what, you will not have to prove your worth to anyone.

"Because I will love you always," he whispered, kissing his son's forehead. The baby didn't stir and continued to breathe softly, and Edward placed him in his crib, sitting back on the chair and watching him until he fell asleep.

"You're still here?"

Marcus turned to see Sir Rikert, wide awake in working the night shift to cover for a sick guard, approach. Marcus shrugged, not willing to admit he felt tired, hoping the knight wouldn't notice the bags developing under his eyes.

"I'm just doing a final check of the palace before I leave for tonight. I want to make sure every guard is at their post."

"It's the royal guard. I don't think too many of them will be goofing off."

"I know, but I want to make sure just in case."

Rikert followed Marcus down the hallways as he counted each guard off. "As happy as I am that you're taking your job seriously, Marcus, just remember to not burn yourself out."

Marcus chuckled as they entered another hallway. "My life is my work, Sam. You needn't worry over me."

"I know. But you look tired. Even you can't deny that."

Marcus pursed his lips. "I'll rest when I get home."

"Just promise me you'll go home tonight."

Marcus nodded. "I promise."

"I'll tell the king to order you to rest if you don't listen to my advice."

"Don't worry. I'm not going to ignore your wisdom, oh wise sage of Audlin." Rikert laughed as he shook his head, making Marcus snicker. "Besides, I have a dog at home that needs feeding. Don't want him chewing on my bow again like last week."

They stopped as they approached the prince's nursery, and Marcus scoffed, shaking his head. "Unbelievable. I thought I had guards stationed at the nursery door!"

"With Sir Ichabod taking over for the prince's security, I think he feels the guards thirty feet away are sufficient."

Marcus scoffed. "It's not good enough, if you ask me." He paused, letting out a sigh. "Though I can't say I'm surprised Malina chose Jacob as her 'personal guard'. She knows I don't trust her."

"It was bound to happen one way or the other," Rikert replied. "Jacob's family is influential. They would've demanded a higher position for him."

"It doesn't make it right, though," Marcus said. "It's just...something doesn't make sense with this. Why Jacob? Malina doesn't do anything unless she has a plan for it."

"I'm not sure. I'll admit it was a smart move on her part, though. It gave her much favor with the nobility."

Marcus frowned. "The people were that angry with my appointment?"

"There are two types of nobles," Rikert said, putting his hand on Marcus' shoulder. "Those who are content and those who are irritable. The content ones were pleased with your new position. The irritable ones, however, were not. And unfortunately the irritable ones outnumber the content ones."

Marcus lowered his eyes to the ground. He hadn't thought of the sacrifice Edward had made to his own popularity for rewarding his friend for his loyalty. "Perhaps Edward should've given Jacob the position instead. It would have been easier on him."

"It wouldn't," Rikert replied warmly. "Even though I am Jacob's friend, I also know what type of man he is. He is not nearly as dedicated, nor as loyal, as you are. Edward was right in putting you in charge, Marcus. The royal family has never been in safer hands."

Marcus smiled, giving him a nod in thanks. "I'll just check on the prince. Make sure he's alright before I head on home."

Rikert nodded as they quietly opened the door. Instead of finding an awake nurse watching over a sleeping baby, however, they found the king of Audlin sleeping on a chair with his son quietly resting in the crib, facing his father.

The knights smiled quietly to themselves as they shut the door back.

"Reminds me of my dad when I was a kid," Marcus said as they walked away from the nursery. "Was King Arden like that, too?"

Rikert shook his head. "Far from it. The queen was usually there but Arden was so busy with the kingdom that he rarely saw his children when they were young."

The men continued down the hallway in the darkness. "I take it Edward takes more after his mother?" Marcus asked.

"Not quite," Rikert replied. "I think he's just wanting to be more of a father than a king."

"Is that a bad thing or a good thing?"

"I guess we'll see, won't we?"

Chapter 19: The Blessed Curse

"We're getting close to the gates," Aldaric said as he finished setting up their nightly camp. He watched as Emmerich grew the flicker starting inside the pile of sticks he'd spent an hour gathering earlier. The young man stared into it, like watching a void, and he made no answer. Aldaric sighed, continuing to speak. Emmerich hadn't changed since their fight near the Edellwood and he doubted he'd change soon, if the past was any indication of the future. "We should be home by tomorrow afternoon. I'm sure your mother will have dinner ready."

He turned around and watched for any change in his son, waiting for some sort of response. Nothing came. "She'll be happy to see you."

Emmerich's eyes glanced up, confused.

"Your mother," Aldaric clarified. "It's been a month since she's seen you. I'm sure she's been missing you."

Emmerich lowered his eyes once more, staring into the fire as it kindled and grew.

Aldaric made his way across from his son and sat down on the cold, hard ground. They were fortunate a warm front had come through and much of the snow had melted in preparation for an early spring. It was still cold, however, and a bitter wind flowed through the air, and Emmerich had to be chilling. He wore the same cloak he had worn in Edeland, and the temperatures weren't as bitter there.

"Are you warm enough?" Aldaric asked, reaching to take off his own coat.

"I'm fine, thanks," Emmerich replied.

Aldaric straightened his coat and pressed his lips together in a frown, unsure of what else to do. He knew his son was hurting, knew he was bottling up all the disappointment and pain from losing Antoinette a second time. As a friend, he knew he had to give Emery space to grieve at the loss, but as a father, he knew he had to step in before Emery went spiraling down a well of despair that would trap him for the rest of his days.

"Son, we need to talk."

"What's there to talk about?" Emmerich asked.

Aldaric exhaled slowly, folding his hands in front of his knees. "I know you're hurting…"

"And talking is supposed to help?"

"I just want to make sure you're alright."

"I'm fine."

"You've barely spoken since we left the Edellwood, Emery," Aldaric said, his voice catching. "I know you're upset about what happened and you have every right to be, but don't shut me out when I can help. You can talk to me about anything."

At least his son looked at him now. Emmerich's face remained emotionless, his eyes glassy. "So it's okay for me to share everything with you, but it's not okay for you to share everything with me. That's a bit hypocritical, isn't it?"

Aldaric sighed, lowering his head. As much as he hated to admit it, Emery was right. He hadn't been honest like he should have, and he was humble enough to admit it. "I was wrong. I know that. I should have told you about Susanna and I. What do you want to know?"

"Did you really have an affair on her?"

"No," Aldaric replied. "What I told you before about your mother and I was true. I left Susanna because I knew the relationship wouldn't last. You've seen the type of person she is. I wasn't about to stay with that."

Emmerich smirked, making Aldaric's heart rise. At least that was some improvement. "Fair enough. So why didn't you tell me sooner?"

"I didn't think it'd be important at first," Aldaric said. "But...I suppose I wanted to put my past with her behind me."

"Why?"

"Because she tried to tear our family apart." Aldaric paused, watching as Emmerich's smirk faded. What he was about to say was only known by Anna, and even she didn't hear the entire story. It would hurt her too much to know. "You were young at the time. There was this one day in the summer when I was summoned to the parlor in Staalberg palace. I thought it was the king willing to discuss some trade deals since we were working on a new agreement. I was alone when I went to the parlor. You were outside with Antoinette taking a walk and your mother was in our room napping. When I got to the parlor, I expected to see the king, but instead...it was Susanna.

"I turned to leave because I didn't think it was proper that we were alone, but she started crying. I didn't know what to do at first seeing her like that, so I asked her what the matter was. I thought it was something wrong with the kids, but she told me it wasn't. She was regretting everything that happened between us and told me she wasn't happy with her life. The king annoyed her and barely spent time with her anymore, and she wanted to go back to the way things were. I tried to tell her that we both made our choices in life, but she wouldn't have it. She wanted to get back together with me.

"I tried to convince her that she was only feeling this way because the king had been busy lately and that she had a wonderful life with John and her children, but she never listened, even when I told her I was happy with you and Anna and didn't want to give you both up. She wouldn't have it. She...she kissed me, told me that we could keep our relationship a secret because she didn't want to give up being queen, either."

Aldaric hung his head in shame. Though it was Susanna who had kissed him and he pulled away from her, he still felt a sting of guilt from it. "I...I won't deny that a part of me still loved her, Emery, before that moment. You never really forget the first woman you've ever fallen in love with. But after she did that, after she tried to pull me away from you and your mother, I...any respect or care I had for Susanna left that day. I never realized how terrible she was until then, and I felt so much regret in ever being with her before I married your mother."

He watched as Emmerich listened intently, his eyes fixed on him. "I guess the reason why I never said anything to you is because I wanted to forget it ever happened. There was too much hurt and regret." He sighed, leaning back as he sat on the ground. "I also didn't want to strain the relationship you had with Antoinette. You two were so close and I didn't want you to pay for my mistakes. But I shouldn't have kept silent with you. I'm sorry, Emery. You should've known regardless of how I felt."

Emmerich's eyes lowered again, his voice becoming soft.

"Thanks for telling me."

Aldaric offered a comforting smile. "Now you know."

"Now I know."

"So...I think it's your turn." He gave a light chuckle as Emmerich rolled his eyes, shaking his head. "It's only fair. I tell you what's on my mind, you tell me what's on your mind..."

"What's there to tell?" Emmerich shrugged as he leaned forward. "It's not like I haven't been rejected before. I'm used to it."

Pity entered Aldaric's heart as he watched his son's saddening expression. He hated to admit that Emmerich had seen the unfairness of life more than most boys his age. It was out of his control, sure, but it hurt nonetheless. "It won't always be this bad, Son. You've went through a lot, but time will prove that this is for the best."

"But she was the one, Dad. I felt it."

"We can't always trust our feelings, Emery. They can change so quickly."

"This was deeper, though." Emmerich shifted in his seat, looking up. "I thought that maybe she cared, maybe she..." He paused, pursing his lips as he looked away, his eyes watering. "I don't understand, Dad. Why wasn't I good enough?"

Emmerich put his hands to his eyes, covering them and holding back tears. Aldaric felt his heart sink within him, and he wished that he could take all the pain his son was feeling and hide it away forever. He scooted next to him and put his arm around Emmerich's shoulder, pulling him close. What could he say to make his son feel better? Even words seemed useless against a broken heart.

"Why is it so hard for people to accept me?" Emmerich asked, his voice catching. "What's wrong with me? What do I have to do to keep people from leaving?"

"There's nothing wrong with you," Aldaric said softly. "You're a good young man, Emery. Antoinette knows this. She always has. She was just deceived by her mother. Try not to take it personally."

"But Antoinette was the one," Emmerich said. "All I dreamed of...all I ever wanted was her. She was my purpose. What do I have now?"

"It'll become clear in time," Aldaric replied. "God will guide you; just don't give up. You have a purpose...you always have."

"But I don't want to be alone, Dad."

"You'll never be alone, Son. You'll always have God, your mother...and me."

"Who will I have when you and Mom are gone, though?"

Aldaric stroked the back of Emery's head as his son faced him with brokenness written on his face. "You'll still have God, then."

Emmerich frowned as he looked away towards the fire once more. "I think He's abandoned me, Dad. Bad things don't happen to favored people."

"Bad things happen to everyone, no matter who they are. Just don't get discouraged. Things will get better, Emery, in time. I promise."

"I'll believe it when I see it." Emmerich shrugged off his father's touch and reached out for his bag, pulling out a blanket. "I'm sorry, Dad. I'm too tired to talk anymore."

Aldaric said nothing as he watched his son fix a bed next to the fire and lay down to sleep.

Chapter 20: The Message

Emmerich was lying on the ground, restless and unable to sleep, his mind moving too fast with thought to allow any chance of recuperation. How had his life fallen so low, his heart cracked into a thousand pieces and his emotions full of despair? What did he do in the past to ever deserve such treatment by fate? He had always been a good man and a good child growing up. He honored his parents, he refused to steal, he never cheated and tried to do everything right. Sure, he slipped up once in a while. Told a lie here, accidentally stepped on an ant while walking through the streets. If he really dug deep, he'd even be willing to admit that he coveted Edward's relationship with Antoinette. But even though it was a sin and jealousy pinched his heart, he didn't think it was enough to make fate tease him with such a thing like the woman he loved marrying him and then leaving for another on the same day. It was like a nightmare from a fairy tale, one of the tragedies the stories of old were filled with.

But no. His situation was no story. It was his life, and somehow the unfairness that plagued him in childhood followed him as an adult.

Too sad to sleep, Emery decided to get up and stretch his legs for a moment. His father rested peacefully near him and Emmerich sighed to himself. The man was supposed to be keeping watch, but weariness wore at him and overcame his desire to stay awake. It didn't matter, anyways. The grass lions were typically more north this time of year and aside from a few squirrels and rabbits, there was nothing threatening out in the wild. There was no need for a watchman that night.

Emmerich walked through the stiff ground, still slightly crunching, and looked up at the sky. Clear, shining stars shown down on him, and had it been any other night, he would have jumped at the chance to chart them. But even the joy of the great beyond was disinteresting to him now, and all he could think of was how much he missed Antoinette and how he wished she had never left.

I wished you loved me, he thought to himself. Tried as he could, though, his emotions never changed. Yes, he was angry. Yes, he was hurt. But no matter how shattered his soul was, he was still in love with her, and he forever would be.

He took in a deep, icy gust of air and slowly exhaled it out, watching the cloudy mist of his breath float high above him. He felt so alone, so lost...so trapped in a fog. If only things had been different...

He heard a snap behind him and turned, seeing nothing in the darkness. The campfire in the distance still shone and he could make out his father's figure lying beside it, still sleeping. Emmerich turned back, feeling a shiver go across his arms and chest, confused as to where the sound came from. He quieted his thoughts, his heart starting to beat quicker inside his chest, until he saw two pairs of eyes light up in front of him.

The sounds of growls nearly put his heart at a stop, and he didn't take time to think as he turned and hurried towards the campfire.

"DAD!" He yelled as loud as his voice would allow him. He sprinted, his heart beating inside his chest so hard that he thought it would burst. Aldaric scrambled up, watching as two

grass lions were chasing his son, and shouted back.

"Emery! Come to the fire!" He reached down and picked up his bow and arrow, rushing forward. Emmerich watched as his father took aim, shooting an arrow towards the two lions, missing. It was too dark, too far away from the safety of the campfire.

"RUN!" Aldaric rushed forward, Emmerich's mind racing faster than his feet as he realized what his father was doing. If the bow wouldn't stop the lions, then he would himself.

"Dad, stay near the camp!" Emmerich said, his voice nearly spent. He turned, seeing the grass lions coming closer, their claws nearly within reach of his legs. He wasn't going to make it. He would be mauled before he'd reach his father in time...

He heard his father scream his name until it was drowned out by the sound of something far louder and more frightening.

Emmerich was nearly overrun when the dogs came. Wolves, more like it, with thick brown fur that covered great, muscular legs and paws strong enough to take on a grass lion. Emmerich nearly ran into his father and Aldaric grabbed hold of him, pulling him back, aiming an arrow at the dueling beasts that battled before them.

"I didn't know there were wolves out here..." Emmerich panted.

Aldaric slowly lowered his bow, his eyes widening. "There shouldn't be..."

With a swipe of a paw and two great bites, the grass lions were gone, leaving the dogs facing the two men backing up towards the campfire. Instead of attacking new prey, however, the dogs suddenly calmed, looking like household pets as they sat on the grass, their tails wagging back and forth and their heads tilted in curiosity.

"What on earth?" Emmerich asked as he looked to his father in question.

"Well this is surprising," Aldaric said as he lowered his bow and stepped forward. "But it is a welcome one!"

Emmerich felt lost, wondering what his father was talking about as he watched him approach the dogs, petting the first one's head. Emmerich stepped forward slowly until he saw the strangest looking men approach. They were covered in furs, their faces painted in dark colors to help them blend into the night air, and Emmerich could only guess who they were from his father's stories.

The Recu, King Erick's fabled "barbarian" clans united under a strange, new ruler named Bohden. Emmerich knew little about them save they stayed to themselves until recently, and even after reaching out, they were still ignored. They were a poor people, scraping off the tundra and barren forests they called home, and Erick would have no dealings with them in Hugellia though they were close neighbors.

"God be with you, Aldaric of Hugellia," one of the men said in a thick accent.

"And with you," Aldaric replied. "Thank you for saving my son and I, but I am curious to know how you knew we'd be here."

"Bohden has seen it," the man replied, making Emmerich take a step back. "And he has sent us to speak with you. He has a message."

"What does he wish to say to me that couldn't be said when I met with him two months ago?"

"The message isn't for you," the man replied. "It is for your son."

Aldaric looked to Emmerich in confusion, and Emmerich gave a nervous gulp in fear.

It was a short ride to the Recu's camp. Emmerich gripped the reins on Waffles tightly, anxiety overwhelming any type of discouragement he was feeling earlier in his mind. He never met Bohden before, never even met a Recu before that night, and somehow he was summoned to speak with them. It was strange tidings, but his father didn't seem fazed. He'd met with them multiple times over the last year, and their oddities were no longer a mystery to him as they once were. Aldaric spoke highly of them, more respectful of their own leader compared to the Hugellian king. Though Erick didn't know it, Aldaric had sent the Recu much trade in secret to promote good relations between them.

The camp was quiet, nearly invisible amongst the grass, and Emmerich and Aldaric were led towards a small tent in the center. Dogs and a few guards spread around them, making Emmerich wonder why they had such a lack of light around the camp. It only dawned on him as he was entering the tent that the Recu weren't even supposed to be in Hugellian territory without letting the king know. Such an invasion could be seen as an act of war.

Emmerich's breathing quickened as he entered, wondering why Chief Bohden risked everything just to talk.

Aldaric and Emmerich stood before the chieftain, and Emmerich got a good look at him in what little light shined inside the tent. Bohden was surprisingly young, maybe a year or so younger than himself, and Emmerich couldn't help but wonder in how a young man (or boy?) was able to unite the scattered clans of the Recu under one leader. Though he had the typical features of a Recu - dark, thick hair and a pale face from lack of sunlight - he also looked different from his kin. While the others were covered in furs and facial hair, looking much like the "barbarians" Erick had described them to be, Bohden was clean-shaven, his hair short and his clothing smooth and tailored underneath a cloak of brown fur. Bohden looked to Aldaric first, and as Emmerich met the chieftain's gaze, he marveled at how piercing his stare could be. Young he was, but a fool he was not, and in his dark eyes there was a glimmer of ancient wisdom not seen in any Hugellian scholar.

"It is an honor to see you, Chief Bohden," Aldaric began with a bow. Bohden turned to a man beside of him and he translated Aldaric's words.

The chieftain replied in his native tongue, giving a nod.

The man beside him quickly translated. "And you, Aldaric of Hugellia."

Aldaric smiled in thanks and then continued. "I thank you for your aid. My son is safe because of you."

The translator relayed Bohden's words. "I am glad to provide it, but that is not why I am here."

Aldaric's brow lowered. "What is it then? Is something wrong?"

"Not with you. I have seen much, but you know what it is I've spoken to you about. That has not changed."

"But your men said you wished to speak with my son," Aldaric continued. "What is it?"

Bohden frowned when he spoke the words, and his translator mimicked his expression. "The message is for your son and no other. I will tell him and he can speak with you afterwards. Agreed?"

Aldaric looked to Emmerich, and the young man shook his head. He didn't want to be left alone with the ruler of a neighboring country...especially a neighbor he had never met before. But one glance from his father told him there would be no choice in the matter. When amongst the Recu, they had to obey, and two of Bohden's guards approached to escort Aldaric outside of the tent.

"Don't leave me here. I don't know these people!" Emmerich hissed beneath his breath as he took hold of his father's arm.

Aldaric put his hand atop his son's and clasped it. "You needn't fear them. They only have your best interest. Just be respectful and kind."

"But..."

"I'm sorry, Emery. There's not much I can do without risking offense to them."

"But you're a diplomat! It's your job to risk offense!"

"It's my job to prevent offense, Emery. Just be respectful and you'll be fine." The guardsmen took Aldaric by the arm and gently pulled him away towards the door flap, leading him out of the tent. Emmerich watched until his father was out of sight, turning back to the Recu chieftain and trying to hide his own growing fear.

They said nothing at first as Bohden looked at Emmerich curiously, his chin resting on the stroking fingers of his left hand. Emmerich stood in silence, looking nervously towards the ground and unsure of what to say or do, until Bohden broke the silence.

"*Recu-vera!*"

Emmerich pressed his lips together, unsure of what to say as he looked at the translator. The man was silent, his hands to his sides and staring back.

"Uhm...pardon?" Emmerich asked, turning to Bohden. "I...I don't know what that means."

Bohden smiled as he set his hands upon his lap. "It is my name for you."

Emmerich's eyes widened in surprise. "You speak our language?"

Bohden nodded. "Yes."

"Does my father know this?"

"No, but I will reveal this to him in time," Bohden replied. "Emissaries of King Erick often accompany your father. I do not trust them, and it is better they think me a fool."

"And why is that?"

"Because an enemy is easier to defeat when they think you are stupid."

Emmerich blinked, unsure of what he was hearing. "Enemy? I don't understand. My father spoke highly of you and acted like there could be an alliance between our countries."

"An alliance will not happen for a long time, *Recu-vera*," Bohden said solemnly. "King Erick will never be a friend of my people, though your father has earned our favor through his kindness." He paused, his lip twitching upward. "Fear not, though. War will not be brought to my lands for now. Hugellia may be our enemy but we are not an enemy of Hugellia. At least not yet."

Emmerich felt his pulse quickening. What madness was

he witnessing? Bohden, a leader barely out of boyhood, spoke like a trickster fond of riddles and flowery speech. "Why do you trust me with all of this information, then? What sets me apart?"

Bohden smiled. "You have always been set apart. The others have not. That is why I trust you."

Emmerich was unsure of how to respond. Bohden's words were more confusing than any logic he had learned in school. It was best to hurry the conversation along and be done with it as soon as possible, lest more strangeness occurred. "I was told you had a message for me. Is there something you wished to be delivered to the king?"

Bohden gave a chuckle, shaking his head. "I could've sent a letter to your father if I wished to speak with Erick. No, my business is done with that idiot of an old man. He is not my concern." He stood to his feet, approaching Emmerich with that piercing gaze once more. "You, on the other hand, are. I have had many visions, and I have never seen your face in them until now."

Emmerich tilted his head. "A vision?"

"Yes."

"What do you mean by a vision?"

"I have seen that which is to come."

Emmerich blinked, unsure of how to answer. He desperately didn't want to seem offensive, yet at the same time didn't want to be taken in as a fool. "So you've seen the future? How?"

"It is a gift few are given in this life," Bohden explained as he walked about the tent. "To know what is to come is both a blessing and a curse, but I am a servant of the One who bestows it, and I cannot ignore what I see." He stopped, turning to Emmerich. "You do not believe me, I suppose?"

"I..." Emmerich swallowed hard, praying desperately for the right words. "I'm just not very knowledgeable about visions, Chief Bohden. I've never had one."

"No. And I doubt you will, but that is not a bad thing." Bohden continued his walk about the tent. "You are saved a lifetime of worry. Regardless, despite what you believe, I must relay what I saw to you. Whether you accept it or not is your decision."

"Very well, then. What is it you've seen?"

Bohden stopped once more, closing his eyes and bowing his head. "I saw you in the midst of a rain storm. The water sprinkled down upon you and you were angry with the water and clouds as it blocked your view of the sun. You cursed the rain until it stopped, but the clouds remained, the sunlight still hidden from you. Frustrated, you looked up to the sky and began to question why the clouds had not moved, but you neglected to see what it was coming behind.

"You survived the storm but it was replaced by a hurricane. The sprinkles became a downpour and the breeze became a mighty wind. Instead of puddles and mud soaking your feet, you were drowning in currents of water, struggling to stay afloat, and you were swept away down a stream as everything you knew was left behind.

"In the end, the currents began to weaken and lower, and instead of being in a river, you then waded in the water. You walked ahead, your legs now strong enough to withstand the current, and you made your way out of the water and towards dry land. You ended in the valley, engulfed by sunlight, and as the storms surrounded you, you no longer looked upon the rain with fear and anger. Instead, you looked up, your eyes forever on the sun that remained in the sky."

Bohden opened his eyes and faced Emmerich once more, leaning forward so they stood face to face. "A storm has already passed for you, Emmerich of Hugellia," he began, searching his eyes. "Yet the hurricane awaits. If you are not strong, you will drown in the current, but fear not! The sun still shines above the clouds. You must remember that."

Emmerich shook his head. "But what do you mean a hurricane awaits? Does that mean something bad is going to happen to me?" His breath panted and his heart sped within him. He had already went through the hurricane in losing Antoinette. How could life get any worse?

"I cannot say much more," Bohden replied. "But you are correct in your interpretations." He lowered his head, frowning. "I'm sorry. I know this is not what you want to hear."

"Of course it isn't! I've already been living a nightmare and I want to escape it, not stay in it longer!"

"I do not control destiny, Emmerich. I only speak of what it is."

"Well I don't believe you," Emmerich said, his voice lowering along with his brow. "With all due respect, Chief Bohden, my life is already at the bottom. It can't get worse. I've lost everything!"

"No," Bohden replied sadly. "Not yet. But you will."

Emmerich's eyes widened in fear, but he said nothing, turning away. He would hear no more. This Bohden, whoever he was, knew nothing of the future! He never would.

"I'll be fine," Emmerich muttered, but Bohden shook his head.

"Take joy in your last moments here, Emmerich of

Hugellia, for the hurricane is about to begin." He returned to his throne, sitting upon it. "Remember what I've told you: the sun still shines above the clouds. It will give you hope when you need it most." He turned to one of the guards, giving him a nod as he left the tent to retrieve Aldaric. Aldaric was brought forth and stood beside his son, his face full of concern after seeing Emmerich's paled expression.

Bohden turned to his translator, speaking in his native language for the man to relay. "Now return home. Aldaric, I will see soon, but it will be many years before we see each other again, Emmerich. God be with you."

The men were not given enough time to respond before they were escorted out of the camp and brought back to their horses.

Aldaric was the first to speak as he saddled to ride towards Kettensburg, too full of confusion to sleep. "What did he say to you? What was the message?" Aldaric asked.

Emmerich remained quiet at first, unsure of whether to tell his father the gloomy words Bohden had given him. "Nothing much," he replied quietly, looking away. "Except he called me *Recu-vera*. Do you know what that means?"

Aldaric's brows rose and he looked at his son in disbelief. "Wait. He called you what?"

"*Recu-vera*. What does it mean?"

"It means 'uniter of the clans' in their native language. That's what Chief Bohden's people call him, and...and...he actually called you that?"

Emmerich looked away, more confused than ever. "It's probably nothing."

"Emery, that's a title not given or taken lightly," Aldaric

replied, smiling. "He's just called you a king."

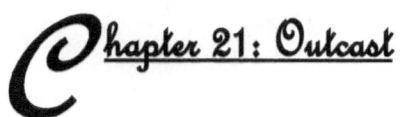

The gates of Kettensburg towered high all around as Aldaric and Emmerich rode into the city. They made their way into the courtyard entrance, trotting through the streets, and Aldaric gave a deep exhale as he looked around.

"It'll be good to be home," he said, looking to his son.

"Yeah," Emmerich replied quietly, his mood somber. "Glad to be back."

Aldaric paused for a moment. "Your mother will be happy to see you, and you'll have to tell her about the name Bohden gave. She'll be thrilled."

Emmerich offered a fake smile. He still hadn't told his father of Bohden's "message"…at least, not all of it. For all Aldaric knew, Bohden had given him a name and that was it. Aldaric took it as a sign of great things to come for his son: respect, purpose, a life of destiny. But little did he know that Bohden's prophecy was far from positive, and though Emmerich told himself that the Recu's words were nothing but fantasy, deep inside his heart, he feared the vision true. He just hoped and prayed it wasn't.

He decided to change the subject, to make his father not bother with Bohden. "Mom will want to know about what's happened with Antoinette. I'd rather not say much just yet. It's still too near."

Aldaric nodded. "I understand. We'll take everything at your pace." They slowed their horses' trot as the crowds thickened in the street corners near the palace. "It's wise to keep everything quiet, anyways. The less King Erick knows, the better. He would not take kindly to what has happened in Edeland. Susanna was always a favorite of his."

"I won't say anything."

"And neither will I," Aldaric said.

They approached the house and led their horses to the stables to rest. Emmerich took his travel bag and slung it across his shoulder, following his father up the steps to the door of their home. Aldaric opened it, stepping inside and calling his wife's name, greeting Anna as she rushed towards the door.

His parents embraced for a long time, their arms wrapped around each other and their lips brushing in a soft kiss. Emmerich watched the looks of joy in their eyes seeing one another, the love they shared for so long being exchanged in a simple glance. It made Emmerich's spirit heavy at the sight of it. How many times had he looked at Antoinette that way, and how many times had she looked back?

There were moments he thought she loved him or at least cared, but…no. If she truly cared, she would've stayed.

He turned away, the hurt of seeing his parents' happiness too much to bear. He trudged up the steps towards his room, staying quiet as he passed them by.

Anna stopped and turned away from her husband, reaching out to her son. "Aren't you going to say hello? What happened in Edeland? Where's Antoinette?"

"Anna…" Aldaric said softly, putting his hand on her arm. She turned, at first confused, until she finally understood.

"I'll be upstairs if you need me," Emmerich muttered, and then turned back and headed up to his room.

Emmerich had been lying down for a while. Energy seemed sapped from his body and his mind was in a fog. At first he was alone in his room, his father undoubtedly filling his mother in on what all had happened with Antoinette and the Recu. Anna eventually came in and sat with him, saying nothing at first as she kissed his forehead and took hold of his hand. He held hers back, thankful for her presence, and they sat there for an hour before Emmerich broke the silence.

"Do you think I'm cursed, Mom?"

Anna frowned as she shook her head. "No. Why would you say that?"

Emmerich shrugged, looking away. Bohden's dire words echoed in his mind of what was to come. "So many bad things have happened."

"Things could always be worse."

"I know. That's what I'm afraid of."

Anna gave him a comforting smile as she brushed a few strands of hair away from his eyes. "Sweetheart, just because bad things happen to you doesn't mean you are cursed. Everything happens for a reason."

"I just had my heart ripped out of me, Mom. What good can come from that?"

"I don't know," Anna replied. "The answer may never be known. Just trust that God works it all out in the end for a purpose."

"Is it my purpose to be alone and miserable, then?"

"No."

"Then what is it?"

"I'm not sure," Anna replied. "But I don't doubt it's big. Even Chief Bohden thinks so by calling you *Recu-vera*."

Emmerich scoffed, rolling his eyes. Bohden could take his words and stuff them. "It doesn't mean anything."

"Emery, he gave you his own title. I've never heard of such a thing."

"Maybe he's just crazy."

Anna smirked. "Or maybe he's right."

Despite the honorary title, Emmerich couldn't help but hope the man was wrong. With the title came a promise of a horrible future full of hardships. He didn't want that at all and would gladly give up some kingly title he'd never receive anyways. "*Recu* is a term for their own people. I doubt Bohden's calling me his heir. That would be an insult to them having a Hugellian rule their clans."

"Then maybe it's not about the Recu. Maybe it has another meaning."

"Or maybe it's just ramblings like everything else he said."

Anna cocked her brow in confusion. "Did he say something else? Your father only mentioned the term."

Emmerich sighed, cursing himself for letting the worries slip his mind. "It's nothing."

"Emery, be honest. If you don't want me to say anything, I won't."

Emmerich faced her, giving a squeeze to her hand. "It's not that I want to keep it a secret. I guess it's just something I don't want to come true."

Anna's eyes beaded in concern. "What did he say?"

Emmerich opened his mouth to speak, but the sounds of rushed footsteps to the door and the entering of a serious-looking Aldaric made him close it back again. Anna and Emmerich both turned, and Aldaric gave a shake of his head. "King Erick wishes to see us immediately."

"Did he say why?" Emmerich asked. Surely the king wouldn't know about what happened in Edeland. Only his mother knew, and she hadn't even left the house.

"No, but with it being urgent we'd best not keep him waiting," Aldaric replied. "He must've gotten word from the gatekeepers that we were back from traveling. He's probably wanting a report on why we were gone for so long."

"What are we going to do?" Anna asked.

"Don't worry. I'll handle it," Aldaric said warmly. He turned to Emmerich. "Say nothing about Edeland and Antoinette. As far as he knows, you stayed in Audlin, and if he asks about what we did, let me do the talking."

"Alright."

The three of them hurried down the stairs towards the king's escort waiting for them, making their way to the palace.

Nerves plagued Emmerich's heart as he stepped into the throne room, King Erick and his two other sons watching him arrive and glaring. From the looks of his kin, whatever they had to say had to be bad, and Emmerich steered closer behind his parents, hoping somehow it would hide him from the king's disdain.

They stopped, bowing in respect and facing his judgment. "You requested to see us?" Aldaric asked, his voice calm.

Erick nodded. "Yes. But my quarrel for once is not with you, Aldaric." He tilted his head, meeting Emmerich's lowering gaze. "I wish to speak with your son. Step forward, Emmerich."

He obeyed, squeezing between his parents and facing the king. "Yes, Your Majesty?"

Erick held up a piece of paper in his right hand, his eyes beading. "Why do you seek to dishonor me?"

Emmerich blinked, his heart starting to race. "I don't understand..."

Aldaric stepped forward. "Clarification is needed, Your Majesty. To what does my son stand accused of?"

"Do not speak for him, Aldaric, for I know your mind. Your son has taken the actions of a boy, but shall be treated like a man when I am through. Now tell me, Emmerich. Why do you seek to dishonor me?"

Emmerich bowed his head, his eyes on the ground. "Your Majesty, I would never seek to dishonor you. You are the leader of this country, my home, and have raised the man who is my father! If anything, I would do all in my power to honor you in my actions."

"Your flowery words are like cattle dung to me, Emmerich!" the king spat. "Do you deny that you went to Edeland and tried to elope with a daughter of their queen?"

"I..." Emmerich looked to his father, his face paling in fear.

Aldaric turned to the king, ready. "Your Majesty, Emmerich was with me while in Audlin. Whatever rumors you have heard..."

"Silence, Aldaric, for you have no permission to speak unless I give it!" He turned to Emmerich as Aldaric closed his mouth. "I have a letter signed by Her Majesty, the queen, in my hand," Erick interrupted, waving the piece of paper. "And it is also signed by a Prince Arnold von Liegen as witness. Do you deny Susanna's charges of trying to destroy the alliance between Edeland and Liegen by marrying the princess as she was bound to Prince Arnold after a treaty sealed the engagement?"

At least the criminal charges brought up by Susanna weren't mentioned. The queen at least kept one part of her deal. "I don't deny it. Lady Antoinette did not wish to go through the marriage and needed my help."

"You are a fool for meddling in the affairs of others, Emmerich!" Erick said. "But you are an even bigger fool for causing a scandal and nearly a war between us, Liegen, and Edeland! Edward's treachery was terrible enough, but this is an outrage and an insult to the van Ketten family! I am ashamed to have even been associated with you!"

Emmerich stood there, frozen, as every word the king lashed at him stung his soul.

"Did you really think you could get away with such recklessness? You, so proud of your mind and your books, who thinks he is so smart and wise! You know nothing of the world, boy, and how it should work, nor do you know anything about life. Royals are meant to marry other royals and anyone who questions such traditions are only after the power and prestige fate has denied them! You are not amongst the princes, Emmerich, nor shall you ever be. You are a disgrace to this family and a disgrace to my nation, and I will not put up with your foolishness any longer."

"Your Majesty, be reasonable!" Aldaric interjected, stepping forward. "He is young and still learning. Are we not all like this at that age? It would be wise to bestow mercy and understanding on him and not..."

"You are lucky I do not punish you as well, Aldaric," Erick interrupted as he turned to his stepson. "For if you hadn't brought your sorry excuse of a son back to Hugellia, you would join his fate. But I will deal with you later. As for you, Emmerich." Erick turned back to him. "I will not chance you endangering this nation again. You are cast out of my presence, and I forbid you to ever enter Hugellia under penalty of death."

Emmerich felt his world stop and his breath be pulled from him. "Wh...what?"

Anna let out a yell as she clutched her son, holding on to him tight and refusing to let go as the guards tried to pry her from him. "I strip you of your citizenship and our family's name, and you are henceforth disowned by the van Kettens."

"You...you can't do this...I..." Emmerich felt his heart pounding, his breath racing in and out of his lungs. His mother's cries nearly deafened him and he staggered into his father's arms. Aldaric held him steady, pulling him close. "I have been nothing but loyal to you! Why would you treat me with such contempt?"

"Your disregard for your nation and king are an act of treason, Emmerich! Now go. The mere sight of you is an abomination to my court. Leave this nation at once and never come back again!"

"Don't argue. Just leave," Aldaric whispered as he pulled Emmerich away from the throne room. The three were ushered out of the palace and sent back home, guards waiting outside to make sure the young man would go.

Aldaric felt numb.

The carriage ride back had been the longest and most draining he had ever been on, even though the distance was short. Anna did nothing but sob, repeating over and over that her son couldn't leave. Emmerich said nothing, his eyes staring back into the void as he shivered, anxiety overtaking him. Aldaric had his arm around his shoulders, holding him close, feeling the weight of his emotions nearly crushing him. There had been moments his feelings towards his stepfather had been strained, but now...after everything that had happened...any disagreement, hurt, or apathy suddenly turned to fury. What a fool he had been to ever want to call the man his father, trying to please him and win over his favor and love so he could be a son just like Ulrich or Ambrose.

Aldaric closed his eyes, taking a deep breath. He couldn't let his emotions cloud reason and judgment. That would help no one, least of all Emery, and he didn't want to become heartless like Erick was. He would never stoop so low.

"We'll get through this," he said softly.

Anna looked up from her tears, her face full of agony. "How could he do this? Edward was even worse and all Erick did was ignore him! How can he be so cruel?"

"Erick is irrational. He has always thought I would take the throne from him and getting rid of our son is another spite against that."

"He should know us better than that, Aldaric. Does he not realize he is separating our family? Have we not went through enough?"

"We're strong. All of us." Aldaric took hold of Anna's hand and kept his arm around Emmerich. "No matter what Erick says, we'll never be separated. We are a family and we'll always be together no matter what distance."

"But what of Emery? Where will he go? He can't just leave!" Anna cried.

"The guards will force him out if he does not leave on his own accord," Aldaric replied. He turned to Emmerich, his son's eyes still staring ahead into nothing. "Worry not, though. I will see what I can do to calm the king and get him to overturn his decision. Erick may be irrational, but time may yet change his mind. For now, Emery, you must go to your Aunt Maria. She will make sure you're taken care of."

"But Audlin is so far away!" Anna said.

"I know, but it is near enough where we can visit and he will be amongst family who will treat him well." He stroked Emery's head, hoping to get him out of the daze. It didn't work. "It will be difficult, Emery, but you must do this for now. If Erick will not change his mind, then your mother and I will come to Audlin and be with you."

Emmerich remained silent, his face showing despair. Aldaric touched his son's cheek to get his attention. "Emery?"

"Bohden was right..." Emmerich whispered as he continued to stare.

"What do you mean?" Aldaric asked.

Emmerich looked up, his eyes suddenly weak. "I'm entering the hurricane."

"Hurricane? What hurricane?" Anna asked.

"It's only going to get worse," Emmerich muttered.

"Son, you'll be alright. I promise," Aldaric reassured.

Emmerich could only lower his head as the carriage pulled to a stop.

"Is there a reason why you're going through my things?"

Edward's eyes narrowed as he looked to his wife, crossing his arms and frowning. She glanced up from his desk, giving a roll of her eyes as she shook her head and went back to her work, his piles of papers and scrolls now neatly piled all around.

"You're very disorganized, Edward. I'm helping you stay on track."

He scoffed, picking up some of the papers and going through them to make sure none were missing. It wouldn't surprise him if she stole some of his work, changed the wording of his decrees, and forged his signature to get what she wanted. "If I needed help, I would've asked for it. Besides, why is tidiness so important to you?"

"It isn't," Malina replied. "But appearances are everything. We can't have a messy-looking king now, can we?"

Edward said nothing, rubbing his brow and feeling very tired all of a sudden.

"By the way, you received some letters today," Malina continued as she went to a stack and handed it to him. "I'm particularly interested in the one from Edeland. Did you know Antoinette got married?"

Edward took the letters and went through them, finding a perfumed parchment towards the bottom. He pulled it out, feeling the dread that rose in his heart. Doubtless it was a wedding announcement between Antoinette and Emmerich. It would explain why Aldaric and Emmerich had left so early after the funeral.

The seal of the letter was broken, proving it already read, but he kept the flap closed, unsure if he was ready to read the words inside. Antoinette, his former bride, his greatest love. It was hard to imagine her in the arms of another, and though he knew Emmerich to be the better man, the thought still pained him. He gave a sigh, swallowing his pride, and opened the letter. Emmerich would make her happy. Emmerich would be loyal and faithful. Emmerich would be the man Edward should've been to her.

But when he read the words of the announcement, he felt his blood run cold.

His Majesty, King John, and Her Majesty, Queen Susanna,
announce the marriage of their daughter, Antoinette,
to Arnold, Prince of Liegen.

Arnold? Edward read the contents of the announcement over again, disbelief coming across his eyes. Had he misunderstood Antoinette's words when they spoke at the funeral? He was sure she agreed that the man she was supposed to marry was Emmerich...

But then the pieces of the puzzle began to fit. Susanna would have never been so giddy had Antoinette been engaged to Emmerich. His mother mentioned to him long ago of Aldaric's betrothal to Susanna, how the breakup was the final nail in the coffin to Erick's disfavor of the Hugellian ambassador.

And then there was the timing after the funeral. Emmerich

left immediately, the same time as Antoinette, but Aldaric left only a few days afterwards. Anna didn't go at all, departing for Hugellia with the van Kettens. Never would she miss her only child's wedding, even if the distance was great.

Edward felt his heart sink, the reality of what probably happened becoming clear in his mind. Emmerich didn't leave to marry Antoinette. He left to stop the wedding.

And from the letter in his hands, it seemed that plan failed miserably.

Edward closed his eyes, his stomach tying in knots as the truth began to take hold. Emmerich's already fragile emotional state had to be in pieces now, and Antoinette...he could only imagine how she felt being forced to marry someone she barely knew.

"I take it you're not happy with the announcement?" Malina asked, her eyes gleaming.

Edward looked to her, his voice weak. "This is terrible news."

"Oh, don't be so glum about it. I hear Arnold is quite the charmer."

Edward frowned. He was unfamiliar with Liegen, but even he had heard of the princes and their wildness. He remembered his father going there for a summit and being appalled that the eldest son had flirted with Queen Maria the entire time.

Had you been faithful, Antoinette would not have been given to a stranger. Now she'll be betrayed over and over for the rest of her days.

The guilt of his actions surfaced in his heart, making him sick.

"My dear king, you look ill," Malina said with a smile.

Edward sat down at the couch near the wall where his secret box was hidden underneath. "I feel ill."

"Worry not. At least Antoinette will have someone to please her in the marriage bed. I can attest to how disappointing that is, marrying a man of no experience."

Edward's head remained bowed, his body leaning forward. "Were you actually interested, maybe it wouldn't be an issue. But it doesn't matter. I am too troubled to think of it right now."

"Wallow in your moods, then," Malina continued as she set the letters down beside her. "On a much brighter topic, I spoke with some of the nobles about expanding the city. Perhaps creating a quarry near the southern edge by the mountain so we can mine extra minerals. Selling the profit could increase the treasury by a great amount." She pulled out a piece of paper, already done up, and held it towards him. "I've signed your name on it and sent it to the house of nobles. It'll be on the agenda during tomorrow's meeting. Here is the copy so you'll know what to say."

Edward's head rose slowly and he glared at his wife, his lips pressed together in a snarl. He was in no mood for her games. He snatched the decree she'd done up and stood to his feet, ripping the parchment to shreds and throwing the pieces in the air. "I am *sick* of this, Malina! Will your mockery of me never end?"

Malina snickered, watching the pieces rain back down to the floor. "Well, so much for keeping your office clean. My, what a messy boy you are!" She paused, meeting his glare with her own confident gaze. "Edward, you should be thankful to have a woman with both experience and intelligence at your side. I am helping you, not harming you."

"I *don't* need your help!" Edward sneered, taking the

papers from the desk and sweeping them off. "I've never needed it! Now for once in your life will you stay away and leave me be?"

Malina smirked. "I see you're taking Antoinette's marriage very well."

Edward's face reddened and he pointed to the door. "Just get out!"

Malina slowly got up from her seat, walking to the door, a smile etched on her face as she left. "Very well. Don't forget the meeting tomorrow, though. I suggest you get there early to read about the new law you just tore up. Hopefully someone will have an extra copy."

He didn't bother listening, heading to the door after she left and slamming it shut. He made his way back to the couch, crashing down upon it and putting his face to his palms. His stomach was in knots, his heart was pounding, and a lump was caught in his throat. He felt wretched knowing Antoinette was in the arms of a scoundrel, and he felt even worse knowing his actions put her there.

I should've helped Emery stop the wedding. He would've been good to her. He would've righted my wrongs.

But he was left out in the dark. Emmerich no longer trusted him and didn't go to him for help, and could he blame him? It wasn't as if Edward hadn't betrayed him before.

Edward sighed, the hurt nearly overwhelming him as he got up from the couch and made his way to the desk, stepping on papers Malina had already gone through. Nothing was secret anymore, his work already exposed to her searching gaze. None of it mattered at the moment. He didn't care if she saw his plans for the country or the decrees he had been working on at night. All he could think of was Antoinette and what that wretch of a man named Arnold was doing to her at that moment.

His worry grew as he thought of her, and in the rashness he embraced when he was younger and more foolish, he grabbed a piece of parchment and reached for a quill.

He had to see her, had to see the woman he betrayed and make sure she was alright.

But he had to be clever, and he wasn't about to be outsmarted by Susanna and her wicked schemes.

He put his hand to the parchment and began to write.

It was early when the bickering started.

Antoinette swerved the spoon in her porridge in small circles as she kept her head down, holding her tongue as Mother went on and on about the latest gossip amongst the nobles. Arnold sat beside her, listening intently as if enamored with her stories, while Bernie only stared at her empty plate, the boiled egg already gone.

"And then Lady Applebridge had the nerve to wear green stockings with that red dress!" Susanna shook her head, scoffing as Arnold looked at her with sympathy. "The poor woman looked like a Christmas decoration. Surely she realized how embarrassing it was to the rest of us."

"Not everyone has the class of a lady like yourself, Your Majesty," Arnold replied, making Bernie roll her eyes. "Some are unfortunate to be so dull that they cannot learn from your example."

"If only I had enough time to teach them." Susanna sighed.

"Yes, because linens and fine silk are clearly more important than a real education," Bernie muttered.

Susanna scoffed. "Perhaps if you took your appearance more seriously, my dear, you wouldn't need an education to make yourself more desirable to others."

Bernie lowered her brow, opening her mouth to retaliate but closing it quickly after a shake of the head from Antoinette.

"But on to more important matters. Tell me, Antoinette," Susanna began as her daughter looked up. "When can I expect the first grandchild?"

Antoinette's eyes widened as she paused from her stirring, Arnold smirking as he met her glance. She didn't know if he said anything about her refusal to share his bed, but if he did, she was more than willing to share his escapades with the local women.

"We've only been married for a short while, Mother," Antoinette answered coolly, taking a sip of her breakfast. "These things take time."

"Young lady, just because your father and I waited to have children does not mean you should. I can attest to the foolishness of having children later on in life. It's more difficult on the body."

"She has a point, dearest," Arnold added, making Antoinette cringe. He was certainly testing her that morning, and she was in no mood for it. He agreed to the terms just like she did, and if he wasn't going to abide by them, then he would lose more than just his bride.

"We already discussed this, *my love*." His nickname felt like vomit on her tongue, and she tried not to make a face when she said it. "I wanted time for us to get to know one another first before we raised a family."

"You'll have all your lives for that," Susanna said with a laugh. "Besides, children can bring you closer together."

"Yeah. I can see how screaming kids and poopy diapers bring out the romance in anyone," Bernie muttered.

Antoinette snickered, mimicking a cough to hide it after Mother frowned.

Arnold turned to Bernie with a confident gaze, his nose in the air. "It is the intimacy in making a child that grows a relationship, Sister. Were you...more experienced...you would know such things."

"Oh, I'm sure you're an expert, then," Bernie sneered back. "By the way, how is Lady Albrecht doing? I heard she was so thankful that you escorted her home last night."

Arnold beaded his eyes, looking back to his meal. "Chivalry is a service I extend to everyone."

"And I'm sure her absent husband is so grateful."

"Oh, how kind of you!" Susanna gleamed as she put her hand on Arnold's shoulder. Even Antoinette understood Bernie's verbal cues. Was Mother so dense that she couldn't see what Arnold's escort really was? "What a wonderful man you are, my dear son-in-law! I should like to tell the ladies all about your good manners. I can't help but brag!"

Bernie rubbed her forehead and sighed.

A courier stepped into the dining room, thankfully interrupting the conversation, and approached the queen with a bow. He reached his hand out, holding a letter, and gave it to her, saying, "A message from His Majesty, King Edward of Audlin." He bowed again, exiting the room, and she took the letter, opening it.

Antoinette leaned forward in curiosity, wondering why

Edward had sent a letter to her mother. Could it be related to the elopement she attempted with Emery? Surely he must've found out. Though the cousins weren't close any longer, she knew their mothers talked, and Edward would be keen to know how she had fared. At least, she thought he would.

"What does it say?" Antoinette asked quietly.

"Well, this is awkward," Susanna mumbled, finishing the letter and setting it on the table. "It is a letter of congratulations on your marriage, dearest."

Antoinette felt her heart sink. Did Edward really not care that she had married another, cousin or stranger? She had hoped for a small reaction, or at least knowledge that he didn't want her to marry Arnold. "I see," Antoinette said, her voice nearly catching. "Does it say anything else?"

"He wishes to fix the strained relations between us," Susanna continued, her eyes still on the letter. "He's invited us to dine with him in Reigal to discuss renewing our old alliance."

Antoinette's eyes widened. He wouldn't invite them over unless he knew something. She'd been with him long enough to know when he was being blunt and when he was being discreet.

"That's interesting news," Antoinette replied. "Still, how very kind of him to put the past behind us."

Susanna scoffed as she looked back up. "Kind, indeed! I think he's up to something. I do not trust that boy and his schemes."

"And what would he be up to, Mother?" Antoinette asked. "We've went our separate ways in life. He knows that our relationship is finished."

"That may be, but I still am uneasy with it."

Antoinette sighed, curious as to why Edward would want to see her. Perhaps he really was regretting the past and was wishing to make amends for his mistakes...or maybe it was Malina wanting to flaunt her victory once more. If that was the case, Antoinette was better off not going to Audlin.

"What do you think, Bernie?" Antoinette asked as she turned to her sister.

"Do I get to hit him?" Bernie asked.

"No, child," Susanna said. "Though it is tempting."

Bernie frowned. "You're no fun."

"If I may," Arnold chimed in, looking a little too perky, "I should like to think of this as a splendid opportunity!"

Antoinette cocked her brow at him, not following. What was he up to?

"What do you mean?" Susanna asked.

"The king of Audlin is requesting our presence to discuss trade and renewing our past friendships," Arnold began, giving his wife a sinister look. Antoinette could only look away, frustrated. "Financially speaking, Edeland would favor such a gain in the treasury, and we could use the extra money to expand your riches, Your Majesty. Also..." Arnold paused for dramatic effect as he turned back to the queen. "I know I am being quite bold in this, but I should like to use this meeting as a chance to show that dreadful beast of a king what he has lost. Allow my wife to accompany me to Reigal. I shall prove to Edward that his loss was my gain and that he was a fool to have ever left her!"

Antoinette frowned at the remark, not wanting to be anyone's show-off girl, but Susanna clapped in delight and laughed, thinking the idea wonderful. "My dear boy, what a genius you are! You tempt me to go there myself just to see the look on Edward's face!"

"Then let us make it a family affair," Arnold replied, and the queen laughed some more.

"Such intrigue! I can't help but love it!"

"Mother, I'd rather not go just to make someone feel regret over his past." Antoinette lowered her head. "It isn't right...it's not..."

"Actually, I'm in agreement with Mother for once," Bernie said. "I say let the bum suffer! I'm game for it."

Antoinette gave Bernie a look, but her sister didn't budge.

"Then it's settled!" Arnold said. "We shall leave for Reigal and attend King Edward's dinner. Oh, what an entertainment this shall be!"

Antoinette looked to her mother, her face in disapproval, but Susanna ignored it, turning to Arnold with a proud smile. Antoinette exhaled slowly, sinking into her chair and ignoring the rest of her meal. She'd been through too much over the past few months, and the last thing she wanted to do was face the original marriage that was taken from her.

But her feelings didn't matter, according to the rest of the family. Never mind that she was still recovering from having Emery taken away. Never mind that her heart was still raw over losing Edward the summer before. Never mind that she still felt so broken and only wanted peace. No, what she felt wasn't important to them. They only cared about the drama they could witness at her expense.

She excused herself from the breakfast table, leaving in haste.

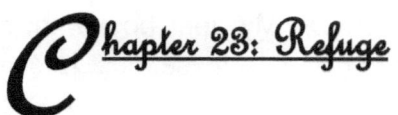

Chapter 23: Refuge

Edward dragged his feet down the hallway, never feeling so tired in his life. Whining nobles, begging paupers, a nagging wife who did nothing but flirt with every man in the room while his son was sick with a cold…he almost wished he could shut himself in a room and lock the world away for a moment just for a few minutes of peace.

But as the king, peace was never an option. It was one saying he and his father agreed upon. No matter what, life would always throw something at him to keep him on his feet.

He listened to the rumble of thunder outside the palace walls, gentle and soothing for a spring rain. Though the day was chaotic, Edward couldn't help but think the rains were there to calm him before he went to sleep. He always found the sound of storms comforting as long as they weren't too violent and shook the windows, and tonight's storm was gentle and relaxing. It was the perfect combination to help him go to sleep.

As he passed the main guards at the front door, waving to them, he suddenly stopped, seeing their leader and another knight arguing amongst themselves.

"You should at least have a guard at his door!" he heard Marcus sneer.

"There are five guards already down that hall!" Sir Ichabod

spat back. "Any more and you'd have an army!"

"The boy is the crowned prince and future king of Audlin!" Marcus continued, his face red. "He is deserving of the greatest protection we can offer, yet you treat him like any other child!"

"I take my duties very seriously, Marcus. The queen has entrusted me with her son and not a scratch has been laid on him!" He shook his head in frustration, putting his hands on his hips. "You run the guard like a dictatorship, always afraid the worst is yet to come! Even King Arden was not this paranoid."

"I'm not paranoid, Jacob. I only seek the protection of the royal family. Forgive me if I can't help but be cautious!"

"Whatever. Do not listen to reason," Ichabod muttered. "I'm going home. The child is well-guarded for the night. If you think it is not enough, then go watch over him too!"

With that, Ichabod turned and walked away.

Edward made his way to Marcus after seeing his friend cross his arms and huff, looking towards the ground. After hearing the footsteps echo on the flooring, Marcus looked up, standing at attention as Edward approached.

"Forgive me, Edward. I didn't know you had overheard our conversation."

"It's fine," Edward replied, noticing the dark circles under Marcus' eyes. Had the man slept at all? It seemed all he ever did was work. "I admire your duty to my son, though Jacob is right. Five is enough guards for the evening watch."

Marcus shrugged. "I'm sorry. I'm just wanting to do everything right."

"You are," Edward replied. "If I didn't think you were, I

wouldn't have kept you in charge."

Marcus smiled slightly, looking back up. "Thank you. I appreciate that."

"Regardless, you look tired. You have done much today; go home and rest."

Marcus frowned. "But…"

"Don't make me order you to go home," Edward said with a smirk. "Rest now. I will see you in the morning."

"But I can do more…"

Before Edward could answer, a knock was heard at the door. Edward and Marcus turned, curious as to who would visit at such a late hour and during a storm. The door guard on duty opened it, seeing who it was, and as Edward peeked at the visitor, his eyes widened in shock.

"Emery?"

The young Hugellian looked exhausted, his clothes tattered and wet from being soaked in the rain. He leaned close to the door post, his arms huddled close to keep him from shivering. "I'm sorry to bother you, Cousin," Emmerich replied as Edward hurried to the door. "But…I need to speak to Aunt Maria."

Edward helped him out of the rain and had Marcus fetch the queen mother.

"There now! A nice hot cup of tea." Maria set the drink in front of her nephew, steam coming up from it. Emmerich thanked her, wrapping his hands around the cup and holding it close to his lips, taking a sip before setting it back down on the table. Edward watched quietly as his mother doted on her nephew, sitting him near the fire, wrapped in blankets even after getting him a change of clothes. Emmerich said nothing as she worked to make him comfortable, his eyes staring off into the distance.

It made Edward curious as to what happened. He had never seen his cousin so distraught in a long while. Eyes gazing into a void, speech barely above a whisper, energy spent...it was as if Emmerich had lost his world without hope of ever gaining it back.

And that's what Edward feared had happened. Antoinette's wedding to Prince Arnold, the failed attempt to stop it....everything had to be related...he was sure of it. Though why Emery was in Audlin was beyond him.

"Can I get you anything else, sweetheart?" Maria asked as she sat in front of her nephew.

Emmerich shook his head. "No. Thank you, though."

"Of course," Maria answered warmly. "Now tell me - why in the world were you traveling in the rain by yourself? Surely your father and mother wouldn't want you to be alone like this! Is everything alright? What's the matter?"

Emmerich glanced up at Edward, his lips pressed firmly together as if he didn't want to talk. Edward could take the hint, especially if his musings were right. If the topic on hand was going to be Antoinette, then Emmerich wouldn't want Edward to hear about it. The humiliation of defeat was best kept quiet in front of the enemy.

But that didn't mean he couldn't spy anyways. "I'll give you two a moment," Edward said, leaving the room. He closed the door, leaving it open with a crack and leaning close so he could still hear and see the conversation without them knowing.

"What's wrong, Emery?" Maria asked after Edward had left. "You look terrible. Are your parents alright?"

"They're well as can be expected," Emery replied, reaching for the satchel at his side and pulling out a note, handing it to the queen mother. "This is from Dad. It explains why I'm here."

Edward watched as Maria took the note and opened it, taking a moment to read quietly to herself. After a few seconds of silence, she soon gave a gasp, looking at her nephew in horror. "You've been banished?"

Edward's eyes widened, his look mimicking his mother's. Out of all the cousins, Emmerich was the one least expected to play with trouble, let alone get into it. Had King Erick gone mad, or had his feud with Aldaric finally reached a breaking point?

"I don't understand..." Maria finished reading the note in a hurry, setting it upon her lap. "Why would Erick banish you? Whatever could you have done to deserve such a punishment?"

Emmerich sighed, leaning forward and resting his face on his palms. "Aunt Maria, I've...I mean, I'm not sure you want to hear this, but..." He paused, taking a deep breath. "I haven't been honest with everyone."

"Sweetheart, whatever it is you've done, you can tell me."

Emmerich nodded, looking up. "It started when Edward came back with Malina."

What followed was a tale that made Edward regret every sin committed. He listened as Emmerich told of how he stood by Antoinette in her hurt, comforting her in Edeland before returning home to Kettensburg. Then came the announcement that she was being forced to marry Arnold.

Emmerich hurried to Staalberg, proposed to Antoinette, and eloped the next morning, only to be found out by Susanna before the marriage could be consummated. What followed were threats and manipulation by the queen of Edeland and Antoinette choosing Arnold, sending Emmerich away. When Aldaric brought him back to Hugellia, the king was outraged at the news and banished him in punishment.

"Dad said for me to go to you until he could talk the king into overturning the sentence," Emmerich continued as Maria leaned forward and took hold of his hand. "I don't wish to be a burden to you, Aunt Maria. If you'd rather me stay somewhere else, I can."

"Nonsense!" Maria exclaimed. "You can stay here as long as it takes. My father is a harsh man, but if anyone can make him see reason, it is Aldaric. And I shall write a letter too! I am his daughter, after all. Surely that should count for something!"

"I don't think he's going to listen," Emmerich said sadly, making Maria frown further. "You know how the king is. He hates my dad. He hates me."

"He doesn't hate you, Emery. You're his grandson. You're family."

"I've never been family in his eyes, Aunt Maria." Emmerich lowered his head further, covering his face with his free hand. "I'll never be family. Aside from my parents, you're all I have."

Maria leaned forward, gathering him in her arms, her face sullen. She said nothing as she held him and kissed the top of his head, and Edward thought it strange she kept quiet.

Probably shocked, he thought to himself, just as he was. But Emmerich's visit could not have come at a more awkward moment. The cousins never did bridge the divide that was dug between them, and for Emmerich to come to Reigal for help, it must have meant he had nowhere else to go. Fate had to be laughing at him somewhere, forcing the one man Edward didn't want to see coming to live with him for who knows how long.

But despite the awkwardness, despite the bad blood between them in the past, Edward couldn't help but pity his cousin as he clutched Maria's arms, burying his face into her shoulder. He lost the love of his life not once, but twice, and after that he lost his country and family. Edward knew he had it rough with Malina, but there was comfort in his son, plus he still had a home, his mother, and his best friend.

Edward's problems were a result of his own actions. Emery's was a result of just pure, rotten luck.

Edward turned to leave the doorway and headed up the stairs, getting ready to have a guest room prepared for his cousin's stay. How long Emery was to remain in Reigal, he didn't know, but he figured his cousin was right in that Erick would not welcome him back soon. The van Ketten family had always been a stubborn lot, and if Erick gave a word, he would never back down from it.

But Emery, too, was stubborn, just like the rest of his kin. Edward could help him as much he could, but whether his cousin would accept it, only time would tell.

For nearly three weeks Emmerich had been away from Kettensburg.

He sat out in the cold air, enjoying the smell of the frost upon the palace gardens. For most in Audlin, the weather was too chilly for a stroll, but for a Hugellian, the weather was like spring, and the smell of the air reminded him of home. Even Waffles enjoyed the crunch in the grass he grazed over, licking the dew off the blades before taking a bite. Emmerich reached forward and rubbed Waffles' neck, taking in a deep breath.

"It's just like home, isn't it?" he asked quietly as the horse neighed back. "All that good, munchy grass."

Waffles took a bunch from the ground and lifted his head, offering some to his friend.

Emmerich smirked, shaking his head. "Thanks, but you keep it. I don't think it'll settle well on my stomach."

Waffles snorted, chewing the rest of the grass in his mouth before bending back down to pick some more.

Emmerich leaned back, resting himself against a tree trunk as he watched Waffles graze. He'd only been in Reigal a little while, but so far it had been tolerable. Aunt Maria had been more than welcoming, giving him his own room in the palace and sending a letter to her father within a day of his arrival.

She'd given him privacy, allowing him to rest from his travels, but best of all she hadn't pushed him in seeing Edward.

Not that she didn't want the cousins to interact. She always wanted them to be close, just like his own parents did, but after hearing about his failed marriage to Antoinette, she was wise enough to keep things quiet. Emmerich didn't want company just yet, especially when that company was the man who stole Antoinette from him in the first place.

But that didn't mean he wouldn't eventually have to face Edward. He just hoped it wouldn't be soon.

Emmerich sighed, closing his eyes and listening to the breeze whisper around him. Moments like this were meant to be tranquil and healing, but his heart still ached in hurt. How did his life take such a dramatic turn so quickly? He only tried to do the right things in life and somehow his world still crashed down upon him.

Was fate angry with him for something he didn't know about? Was God punishing him for not being good enough? Bad things were only supposed to happen to bad people, so what did he do wrong?

And then his thoughts drifted to the one person that pained him the most. Antoinette, his wife, the best friend he ever had. Losing her once was painful enough, but losing her twice was a devastation he never thought possible.

It was strange to Emmerich that she still filled his senses after weeks apart. The sight of her smile plagued his thoughts. The sound of her voice echoed in his ears. The touch of her lips tingled on his own. The smell of her hair lingered in the air.

And yet his senses betrayed him. When he looked around, all he saw was a foreign land that he didn't want to be in. When he listened, he could only hear silence save the occasional gust of wind that came through the air. His body felt nothing but wool and cotton scratching against his skin. The air even smelled musty, doubtless from the rain that poured down the day before.

Without her, his world was nothing. Without her, beauty in life was gone and there was nothing but the void of the space before him.

I need you.

His friend, his lover, his wife. And instead of being in his arms that very moment, she was in the arms of another, forever bound by a matrimony he thought she didn't want.

If only he hadn't been blind in opening his arms so wide and his heart so freely. He wouldn't have been as broken as he was now.

He drifted away into memory, reminiscing of the short time he had with her. Their time in the garden where he confessed his love. The moment she gave him a chance in the apple orchard until Waffles made them both laugh so hard they cried. Dancing in the rain. His first kiss, when he swore the world stopped and time stood still as he relished his soul touching hers. The look on her face as they said their vows on their wedding day. He had never seen her so beautiful, and when he looked into her eyes, he got a glimpse of eternity.

Now all he saw was clouds, covering up the sun that once shined overhead.

His thoughts were interrupted as he heard the crunches of footsteps coming near him. Waffles made a grunt as he shifted in his stance, and Emmerich opened his eyes, turning towards the noise. He wondered if Aunt Maria sent him a messenger to let him know lunch was ready.

But what greeted him wasn't a common page boy. It was

Edward, and it made Emmerich's blood boil.

The last person he wanted to see was his cousin. If anyone deserved the heartache that he was going through, it was Edward. But no...fate had other plans. Edward broke his love's heart, so he got a wife and son. Edward betrayed his family's trust, so he got a crown upon his head and a country to rule.

If ever there was proof that life wasn't fair, it stood in the form of the two cousins now staring blankly at each other.

Emmerich was the first to speak, giving a scoff as he looked away towards Waffles. "What do you want?"

"I wanted to check on you. You've been out here for hours."

Edward's voice was soft, calm like he wanted to be friendly, but Emmerich knew better. Edward only came to gloat and laugh at him for losing Antoinette a second time.

Emmerich shook his head, stifling sarcasm. "I wanted time to myself. Guess I won't be getting that now."

"I didn't mean to interrupt," Edward said, looking down to the ground. "I just...I know you've been through a lot and..."

"I'd rather not talk about it," Emmerich replied.

"I overheard what you told Mother," Edward said, looking back up.

Emmerich's eyes widened in anger. "You were eavesdropping on me? *Do you care nothing for privacy?*"

"I was worried about you. I still am."

"You can drop the niceties, Cousin." Emmerich gathered his knees to his chest and rested his chin on his arms. "You needn't feign concern when our only company is a horse."

Waffles gave a grumble as he paused from his eating, almost offended by Emmerich's remark.

"I'm not pretending, Emery. Not this time." Edward paused, rubbing his arms to keep warm in the cold. "I just wanted to let you know that even though the past has been rough between us, I don't want the present to be that way. I'm here for you. If there's any way I can help you, I wish to do it."

Emmerich beaded his eyes, saying nothing. Edward always lied and always betrayed. He would never be worthy of trust no matter how hard he tried to say otherwise.

Edward waited for a response, clearing his throat when he knew one wasn't coming. "How are you holding up? I mean...after everything?"

"How do you think?"

Edward lowered his head for a moment as if gathering his thoughts, but after a quick gulp, he lifted his head and attempted to speak again. "I know how difficult it is to lose her..."

Emmerich's fists clenched, but he was too tired to become angry this time. Edward was a fool - always had been, always would be - and it would be folly to waste his time on someone who was only there to make him suffer more.

He turned his head away, leaving Edward standing in the cold with an awkward silence standing between them.

"Emery?" he asked.

"Go away, Edward," Emmerich muttered. "I told you. I don't want to talk."

Edward stood there for a moment, unsure of what to say, until he nodded and spoke quietly. "Alright. I'll...I'll have the servants prepare you lunch, if you're willing to eat."

"I'm not hungry. Just go."

Edward said nothing as he gave a final glance before walking away back to the palace. Emmerich listened as his cousin's footsteps faded into the distance, and once he couldn't hear them anymore, he lifted his head and watched as Edward walked towards the main doors.

Emmerich shook his head, leaning back against the tree and stretching his legs as he closed his eyes and returned to his melancholy.

"Ugh. How pathetic." Malina rolled her eyes as she gazed out the window, watching as Edward's cousin and his horse sat in the gardens and wasted the day away dreaming. She wanted to laugh when one of the nobles told her about the latest gossip, how the Hugellian tried to elope with the Edelandian princess and failed. "The man is rejected by one woman and it's as if the entire world has stopped for him. Really, Edward. I'm starting to think weakness is a family trait."

Edward was finishing taking off his boots, sitting on the bed and refusing to look up. "He's loved Antoinette since childhood. Losing her has been difficult for him."

"And yet you lost her as well, but you're much more chipper. I guess she wasn't as important to you, hmm?"

Edward frowned as he stood to his feet, finally comfortable. "She was very important to me. She still is."

"Darling, how rude of you!" Malina replied with a pout as she playfully tugged at his tunic. "One thing you should never tell a wife is that you're still in love with the other woman."

Edward ignored her teases, lowering his brow. "I never said I was still in love with her."

"And yet you and I know that is a lie you are terrible at telling." Malina laughed, letting the fabric go and returning to the window. "What that girl has, I don't think I'll ever understand. You never bedded her, so it's not like she ever pleased you physically. Her looks are average, at best. Nothing near as perfect as me. She has a lack of confidence, too, if I'm being picky. Poor girl gets trampled on more than a dirt road on market day."

"She is a good woman, Malina. It is a pity you fail to see why an angel would be more desirable than a devil."

Malina gave a laugh as she circled her husband. "And yet who did you choose? You wicked sinner, you…"

Edward looked away, remaining still as she took hold of his collar to play with it. "Pity that you ever thought she'd want to be with you," Malina replied. "As if a saint could ever love a sinner. But enough about your relationship with her, Edward. You must be relishing in hearing your kin has failed so miserably!"

Edward met Malina's gaze with a grimace. "You think you know my heart, yet you know so little. I take no joy in Emery's pain."

"Oh really?" Malina asked, her brows rising in playful surprise. "You, who hated your cousin? I would think you'd be happy at seeing his only company being a gluttonous horse."

"He is hurt, Malina. He needs encouragement."

"Darling, he needs a prostitute. He'd forget all about that girl once he bedded a real woman."

Edward removed her hands from his shoulders, backing away from her grip. "You filthy wretch! Is that all love is to you? Satisfying your lusts with whoever is willing?"

"Love is for stories, Edward. Real relationships are about passion." She paused, giving a lick of her lips. "And pleasure. If you understood this better, I could never keep my hands off you."

"So what? Do you find your pleasures elsewhere since I'm so terrible at providing for you?"

Malina blinked, feeling a moment of unease. Though Edward was smart enough to know she was not one for commitment, she could never admit to infidelity. That would give him leverage to remove her as queen, to take away her power and send her back to Verloris. No, she hadn't the time to deal with a mess like that just yet. She needed more favor with the people before she could test Edward's patience.

"You put words in my mouth that are untrue, Edward. I may not be like your Antoinette, but I am faithful. Have you ever seen me with a lover?"

Edward snickered, putting his hands on his hips. "Not yet."

"How cruel you are to me, accusing when there is no evidence of unfaithfulness!" Malina whined, feigning anger. "Really! Have I ever given you doubt?"

"You've given me doubt since the day we first met," Edward replied solemnly. "You are such a fool, Malina. You may win men's desires and lusts, but you will never win a man's heart. Do you know why? Because there is no love in you." He faced Malina with eyes glaring. "You mock my cousin and I for loving a woman like Antoinette, yet despite her lack of experience and what you think is insecurity, she holds both our hearts and always will, no matter who we marry. You pity us, Malina, but I pity you, because you will never know what it's like to have the unwavering loyalty of someone in love, because you have never been capable of it yourself."

Malina smiled at the thought that Edward believed himself to be so clever with his words. Oh, what a fool he really was. "And yet despite all that love, you betrayed her and she betrayed your cousin. Love, my dear Edward, has made your lives full of hypocrisy and misery, while passion has made me true and content. So who is the right one after all?"

Edward's face sunk at her words and he backed away, saying nothing, Malina smiling at her easy victory.

Chapter 25: Preparing for Dinner

"The university here in Reigal will more than suit your academic needs, Emery," Maria said as she and her nephew sat down for breakfast. She tried to sound cheerful, but Emmerich found that even his aunt's sanguine nature was not enough to bring him out of his mood. He appreciated the thought, however, and faked a small smile to appease her.

"I'd like to visit it. It would be a shame to see my studies go to waste."

"Exactly!" Maria replied after taking a bite of salted pork. "The sooner you become busy, the quicker you shall feel at home. What was it you were studying again? Philosophy?"

"I only took a class," Emmerich clarified as he stared at his toast, barely touched. He still didn't feel like eating much, despair hampering his appetite. "I was studying the liberal arts like Dad. I was just starting my courses on political science."

"Well we have a wonderful science academy here," Maria added. "And the library! You'll feel as if you're in Heaven, Emery. So many books to read. I know you'll enjoy it as much as the other students."

"I'm sure I will, Aunt Maria." He paused, giving her a real smile this time. "Thank you. Your kindness…it has brought me much comfort since I've arrived, though I am not surprised of it. You've always been so good to me."

He thought she'd smile back at him, but he could've sworn he saw her eyes tear up. She cleared her throat, taking a sip of tea, and gave him a quick grin before looking away, facing the door that opened.

Emmerich turned to see who had entered. Edward, typically busy save the few times he'd seen him, had walked in, his hands holding on to a large stack of papers.

"Forgive me. I hope I'm not interrupting anything," he said, turning his gaze away from Emmerich after making eye contact.

Emmerich returned the sentiment, looking down at his food and poking the toast with his knife.

"Nonsense. We were only eating breakfast," Maria said cheerily as she waved Edward into the room. He walked further in, standing behind a chair at the table. "What is it you wish to tell us, Edward? I hope it is good news."

"It's not so much news as an announcement," he replied, giving a pause as he turned back to Emmerich. "We are having guests later in the week."

"Guests?" Maria asked. "I was unaware we were having a party."

"Malina was supposed to tell you. I take it she didn't?"

Maria shook her head, giving a huff. "As if she ever would."

Edward frowned, though he didn't seem surprised. "Forgive me. I've been busy of late and should've told you myself. We are having a dinner and meeting with the royal family on Saturday. They should arrive by the afternoon in time for the meal and will stay the night so we can talk the next day."

"The royal family? Which one?" Maria asked.

Edward hesitated, pursing his lips as if unsure he wanted to say anything. Emmerich's eyes rose and he kept his knife still. There were few royal families in the surrounding areas that he was favored by at the moment. Unless Edward was meeting with Braiden, Emmerich was certain he'd be faced with a family he didn't want to see.

"It's the van Echts."

Maria's face paled as she fell back into her chair. "Oh Edward...the timing!"

But Emmerich would have none of it. "Is this some sort of joke, Cousin, inviting Antoinette and her family here?" he asked, dropping the knife to the table. "If it is, it's in poor taste!"

"I'm sorry," Edward said with a frown. "I had sent the invitation before I knew you would be here. Had I known the situation, I wouldn't have sent it."

"What is the purpose of this dinner?" Maria asked.

"I was trying to foster better relations with Edeland."

Emmerich wanted to scoff at Edward's words. As if the man really cared about politics. He only wanted to see Antoinette, doubtless hearing about her wedding to Arnold and wanting to see the truth for himself. "I'm sure you were," he said sarcastically. "Nice job, by the way. You certainly know how to make your guests feel welcome."

Edward frowned. "Emery, I swear this was not intentional."

"No one is saying it is, Edward," Maria added, but Emmerich only rolled his eyes.

"The one person I don't want to see is the one person you invite to dinner." Emmerich gave a laugh in bitterness. "This is low Edward, even for you." He turned away, shaking his head in disbelief. "I don't even know why I came here."

"Emery, I promise you won't have to see them. I'll keep them busy and you can do whatever you want!" Maria reached for his hand to hold it, but he pulled away. He knew she meant well and was honest in being caught unawares, but even her love wasn't enough to keep him there. It wasn't enough to give him the strength to face Antoinette again.

He stood to his feet, excusing himself from the table. "I've overstayed my welcome. I'm sorry, Aunt Maria, but I can't remain here. The possibility of seeing Antoinette again is too much for me to bear."

"But where will you go?" Maria asked, her face full of concern. "Your parents wished you to stay here!"

"Braiden is nearby," Emmerich muttered, though in truth Braiden was also the only nation he felt he could go to without feeling threatened by family or enemies.

"But you can't go, Emery! You'll be all alone! We're your family - we'll be here for you."

Emmerich looked to Edward, who only looked back, and lowered his brow. "I'm sorry, Aunt Maria. I think I'd be happier being alone."

With that, he left the room.

Malina watched as Edward's cousin began throwing his few belongings into a bag.

She had heard of Edward's announcement that the van Echt family was coming, how Emmerich took it poorly and now threatened to leave for Braiden. She smirked at how juicy all the gossip was, feeling left out knowing she had little to do with the chaos between the cousins. She watched from across the hall, safe in the shadows of an empty guest room, trying to contain the laughter that wanted to spew from her lips as Emmerich threw one of his shirts to the bed in frustration, bending down and stifling a sob.

What a pathetic boy, she thought to herself, and yet she couldn't help but be elated by his predicament. She was never fond of the Edelandian princess that seemed to hold so many hearts. Though Malina would never admit to it, a part of her was jealous that Edward still favored Antoinette over her. Not that it mattered, really, since Malina could have so many other men. No, what bothered her more was the fact that Antoinette was adored more than she was. Malina wanted to be first in every man's heart, not everyone save the king and his cousin.

She eyed Emmerich carefully, guessing well that he and the Edelandian girl had to have been close. She saw little of them when she first came to Audlin, but she remembered the way they stood by one another. His arm around her in a protective embrace. Her teary eyes constantly seeking his for comfort. The way they both stood so close to each other that they practically walked as one.

It made her sick thinking the Edelandian girl had yet another man at her command, and Malina was not one to lose so easily. There wasn't a man she couldn't conquer, and Emmerich van Ketten would be no exception.

She licked her lips hungrily as she eyed him from the darkness, her mind already wandering at all the things she could do to make him *beg* for her instead of Antoinette.

"I know that look."

Malina froze, her eyes widening as she quickly turned to see a familiar face standing behind her.

"Malum?" she asked quietly, turning back to the Hugellian. "It's been a while since I've seen you. Where have you been?"

"Places," he replied.

The answer was cryptic, and she knew she would get no more. Malum was a man of many secrets and his mind was like a guarded castle. She'd have to break down the door to get in. "What are you doing here?"

"I should ask you the same."

"Observing," she said casually.

"And?"

"And what? Can I not watch the happenings of my own palace?"

She felt a grip on her arm, turning her around in a slow motion to face her speaker. "He is not your concern."

"Darling, I don't see why he can't be," Malina said. "There's no harm in a little fun with the guests."

"Your 'fun' will bring him ruin. He is not to be touched."

"And why not?"

"Because he will be one of us."

"Really, Malum! What do you think I'm trying to do?"

His grip became firm and he leaned forward, staring at her with a calm face. She didn't know how to interpret the ease he had when controlling his emotions. "You seek him to spite Lady Antoinette. You waste your time - he will not bother with you."

"I have a way with men." Malina grinned confidently.

Malum snorted. "The weak ones."

"And the strong." She paused, giving him a glare. "I have controlled kings and nobles alike. Even you know how effective I can be. Your Velori seek my company often. You must admit my charms have been helpful, especially with Vacius."

"Your lover is a failure, Malina. Even you are not so daft to be blind of this."

Malina opened her mouth to give a remark back to him, but before she could speak, she heard footsteps approach. She and Malum both became silent as they watched Edward hurry to the guest room where Emmerich stood, packing.

"Cousin, wait!" Edward's voice echoed as he entered the room, Emmerich pausing from his work and lowering his head.

"And now I've lost my opportunity," Malina muttered spitefully as she crossed her arms. "I hope you're happy, Malum, for..."

"Quiet." His voice was harsh, yet near a whisper as his eyes beaded towards Edward and Emmerich conversing.

"Whatever for?" Malina asked, perturbed.

"I must observe this," he muttered, and she closed her mouth, watching the conversation in silence.

"Get out of my room, Edward."

He stopped at the door, keeping still as Emmerich stood and faced him with an all too familiar glare. Edward understood that his cousin didn't want to see him, especially after the announcement that his ex-wife could be visiting, but something pricked at his conscience in seeing Emmerich's sorry state. The poor man was at his lowest, trapped in despair and the product of one rotten break after another. Edward couldn't help but feel sorry for him, but even more than that, he felt guilty. Had he not courted Antoinette in the first place, or had he not married Malina, Emmerich would have been spared the hurt.

"I'm not leaving," Edward said quietly, facing the glare with heavy, sorrowful eyes. "And I'd rather not see you leave, either."

"A little late for that," Emmerich huffed as he went back to packing his bag.

"Where would you go?"

"I told you," Emmerich replied. "I'll take my chances in Braiden."

"They're nothing but cheats and greedy businessmen. You'd be better staying here with us."

"I'll take my chances." Emmerich stuffed one last tunic into his bag, taking a deep breath. "There's nothing for me here, anyway."

He lifted his bag and slung it over his shoulder, heading towards the door. He was about to walk out until Edward stood in front of him, blocking the exit.

"Wait."

Emmerich looked up, perturbed and giving a sneer. "Move."

"No."

"Edward, I'm too tired to argue."

"I know. But hear me out - please."

Emmerich rolled his eyes as he backed up and crossed his arms, looking more impatient than attentive.

Edward sighed, knowing the conversation would be anything but pleasant.

"I want you to stay."

Emmerich scoffed. "You really expect me to believe that?"

"I'm serious."

"I am too. If you're going to lie, at least make it creative."

Edward sighed, unsure of what else to say. His cousin had been so used to being treated poorly that he almost came to expect it. It made Edward curse every moment he had dishonored his kin. "Emery, I know nothing I can say will make you believe me, but Mother and I want to help you. You've been through a lot and we don't look at that lightly."

"Save it." Emmerich pulled his bag higher on his shoulder

and stepped forward, clipping Edward to the side and forcing his way past the door. "I'm going. Give Aunt Maria my regards. I'll write her when I arrive in Braiden."

Edward stifled his desire to smack the wall and hurried after his cousin, trailing close behind. "At least stay a few more days to gather supplies. You needn't journey with just a bag and your horse."

"I don't need anything. I *used* to be Hugellian, remember? They train us to survive on the land."

"But Emery..."

Before he could speak any more, however, both of them stopped as a messenger approached. The older man gave a quick bow to Edward before turning to Emmerich, holding out a thick letter.

"Sir, you have a message from Kettensburg," he said. "It's just arrived from your mother."

A glimmer of hope entered Edward's heart. Perhaps King Erick had some sense after all and listened to Aldaric in allowing Emmerich back home.

The letter was taken carefully, Emmerich thanking the man for bringing him the news. He opened it quietly, reading the contents to himself, making Edward want to peek over his shoulder just to get the information from Anna quicker.

"What's it say?"

"It says it's for me, Edward. Mind your own business."

Edward backed away, frowning. "I only wondered if you heard news of returning."

Emmerich continued to read, his face sinking further after each minute. After Edward asked again for information, he finally sighed, keeping his head down.

"The king has not changed his mind," Emmerich muttered. "Mother says I am to remain here. She and father wish to visit within the next few weeks."

Edward was perturbed that the king still remained senseless, but he was glad Emmerich's mother requested he stay in Reigal. At least then he wouldn't have to explain to Aldaric and Anna why Emmerich ended up with a cesspool of scoundrels in Braiden.

"I'm glad they'll be here," Edward said kindly as Emmerich looked up. "They'll provide you with good company and comfort. Now come, Cousin. Put back your bag and return to your meal with Mother. You needn't leave just yet."

"I can send my mother a letter to tell her where I'll be." Emmerich looked back down to the paper, preparing to finish the rest of the note. "This hasn't changed my mind, Edward. I'm still going to Braiden. I can't face An..."

Emmerich paused, a deep frown coming across his face. Edward leaned forward in concern, trying to see what was on the note, but this time Emmerich didn't try to hide it. He was too stunned, too confused to move, and Edward speedily read the contents of the paper nestled underneath Anna's letter.

My dearest Emery,

I'm sorry for the way things transpired in Staalberg. I had no choice but to send you away. Mother's mind could not be changed and no matter what I said or did, she would not allow me to stay married to you.

I know you're hurt and I'm sure you're angry, but please...I must speak with you. There are things you must know about why I did what I did and I can't put them in a letter lest they be found by Mother.

Please write your response to Father Thomas Meuller here in Staalberg. He is trustworthy and will not tell the queen of our correspondence.

You asked me to trust you, Emery, and I do. Now I ask that you trust me. Write back as soon as you can.

Yours, Antoinette

Edward had barely finished reading the letter before Emmerich wadded it up and stuffed it into his pocket, turning to Edward in a fiery stare. "Once was cruel enough, Edward! Now you write a second note? Is the letter from my mother a forgery as well?"

Edward's eyes widened in surprise. "I forged no letters to you!"

Emmerich held up the wadded paper and waved it in front of Edward's face. "This is just like when you came back from Verloris, writing a letter and acting like Antoinette wanted to speak to me! You're a bigger wretch than I thought to do this a second time! When will you stop?"

"I swear to you on my father and brother's graves that I did not forge any letters to you. Not the first you spoke of and certainly not this latest one. I have not the talent for mimicking penmanship! You know this."

"It's not like you haven't written fake notes before."

"That may be true, but when I wrote them, I only copied the words and not the handwriting!"

Emmerich gave a huff, shaking his head as if still wanting to deny it. But Edward saw the conflict in his cousin's eyes. He was beginning to doubt, and even though emotion often clouded Emmerich's judgment, reason still prevailed when the evidence was clear enough.

"Someone else must've wrote it, then. Maybe it was Lady Bernette. Antoinette did accuse her the first time."

Edward shook his head. "She's capable of it, but I don't think this is her work. This is Antoinette's handwriting."

"The first note was in her handwriting as well, yet Antoinette denied it."

"But look at the folding," Edward said, straightening the letter and pointing to the creases. "It's been folded from left to right first, and then from top to bottom. Antoinette always folded her letters that way. Everyone else I've known has folded them only top to bottom."

Emmerich looked at the paper, saying nothing as he rubbed his brow. "Edward, whether it's from her or not, it pains me to see her. She made her feelings clear in Staalberg and I must learn to accept the fact that she never cared for me."

"Don't say that." Edward paused, not willing to tell the words he was about to speak. It pained him to admit them, but seeing the hurt upon his cousin's face forced him to swallow his pride. "She's always cared for you, Emery. Even when she and I were together, she spoke of you often, and when she talked, she had this look in her eyes that she never gave anyone else. It was like you were there and only she could see you. She eventually gave me that look after a few years, but with you, she always had it."

"She made her choice, Edward. She chose Arnold, not me."

"I know," Edward said quietly. "But regardless, you need to hear her out. Maybe the choice wasn't as easy as you think it was."

"Edward, a choice is a choice. If she really wanted to marry me, she would've stayed and..." Emmerich stopped, his voice catching. Seeing his cousin break down made Edward's spirit hurt.

"That's not always true, Emery."

"Of course it is. It always is."

Edward pressed his lips together, holding them shut for a moment. He thought back to that one night in Verloris when Vacius, the Velori, dragged Marcus away to the dungeons and Malina offered him a choice: marry her and let Marcus live or reject her and let him die. As much as Edward loved Antoinette, as much as he didn't want to leave her, the mere fact that a man's life hung in the balance of his decision was reason enough to decide what he did.

"Look," Edward continued after a pause. "She asked you to trust her. If you love her like you've always said you did, then you'll hear her out."

"But..."

"No. You and I have known Antoinette for a long time, and we both know she is not a woman willing to break someone's heart so carelessly. There is a reason she sent you away, Emery, and I speak from experience when I say sometimes these decisions are made because things more important than our hearts are at stake."

Edward set his hand upon Emmerich's shoulder, clasping it. "Stay a little while longer, not for me or my mother or your parents, but for her. We both know Arnold is a fool, and this letter sent by Antoinette may even be a cry for help. Would you really miss a chance in saving her?"

The thought of Antoinette being harmed made his blood boil - a sentiment that Emmerich shared wholeheartedly.

"Very well, Cousin. I will stay until we speak." Emmerich

exhaled slowly, lowering his bag from his shoulder. "But if this is a jest or if Antoinette has no need of me, then I will depart for Braiden. I do not wish to be here any longer."

"I can agree to that." Edward unclasped Emmerich's shoulder after an expectant look from his cousin and returned his hand to his side. "I will tell my mother of your staying, then."

"Thank you. I will unpack my things."

Their farewell was cold, even distant, but it was the longest conversation Edward had with his kin in a long time. He wasn't about to push himself any further, yet he couldn't help but be pleased with the progress.

He just hoped whatever Antoinette had to say would not harm Emmerich further. As he watched his cousin leave, he couldn't help but say a prayer for him. Despite his silence, Emmerich truly was hurting deep down inside.

Edward sighed as he returned to his mother to tell her the news.

"You're not packed yet."

Antoinette looked up to see Arnold leaning against the wall, his arms crossed and his lips curled upward in a smug grin. She looked away, lowering her eyes to the ground as she continued to walk down the palace hall. Arnold stood up and followed, walking alongside as she spoke.

"I already told you. I'm not going to Reigal."

"But it will be so much fun," he replied. "Your lover will be there."

"I do not wish to see Edward," Antoinette answered. "My heart is too raw for that."

"Silly girl. I wasn't talking of Edward."

Antoinette stopped, giving Arnold a concerned glance. "What do you mean? Has Edward left the capital?"

"Oh no, Edward will be there," Arnold replied casually, tilting his head. "I'm actually speaking of the Hugellian. You know, the one you eloped with?"

Antoinette's eyes widened. "Emery?"

"Indeed. It's a grand stroke of luck for you, isn't it?"

Antoinette's face sunk as she thought about it. It *was* a stroke of luck, almost too good to be true. Surely Arnold was lying just so she would go and be forced to see Edward, being reminded of her first failed relationship.

"Why would Emery be there?" Antoinette asked. "He and Edward hate each other. Besides, Emery is in Kettensburg with his family."

"No he isn't."

"Why would he not be in Kettensburg, then? Is he with his father at a meeting with another ambassador?"

"Not at all. Didn't you hear the news?" Arnold stifled a chuckle, making Antoinette worry. "King Erick banished him from Hugellia because of that little stunt you two pulled. He was forced to go to his aunt for help."

Antoinette felt her heart want to stop. Her stomach soured at the thought that such a punishment had befallen Emmerich, all because he tried to help her. "No...no, that can't be right. Mother kept everything quiet and..."

"Your Mother sent a letter to King Erick as soon as Emmerich and Aldaric left. He was informed when they arrived home."

"But why would Mother do such a thing? She promised to stay silent!"

"I don't know the queen's reasoning," Arnold said, his face too composed for Antoinette's taste. "I would guess she'd be afraid of you trying to contact the man, though. Now that he's left home, you can't exactly reach him too easily now, can you?"

Antoinette's lip quivered. She could only imagine the hurt going through him, losing his wife, parents, and home in such a short amount of time. Her heart ached at the thought, and she wanted nothing more than to go and gather him to her arms. But now that he was no longer home, how would she be able to reach him? She knew he wouldn't stay at Edward's long. The cousins would fight constantly living in the same house.

"How do you know he's in Reigal?" Antoinette asked, trying to regain her composure.

"Lady Albrecht is quite the gossip. She hears news even before the queen."

The news wouldn't be secret long. Doubtless Mother would hear about Emery's departure before the day's end. "Why are you telling me this, then? Once Mother learns of it, she will make sure I'm not allowed to leave for Reigal tomorrow."

"Antoinette, you sting me with your accusations," Arnold said with a pout. He took his finger and caressed her cheek with it, making her cringe. "You know how much I adore you. What sort of husband would I be if I kept secrets from you?"

She turned away, perturbed. "I know you well enough that

you could care less about my feelings. What's the real reason you're telling me this?"

"Sweetheart, don't you believe me?"

She only lowered her brow.

"Ouch. You're worse than your sister with that look. Fine." He crossed his arms like a toddler being denied his toy. "Your Mother will not allow *me* to go to Reigal unless *you* go. She doesn't want you left alone in case you get tempted to find your lover."

"Then this is all pointless. Mother will not allow me to go to Reigal if Emery is there."

"But that's where I come in. If you go, then I shall speak to your mother. I can convince her that you should be allowed to see Emmerich."

"She won't allow it, Arnold."

"Of course she will." He grinned, his look seeming almost sinister. "As long as I'm there, that is. You have to admit she'd love seeing me parade you in front of him."

Antoinette felt a rage at the thought, being seen as nothing but a show for her peacock of a husband. "And what makes you want to go to Reigal so bad?"

"There's someone I want to meet."

"Oh? Does Lady Albrecht have family there?"

"Of course not. But there is a woman I've heard much about. I should like to…get acquainted."

"Who is she?"

"A woman you need not be concerned with. I'm sure you

don't mind my indiscretion."

Antoinette frowned, but shook her head. As much as she hated his tendency towards infidelity, this was one opportunity she didn't want to pass up, mystery woman or not.

She had so much to say to Emery. So much to confess and be honest about, and he would benefit to know why she sent him away.

"You'll convince Mother to allow me to go?"

Arnold nodded. "If I can't, I shall take you there myself."

"And all you want in return is to see this woman of yours?"

"Well," Arnold whispered as he leaned closer. "I could think of a few other things *you* could do for me."

Antoinette suppressed the urge to punch him. "Unless it's taking you to confession at the church, there's not much I'm going to do for you. You know what we agreed to and I am *not* going to be like all your other women."

Arnold frowned, but his face quickly softened as he leaned back. "Fine. You can't blame me for trying. It's only a matter of time before you come crawling to me, anyways. You might want to see that Hugellian, but who says he wants to see you? Were I in his place, I'd never want to be with you again."

She paused for a moment, a hurt look coming upon her face. She did what she had to do to save him. Surely Emery would understand that...

She hardened her look, not letting Arnold have the satisfaction of bothering her. "I don't care about your opinion on this, Arnold. Do you agree to my terms or not?"

"A deal's a deal. It's not like we haven't done this before."

Antoinette exhaled in relief, putting her hands on her hips. "Very well. Convince her and I'll go pack my things."

"Splendid!" Arnold said in feigned delight as he gave her a sarcastic look. "I will go speak with her now."

She watched as he went down the hallway towards Mother's parlor, not looking back

Chapter 27: Facing the Fire

Emmerich stood in front of the mirror, looking at himself from head to toe. His clothing was tailored to perfection, a shirt of dark brown and black matched with trousers and boots fit for a king. Technically, however, they did belong to the king, but Aunt Maria promised her nephew that Edward could no longer fit in the clothes anyways and that he was welcome to wearing them since he only had a few outfits that were brought from Hugellia.

Despite the fanciful clothes and spacious room, Emmerich found himself missing the comforts of home. He'd gladly trade the silken comfort of Audlin's royalty for the woolen tunics of Hugellia, and though the palace was a nice place to stay, he still longed for the comforts of home. His small two-story in Kettensburg, the narrow staircase only one person could climb at a time to get upstairs, his bedroom with its bed against the wall and so many piles of books that you had to be careful where to step lest you trip…

He sighed, looking away from the mirror. It was best to forget about home, no longer being welcome there. Hugellia was just another piece of the past that was taken from him and forced into memory, like everything else that was dear.

Antoinette was supposed to arrive within the day. At least, he thought she would. Edward and Maria never did get confirmation that all of the van Echt family would arrive, but deep in his heart, Emmerich felt like she would be there. He sensed it, as strange as it sounded, but the thought of seeing her filled him with dread. He was trying to let go of the pain her leaving caused him, and seeing her face would just add to the difficulty of forgetting.

"You look nice," Aunt Maria said from the door, watching him as he smoothed the wrinkles in his shirt. He looked up, giving her a small smile, and approached.

"Thank you for letting me borrow these," he said. "I'm sorry I wasn't able to bring more of my things from Kettensburg. The king didn't give me much time to pack."

"You're welcome to anything here, Emery," Maria said warmly. "You know we're more than happy to care for you."

"I appreciate that. Mom said she'll bring my belongings when she and Dad come here."

"I'll be glad to see them and talk." Maria paused, giving a frown as she put a hand on her nephew's arm. "Edward told me of the letters she sent. I'm sorry my father hasn't changed his mind on allowing you back. I'll be sure to send another letter. I won't give up until he listens."

Emmerich patted her hand, thanking her, wondering if Edward mentioned how his mother's letter also contained a supposed note from Antoinette that had been sent to him in Kettensburg. If Maria wasn't going to mention it, he probably wouldn't either. It was awkward enough that he tried to elope with the woman that was once destined to be Maria's daughter-in-law. Thankfully Maria didn't seem to mind that they were together, but it was still something Emmerich didn't like to talk about.

"The van Echt family will be arriving soon. I'm having dinner prepared for them." She stopped, her face scrunching a little as if she didn't know whether to speak more. "Do you... I mean, only if you want... are you going to join us?"

Emmerich looked away, keeping his hand atop hers. She meant well in her invitation, but he knew he would decline. If Antoinette was going to be there, and if the letter was legitimate, she would seek him out. He wasn't about to face Susanna, Arnold, and Edward all in the same room. No one was that brave.

"I'll think about it," he answered, trying to be polite. She nodded and smiled, but in her eyes, she looked like she knew he didn't want to go, and she could understand why.

"Alright," she said, patting his arm and letting it go. "But don't forget to eat. I don't want you losing any weight under my watch. Your father would never forgive me if you got unhealthy."

He smiled back. "I know. Don't worry - I won't skip dinner."

"Good." She turned to leave the room. "I'll check on you later, then. I'll send a servant to let you know when our guests arrive."

"Thank you," he replied, and watched as she left.

Antoinette found herself twisting her fingers in the sash of her dress. A nervous habit, to be sure, constantly fidgeting with whatever she could get her hands on as she sat trapped in the carriage with her husband and sister. She was fortunate Mother and Father were in the other carriage with her two brothers, but still... even that was probably more peaceful than what she had to put up with.

"Ugh. We need to make a stop. One more minute and I

swear I'm going to vomit."

Bernie sprawled about her seat, mimicking sickness, as she flailed her arms and moaned.

"The smell...it's like a pig bathed in old vinegar!" She looked to Arnold and made a morbid face. "For the love of all that's good, man, why don't you bathe?"

Arnold only rubbed the bridge of his nose, shutting his eyes and trying to drown out Bernie's insults. Antoinette had been listening to them bicker the entire trip there, and though she first thought it funny, even she was starting to tire of it. Not that she didn't want to hear Bernie's insults towards him. She just didn't want to hear his insults towards her.

"I bathe every day, thank you," Arnold replied, desperate to keep his voice in check. "It is unfortunate that I must remind you it is your own self that smells."

"Wow. That's the best you have? I say you stink and all you say is I stink back? Pathetic." Bernie sat up and crossed her arms, smirking. "You're so smelly, people mistake your room for the outhouse."

"These insults are childish, Bernette."

"I know. I had to dumb them down for you to understand them. Should I go lower?"

"No wonder you're still single. It's a miracle anyone puts up with you."

"And it's a miracle no one's died from smelling your dog breath. Can we open a door?"

On and on they bickered, Antoinette forced to listen as they continued without a moment's peace. She turned her head, gazing out the window at the mountainous countryside, desperate to get her mind on other things. She was so nervous about coming back to Audlin and dining with Edward and his family, stuck with seeing the woman who broke her engagement to the man she called her first love.

But even worse than that was seeing Emery, her childhood best friend turned husband after an elopement that eventually failed. She could never forget the look of disappointment he gave when she showed him the annulment papers, how his heart broke in seeing their secret caught.

She tried to downplay it so Mother would leave him alone. Emery was in danger of being imprisoned and she had to pretend disinterest to keep him safe. But he didn't know that, and he left thinking the woman he loved since childhood only used him to escape an arranged marriage, casting him aside in favor of the other man.

She wished he knew the truth, how her heart broke as much as his when she learned their dreams shattered and their plan was ruined; how she sobbed for days after he left, unable to sleep because she felt his hurt in her soul and she couldn't do a thing about it to comfort him.

But there was one more thing she could do, one more thing to make all of the pain and hurt worthwhile. She could tell him the truth, and at least he would know after all of the hurt, he was still the one who held her heart.

How would he react in seeing her again? Would he be glad? Sorrowful? Angry?

Would he even listen if she could talk with him like she wanted, to explain the real reason she sent him away?

She could only pray he was faithful in his trust, that he would still be willing to love her even though it seemed she would never love him.

"Heavens, are you always this annoying? You're like a

parrot that repeats itself!"

Antoinette's thoughts were interrupted by Arnold's complaints, his face turning red as he glared Bernie down in fury. Her sister only laughed as she leaned back in her seat, enjoying the fact she was making the prince so miserable.

"What's annoying is your face. Reminds me of a horse's rear after a bowel movement."

"You have no decency about you."

"And you have no hygiene. You've got something between your teeth, by the way."

"You nuisance of a girl!" He turned to Antoinette in a huff, clenching his fists like a child throwing a tantrum. "Are we in Reigal yet? Because if we aren't, I'd like to switch carriages!"

Antoinette could only sigh as she rested her head against the door.

"You've never said no to me, Malum! Not once!"

Malina glared at the Velori leader with her muscles tensed, wanting to smack the emotionless look upon his face. How could he deny her such a harmless want? Never had he stopped her intrigues. Never had he cared about her plans when they didn't include him.

"I don't care. You can't touch the Hugellian."

"Why not?"

"To gain an ally, you must help an ally."

"He'd get plenty of help with me by his side."

"Your main concern is Edward, not his cousin."

Malina fumed. "My main concern is taking control of Audlin, and that is what I've done *on my terms*. I'm winning the nobles. I'm extending our alliances. Does it matter if I have a little fling? Why is this man so important?"

"Your contributions have been minimal. While you win over the nobles, Edward gains the peasants. You're extending alliances, but Edward is connecting with people who will strengthen him. I gave you clear instructions, Malina, and you have not heeded them. The only reason you remain is because you are needed to take the throne."

"And what better way to do that than to use his cousin?"

"Emmerich is not a usurper, Malina, nor will he find favor with you. Your last impression left upon him sealed that. Leave him to me."

"You?" Malina shook her head, letting out a huff. "Why is this man so important, Malum? He is nothing but a weakling who pines over a woman he can't have!"

"Were you intelligent, you would see matters differently." Malum's face didn't change as she seethed at him. Her looks would make others tremble, but with him, there was nothing. "He is integral to later plans. Honestly, Malina, did you really think I'd stop at Audlin?"

Malina blinked, wondering if she was starting to understand. "You don't just want Audlin and Verloris. You want Hugellia as well?"

"There. It wasn't so hard using that brain of yours, was it?" He smirked.

Malina's eyes widened. "So you want Emmerich to help you conquer it."

"One step at a time," Malum reminded. "But until then, do not touch him."

Edward stood silently by the window, watching and waiting for the carriage to pull up. If he had his guesses right, Antoinette and her family would be arriving any minute, and he made sure the palace staff was ready to receive them.

"Are you nervous?" Marcus asked as he stood beside his friend, looking out the window.

"A little."

"I'm sure she'll be glad to see you."

"As I will be her."

Marcus nodded quietly. "Will you introduce her to Calimus?"

"I'd like to, but then she may not want to see him."

"Depending on how tonight goes, anyways."

Edward chuckled. "Indeed. With Emery here as well, I think we'll have an interesting evening."

"A night to remember?"

"Or a night to forget."

Marcus snickered, shaking his head. "I understand. Holidays were always exciting for my family back in Circh. Fights, arguments, carriages suddenly missing wheels or horses being let out of the stable…"

Edward's eyes widened as he turned to Marcus. "I guess I

should be glad I have you here, then."

"There's nothing I haven't seen. I'll be prepared."

"True, but you've never seen Susanna and Bernie at their worst."

"I've seen the princess. She and I had a memorable meeting when you came back from Verloris."

Edward looked back to the window. "I remember you telling me about that. You looked awful."

"She beat me up. I'm still sore from where she headbutted me."

"At least you're man enough to face her."

"Barely."

"I guess I shouldn't make fun," Edward said, remembering the past. "She gets worked up easily but don't let her fool you. She's got a good heart."

"And a good punch."

"That too. But I'm sure she'll be fine this time around."

"I'm wearing armor underneath my tunic. I'm not taking any chances," Marcus mumbled.

Edward laughed but quickly silenced himself as the carriages pulled up to the front.

Chapter 28: Greetings

It was almost surreal stepping back into the royal palace not as a resident, but a guest.

Antoinette looked around the foyer, marveling at how much the decor had already changed since she last stepped inside. Malina's input, no doubt, but she noticed a bit of Edward's flare. Despite the extra stone and red splashed about, there were blue drapes on the windows. It clashed, but then again, Edward always liked blue. He said the color reminded him of the dress she wore when they first met. Reigal blue, a color rarely seen in Edeland, its deep shades made from a unique dye from the mountains surrounding the city. Mother insisted she wear it to impress the future king, Stephen, but it impressed his brother, instead.

She couldn't help but smile at the memory, but it quickly faded once she saw Edward approach with his guard, mother, wife, and child. He and Malina were distant from each other, a coldness between them like invisible hands pulling them apart, despite the fact that the woman remained near him and smiled profusely. Their child (a son, she had heard from the rumors) remained quiet save the occasional coo. His eyes never left his father, and every so often Edward looked back at him to smile. It pained her to see such a bond between father and son, and she couldn't help but think Edward would've made a good father to her children had he stayed.

She shook her head, pushing away the past. Edward may have had a child, but he made his choice and she made hers. But despite her eagerness to forget, she noticed Edward was no longer as proud like he was before. The poor man looked worn out, exhausted, and sadness dwelled in his eyes like she had never seen since his brother died. He met her glance, but she looked away quickly, scanning the room for the man who deserved her affections.

Hope diminished at the emptiness before her. Emery was nowhere to be seen.

Did he know I'd be here? Did he leave?

She hadn't the time to answer those questions as conversation between the families began.

"Welcome to Reigal," Edward said as he gave a polite nod to Susanna and her husband. The king and queen nodded back, though Susanna's lip turned in disgust after seeing the clashing drapes. "I trust your trip was pleasant?"

"Quite pleasant," King John answered. "We even saw some deer upon the road. Lovely animals. My boys and I were tempted by the hunt and…"

"I see you've redecorated the place," Susanna interrupted as the king gave a sigh and lowered his eyes. "It's quite…quaint. You're doing, I presume?" She turned to Malina, narrowing her eyes. One minute into conversation and already there was a challenge for dominance. Antoinette couldn't help but cringe.

"I thought I'd liven up the palace with a touch of home," Malina replied as she turned to Edward, lifting the baby a little higher as if to show him off. "Though Edward desired the drapes. They clash, I know, but how could I say no to my sweet love? After all, he never says no to me. By the way…" She paused, holding the baby forward for Antoinette to see. "I believe you haven't met our son Calimus."

"Calimus?" Susanna asked. "I daren't say I've heard of the name before."

"He was named after my father, the king of Verloris," Malina replied. "Though I think we should have named him after Edward. The boy is a spitting image of him, don't you think?"

She looked to Antoinette and she couldn't help but agree. Though some features were of his mother, the baby looked so much like Edward. Blue eyes, dark hair, a defined face. He even had Edward's goofy grin, or at least it was an attempt at it.

"He is a beautiful baby," Antoinette said quietly, forcing the words from her lips as she felt her heart break. "You must be very proud."

"He is perfect in every way. Of course, Edward and I will have more soon. I don't think I've ever seen a more doting husband and father," Malina said, making Antoinette's face burn in anger. Despite the attempt at forgetting the past, the hurt was still there and probably always would be. She met Malina's stare with her own, though it was clearly less intimidating, and Malina only smiled back.

"I think he likes you."

Antoinette and Malina's private war was interrupted as Edward spoke, nodding towards Calimus. The baby stuck out his hand, reaching for Antoinette and cooing.

She looked at the baby as he looked back at her, feeling her lip quiver. *This is what you could have had.*

"Would you like to hold him?" Edward asked.

Antoinette shook her head, trying to be polite. "No thank you. I wouldn't want to separate him from his mother."

Malina smiled further as Antoinette lowered her gaze.

Edward cleared his throat, changing the subject and turning to the other guests. "I hope the accommodations are to your liking, Queen Susanna. I've prepared rooms for you and your family."

"Of course," Susanna replied. "And I hope you gave Antoinette her own room this time. She needn't share with Bernette. Being a married woman now, she refuses to be away from her husband. Silly things can't keep their hands off each other, you know."

"So I've heard. Of course congratulations are in order for your marriage." Edward's face turned red, his voice sounding perturbed, and Antoinette blushed. If only Mother knew the truth about her and Arnold's "loving relationship". But Arnold was quick to run with it. He wrapped his arm around Antoinette's waist and pulled her close, his lips near her ear.

"Play along, sweetheart, if you want this show to be good."

His whisper reminded her to stay on track, to not be distracted by Malina or Edward. She put her hand on his chest, showing off her ring. Arnold lingered his lips near her ear, tickling it with his breath, and she let out a fake giggle.

Guilt rose at seeing Edward's reaction, and she noticed his jaw tensed when Arnold kissed her cheek.

"Forgive me," Arnold said, clearing his throat and lifting his head as he faced Edward. "I'm afraid talk of getting a room has reminded me of other matters. You understand how it is to be newlywed, I'm sure. Anyways, I'd like to introduce myself to you. Prince Arnold von Liegen, husband to the beautiful woman standing beside me. It's a pleasure to finally meet you, Prince Edward."

He stuck out his right hand, his left remaining around

Antoinette, and Edward frowned, staying still for a moment. After an awkward few seconds of silence, however, he finally relented and shook the man's hand, giving it a hard grasp.

"It's King Edward, actually," Edward replied, clasping Arnold's hand even harder, making his fingers turn red. Arnold gave a frown and looked to Edward in confusion as he muttered an apology.

"Of course, of course. Forgive me, Your Majesty. News travels slow to Liegen and I'm afraid my wife has been distracting me from other things."

"I'm sure," Edward replied, his voice low.

Arnold began to stammer. "Uhm...that's quite a grip you have, Your Majesty...uhm..."

"Oh, my apologies *Prince* Arnold," Edward replied, letting go of his hand and smirking. "Knight's hands. I'm so used to grasping a sword, I guess I don't know my own strength."

"Clearly," Arnold muttered, turning his sights to the queen. "And you must be Queen Malina. It is an honor to meet you!"

He took her hand and kissed it, making the woman giggle in delight. "Such a wonderful gentleman, you are! But you also look familiar. Have we met?"

"No, Your Majesty. You may have met my eldest brother, though. He visited Verloris five years ago with my father."

"That's right," Malina said. "Now I remember. What kindness they showed us! And your brother was quite the guest."

"He speaks of you still, Your Majesty," Arnold replied, his eyes looking at the queen from head to toe. "Though...if I may be so blunt...his stories do not do you justice. You are even more beautiful than the description they gave."

Malina licked her lips as she looked at him, ignoring Edward's eye roll as he interrupted. "Not as beautiful as your wife, of course, Prince Arnold. I daresay none could equal the radiance she displays both inside and out."

"Edward!" Malina hissed, and Antoinette couldn't help but smirk at his words, but before anything else could be said, Maria stepped forward with a forced smile.

Antoinette breathed a sigh of relief as the queen mother went to work doing damage control. She repeated pleasantries about settling in to their rooms and dinner being served, and then Edward added something about talking terms for a new peace agreement in the morning with Susanna and John. Antoinette listened to the conversations that followed with a disinterested ear until her eyes noticed something move near the corner by the hallway.

She remembered the figure whose eyes stared longingly back at hers, and her heart fluttered. Emery stood in the distance, watching and waiting, and in her excitement to see him, she gave a smile back.

But instead of meeting her joy with his own, his head lowered and his eyes closed in hurt. He turned, his lips pressed firmly together as if in pain, and walked away.

"So...whose dinner should I put the bugs in? I've got a beetle/earwig concoction that's guaranteed to make someone mess their pants in fright!" Bernie's whispers would normally make Antoinette laugh, but Emery's look was too distracting. The man was so hurt after seeing her, but in his eyes she could still see love. Love that had been hurt, yet love that was true. It took every ounce of strength to not push everyone around her out of the way and chase after him.

But she couldn't cause a scene...not now, not ever. She knew what Mother would do if she found out where her daughter's heart really lied.

"Maybe I could sneak into the gardens and get another jar. That way I can give it to Malina *and* Edward," Bernie continued quietly, leaning close. "What do you think?"

Antoinette frowned. "I'd rather not think right now."

"I know, I know," Bernie replied. "You should have the honors of pouring them in."

Antoinette lowered her head, not wanting to say anything as she tried to think of a way to get to Emery.

"Quick! Act natural. Mr. Grumpy Guard is watching me." Bernette turned and gave an innocent wave to Sir Peterson, who only smiled politely before frowning again. "Maybe I should make a third batch," Bernie muttered under her breath. "Poor guy's got a boot up his rear that needs to fall out."

"Dinner will be ready in an hour," Maria said, interrupting Antoinette's thoughts. "I'll let you settle in your rooms and call when we can gather in the dining room. For now, make yourselves at home and freshen up. If you need anything, please let us know."

King John and Queen Susanna thanked her, following a few of the servants towards the guest quarters in the east wing. Antoinette was led quietly beside Arnold, but as she passed Edward, she was stopped for a moment as he gently grabbed her hand.

"It's good seeing you again, Antoinette," he said quietly, his eyes meeting hers. She was about to say the same to him, but before she could answer, he let go of her hand and walked away.

She was confused at the abrupt ending, and Arnold pulled her along to keep up with the group, but a strange feeling in her palm made her check what had suddenly ended up in her hand.

A small note, written and folded, was there. She quickly unwrapped it, Arnold giving her a puzzled look, and read the contents before hiding it in her sleeve.

Palace chapel, 10 minutes. We need to talk.

"Meeting your former lover in the chapel?" Arnold whispered to her with a smirk. "Try not to be too loud. Sounds are amplified when the ceilings are high."

She gave him a sneer as she shook her head. "I'm not that kind of woman, Arnold. Besides, there's other people in the chapel praying. We won't be alone, I'm sure."

"Of course," Arnold replied. "I doubt he'd order everyone out of the room to give you privacy."

Antoinette said nothing as they were taken to their room.

Edward kneeled quietly at the pew, hands folded and head bowed in prayer as he begged the Almighty for help. Help for himself, help for his cousin, help for Antoinette, and help for Arnold because more than anything, he wanted to pummel the man into the ground for flirting with another woman in front of his wife. Edward didn't care that it was his own wife Arnold lusted after. He could have her. But no one hurt Antoinette, if he could help it. Her heart was broken enough and the pieces needn't be played with.

He waited, listening for the doors to open and the footsteps of his beloved to walk down the aisle towards him. When she came, he remained still and faced his eyes forward, hoping not to rouse suspicion from the two nuns praying silently at the front.

"You read my note?" he asked as she knelt beside him, mimicking his pose.

"Yes," she replied, "but I don't have a lot of time, Edward. What's this about?"

"I'm sorry. I won't keep you long." He paused, his heart beating fast. He was so nervous talking to her all of a sudden, as if they were young again, and he overanalyzed each word he planned to say in hopes of pleasing her. He'd messed up so badly in the past and he was so afraid of making things worse for the future. "I just wanted to talk about your marriage and…"

"I'd rather not talk about that."

He nodded slowly, seeing the look of impatience on her face. Was she wanting to get back to Arnold? From the looks she gave a moment ago, she seemed disinterested in him. Even the smile she gave when he nibbled her ear and drew her close seemed fake.

"Antoinette, please let me get this out. This isn't what you think it is."

"Edward, you had your chance with me and blew it. I don't want another apology. I don't care anymore." Her answer was cold, but he noticed she didn't look at him when she said it. Poor girl was still a terrible liar and probably always would be.

"This isn't about me, Antoinette. I know the mistakes I've made, but that isn't the point. I want to talk about what happened with you and Emery."

Her face turned and she looked at him with wide eyes.

"What about me and Emery?" Her voice was accusing, but he noticed a hint of fear, as if some deep, dark secret was about to be found out.

"Emery is here, Antoinette. Erick sent him away from Hugellia."

She frowned, looking back towards the front. "I know."

"And you know why Erick sent him away, right?"

"Yes. Do you?"

"Emery told me everything." He paused, shrugging as she frowned further. "Well...he told my mother everything. I only overheard it." He leaned closer to her, his voice quieting. "I know of the elopement and I know that the marriage was annulled by you."

Antoinette closed her eyes, bowing her head and giving a sigh. "Edward, please. This isn't the time or the place to..."

"What happened?" Edward asked. "Why did you leave him?"

"Why would you care?"

"Because he's my cousin. Because you and I were once betrothed. Because I want you both to be happy."

She laughed at him, shaking her head as if in disbelief. It hurt that she had such little trust in him like she used to, but then again...he shouldn't have been surprised. He barely trusted himself, either.

"It doesn't matter."

"It *does* matter, especially when my cousin is so depressed he neither eats nor sleeps."

Antoinette's scoffing stopped, and she looked at him with concern. "How bad is it?"

"If it wasn't bad, I wouldn't have said anything."

She frowned. "I didn't mean to hurt him, but there's nothing I can do about it. He knew that Arnold and I were engaged."

"He also knew you didn't want to marry the idiot."

He expected a reaction for that remark, but she gave none. Even more proof that her love for Arnold was nothing more than a ruse.

"Arnold was the better choice, Edward."

"You and I both know that isn't true."

Antoinette looked back at him, her brows lowered. "Don't lecture me on choices. I know what I'm doing and you have no right to say anything."

"Arnold is a fool and a cheat, Antoinette. Even I can tell he is nothing but a flirt to every woman he sees!"

"Arnold was just being friendly. It was your wife who was the flirt."

"This isn't about her. It's about you." He paused, frustration building up. "I know you, Antoinette. We can pretend the past never happened and that we're just two strangers in the same room, but we both still have that connection that was there before I made a mess of things. You don't love Arnold and you loathe him like I loathe Malina. I can see it in your eyes."

"You don't know me anymore, Edward," she said quietly. "Just like I don't know you. I love Arnold."

"You're in a church, Antoinette. You shouldn't be lying with

God watching."

She was about to say something, but closed her mouth quickly, shaking her head. "Edward, what is it you want from me? I'd rather not be mocked right now. I'm not in the mood for it."

"I'm not mocking you. I'm just saying that I don't think you left Emmerich willingly."

She bowed, her forehead resting on her arms in frustration. "Edward, stop pretending you care. You don't."

It hurt him seeing the damage his leaving had caused, how she truly believed him incapable of ever loving her. Were he not bound by the laws of matrimony, he would've gathered her in his arms right then and there and proved how much he still loved her, but there was nothing he could do. The only proof he could provide was words, and that meant little to her.

"Doubt me, then, but know that I doubt you. You cannot deny that you and Emery have always been close, even from before we met, and whether there was attraction between the two of you or not, you still wouldn't have sent him away like you did unless it was for a reason." He paused, looking at her as she looked back up at him. "I overheard that Susanna was threatening. I know your mother, Antoinette, and it would not surprise me if you married Arnold to save Emmerich from her wrath."

Antoinette looked away. "You know nothing."

"Maybe. Maybe not. But I do know this." He swallowed hard, fighting the urge to put his trembling hand atop hers and hold it once more. "Your marriage...I understand it. I know the pain of sacrifice and I know what it is to be bound to a person you do not care for." He watched as her eyes slowly met his, and he knew she was listening carefully. "The hurt...the pain...the many nights you stay up wide awake because you ache for what you used to have so ardently…it never gets better. I can pretend I'm happy with Malina, but I'm not, and I never will be because you were the one I wanted to spend my life with."

Her lip quivered, and her harsh look began to fade. Instead of watching him with anger, she now watched him with pity and an all too familiar understanding.

"Did you marry Arnold to save Emmerich from your mother?"

She looked away, her face scrunching as she tried to stop the quiver in her lips. "I made the choice I had to make."

"So you saved his life."

Her eyes remained ahead and she said nothing.

His heart became heavy at the notion. Here he had thought separating himself from Antoinette would prevent her from further hurt, yet time was proving he had never been more wrong. Already she was following in his footsteps. Already her life was being affected by his decisions even when he walked away.

"I guess we understand each other, then," he said, watching as she faced him once more curiously. "Though I wish we didn't. I'm sorry…I thought leaving would save you from all of this."

Her expression was foreign to him. Was she hurt? Understanding? Angry? A combination of all three? He didn't know for once, and that worried him. She had never been able to mask her feelings before.

"If there is *ever* a time that you need me, Antoinette…" He stopped, his hand going atop hers. No matter what she felt, she needed to know he still loved her, even if he was limited in how he could show it. "I'll be there to help you. Emery...will be there to help you. You don't deserve to go through this life uncared for."

He meant it in a friendly way, but he wondered if she even noticed. Her eyes became teary, but she pulled her hand away. "Stop pretending you'll be there for me, Edward. When I needed you most, you left." She got up from the pew, facing the floor. "You made your choice and I made mine. Now stop questioning my decisions and let me live my life in peace. Our relationship is in the past now and I wish to forget it. Do not speak to me again!"

With that, she stormed off, leaving him alone in the church.

Chapter 29: The Dinner

Bernie was never one to enjoy parties, but this was one she'd been looking forward to for a while.

Chaos. She'd have the best opportunity to get revenge on so many people; there wouldn't be a box big enough to contain all her excitement. Edward, Malina, Arnold, Mr. Grumpy Guard...the possibilities were as endless as they were perfect!

The only problem was not bringing enough bugs to the dinner to give everyone fright after they ate. No, it wasn't anything that would make them terribly sick, but it was enough to send everyone clamoring out of the room and not wanting to eat another bite. It'd more than become the greatest entertainment she'd witnessed since releasing the pig and chickens in Mother's kitchen.

Never had she felt so evil, and never had it felt so much fun!

She tiptoed quietly towards the dining room, noticing the servants were just finishing setting the table and bringing out a few dishes ready to serve. She only had a few minutes before the guests started arriving, so she had to be quick before getting caught. She waited until the last servant left, rushing into the room and heading for a large salad bowl near the door that would be served to the families first.

She snickered quietly to herself as she took out the small

jar of bugs from her pocket, lifting the lid off the salad bowl and setting it to the side. She opened the jar and dumped the bugs into the cabbage, giving it a quick stir with her hands.

"There you go, my lovelies..." she whispered, stifling another chuckle. "Now don't forget to be on your best behavior! I really want you to impress Malina, Edward, and Arnold." She paused, giving a wicked grin. "And don't forget Mother. I'm sure she'll enjoy you all so much!"

She put the empty jar back in her pocket and closed the salad lid, feeling confident her plan was going so perfectly!

"Dinner hasn't been served yet, Your Majesty."

She froze, turning to find familiar brown eyes staring back at her with arms crossed. Mr. Grumpy Guard stood before her with his typical, serious face.

She wanted to curse her rotten luck, but hoped she hadn't been caught. Going by the expectant look he gave, however, she figured he didn't know about the bugs...yet.

"I'm sorry. I didn't eat much lunch on the road today. Everything smells so good!" She made sure she smiled to throw him off, but it didn't work. His seriousness remained, probably because fermented cabbage didn't smell good for anyone.

"The king requested that all the guests be present before dinner is served. If you like, I can get you some appetizers or something to drink for now."

At least he was polite about it, but it didn't matter. Her work was done, anyways. "I'm fine. I'm more than happy to wait."

"Of course," he said, but after a moment of awkward silence, she noticed he still hadn't left.

Typical, paranoid guard. Did he not trust her with

something as simple as salad? Surely he didn't suspect her of foul play…even though it was true.

"So…are you going to stay here until everyone arrives?" she asked, hoping he wouldn't take off the lid to the salad bowl and spoil the surprise.

"I'm here to serve the king's guests and make sure everything runs smoothly," he replied. "If that requires me to stay here, then I'll stay."

"Okay…" Bernie nodded, unsure of what to do. She couldn't leave the salad alone lest he check it, but she didn't want to stay in the room with him and be under his guarding eye. "How long until the guests get here, again?"

"Dinner is to be served in five minutes."

Great, she thought to herself. *Five minutes stuck with Mr. Grumpy Guard.*

"I guess I'll stay here, then. No sense in walking back to my room when dinner will be served by the time I get there." Bernie found her seat at the table and plopped down upon it, crossing her arms and leaning back.

"Whatever you wish, Your Majesty," he said, and she noticed him still standing by the doorway, not moving an inch.

She wanted to sigh in frustration. What did it take to get rid of him? Or at least make him more laid back? Even Antoinette wasn't this stiff at her most serious, and that was saying something!

"So…what do you do, Sir…?" She had to remind herself to not call him Mr. Grumpy Guard. She swore one day it'd come out, though. Sometimes she just couldn't help it.

"Peterson," he replied. "My name is Marcus Peterson. I'm the head of the royal guard here."

"I see," she said, giving a polite nod but secretly not caring. All she knew about him was that he was the knight who defended Edward when the scum came back with a wife from Verloris.

"So...you're Edward's bodyguard?"

"The head of it...yes."

She nodded, getting another gleam in her eye. "How lovely! Tell me, will you be joining us for dinner tonight? I do hope you can take a break from your duties and dine with us."

Sir Peterson looked at her in suspicion, almost as if he didn't trust her. Surely she wasn't *that* obvious, was she? "The king expects me to remain with my duty. It is kind of you to ask, but I'm afraid I will be unable to dine with you."

"Oh, but at least get a small plate to eat during a break," she replied. "I insist that you not go hungry. Not only are you protecting your king, but my king as well. I appreciate that you are making sure my family and I are coming to a very safe palace."

"That is kind of you, but..."

"Nope. I'll make sure you get a plate of food for your dinner. You look like you could use a good meal, anyways."

"But..."

"I insist!" she replied, grinning widely. "After all, no good knight should go hungry!"

Sir Peterson was about to say something until the servants came into the room, adding the rest of the dishes and taking their stations for dinner to start.

Emmerich stood by the window, watching a sprinkle of rain slowly turn to a drizzle outside the palace walls. He was safe and warm in his aunt's library, but the sound of the rain brought back painful memories of Bohden's words: trapped in a hurricane, drowning in a current, struggling to survive until he came to the valley. But even when he made his way out, the rains still surrounded him. The pain, the suffering, the unfairness of life...no matter what, it would always plague him. No matter what, he would never have the life he wanted to live.

And seeing Antoinette walk in with Arnold's hand around her waist was just another painful reminder of that fact.

He remembered the look she gave him, how for a moment he thought he glimpsed that familiar love he saw in her eyes when they were at the church reciting their wedding vows. It told him she cared; that despite her lack of words, she really did love him like he loved her. But then reality set in as he saw Arnold once more, and he remembered who she chose to spend her life with. He was the rejected one, the one she didn't trust or care for, and after that realization, he couldn't help but look away and return to the library to find peace.

Would she seek him out? He was doubtful. With her mother and Arnold there and with Edward nosing about, there was little room for him and Antoinette to have any private talks. Even if they could, he didn't know what they would say to each other. There was nothing left to say after Staalberg, and anything more would just bring him heartache.

But then he remembered the note his mother had sent him from Kettensburg – a hand-written letter supposedly sent by Antoinette earlier, asking to speak with him. What could be so important that she wanted to talk with him in private? Unless his suspicions were correct and someone else sent the note... but who else would?

Perhaps it was Susanna, hoping to trap him further. Perhaps it was Bernie, hoping to get him and Antoinette back together.

Or perhaps it really was Antoinette, and this was her way of crying out for help.

He didn't know what to think anymore, didn't know whether to chance it or play safe. Were he to risk and meet Antoinette, he'd put his heart...maybe even his life...on the line. Was he willing to go through with it again, even if it meant keeping her safe and happy?

His thoughts were interrupted as a servant stepped inside the library and brought him a sealed note. He thanked the young man and opened the letter, curious as to who it might be from. When he opened it, he found the ink was still wet as if the words were just written, and he read silently to himself.

My dearest Emery,

Fate has been kind to bring us together today. Please...I must speak with you, but not in front of watching eyes. I will go to your bedroom at ten tonight so we can talk in private.

Yours lovingly,

Antoinette.

The letter looked to be in her handwriting, folded in the same way as the one before. Surely it was Antoinette who wrote it, but why would she meet him in his bedroom? Did she not understand that it would make her look indecent, much less make it look like they were having an affair with each other if caught?

He didn't know what to make of it, but he knew what he had to do. He would listen to what she had to say...if it really was her...but he would also protect her reputation.

He wouldn't open his door, but that didn't mean she couldn't speak from outside it.

He placed the note inside his pocket, returning his sight to the rain outside.

"Where were you?"

Susanna's demanding tone was no surprise to Antoinette, but she dreaded having to hear it nonetheless. She sat up straighter in her chair near the window as Arnold smoothed his coat, waiting for Mother's words of accusations to fly.

"Speak, child! I visited your room after settling in and found you were not there! Where have you been?"

"Not seeing Emmerich, if that is what you're implying," Antoinette replied, her tone more than a little harsh. "My husband knows of this. Edward sent me a note and wished to speak with me in the chapel. That is all."

Susanna's frown did not leave her face. "And what did you speak of?"

"He asked me about what happened with Emmerich and I told him the truth. I told him I chose my husband and that the matter should be dropped."

Susanna turned to Arnold, probing. "Is this true?"

"Yes, Your Majesty," Arnold replied. "I followed her and watched from the church doors in case she needed me. What she speaks is the truth. After that, we returned here to ready for dinner. We have seen nothing of Emmerich van Ketten, though I must admit I'm disappointed. I wished I could've seen the look of defeat on his face!"

"In due time, my precious Arnold." Susanna turned back to Antoinette. "He still might be at dinner. Whatever the circumstance, Antoinette, you must not show yourself to that boy. Do not look at him. Do not speak to him. If that is too difficult for you, you and Arnold shall leave dinner early and return to your room. You are not to leave your husband's side. Understand?"

"Yes, Mother."

"Good. Now hurry up. We're due in the dining hall. Your father and I shall meet you there."

Antoinette nodded, watching her leave the room and shut the door. She stood from her chair and went to the mirror to fix her hair quickly before following, but Arnold's voice made her pause.

"You're getting better at this."

She went back to her hair, brushing it. "Better at what?"

"Deception."

Arnold's grin made her feel uncomfortable. She never was good at deception and never wanted to be. It was strange how time had changed all of that. "I don't take that as a compliment."

"You should, my little vixen. It makes me wonder what else you've got hiding there."

"Nothing of your concern."

"So mysterious and so feisty!" Arnold said, approaching her from behind. He put his hands around her waist and looked at the mirror with her, smiling. "Look at us. So similar, so alike. We really do make the perfect couple, don't we?"

"I'm not like you," she replied, squirming her way out of his grasp.

"Not yet, but you're getting there," he said as he watched her head to the door. "Practice makes perfect, right?"

She said nothing as she left the room, heading towards the dining hall.

Marcus was not one to distrust royalty, but when it came to Princess Bernette, he *knew* not to let his guard down.

Something about the way the girl smirked at him, her look almost beckoning him to question her. She was hiding something – he was sure of it – but he couldn't do a thing until she left the room. He couldn't go accusing a guest of the king, especially when she was present. That would throw out any attempt at good relations with Edeland, not to mention make him look disrespectful.

But she wouldn't let up. There she sat at the table, her eyes occasionally going back to the salad bowl waiting to be served, and he stood his ground. What she had planned, he didn't know, but he suspected it had something to do with that salad.

As the guests started to arrive, he hurried to Edward, gently putting his hand on the king's arm and whispering.

"Edward, I think we have a problem."

Edward's brow rose, but he quickly hid his concern as the guests found their seats, busy conversing with the queen mother and Malina. "What is it?"

"I think the cabbage salad has been tampered with."

"How?"

"I don't know, but I suspect Lady Bernette. She's been here for five minutes."

Edward tried to hide the laugh that wanted to come out, but it was a struggle. "Marcus, you're being paranoid. Bernie's not going to poison anyone."

"But she keeps looking at that salad bowl!"

"It's probably because she's hungry."

"I don't think..."

"Marcus, relax," Edward said, clasping his shoulder. "You worry too much. Bernie's not the one that would cause any trouble tonight. I'd be more worried about her mother."

"Edward, I'm sorry, but that girl is up to something. You can see it on her."

"I've known her longer than you, Marcus. She's a little high-strung, but not devious. Now relax! Take your place at the door to stand guard. If anything does go amiss, you'll know what to do."

"But..."

"Go, Marcus. I've got enough on my plate dealing with my wife and Susanna." Marcus watched as the king took his seat, greeting his guests and welcoming them. He sighed, taking his place at the door, knowing in his heart that he was more right than what Edward wanted to believe.

He remained vigilant regardless, especially after he heard Lady Bernette request that the salad be served first.

The servants complied, hurriedly dispensing the salad onto bowls that were given to the guests. Marcus got a quick look at the food and didn't notice anything amiss with it, and for a moment he wondered if Edward was right in that he was worrying too much. As the drinks were poured and bread was set on the table, the conversation of the evening turned his thoughts elsewhere.

He watched as Malina and Prince Arnold sat next to each other, conversing and laughing to themselves. It didn't take a smart man to see that the two were flirting, and though Edward had been used to his wife's antics, he noticed Antoinette looked hurt over the matter. Poor woman; he couldn't help but wish fate had been better to her. She was a kind soul and deserved a better man than Arnold. In truth, she deserved Edward.

"I hear your nephew is staying here," Susanna said, turning to Maria. Marcus' eyes widened at the conversation. Edward had said little of Emmerich's predicament with Edeland, but he knew enough. He'd heard of the failed elopement and how Susanna stepped in to stop the marriage.

Maria frowned as bread was handed to her by one of the servants. "Yes, he is staying here at the moment as our guest. I'm sorry he was unable to attend the dinner tonight. I don't think he's feeling too well."

"Well, do give my condolences to him. I would give them myself, but don't wish to catch whatever illness he has."

Maria frowned further, only nodding as she turned to her food.

After a prayer was said by the king, the guests turned to eat, but after a quick bite by Susanna, she suddenly brought her napkin to her lips.

"Heavens! It feels as if something's moving!" she mumbled, her mouth full before spitting the food contents into her napkin. Marcus noticed the other guests eating their salad, but his eyes narrowed as he looked to Lady Bernette. She only touched the bread, motioning for Antoinette to do the same, watching her mother intently with a grin on her face.

"What is this salad made of?" Susanna asked as she opened her napkin to see what she'd spit out. Before she could speak any further, however, she let out a scream, flinging the napkin across the table, its contents landing on Arnold.

"INSECTS!" She let out another scream, her husband trying desperately to calm her, as some of the other guests took a deeper look at their salad and let out a few yells.

"Bugs? How did these get here?" King John asked.

"This is great!" Caspar and Robert exclaimed together, digging further into their bowls and pulling more of the things out onto the table.

Antoinette only put her hand on her stomach, looking to Bernie, as Malina stood to her feet, pulling one of the servants to her by the shirt. "Have you no decency in serving this garbage to our guests? How dare you not check the food before serving it! I could've been made deathly ill!"

Arnold only wiped the contents of Susanna's napkin off his face, cringing, as Bernie laughed.

"At least we know the salad's fresh!" she cackled, and Marcus could only glance to Edward and Maria as the queen mother tried to calm everyone down.

Edward met his gaze, shaking his head as he leaned back in his chair. "Told you," Marcus mouthed as the king rubbed his brow, shutting his eyes and giving a groan.

Marcus turned back to Bernie, arms crossed as she finally met his stare.

All she did was smile and wink at him, holding out her plate. "Looks like we'll be ordering from a tavern. Any good suggestions?"

He only took the plate and frowned, leaving to help the servants and Maria calm the chaos.

Chapter 30: Antoinette's Choice

"The nerve of that girl!" Arnold spat as he paced within his room, Antoinette lying on the bed in her nightgown and robe, wringing her hands. She felt terribly nervous, more nervous than she had ever felt, and the insanity that was dinner didn't help matters. It took a long time to get Mother to sit down and eat. The hysterics then led to a great argument, and until Edward stepped in between the two fighting queens and compromised, barring all formal dinners for the time being, the night threatened to be nothing but chaos for the rest of the trip.

Of course, Arnold was still fuming, especially after being pelted with Mother's half-chewed up food, and he hadn't quieted about it. "Your sister is a monster, Antoinette. I daren't say I've ever met a girl with such childishness! She should be sent away!"

"She meant to get back at Edward and Malina for what happened last year," Antoinette replied. "Don't take it personally."

"But did you see the way she laughed at me? There is something wrong with that girl. Something terribly, terribly wrong!"

Antoinette only sighed, lowering her head, counting the time to ten when she was supposed to meet with Emery.

"Are we still agreed about the arrangement?" Antoinette

asked, wanting to change the subject. She looked up to Arnold as he looked back to her.

"Yes," he replied. "I expect this room to be occupied, however. Don't plan on returning until five in the morning. That's when the guards change shifts again. We'll have a two minute window to go about the hallways unawares."

Just like at ten. "Are you sure we won't be caught?"

"My source says it should be fine. She knows her way about the palace and its workings, plus she can manipulate them when she wants to."

"Is your 'source' your special guest tonight?"

Arnold grinned. "Perhaps."

Antoinette couldn't help but wonder if it was Malina. The way they spoke to each other, flirting and batting their eyes all evening. It made her sick just thinking about it. "I don't think Edward would appreciate you sleeping with his wife."

"Who said I was doing that?"

"I know you, Arnold. I'm not stupid."

"Is it any different from you sleeping with his cousin?"

Antoinette's eyes widened. "I never said I was going to do that. I'm only going to talk."

"Of course. But I know you, Antoinette. I'm not as dumb as you think, either."

He approached, putting his finger to her collarbone and grazing it downward, fingering the necklace she wore and lifting it gently from under her gown. In his hand he pinched the ring Emmerich had given, setting it in front of her line of sight.

"Need I get any more proof than this?"

She snatched the ring from his hand, stuffing it back down in her gown to hide it lest Mother would see. Arnold only chuckled, stepping away as a knock on the door was heard.

"Come in," Arnold replied, and in stepped Susanna.

"I was only wanting to check on you two," she said as she shut the door. "Maria says Emmerich is still here."

Antoinette let out a scoff. "Mother, do you not trust me? It's insulting that you'd think I'd leave my husband!"

"It's not that I don't trust you, my daughter; I just don't trust that boy!"

"You needn't worry over anything, Mother," Arnold replied warmly, his charms calming her. "I will watch over Antoinette tonight and make sure nothing happens."

"I should like to check throughout the night, regardless."

Antoinette's eyes widened in panic. She couldn't be caught sneaking out of her room to Emmerich's. She looked to Arnold, hoping he would come up with an excuse. No matter what she said, Mother wouldn't oblige.

"You worry so much, Mother!" Arnold said warmly as he took his hand in hers and kissed it. "But...if I may speak freely with you...I was hoping Antoinette and I would have some...privacy...tonight."

"Privacy?" she asked.

"Yes. We've been speaking of having a child, and...well...you know what must be done to create one." He paused, adding for dramatic effect. "I think Antoinette would be more in the mood if we knew we wouldn't be interrupted."

"Oh..." Susanna's face brightened and she nodded in agreement. "Of course, my dear prince! I shan't interrupt you, then. I trust my daughter will be in good hands with you tonight, though I hope you don't mind me checking on you two in the morning."

"Of course, Mother," Arnold said with a smile. "And thank you."

Susanna grinned widely as she looked at her daughter, making Antoinette want to scoff at the sight of it. "Have a pleasant evening, then. See you in the morning!" she called, and Antoinette offered her a polite smile that quickly turned into a frown once Mother left the room.

She turned to Arnold. "You're a little too good at this."

"You have to be, living the life I live."

She smirked, shaking her head. She wasn't surprised by Arnold's "talent" for deception, but she had to admit it came in handy. Though she didn't want to be like him, she couldn't help but admit it had its perks.

It was another hour before ten, and she patiently counted down the minutes until she could leave to see Emmerich.

Emmerich stood in front of the hearth, his senses heightened from nerves getting the best of him. His heart raced, his palms sweated, and his body tensed at the thought of Antoinette visiting his room. What did she want to say? Was it really her that was going to be at the door? What if it was all a trap by Susanna, another method of humiliating him and ripping his heart out, stomping it on the ground?

He listened for a knock at the door, dreading its sound and what it might mean.

He didn't have to wait long as ten approached, and a gentle *tap tap tap* was heard from behind him. He turned, his heart racing faster now, and he spoke.

"Who is it?"

He heard a soft voice answer from behind the door. "It's Antoinette."

He approached, keeping the door closed as his thoughts churned within him. He knew her voice, knew it was really her, and that made him wonder all the more. She really did want to speak to him, but what about? His heart couldn't take much more rejection. He was already mad with grief and didn't need more.

"What is it you want?"

"May I come in?"

He lowered his head, letting out a sigh. "It's not proper, Antoinette. You're a married woman and it would look indecent if you were in my bedroom."

"Emery, please. The guards will be back any moment and I don't wish to get caught!"

"I'm sorry, Antoinette. Your reputation is still important to me."

He heard a scoff, but he remained still. Even if she no longer cared, he did. "Emery, Mother doesn't know I'm here. If she finds me at your room, she will suspect something! Now let me in so we can at least keep this private!"

His thoughts changed, and he realized the truth she spoke. Though he was right in keeping his distance, she was also right that Susanna would suspect something that wasn't there. He muttered a curse to himself, quickly opening the door, swearing the conversation would be nothing more than quick talk.

She rushed inside before closing the door quietly, and he watched as she turned to face him.

Antoinette was dressed in her nightgown, covered by a robe, her hair down and straight. She looked simple…plain…but that was when he thought her the most beautiful. It reminded him of when they were children, sneaking out to the parlor after being sent to bed so they could read stories to one another, falling asleep on the couch and being scolded by their parents the next morning. Those were the moments that he first realized she was beautiful to him, and now, as she stood looking so similar in her older age, he realized she was still the object of his affection.

"It's good to see you again," she said, her hands wringing together. Doubtless she was nervous like him.

"It's good to see you," he replied awkwardly, unsure of what to say.

They stood there for a moment, watching and waiting for the other to speak. When nothing was said, Antoinette broke the silence.

"You got my note?"

Emmerich nodded. "Yes."

"Thank you for hearing me out."

"Of course."

"I…I know this is awkward," she began, meeting his gaze. "But I knew I needed to explain myself. What happened in Staalberg…after our marriage…it wasn't what I planned."

Emmerich lowered his gaze. It wasn't his plan, either. If things happened the way he wanted them to, he'd be back in Kettensburg, asleep with Antoinette at his side.

She continued, noticing his silence. "Emery, I wanted you to know that...it's you I really wanted. I don't love Arnold. I never did."

Emmerich gave a scoff, shaking his head. "You really proved that, didn't you?"

"Emery, you don't understand."

"What I don't understand is how you can pretend to care for someone, lead them on all the way to the altar, and then leave! I love you, Antoinette. I still do. But...my word, you shattered my soul! If you didn't agree to our marriage, you should've told me from the beginning!"

"Emery, what I said to you in Staalberg after I sent you away...it was all a lie." She reached from inside her sleeve and pulled out a piece of paper. It was crumpled, yet familiar, as she forced it forward, opening it up for Emmerich to see. He looked at the contents and noticed the word that he dreaded on the top: *annulment.* It was the paper she had him sign before he left.

There at the bottom was his signature, but where she was meant to sign was blank.

He looked up at her, confusion in his eyes.

"I never signed the papers. I never married Arnold. I made a promise to you, Emery, that I would be by your side until death and that's what I intend to do." She paused, looking at him with a warm smile as she put her hand to his cheek, caressing it. "*You* are my husband, Emery. Not Arnold. Not Edward. Not anyone else. It's just you."

He lowered his brow, still not understanding. "How can this be?"

"I made a deal with Arnold in secret. In exchange for my silence on his infidelities, as well as giving him some other things…"

"What other things?"

Antoinette sighed, pausing for a moment. "I agreed to give him my dowry. He inherits my entire estate – money, titles, lands…anything my parents will give me when they die."

His eyes widened. "Antoinette, you shouldn't have done that. You needn't give up everything you own for me."

She shook her head, ignoring his objection. "In exchange for all of that, he agreed to pretend to marry me in order to appease Mother. He told her he turned in the signed annulment. We set up the church and ceremony like any other wedding with a few exceptions. Bernie was in on the secret and was to make a distraction during the vows so we didn't have to say them, and the priest from Liegen Arnold insisted on performing at the ceremony was no priest at all, but an old friend. We've been pretending to be married ever since."

The entire story was too much for Emmerich to handle and he sat on the bed, facing the hearth. Antoinette had never been a good liar, and for her to be able to fool her mother this long was a testament to how desperate she was to keep it a secret. But even that wasn't enough to comfort him, wasn't enough to make him take her in his arms again.

"So what are you trying to say by telling me all of this?" he asked.

"We can still be married, Emery. It may not be a normal marriage, but we can still be together."

"So you're saying you and I can be together while you pretend to be married to Arnold?"

"Yes."

"It's not feasible." He shook his head as he turned away from her disappointed face. "For one, I'm not allowed back in Staalberg. Two, how do we know Arnold will keep his end of the bargain? And three...how long do you think we can actually keep this up? I know you, Antoinette. You may have been able to fool your mother with Arnold and Bernie's help, but you're not a liar. You're not one to keep this deception going on for a long time. Besides..." He paused, taking in a deep breath. "None of this proves anything to me. How do I know you're not doing this because you feel sorry for me? I don't need or want your pity, Antoinette. I only wanted your love."

"But you can have it this way."

"I sacrificed everything for you," he said, his voice catching. "I gave up my home, my family, my life. I know your mother doesn't support us, but it shouldn't matter. I don't want to ask you to give her up, Antoinette, but if she won't allow me to be near you, the only way we can be together is if you leave her."

"Emery, you know I can't leave my sister."

"We can take her with us. I told you that I would take care of Bernie, too."

"And where would we go? You're no longer allowed in Hugellia."

"We can stay here in Audlin. Change our names, live life the way we want to live it. Circh is far away and large enough to be the perfect hiding place."

"Would you really be willing to risk it?" Antoinette asked.

"You know Mother would follow us!"

He looked up. "It's less risky than living a lie like you're suggesting."

"It's still living a lie, though, Emery! How is it any different?"

Emmerich rubbed his brow in frustration. Though she was right, there was still something else. "It's different in one thing, Antoinette: Arnold's not in the picture. I can't share you with him. I won't."

"Arnold and I have nothing going on," Antoinette said, anger in her voice. "I have not been with him at all, though I can tell you he's been begging for the opportunity."

"Then why can't you leave him?"

"I can leave any time I want, Emery. That's not the point. The point is Mother. If I leave Arnold, she will chase after me and never stop."

"But if we go into hiding..."

"Do you really think that would stop her?" Antoinette asked as she faced him, her cheeks red. "Look at how quiet we were in our elopement, and yet she still found out! No matter where we go or what we do, she will hunt us down."

"And don't you think she'll find out about us quicker with this secret marriage of yours?"

"It'll give me time to calm her down and reason with her, Emery. I think she could eventually see the error of her ways."

Emmerich snickered in sarcasm. "You have more faith in her than I do."

"I'm sorry. There's nothing else I can think of."

"No, Antoinette. I'm sorry." His face sunk in sorrow, and he met her fury with teary eyes. "I love you. God knows I have thought of you more this past month than I have thought of you my entire life before then. But I can't do this. I can't live a lie, pretending you are married to another man who would love nothing more than to weasel his way between us. I want to spend my life with you and live the rest of my days as your husband, but I want you to be there because you want to be."

"Emmerich, what proof do you want?"

"I don't want your proof," he said sorrowfully. "I just want to know that you're here because you want to be. I don't want your pity and I don't want any lies. You said so many things in Staalberg...so many things that showed you didn't care..."

"I had to say those things because Mother was watching. If I was truthful, she wouldn't have let you leave."

"I was willing to face her for you, Antoinette. I don't fear her."

"I know you don't," she said softly. "But I do."

"So you fear her more than you care for me?"

She frowned. "That's not what I'm saying."

"Then what are you trying to say?"

"That I love you." She paused, gently running her fingers through his hair as she stood before him. "I know I wasn't too clear on that before, but...I think I was just scared. After everything that happened with Edward, I was afraid to open up again. I was afraid of getting hurt."

He rested his hands behind her back, holding her close. "You know I would never hurt you."

"I know. But I hope you know I didn't want to hurt you."

She stopped, lifting his chin and cupping his face with her hands. "There is nothing more that I want than to have a normal life with you.   But Mother...she won't allow it.   I learned the hard way when she called me to the throne room after our elopement.

"She threatened you, Emery.   Threatened to have you imprisoned and tried, but I feared she would go even further than that. I wouldn't have lied if I didn't fear for your life. Her anger was so great and I...I couldn't chance losing you. I couldn't risk seeing you at the hangman's noose."

"I would've given my life for you, Antoinette," he whispered softly.

"I know.   And that's what worried me."   Her fingers caressed his cheek as she remained close.   "I've had too much loss, Emery, and I refuse to lose anyone again. I love you. I love you more than anyone now and anyone I've loved before. And I wish to remain married to you, if you'll have me."

"But we'll be living a lie. You'll be with Arnold."

"I have enough leverage to keep him away. If it becomes a problem, Bernie will go after him."

Emmerich snickered at the thought as Antoinette smiled back at him, her fingers returning to his hair. His eyes closed and he rested his forehead upon hers, his arms still around her waist. "I don't want us to be apart."

"Neither do I, but time will eventually reward us. Arnold will slip up and show himself as the fool he really is. Mother will see his infidelities, and when that happens she will see how much better you are than he. She will see the truth, Emery, and in time, we will be able to be together out in the open without any fear or threat to your life."

"I don't mind risking it."

"But I can't risk you. If you were me, what would you do? Would you be willing to risk my life by running away?"

He sighed, wondering if he really could. If the roles were switched, he'd keep his distance from her as much as he could, just so she would be safe. But if there was a way for them to still be together in secret, he would take it. When he thought of it, there was less chance of being caught if she was pretending to be married to Arnold. If they ran away, Susanna would hunt them down and execute him as a kidnapper.

But the thought of being away from her...the thought of trusting their secret with Arnold...was it truly worth it?

"Emery, please..." Antoinette said softly as she stroked his head. "I've trusted you and now I ask that you trust me. We can make this work. I know it."

And wasn't that what a marriage was? A relationship built on trust?

He opened his eyes as he remained at her shoulder, noticing the necklace upon her chest. Deep down in the crevice of her shirt was the ring that he gave her for their marriage, dangling from the chain around her neck. It was close to her heart, and he was warmed at the sight that she still had it.

It was against his better judgment. It threw reason out the window and risked so much by living a life of deceit. But if this was what it took to prove his devotion to his wife, he would do it. His father once told him that love could make a man do foolish things, and now...he would see the proof in that.

He lifted his head, meeting her gaze. "I don't want to lie. I don't want to deceive people." He watched as her expression sunk and her eyes started filling with tears. As her lip started to quiver, he stilled it with a kiss.

She gave a gasp as she looked to him in wonder, and he could feel her heart start to beat faster as he gazed at her curious eyes. "But..." he began softly, "I love you more than any of that. I trust you, Antoinette. I don't want to do a secret marriage, but if it means staying with you, I'll do it. As long as you'll have me, that is."

"I'll have you," she said with a laugh, throwing herself into his arms. "I'll have you for all eternity."

He gathered her close, hands behind her back slowly climbing up to her shoulders as she kept her forehead against his. His lips parted, joining with hers in an almost forbidden touch. For a moment he felt as if he were kissing another man's wife, and so stopped, but after remembering her confession and the truth that they were still married in the sight of God, he pushed the guilt from his mind. Antoinette eased forward, mouth agape and breath being held in anticipation, and he kissed her once more. Deeper, longer, the tip of his tongue gently caressing hers and making her groan for more. He happily obliged, clutching the fabric of her robe, and she arched her head back. His lips soon left hers to explore new areas, moving down her neck and shoulders towards her chest.

"Emery..." Her voice was in a pant.

He stopped, looking up as he steadied her. Bless it, if he didn't let passion nearly overwhelm his self-control! He had been away from her for so long, and he missed her so much...

"I'm sorry." He swallowed hard, the sight of her beauty racing his heart so fast he thought it'd burst. "I didn't mean to go so far...that is...if you weren't ready...I mean..." He paused again, watching as a smile crept up on her face. "You came here to talk. I didn't mean to get carried away..."

"Emery." His name sounded so soft on her voice, and she

slid her hands around his waist, grasping his shirt and pulling it out where it had been tucked in. She leaned closer towards his ear, her hands gliding to the front as they remained hidden underneath the fabric. He felt her breath tickle his ear, desire turning to fire as she whispered, "Don't stop. Not yet."

"You want to...?"

"We never did get to celebrate our wedding night," she said, blushing, as her eyes lowered for a moment. "I thought...while we have the chance..."

His smile faded at her words, and his hands stilled. "While we have the chance," he repeated quietly. What they were doing now would never be the norm like most couples. Intimacy would be rare, each moment a mere blink. The thought of being away from her...

"Sweetheart." She gently kissed him, interrupting his thoughts. Her eyes met his in a loving glance, soothing his anxious soul. "Don't think about tomorrow."

Time never made his heart grow fonder. It made it ache in pain every second. "But I don't want us to be separated."

"We won't be," she said softly. "Not when we are one."

"Well we're not one yet," he teased as he lifted his fingers to her hair.

She eyed him playfully, her smile widening as her hands begin to drop. "We can fix that."

He grinned. "Yes, we can." He could barely get the words out before ecstasy took over, her touch and voice and taste and beauty overwhelming every sense in his body like a volcano unable to contain its fire. He returned the favor, her knees buckling from the touch of his lips on the places he hadn't kissed before, making her laugh out in delight. They barely made it to the bed before passion consumed them, the warmth in between their skin growing hotter than the hearth blazing at the end of the room. But it wasn't lust that drove Emmerich wild as his fantasies became reality, their clothes on the floor and their bodies tangled in a web of limbs and sheets. It was simply the fact that she was there, loving him as much as he loved her, and it was real. He waited so long to express his caring for her, bottling up every intimate desire over the years and saving it for their first night together, and now…he could give it to her, every piece of his once-shattered heart. And it would last for all eternity.

His mind couldn't help but swoon as the woman in his arms covered every thought.

My friend…

Bohden's vision drifted away as Antoinette's features took over his memory.

My lover…

"I love you…" Her words amidst the rhythms of passion made him forget hearing that he was disowned by his kin.

My wife…

A wave never felt before suddenly crashed upon him, taking his breath away. He collapsed beside her, breathing hard and gasping for air as the most wonderful feeling buried the despair that plagued him for so long. His wife followed him as she closed her eyes, pressing her lips together, her voice caught in a moan. He laid there, his gaze meeting her lovely form, and he realized that he had never felt so close to someone in all his life. He felt bonded to her, body to body and soul to soul, and his arm draped casually across her, his hand resting above her heart, feeling the heavy pound pulsating through his fingertips. Surely this was what the Almighty meant when He said that the two would become one, and never was he happier to join his soul with another as he was at that moment.

"Oh Antoinette..." His voice was so weak as exhaustion threatened to overtake him, but he fought with the sleep that wanted to wash over. He would bask in every minute with her, every moment that he was in her presence. "You're...you're so amazing...so...I love you so much..." He watched as she turned, resting her arm on his chest and leaning over him as he laid on his back, their faces a breath apart. He wrapped his arms around her, the feel of her skin so soft on his hands.

"I love you, too," she replied with a smile, wiping a few strands of hair away from his forehead. "Can we stay in this moment forever? I don't want it to end."

"Then don't let it end," he whispered, gathering her close as love overtook them both in the night.

Chapter 31: The Adulterer

Edward knew he was in a nightmare, but no matter how hard he tried to wake up, his mind wouldn't allow it.

He saw the palace burning. Riots, looters, angry mobs surrounding him as the fires rose high, eating up the sky above. He looked around, desperate for help, but as he searched the crowds, the only familiar face he saw was one.

Stephen, his older brother, pale with a wound upon his chest, circling him like a vulture and cackling in delight.

"I told you this day would come."

His voice had an echo that only a ghost could give, and Edward fell upon his knees, covering his ears. The crowds were shouting so loud, calling for his death, but it was Stephen's voice that drowned out all other noise.

"Your sins will find you."

He pressed against his ears even further, desperate to block out Stephen's voice. "I said I was sorry. I'm forgiven! The past is in the past!"

Stephen laughed as he faced him. "You were sorry for what happened with Antoinette. You never apologized for me."

"I apologized for everything. I said I was sorry!"

"But you still must pay." Stephen looked at him and grinned. "You will be abandoned, Edward, just like you abandoned me."

"No I won't."

"Mother will disown you."

"No…she loves me…"

"Marcus will turn against you."

"He will stay loyal!"

"Calimus will hate you."

"No…I won't lose my son!"

"You will lose everything, Edward," Stephen replied. "I will make sure of it."

He then saw an image of a Velori approach him, Malina standing behind with a wicked gleam. As she walked through the crowds, the people sang her praises, cheering her name and calling her their queen.

"You will pay for your crimes," she said to him, and she pointed to his face, urging the Velori forward.

He recognized the man who approached with sword drawn, and he froze, meeting Vacius' beaded gaze.

"Vacius…don't do this…"

"I must, for my lady."

"But she will betray you too!"

Vacius said nothing as he lifted his sword and swung.

Suddenly Edward gave a gasp, his eyes opening wide in

fright as he sat up, wheezing. His body was drenched in sweat and he was shaking, and as he wrung his hands in his hair, he noticed the place beside him was empty.

Malina. She had fallen asleep with him hours before. Where would she be now? Though the dream certainly put him on edge, his wife now missing made him even more nervous. Perhaps the dream had been a warning to him, that Malina was being more crafty than he thought. He put his hand to where she had laid and noticed the sheet was cool. She had been gone for a while, doubtless for a few hours, and he remembered the guard change at ten. If ever there was a time she could sneak out of the room, it would be then.

He hurried up, ignoring the fact that he was still in his nightclothes, and stormed out the door. Had he not noticed Malina's eyes constantly looking towards Arnold? Not that it mattered she fancied him. It was no surprise. But if she was to whore herself with a man vowed to be with Antoinette, he would never forgive himself. He caused Antoinette enough pain in her life and he wasn't about to let Malina do more damage.

Besides, catching Malina in infidelity could only help him, especially since she was trying to undermine his authority. With proof of infidelity, he could divorce without scandal and be rid of her once and for all.

He hurried towards the guest bedrooms, a guard stationed at the edge of the hallway looking at him curiously.

"Your Majesty? What are you doing up at this hour? Is something wrong?"

Edward's words came out like a grunt. "The queen is not in our chambers. I awoke to find her missing. Have you seen her?"

"No, Sire. I've seen no one trespass these halls since I

arrived."

Crafty, clever girl. He knew she would arrive during the guard change. "Follow me. I may have need of your services."

The guard nodded, hurrying along.

Edward went to the last guest bedroom at the hall where Arnold and Antoinette had been sent to stay. His blood started to boil as he heard noises coming from their room, and he knew it to be too late in the evening to hear laughter instead of snores. He approached the door, listening intently, as he heard Arnold speak.

"That's it, my little vixen. You know what I like."

He heard a woman's giggle, but it was so soft, he couldn't make it out. The knight beside Edward blushed, stuttering. "Sire, what are we doing?"

Edward hushed him quietly, listening some more, trying to see if it was really Antoinette in there with him. Sure enough, Arnold gave him his answer.

"You naughty girl, you! I don't think I could ever get Antoinette to do that!"

That was all the proof Edward needed. He knew it was Malina and Arnold in there, and he was about to expose the cheats they both were. He turned to the guard, his voice low. "Open the door."

"But..."

"I said open it!"

The knight's shaking hand fumbled for the knob, but nothing happened. "It's locked."

"Then kick it down!"

The knight nodded, putting his foot to the door and kicking it open. Instantly a gasp was heard from the woman, and as Edward stepped in, he felt both victory and loss.

The woman in the bed hastily covering herself with a sheet was not Malina, but one of the palace servants. He couldn't even recall her name, only that she was young and beautiful. But his heart burned at seeing Arnold atop her, loving on another woman instead of his wife. Antoinette was nowhere to be found, and Edward guessed she had to be in Bernie's room. Regardless, his temper rose, and Arnold would receive no mercy from him.

"HOW DARE YOU!"

Edward's shout was probably heard throughout the palace as he lunged at Arnold, who quickly tried to get away. The guard stepped in to defend the king, and in the midst of all the commotion, the poor servant girl ran out of the room, ignored and not being chased. Edward didn't care. If he saw her again, he would deal with her, but now all he cared about was Arnold.

He took the man and threw him out of the room, Arnold's body shaking in fright. He stammered as he backed away towards the wall as Edward approached, heaving.

"Have you no decency, Edward, to barge in my room unannounced?"

Edward didn't care for Arnold's petty excuses or arguments. He only cared that he shattered his vows to Antoinette. "You made a promise to her. How *dare* you go against that and defile her bed with a whore!"

Before Arnold could answer, Edward grabbed the man again, pinning him against the wall and kneeing him in the groin. Arnold gave a high-pitched shout, his breath being knocked out of him, and Edward threw him to the ground once more.

"I knew there was something rotten about you," he said as Arnold tried to get back up. "I hoped I was wrong. Antoinette doesn't deserve this, you beast! She deserves someone who will be faithful to her and love her."

"Like you?" Arnold said with a laugh before being kicked in the groin again.

That was all it took to set Edward off, and as Arnold screamed for help, Edward set his fist to the man's face.

"I never knew I could be so close to you."

Antoinette felt Emery's hands go across her chest and towards her back as he finished helping her dress, tying the ribbon to her nightgown and kissing her neck when he was finished. She lifted her hand to his head, touching it and holding him steady, giving a slow breath as she felt desire rising back up.

"I've never felt so loved," she said as she turned around, smiling. She eyed him playfully, not wanting the night to end. "We still have some time to spare before the guard change, though."

He grinned, his hands lowering to her hips. "What did you have in mind?"

"I could think of something." She moved to kiss him, but after hearing a scream, she stopped, pulling away.

"What was that?" she asked.

"It sounds like a little girl."

Another scream was heard, this time louder and calling for help.

"Could someone have broken in?" Emmerich asked, and he led his wife to stand behind him as he went to the door to lock it.

A third scream was heard, and Antoinette knew the voice that gave it. *Arnold.*

"Wait...something's wrong..." Antoinette hurried forward and opened the door for a peek, noticing the guard in the hallway was running away.

"Your Majesty! What's going on?" the guard called out, and that was when Antoinette heard Edward's voice, loud and clear.

"You wretch! You monstrous beast! HOW COULD YOU DO THIS TO HER?"

"Oh my..." She turned to Emery, putting her hands to his face. "I have to go. It's Arnold. I think he was caught with a mistress and..."

"What are you going to do?"

"I might not have to do anything," she said, her smile widening. "Our prayers may have been answered even quicker than I thought!" She kissed his cheek, hurrying out. "I can't be seen with you, though. Not yet. I'll let you know what we can do next!"

But Emmerich's face sunk at her leaving. "No...wait..."

"I'm sorry! I have to go!" With that, she ran down the hallway, leaving Emmerich at the door.

She hurried and followed the guard only to find Edward upon Arnold, the former in his nightclothes and the latter completely nude, engaged in a brawl that proved Edward the victor. She looked around noticing only another guard and Mother rushing out from her room, followed by a few more curious onlookers.

Doubtless Edward had caught Arnold in an indecent situation, and he was about to get vengeance for it.

But she couldn't let Edward kill the man lest Mother seek Edward's head, too.

"Get off him," Antoinette said, though her voice didn't show much anger. She gently pulled Edward away, feeling rather glad he was still willing to defend her honor.

"I caught him with another woman," Edward said, panting.

"Who?"

"One of the palace servants." He paused, catching his breath. "Malina was gone, too. I thought they were together."

"You idiot," Arnold muttered with a cough. "I'm not stupid enough to bed a queen."

"But it's not surprising," Antoinette said, her arms crossed. "Looks like your secret affairs have been exposed."

"Silly girl," Arnold replied as Mother neared. His voice lowered to a whisper as he looked at Antoinette. "You reveal my secret, I'll reveal yours. I'm sure you know who she'll side with."

Antoinette's eyes widened in fear as Edward looked at her in concern.

"Secret? What secret?"

Antoinette ignored him as she kept her eyes on Arnold. "You wouldn't."

His smirk remained as he challenged her with his stare. "Want to put it to the test?"

Antoinette stood frozen as she realized Emmerich was still in danger. No matter what, Arnold would look out after himself in the end.

"Antoinette?" Edward repeated her name, but she stayed quiet, and he picked up Arnold once more, pushing him against the wall.

"If you've threatened her in *any* way..." he began, but Susanna's shrill yell stopped him from speaking more.

"GET YOUR HANDS OFF OF HIM!" Susanna smacked Edward in the face, shoving him off of Arnold as the man slid back down to the ground. "THE NERVE! WHAT MADNESS IS THIS?"

"I should ask you the same, Susanna!" Edward yelled back, glaring her down. "I caught your son-in-law in bed with another woman! He's been cheating on Antoinette!"

Susanna looked to Arnold, her eyes beaded. "Is this true?"

"Of course it isn't, Mother!" Arnold replied, his voice weak. "I was in the throes of passion with my wife and Edward had been spying on us. When Antoinette and I were through, he burst open the door and attacked me in a jealous rage!"

Susanna looked up to Antoinette. "I saw you coming down from the other hallway. Where were you?"

"I...I was..." Antoinette felt her heart beat faster as Arnold looked to her, his eyes fixed. She couldn't risk Emery's life, could she?

"Were you with *him*?" Susanna seethed as she approached Antoinette, grabbing her by the collar. "If I find you were with that wretched Hugellian again, I will rid of him myself!"

"Don't you *dare* threaten her!" Edward said, taking Susanna's hand off of Antoinette's collar.

Antoinette looked back to Arnold, his face beaming. "I know where she was, Mother," he said.

Susanna turned to him. "Where?"

"The bathroom," Antoinette blurted out before Arnold could reveal the truth. "Arnold and I were in our room like he said. I had gotten up to use the toilet, and after I had left, Edward came in and attacked Arnold."

"What she says is true, Mother," Arnold replied, his eyes remaining on Antoinette in triumph. "You can see by her appearance that she is right."

Antoinette wanted to breathe a sigh of relief, but Edward's reaction would prevent it.

"My word..." Edward said, his face full of horror. "What hold has he over you that you would lie like this?"

"I'm not lying, Edward," Antoinette said as she kneeled down, covering Arnold with part of her robe.

"Antoinette, this isn't you..."

"You foolish boy!" Susanna yelled as she slapped Edward again. "You dare call my daughter a liar to her face?"

"I know your daughter," Edward said, his voice cracking. "And I know she is not a liar. At least...she used to not be." He paused as he looked back to her, and she met his sorry gaze with her own. His breath was heavy as his eyes filled with tears, and he started to back away. "Antoinette, don't follow my path. Don't hide the truth, thinking that it can protect you. It can't...it won't..."

"I'm not like you, Edward," Antoinette replied.

"Please don't be..." Edward swallowed hard, his voice catching. "I beg of you...don't repeat my mistakes..."

"I've heard enough. We've overstayed our welcome!" Susanna spat as she helped Arnold stand. She turned to one of the guards. "Get our carriages ready, now!"

Antoinette remained at Arnold's side, though her gaze never left Edward's. They looked at each other, his eyes so sorrowful, and she suddenly began to question every lie she had ever told.

Did she make the right choice being secretly married to Emery? Or would he have been safer if she had pushed him away altogether?

It took every ounce of strength she had to fight away the tears that wanted to stream down her face. She was screaming inside with no one to hear, and she began to pray desperately for help.

"And you!" She heard Susanna's yell as the woman stood up to Edward, her face an inch away from his. "If you *dare* lay a hand upon my dear Prince Arnold again, I will send an army after you! Your father was never so foolish to insult his guests like this and I am ashamed that you would ever be this way!"

She slapped him again, and he said nothing as he looked back to Antoinette.

"You needn't return with them. You'll be safe here. Stay...please..."

Antoinette knew he was sincere, but she couldn't take the risk. If Mother would send an army after Edward for hitting

Arnold, she could only imagine what she would do if she knew Edward was hiding her and Emmerich.

"I'm sorry, Edward. I'm going with my husband. I told you...never speak to me again."

She helped Arnold up, leading him to the bedroom so she could nurse his wounds and help him dress. Before she left Edward, however, she looked back one final time to the hall she came from, Emmerich standing there in the shadows and silently watching with a frown.

She mouthed a quick apology before turning away.

I love you, my sweet Emery.

When she entered the room, she couldn't stop the tear that streamed down her cheek.

That's why I have to walk away.

Malina was in the throes of passion when she first heard the commotion.

She pushed Vacius off of her, urging him to be silent. He grunted, perturbed, as he returned his lips to her body. "No. I've barely seen you at all, Malina. I will not be denied this!"

"You fool!" she hissed, pushing him off again. "It has nothing to do with that! Listen!"

She then heard arguments, yells between Edward and Susanna and accusations of him beating Arnold. Malina couldn't help but grin at the thought of it, and she hurried up, dressing.

"What are you doing?" Vacius asked. "Do not leave me just yet!"

"I'm sorry, my lover, but when an opportunity presents itself, I must act." She knew with Edward awake that he would be wondering where she was at. He had already questioned her faithfulness before and couldn't be given the opportunity for proof. "I must get Calimus now. Stay hidden and I will join you once more when the time allows."

"But Malina..."

"Be gone, Vacius, 'til I have need of you!"

She hurried to Calimus' room and snatched the baby from his crib, not caring if it woke him up and caused him to cry. She tried to bounce him to quiet, but after that didn't work, she thought it best to present herself to the king with a screaming baby anyways.

She hurried down the hall, slowing once she saw Susanna storming back to her room in a huff.

"Your Majesty, is something wrong?" Malina asked sweetly as Calimus started to quiet.

"Ask your beast of a husband!" Susanna spat. "He just nearly killed my son-in-law!"

Malina's eyes widened in fake surprise. Oh, this was too good to be true. Malum always said the best opportunities came at the spur of the moment, and this was no exception. "Good heavens! Is Prince Arnold hurt?"

"Beaten and bruised, but Antoinette is overseeing his care," Susanna replied. "Never have I been so insulted in my life!"

"Forgive my husband, Your Majesty," Malina replied. "Sometimes he is not wise in his decisions. But fear not! I shall see that this matter does not go unpunished!"

Susanna only scoffed as she entered her room, slamming the door.

Malina grinned, approaching Edward as he rested against the wall. When he saw her approach, he hurried to his feet, clenching his fists.

"*Where were you*?" he demanded.

"With our child," Malina replied as she bounced Calimus once more. The boy still cried, but after looking at Edward, he began to settle down. "I felt as if I should check on him, and when I came to his crib, I saw him crying. I've been trying to settle him ever since. I think it's his stomach."

"That is not the cry he makes when he is sick, Malina," Edward seethed, taking the boy in his arms and quieting him. "It is the cry he makes when he is tired."

"Believe me or not. I do not care," she muttered. "What I do care about is you beating our guest. Want to explain?"

She could see he was in no mood to talk, but that didn't mean she couldn't make him squirm. "No," he answered. "Now take our child back to his crib so he can sleep."

He handed the boy back to Malina, making him whimper. "Not even a little information?" she asked with a pout.

"Just go," Edward said. She turned to walk away, but before leaving, she heard him speak. "I know you weren't with our son, Malina. It's only a matter of time before I catch you."

She smirked as she walked back to the nursery. Oh, how she would love to see him try!

Emmerich sat on the bed, feeling the warmth of the sheets beneath his fingers.

He could still feel Antoinette in his arms, the smell of her breath on his lips and the touch of her skin against his. Never had he known such ecstasy in loving her, and never had he known it to be taken away so quickly.

Was that what his marriage was going to be? A quick visit followed by weeks, maybe months or years, of isolation? No sooner had Antoinette come back into his life did she have to leave once more, all because of Edward beating Arnold senseless out of jealousy.

But despite his anger towards his cousin, he felt more hurt at how Antoinette handled it all. She had the perfect opportunity to expose Arnold as the fraud he was, yet she didn't take it.

He couldn't hear the words spoken between them, but he knew when he saw her look back at him with a frown that their marriage would still have to be a secret. They'd still have to be separated. He'd still be denied his wife, and how he was ever going to see her again was anyone's guess.

He sat amidst the sheets once reserved for passion and lowered his head into his palms. Already the marriage was proving difficult, and he didn't know if he had the strength to handle it.

A knock was suddenly heard at the door, and his head shot up. Perhaps it was Antoinette coming back. He hoped to at least tell her good-bye before she left.

He rushed to the door, opening it, only to find that it was Edward who stood in front of him.

"We need to talk."

Emmerich moved to shut the door, his anger rising, but Edward blocked him, pushing the door open and entering the room.

"Edward, get out!" Emmerich said, cursing his lack of speed.

"No. Not until you hear what I have to say." Edward paused, taking a look about the room, his eyes going to the bed. "This place is a mess. Do you always sleep this wildly?"

Emmerich felt embarrassed as he cleared his throat, searching for an excuse. "I toss and turn a lot when I can't sleep."

"Then why are you not in nightclothes?" Edward asked beneath his breath.

Emmerich blinked, his face flushing in embarrassment. "Uhm..."

"Save it. I'm in no mood for another runaround," Edward began, putting his hands on his hips and turning to his cousin. "I want to know what's going on *now*."

"There's nothing going on, Edward."

"Susanna is frantic about Antoinette seeing you and Arnold has mentioned he is keeping a secret about her. I may have been considered the dumb one in the family, but I'm not as dumb as you all think. Antoinette was about to let me expose Arnold for the crook he is until he threatened to expose her secret."

Emmerich's eyes widened. Arnold had threatened her? His heart burned at the thought.

"She wasn't about to support him until Susanna mentioned you," Edward continued. "So either you start talking, Emery, or I will go to Edeland myself and find the truth. Antoinette was here tonight, wasn't she?"

Emmerich remained silent, unsure of what to say. He didn't want to let their secret out, especially if it involved Edward knowing. He would sabotage their marriage. He would do everything he could to try and ruin his life with Antoinette just like he had done in the past.

"Emery, for the love of all that is good, you wouldn't have a wreck of a room for no reason! Besides, I know it when two people have just had..."

"Edward," Emmerich interrupted, lifting his head. "It's not what you think."

"It's exactly what I think," he replied. "And if you care about Antoinette like I do, you'll do everything you can to get her out of this mess."

Emmerich's face softened, and he looked at Edward with tired eyes.

"I know what it is to be a liar," Edward began. "And I know the consequences it gives. I refuse to let Antoinette walk my path in life, and if I can stop it, I will." He paused, letting out a deep breath. "But I can't do anything without your help. I need to know what's going on."

Emmerich lowered his head, praying he would make the right decision as he opened his mouth to speak.

Chapter 32: A Need to Let Go

Edward hadn't felt so much anger since Malina first met Antoinette. His blood boiled, his face reddened, and his fists ached to hit something. Adrenaline was still rushing through his veins after his attack on Prince Arnold, yet it threatened to remain as his foolish cousin continued to elude him.

"There's nothing going on," Emmerich repeated with beaded eyes. "And if there was, I can handle it. You've messed up our lives enough, Cousin. We don't need you anymore."

It took every ounce of strength he had to not scream out a curse. "Heavens, man! Can you not see I'm trying to rectify my mistakes? From the bottom of my heart, I want to help you!"

"You tried to help me in the past and I lost the only woman I ever loved," Emmerich said, his anger trying to remain in check. "Forgive me if I don't have much trust. The past has taught me much. I don't need your help."

"Yet you still remain a fool," Edward muttered, noticing Emmerich's jaw clench. Good. Let the man get furious. Let him lower his guard and slip up the truth! Perhaps then Edward would get the answers he needed.

"I'm in no mood for this." Emmerich's voice was low as he stood, pointing to the door. "I've been mocked enough as it is, so just go. I don't want to see you."

"All I want is an answer," Edward continued, edging closer. "If you don't want me meddling in your affairs, that's fine. I can respect that. But I will *not* sit idle and let Antoinette be blackmailed by some sniveling coward of a prince! Now please – I beg of you – tell me what it is that Arnold is holding over her!"

"There's nothing, Edward."

"God bless it, Emmerich!" Edward turned around, wringing his hands in his hair out of frustration. He wanted nothing more than to shake his cousin by the shoulders to add some sense to him, but there was nothing he could do. As much as he tried, Emmerich refused to trust, and once again the past was affecting the future.

Edward turned back and faced his cousin with an unbridled fury. *"What if Arnold threatens to harm her? What if he already has?"* He could see the anger rising in Emmerich's eyes at the mere thought, but his next words would see that anger released. *"Do you care nothing for her?"*

"I care for her more than you ever could!" Emmerich spat, his muscles tensing. "But for once in your life, Edward, stop meddling in our affairs! If Antoinette is being threatened, then I will take care of it! She's not your concern, but mine!"

Finally, he took the bait. "So there is something going on between you two?" Edward asked.

"I never said that."

"Your room and your words confirm it."

"And whether it's true or not, it still isn't your concern!" Emmerich replied.

"I don't feign assistance out of jealousy, Emery. I promise I'm happy that she's with you."

"She's with Arnold, Edward. I don't need the reminding."

"You can't deny she was here," Edward continued, his voice firm. "Is that what the secret is? That you two are having an affair?"

Emmerich's face reddened. *"I'm not having an affair."*

"Emery, please be honest. Trust me; I've been down this road before. Even if you have the best intentions, an affair will bring you nothing but trouble. If Susanna learns of this, it can endanger both you and Antoinette and..."

"This is not the same situation, Edward. I am nothing like you! I NEVER betrayed the ones I loved and I NEVER lost my integrity. Stop pretending you are such a saint when you and I both know there's not a holy drop of blood in your body!"

The cheap blow fell hard upon Edward's pride. Though there was little of it left, it was still there deep down inside, and he couldn't help but feel winded from being reminded of his past failures. But despite the reminder, despite feeling the guilt rise, he had to be strong. He couldn't be paralyzed by it, especially if Antoinette needed him.

"I know I've done much wrong," Edward continued, keeping his voice in check. "I don't ask that you forget what I've done. I ask you to forgive it. But we can't move forward and help each other until you are willing to move on. I'm willing, Emery. I want to put the past behind us. You don't have to trust me and we don't have to be friends. Just let me be your family."

"You never were my family, Edward. Nor will you ever be." He pointed to the door once more, his voice snarling. *"Now get out."*

"Fine! Keep your grudges! But I will not allow Antoinette to be bullied. I will not ask you again. What is the secret Arnold holds against her?"

But Emmerich would hear none of it. He pushed his cousin out of the room, yelling, *"GET OUT!"* before slamming the door, leaving Edward in the echoes of the hallway.

Edward tried to open the door once more, finding it locked, and soon resorted to pounding it with the ball of his hand. "Open this door, Emmerich!" Edward said as he banged on the door. "I'm not going to leave until you tell me what you know!"

"Edward!" The voice of Maria soon interrupted Edward's anger, and he turned to see his mother rush towards him, still in her nightclothes. "I heard yelling. What's going on?"

"Tell Emmerich to open the door!"

"Why?"

"Because he knows something about Antoinette and he's not telling!"

Maria sighed, rubbing the bridge of her nose as she shook her head. "Is this related to the naked man who got beat up in the hallway?"

Edward paused from his pounding on the door and looked at her, hoping to hide his guilty expression. "You heard about that?"

"Susanna was very detailed in her complaints before she left."

"I'm sure."

Maria looked to the floor and scoffed. "Why were you so *foolish*, Edward? Why concern yourself with Prince Arnold?"

"I caught him having an affair on Antoinette."

"And that gave you a reason to nearly kill him?"

"No. It gave me a reason to humiliate him like he humiliated her."

"Well apparently she wasn't humiliated, Edward. According to Susanna, she's the most livid."

"That's not true." Edward put his hands on his hips in defense. "When she arrived, she wasn't angry at me. She was glad I hit the man! But then Arnold threatened to expose some secret. She lied for him, Mother, because she was afraid of what he might do."

"So why are you at Emmerich's door?"

"Because the secret is connected to him. At least, I think it is." Edward turned back to the door to pound it once more. "But bless it, he won't tell me!" He swung back his hand, but before it hit the door, Maria took his wrist and lowered it.

"Not again, Edward. Leave your cousin be."

"But if Antoinette is in trouble..."

"Come here, Edward. Into the guest bedroom."

She took his hand like he was a child about to be punished, leading him away from Emmerich's room and down the hallway into a small room near the corner. They entered and she quickly closed the door, shutting it quietly so as not to attract any attention. She motioned for Edward to go to the cushioned seat by the window. "Sit."

He obeyed with a huff. If she was going to treat him like a child, then he was going to act like one!

Maria stood before him with arms crossed. "This has got to stop."

"What?"

"Getting in Emery and Antoinette's business," she replied. "Or anyone's business, for that matter."

"I was only trying to help."

"Beating a man is not helping, Edward, nor is hounding your cousin."

Edward leaned forward and rubbed his forehead. "Mother, Arnold is blackmailing Antoinette! Emmerich knows, and if he's not careful, it will fall on him too!"

"I know this hurts you, Son, but it is not your concern."

Edward sat up straight, narrowing his eyes and raising his voice. "Not my concern? *How can you say that?*"

Maria exhaled slowly, lowering her head. "Edward, I know you're hurt over Antoinette and Emmerich trying to elope."

"That has nothing to do with it."

"You can't deny that it bothered you."

Edward sighed, shaking his head. The truth was, in a small way, it *did* bother him. He wasn't ashamed to admit he still loved the woman and wished it was he who married her. But it wasn't jealousy that drove him into attacking Arnold, nor was it what made him beg his cousin for information.

"Mother, none of my actions are out of jealousy. Everything I did is because I love Antoinette."

Maria looked at her son in the eyes, her face emotionless. "And that is the problem."

"Problem?"

"Edward, your greatest strength has always been your love. You are a man who cares with all of his heart, soul, and body. But it is also your greatest weakness. Though I know you still love her, you must realize that she's no longer your concern."

"But if she's being hurt..."

"It is still not your concern."

Edward's mouth dropped agape. "And why isn't it?"

"Edward, she is not your wife!"

He lowered his head, remembering the pain of losing her. "I know. But that shouldn't matter if her safety is at stake."

"She is a grown woman who has made her decision."

"And what if she chose Emery instead of Arnold?"

"Then she is still not your responsibility." Maria paused, putting her hand on her son's cheek. "I know you still love her and I know you want her to have the world, but you must realize you made your choice and she has made hers. You have to let her go."

"Let her go?"

"Yes."

Edward huffed, lowering his brow. "I can't."

"This is not a choice, Edward. You are the king of Audlin and must make sacrifices."

"By refusing to love?"

"By putting your country's needs and wants over your own." Maria removed her touch from him and stood firm. "You nearly started a war tonight, Edward, because of petty jealousy. You were fortunate they handled it as well as they did, but if this happens again, you might not be so lucky."

"But Antoinette was being betrayed."

"And you nearly betrayed your country with your rashness. I'm sorry, Son, that her marriage has hurt you, but you must let her go for the good of Audlin."

Edward stood to his feet, not wanting to hear any more. "No. I won't do that...not when she could be getting hurt."

"I don't like it either, Edward, but as king, you must put your personal grievances aside! If you pursue this matter with Antoinette, you could bring us to war. Susanna is volatile enough to fight you if goaded into it!"

"So be it. I'll fight anyone as long as Antoinette stays safe."

"Do you hear yourself?" Maria scoffed. "You lament your woes in Emmerich not letting go of the past, and yet here you are doing the same! Son, I beg you, please...listen to your mother. Let Antoinette go!"

"No."

"Oh Edward," Maria said quietly. "Your father worried over this. You cannot put the people you love first as king. Your nation will suffer when you let it cloud your judgment. Arden knew this. It was why Audlin came first in our lives. You can see how it made us prosper."

"And you can also see how it destroyed our family," Edward replied. Maria only looked away, and he wondered if she secretly agreed with him. "I will not let Audlin suffer, Mother. I promise you that I take the crown seriously. But I will also not let the ones I love suffer for it, either. I love Antoinette and I refuse to see her hurt."

"I know, Edward, but again...she is not your responsibility." Maria took her son's hand and lifted it, pointing to the wedding band on his finger. "Your responsibility is to your wife and son. You made your choice, Edward. Now you must learn to live with it."

She released his hand, and suddenly Edward felt very cold, the realization of what his mother was trying to convey suddenly becoming too heavy a burden to bear. "Malina is your wife, Edward. The woman you bound yourself to. At the risk of another adultery, stay faithful to the wife you have chosen and let Antoinette go."

Edward knew what she was trying to say, but it pained him still. He never planned to leave Malina and have another affair. He knew better, promising God to be pure in mind and body regardless of how he felt about his wife. But at the same time, there were past mistakes to be rectified. Antoinette would never be his wife, but that didn't mean he couldn't keep the promises he made to love and care for her always.

"I didn't choose Malina, Mother," he said before turning to leave the room. "I will remain faithful to my wife and son, but I cannot sit by and let the woman I love be hurt."

"Even if it risks your country?"

"I'm sorry, Mother. The ones I love come first."

He walked out the door, leaving his mother in the room and hearing her final words.

"Then you will lose your country."

No. He would prove her wrong. He would take care of both his country and his loved ones without the need for sacrifice. Just because his father didn't do it didn't mean he wasn't capable.

He went down the hall and towards the front window, looking out into the evening to find Antoinette helping Arnold get into their carriage.

"I'm glad to be rid of this place," Arnold muttered painfully as he limped into his seat.

Antoinette ignored him as she turned to look behind. "Isn't Bernie coming?"

"She already left with Mother and the others," Arnold muttered.

"But I told you I wanted her to ride with me. Didn't you tell the servants?"

"I did, but they said your mother insisted she ride with her. I think it was punishment for what happened at dinner."

Antoinette frowned, and Edward watched as she looked up towards the front windows of the palace before stepping into the carriage. At first Edward thought her to be looking at him, and his heart lifted at the thought, but then he realized she wasn't. Rather, her gaze went more towards the right, and he turned to see Emmerich down the hall, watching through the window as well. His hand was up and pressed on the glass as if reaching out to her, and he watched as Antoinette met his gaze, staring back for a long time. The sight made Edward's heart heavy, and he realized the truth in his mother's words.

Let her go.

She made her choice, and her choice wasn't him.

Her choice was Emery.

He watched as she entered the carriage and the guards closed the door. They rode on slowly into the night, back to Edeland in the distant east.

No...she chose Arnold.

He watched for a long time as the carriage soon became a speck in the distance. After the carriage was gone, Edward turned back to his cousin, noticing he had already left. Undoubtedly he was hurt at seeing the love of his life gone once again. Though Maria would've scolded him against it, Edward felt as if he should check on his cousin once more before heading back to bed. Though he was at risk for getting kicked out again, it would bring him peace of mind to know that Emery knew he wasn't alone.

Edward slowly went back down the hall towards Emmerich's room, giving a knock on the door. "Emery? Are you alright? Can I come in?"

There was no answer. Typical.

"Emery, I know you're angry. I just wanted to let you know that I'm here for you and that I'm sorry for earlier."

Still no answer. Not a breath, not a sound.

Edward was slightly perturbed, but at the same time he wasn't surprised. Emery was the type of person to shut everyone off when wanting to be alone. It didn't matter, though. He'd still wish him a good night.

He put his hand to the knob and found it unlocked to his surprise, and he gently opened the door. "Emery? I just..."

When he saw the room, he paused.

There was no one there. Emery was gone, as was his travel bag and some of his belongings, and soon Edward was filled with a new panic.

Oh Cousin...what are you doing?

Edward rushed down the hall and out of the palace towards the stables, running as fast as his feet could carry him. He hoped he was wrong, hoped and prayed to God that Emmerich didn't do what he thought he was going to do, but after seeing the stable stall open and Waffles gone, a pair of hooves and feet leading towards the east, Edward knew his fears were correct.

Emmerich had gone to Edeland, and there was nothing he could do to stop him.

To be continued in

Book 4 of The Ripple Affair Series,

"Heart of Deceit".

Turn the page for a preview of Chapter One...

Chapter 1: The Challenge

Bernie was never one to quit while she was ahead.

The memories of dinner earlier replayed in her mind, enough to inspire an encore of such a wonderful show. She snuck into the gardens, gathering more bugs (or performers, as she liked to call them), and took them back into the kitchen to their stages atop the morning pastries that had been set out to cool after a late baking.

She was careful to be quiet while everyone slept, and she giggled to herself as the last centipede was lowered onto the food, completing the mission for the night.

"There," she said with a rub of her hands. "Now remember to be on your best behavior and dig in real deep through the crust. You don't want to be caught before being served!"

She was about to do one last check until a voice from behind made her freeze. "Served to whom, exactly?"

The sound made her cringe, for she knew who it was that stood waiting for her, though how he was able to see so clearly in nothing but moonlight and lantern flame was beyond her. Mr. Grumpy Guard, also known as Sir Marcus Peterson, waited patiently for an answer and said nothing as she turned to face him.

She had to play it cool before saying a word. He was by no means dull-witted or slow — no, his paranoia proved his intelligence – so getting away would be a challenge. Luckily for her, she enjoyed stretching her abilities, and the knight would be perfect practice for just how creative she could be in getting out of a bind.

"Serving me, of course," she replied cheerily, meeting his sour look with a grin. "Sorry. Since dinner was a little too lively, I got hungry and wanted to get a snack. Can't blame a girl for getting food."

He lit another lantern so they'd have more light. "Why didn't you ask one of the servants for assistance?"

"Didn't want to bother them. It's pretty late."

"It would be no inconvenience. Many remain on duty through the night."

"Yeah, but just because you don't sleep doesn't mean other people stay awake."

He frowned further. "Then you should've asked one of the guards stationed in the halls. They remain awake every night and rest during the day."

"Alright; you got me." She lifted her hands in surrender, seeing as the man clearly had an excuse for the palace staff. Audlin he could account for, but there was one thing he missed. "I didn't want my mother to know I was snacking. She's so picky about what I eat, and I didn't want her to find out I was sneaking a pastry."

His look softened until he noticed her hand trying to slip behind her back. "So the jar is for holding your snack, I take it?"

Her eyes widened for a second before she calmed herself. Bless it, if the man wasn't so observant, she'd have been out of the room in no time! She fumbled the jar forward, shrugging as if it was commonplace to bring a jar when getting a pastry. "Yeah, uh…it's an Edelandian thing. We mush them in the jars and eat it with a spoon." Far from the truth, but she hoped his lack of experience with foreigners kept him ignorant.

"And the grasshopper in it is supposed to add flavor?"

She looked at the jar, acting quickly to hide her frustration. Apparently she forgot one. She made a grimace as she held the jar forward, ushering it towards the knight. If her words couldn't fool him, maybe her actions could. "Ew! Take it away! I don't like bugs!" She forced the jar into his hands, jumping and shaking her arms in feigned fright.

"So you didn't notice the giant grasshopper in the jar when you picked it up?" he asked.

"It's nighttime. I didn't see it."

"But you have a lantern."

"I was looking for the pastries with it."

"Well, then," Marcus replied, finally showing a grin. "Normally protocol requires me to fetch a servant for you so that the bakers know their pastries were taken with permission, but seeing as you and I are both already here, I can take their place. Here." He picked up a pastry from beside her and held it in front for her to take. She gave a gulp, remembering it to be the same pastry not one, but *two* earthworms squiggled into. "One pastry snack for a hungry princess."

He put the pastry on her palm, and she looked up, faking a smile. "Thanks. I'll…uh…just take this up to my room now. Best to not disturb anyone else."

"Oh, no," Marcus said. "At least try it here. If you don't like it, you'll be close enough to the other pastries to see if you like them."

"Well...this is a plain jelly pastry," Bernie said. "I prefer mine with fruit. I think the ones over here have some berries..."

"I'm sorry, Princess. Those are reserved for the king and queen. As much as I'd like to share those with you, I'm afraid I can't." He smiled further, leaning forward with crossed arms. "At least *try* the jelly one. You never know - you may find it's quite appetizing. The baker is known for putting in the best secret ingredients."

His look never left hers, as if he were challenging her to try him. Of course, that made her want to accept the challenge all the more, and she met his gaze with her own defiance. She took the pastry firmly in her hand and planted it to her lips. Mr. Grumpy Guard could never make her admit to defeat!

"You know what? I think you're right. Might as well try it. After all, I sure am hungry!" Then she took half of the pastry, stuffing it into her mouth, making the knight's face grimace in shock.

She stood there proudly at first, but after feeling a squirm of one of the worms near her tongue, she suddenly realized eating bugs wasn't as pleasant as she thought it was.

She held it together, refusing to give the man the satisfaction of proving her guilty in ruining dinner. She swallowed the worm whole, along with the pastry bits, holding the other half of the food proudly in her hand. "That was tasty! Want a bite?"

He shook his head, still looking at her in shock. "There's a worm coming out of that pastry..."

She looked down at it, seeing worm number two peeking its head (or tail? She really couldn't tell which end was which) out of the jelly, and that was all it took to put her in a panic.

She just ate a worm. A living, squirming, dirt-loving worm, all just to prove a man wrong.

It didn't take long for the gagging to start, and she rushed forward to the nearest basket, vomiting what she ate only seconds before into the bin. Marcus rushed forward, now looking panicked, and as Bernie looked into what she threw up, seeing the worm she ate alive and squiggling still, she suddenly felt a new sickness come upon her, and whatever she ate for dinner suddenly came up, too.

Victory never felt so terrible.

About the Author

Erin Cruey is the author of *The Ripple Affair Series* and *The Adventures of Captain Patty*. When she isn't busy writing, she's trying to come up with the next big bestseller...or figure out how to make her apple muffins not come out of the oven so crumbly. She currently resides with her family in the United States of America.

For the latest blog posts, news, and book releases, visit http://erincruey.com.

Other Books by Erin Cruey

The Ripple Affair Series

The Ripple Affair

Reign of Change

When Dreams Break

The Adventures of Captain Patty

Captain Patty and the Nameless Navigator